I0729956

Table of Contents

Chapter 1	2
Chapter 2	8
Chapter 3	16
Chapter 4	22
Chapter 5	28
Chapter 6	34
Chapter 7	40
Chapter 8	50
Chapter 9	54
Chapter 10	62
Chapter 11	68
Chapter 12	74
Chapter 13	78
Chapter 14	82
Chapter 15	88
Chapter 16	98
Chapter 17	106
Chapter 18	112
Chapter 19	118
Chapter 20	128
Chapter 21	140
Chapter 22	150
Chapter 23	160
Chapter 24	174
Chapter 25	186
Chapter 26	192
Chapter 27	200
Chapter 28	212

TABLE OF CONTENTS

Chapter 29	226
Chapter 30	232
Chapter 31	242
Chapter 32	254
Chapter 33	260
Chapter 34	266
Chapter 35	274
Chapter 36	282
Chapter 37	288
Chapter 38	294
Chapter 39	302
Chapter 40	308
Chapter 41	318
Chapter 42	326
Chapter 43	332
Chapter 44	340
Chapter 45	346
Chapter 46	352
Chapter 47	358
Chapter 48	364
Chapter 49	370
Chapter 50	382
Chapter 51	398
Epilogue	404
Acknowledgments	2
Book 2: Prologue	1
Book 2: Interlude:	5
Book 2: Chapter 1	9

Rachel,
You wanted a new vampire romance novel to read.
Well, I hope this meets one or two expectations.

Anna,
Thanks for helping me give a certain someone
some depth.

Trent,
Thanks for not complaining too much when I took
your idea and made into a mushy romance. And
thank you for being a continuous source of
inspiration and support for my heavy time
requiring hobby.

Chapter 1

They train you how to fight and hold a gun, but they can't teach you the sound of death in the air—the crack of a bullet meant for you, or the silence before everything falls apart.

Peering over my weapon, I scan the darkness, holding my breath as if the air itself is bracing for what comes next. Three years into this war with the Turig, and I still haven't gotten used to the waiting. Command calls them "enhanced genetic combatants, or EGC's" but that sanitized language doesn't capture the cold precision in their eyes or how their metal armor-fused bodies shrug off wounds that would kill a non-modified human soldier.

The battlefield is a brutal landscape. Out here, trust is a fragile thing. It isn't a given—it's earned in blood and sweat. Every decision is a gamble with lives you can't afford to lose. I feel it in every mission. *The battlefield doesn't just take skill; it strips you bare—demanding pieces of your soul.*

And the connection with your team can be the difference between making it to the next fight… or fighting to make it out alive.

I peer around the corner of the building where I'd recently taken cover and snap back instantly—a crack in the air following the chip of concrete from impact with the opposing wall.

"Could really use an ETA on backup here, guys." I exhale, shoulder pressed against the wall. Nothing gets the heart pumping like a close call with a bullet.

The adrenaline clouds the fear, but it's there. I can't shake the feeling that every bullet, every step I take, might be my last. This mission was supposed to be routine—secure the target, extract intel on Turig armor capabilities, get out. Command said this could be the breakthrough we needed after losing three major cities in the Northern Sector last month. But Command isn't here, feeling the wrongness in the air

My comm statics with the incoming response. "Two minutes."

Four of my guys fall in line against the wall alongside me. "I think this mission may be a bust. I'm low on ammo." Lungram, my second, says with a heavy breath.

"Air support should be here any sec—" The explosion around the corner makes me flinch away from the exposure of the road. "Scratch that."—I raise my hand and throw a fist toward the street—"Move!" I count each person as they pass me, weapons raised, out from the safety of cover. I shoulder my weapon and rush after them, scanning over the fire and destruction for the next pit stop.

Sweat trickles down my temple as I scurry over chunks of broken asphalt. There's an unmistakable aroma in the air, churning with the smoke and dust, before the sky unleashes a new version of watery hell upon us.

The city was once a thriving hub, now just another casualty in a war no one is winning. *If we don't secure the target, it'll all be for nothing.*

We settle in behind new cover. Water drips from the edge of their helmets and they stare at me, waiting on my signal. *Every one of these guys is looking to me. Relying on me to get them out of this mess safely. This should be our final push.*

"Once we get in there, shit is going to get real. Anyone not taken out in the blast will be waiting for us. Lungram"—I slap my final mag into his palm—"don't go spending it all in one place." He nods, tucking it into an empty compartment on his chest plate. *Lungram may be new to the team, but he's my second for a reason. He knows how to make every shot count.*

I meet eyes with every one of them before taking a deep breath and ready my weapon to run across the final exposed stretch of road.

Intel last placed our target within the building at the end of the street, barely hanging on to its original form—holes expose the hatch pattern of rusted rebar throughout the cracked concrete exterior finish. Window treatments flutter with the breeze beyond broken glass. Tall palm trees smolder in a struggling battle for their own life.

Unease settles in my gut when we reach the building with no enemy fire. Uncertainty of what awaits inside gnaws at me. We line up beside the door, eyes scanning and weapons ready for defense should a round find us while we wait. With everyone caught up, I lead the sweep and enter through the doorway, clearing the room while my guys follow as flawlessly as a rehearsed drill.

The second and third stories clear before we make our way to the roof.

"Hale, there's nobody here." Lungram says.

Frustrated, I head back inside. "This makes no sense... the intel was solid." I growl through my teeth as they follow me

No sign of the target. A bust like this doesn't just stain my record, it's one more reason to doubt we'll ever win this war.

The pattering sound of footsteps in the distant stairwell is faint, but undeniable. I put my hand up to silence my team and motion for them to take a defensive position.

Maneuvering closer to the stairwell, I take my stance—with heart racing and breath held, listening. The silence, shattered by thundering footsteps, grows deafening until they round the corner. I fire into the leading man, catching his fall through the corner of my eye as I kick in the door behind me—slipping inside to take cover. I unload into the men who flood the hallway over his still body just beyond the door.

Reaching for my last magazine, I curse—*I gave it to Lungram.* I swing my rifle to my back, drawing my pistol. The doorway darkens as a soldier in full Turig armor steps inside, his gun fixed on me. I fire.

His shoulder jolts backward, taking the bullet as though playing with bubbles. I fire again as he advances toward me—unphased. I growl, willing his steady advancement to be a bluff. The lack of a sheening glimmer on his elbow switches my aim.

"Your efforts are futile," his voice is a mechanical growl behind the mask's scrolling red-and-blue lights. "Surrender now, and we may allow you to negotiate your freedom."

That insignia. Three black crescents offset over red ones. Burned into my memory from three years ago. My squad. My friends. All slaughtered by the Turig.

The military intelligence briefing from this morning

flashes through my mind—these advanced units were designed to be more than weapons. They're strategic assets, capable of learning, adapting, even negotiating when it serves their purpose. But I'd seen what happened to "negotiated" prisoners. The experiments. The conversion attempts. The empty eyes of the few who made it back.

I watched him kill you... and yet. You'll die this time. I'll make sure of it.

"Not again, bastard!" I snarl, unloading my magazine into the mask. The click of an empty chamber silences my rage, but I don't stop. The knife in my hand feels like justice. I lunge, driving the blade into his neck again and again, desperate to sever his spine and end this nightmare.

Inky black fluid spills onto my hands from the fresh wound, trickling down his black armor. "Just fucking die, you piece of shit."

"They did not train me to die. Your resistance seals your fate. This war will outlast you." he growls through the crackling speaker, jerking forward with inhuman strength.

His blade carves through my side like paper—the pain nearly wrenching the air from my chest. His unrelenting force, an unusual testament to what we're fighting. My grip on my weapon weakens, but I refuse to let go.

I watch with horror as the inky blood turns dark and viscous. Seeping from his wound. Mixing with my blood. The military scientists had warned us about Turig blood contamination, but in the heat of battle, there's no time to worry about protocols.

Not yet.

I won't let him win.

The stench of blood and sweat chokes the air, laced with the metallic tang of spent bullets.

Prying the rifle from his hands, I swing it at his head. With a satisfying crunch of cracking his glass mask, I reset my position, prepared to take him out. With a final desperate swing, I smash his rifle into his mask, glass shattering under the blow. My leg buckles as his knife rips through my calf, but I force myself to move. I yank the mask away, exposing his icy, soulless eyes.

"They'll come for you, as they came for me…" his heavy accent is less cold without the mask. But his grin is unswaying as he rips his blade into my leg.

"Say goodnight, asshole," I hiss, driving the rifle barrel

into his eye. His scream chokes off, and he goes still.

I gasp for air, thrusting the rifle to the floor beside me.

"Roll call." I choke. Voices follow the static over my intercom, which turns into a high-pitched ringing. The room tilts and I stumble backward. The edges of my vision blur, the pain crawling over me like fire.

This can't be it. Not now.

"Hale..." A voice breaks through the growing haze. "Hale, where are you?"

I manage only a grunt before the room spinning takes hold.

I never did believe in fate. But right now? Maybe I was wrong about it. I was meant to die by a Turig's hand.

My vision pulses and I try to refocus my resolve as the pain hits like a freight train. But my legs give out.

Lungram, get them out. This mission doesn't end here... it can't die with me...

Chapter 2

Pain is a cruel way to learn you're still alive.
The sharp sting in my ribs wakes me before the sterile hum of the machines around me registers.

They say if you wake up in the hospital, you're one of the lucky ones.

I don't feel lucky.

A cough erupts, saliva clinging to my throat. I clench my teeth, the sharp pain in my side ripping the air out of me. Bright lights force me to squint. Vision blurry, I slowly scan the room, blinking for clarity. White walls. Sunlight slanting through open blinds. Cabinets in the far corner. Machines humming at the head of my bed, spitting out numbers I can't read.

My blurry vision sharpens just enough to make out a chart on the wall—a row of numbers paired with smiley faces, their expressions ranging from weeping to grinning. *How juvenile.*

Movement shifts in my peripheral vision. A figure—too still to be a nurse. I blink again. Harder. And again.

A woman. Maybe early twenties. Red curls pulled back in a loose knot, wisps escaping near her temples. She's wearing scrubs, perched in a chair beside the bed, hands folded neatly over a clipboard in her lap.

I guess she is a nurse.

Her posture's calm, but her expression isn't. I try to speak but only manage a rasp.

She leans forward slightly, and that's when I catch her eyes—clear and blue, almost unnaturally so. They lock onto mine with steady focus, and for a moment, the room steadies with them.

"You're awake," she says quietly, like she wasn't sure I'd make it this far. "Don't move too much. He tore through half your side." She marks on the board and stands.

"Do you know where you are?"

I open my mouth to speak but hesitate, not wanting to trigger another cough.

She turns to me and moves to the IV stand by my bed, her blue eyes catching the light with a calmness that feels out of place in my storm of pain. "Are you in a lot of pain?"

Breaking my stare on her, I look at the chart.

The crying face seems dramatic, the grinning one, ridiculous.

I settle on the midpoint. Her glance follows my eyes, and she moves toward it, pointing first at the crying face. I don't react and wait for her to move along the chart. When she gets to the halfway mark, I nod.

"I see." She picks up the clipboard from the counter and lifts one of the pages, marking on it. "Mr. Hale,"—she walks toward me, her footsteps measured and soft—"you're in the Emmen base hospital. Do you remember anything about what happened?"

My mind races, but nothing comes clearly—just fragmented flashes of blinding pain and shouts that seem too far away. It's like trying to pull a memory from the depths of a fog that keeps thickening. I glance at a cup on the wheeled tray next to me. She reaches forward and picks it up before I can and brings it to my lips, tipping it upward slightly. I close my eyes and sip, the cool water slipping down my dry throat. The sensation is sticky at first, but it goes down easier after the first two gulps—relief trickling in it's wake.

"Thank you," I rasp and glance at the badge clipped to the bottom of the V in her top. "Eden."

She smiles, placing the cup back down with precision. Her hands linger in front of her for a second too long before folding together. "My pleasure, Mr. Hale."

"Ben, please."

With a nod, she moves back toward the cabinet. "Ben. Do you remember what happened?"

The memory is elusive, like a shadow slipping just out of reach. "A fight."

"And do you recall what attacked you?" She returns to my bedside, a tray of bandages and differently colored wraps in hand.

I hesitate, feeling through the weight of the question. "It would be classified, Ma'am."

Her glance sharpens, locking onto mine for a heartbeat longer than necessary. She presses her lips together, as though considering her next words, before grabbing for the edge of the blanket covering me. I grit my teeth when she lifts my leg from the bed. The sharp pain shoots through my thigh like a live wire. She carefully places a small block from the tray under my ankle, resting my leg on it.

"No offense meant." I add quickly, trying to keep the tension from the room.

She clears her throat, her hands steady as she begins unwrapping the bandage from my leg. "My attempt at information is to test your memory. Nothing else."

Her words seem sincere, but something in her gaze keeps me on edge. I glance at her as she works, her calm presence grounding me amid the chaos. Yet, beneath her composure, there's a control that feels deliberate and guarded.

We remain in silence until she removes the block and gently lowers my leg back. Moving to the other side of the bed, I watch her just a moment more as she pulls the sheet away from my torso. She touches my ribcage gingerly, and I flinch, fisting the fabric as my eyes roll into my head.

"Sorry," she whispers. I meet her eyes. Wispy red bangs frame her slender, round face, and full, glossed lips twist into a soft, sympathetic smile that contrasts sharply against the intensity of the pain. Her cerulean eyes meet mine, full of concern. "I need to redress this one as well. But it will be less pleasant than your leg."

I lean my head back and stare at the ceiling, trying to steady my breath. The sterile whiteness above me is almost too bright. It's harsh, like an overexposed photo. "I can take it. I'm a big boy."

She chuckles, a little snort escaping through her nose. "I was just trying to prepare you."

My heart flutters unexpectedly at the sound of her laughter. I look back at her, a smile tugging at the corner of my lips. "Thanks."

Breaking our brief eye contact, she peels the bandage from my side, her expression tightening in response to what waits underneath.

Her eyes linger on my wound a moment too long, an

unreadable concern flickering across her face. The clinical mask slips for just a second before she composes herself.

"What's wrong?" My smile fades, worry creeping in. Under the harsh hospital lights, the wound has an unusual dark tinge around the edges, where the Turig's inky blood had mixed with mine. Eden's fingers hesitate over it, her brow furrowing slightly as she notices the strange discoloration.

Her eyes meet mine, professional detachment firmly back in place, though uncertainty lingers in her gaze. She forces a gentle smile, her eyes softening. She replaces the bandage with careful hands, then stands up, gathering her supplies and the old wrap. She walks to the sink, tossing them into the bin with a quiet thunk. After snapping off her gloves, she turns on the water, the sound filling the silence. "I just need to see the doctor for a moment. Excuse me."

Her hurried exit leaves a strange emptiness in the room, the unspoken truth lingering in the air.

I lift my arm, wincing at the sharp protest from my body, and look down—a fresh, clean bandage now covering the wound. The previous sight of raw, darkened flesh haunts me.

With a sigh, I stare out the window, my mind drifting back to the incident. Images flash—blood, the searing pain in my side, the fight.

My team...

The thought hits like a punch to the gut, and I sit up quickly, grabbing at my side, the motion causing a fresh spike of pain. I fall backward onto my other elbow for support, trying to catch my breath.

Swinging my legs off the bed sends a sharp jolt through my calf. "Fuck," I mutter under my breath, the pain radiating upward. I drop my feet to the floor, the cold surface a welcome relief. I tug at the tubes attached to me, resisting their pull as I slowly push myself upright.

Looking over my shoulder, I disconnect the cables for the heart monitor with a firm yank and grip the IV stand to drag it with me. As I hobble toward the door, I lean on it for support more than I care to admit, mostly hopping on my good leg.

"Hey!" I call out to get someone's attention.

A head pops over from the nurses' station, and I start toward them. "You shouldn't be up!" A man with salt-and-pepper hair rushes over, grabbing my arm. "What the hell is wrong with you?"

"You don't understand." I growl through my teeth. "My

team"—I breathe, pressure building in my chest—"I need to check on my team."

"We've been in contact with everyone necessary." He guides me back into the room and sits me on the bed.

I lock eyes with him, my gaze sharp. "I can't sit here and wait for them to tell me if my team made it." My voice sharpens, the memory of their shouts echoing in my mind.

"Try to relax." He eases me back into the bed, but I grab him by the collar.

"Listen to me"—I glance at his badge—"Rigby. I need to speak with my Commander." Our faces are nearly touching, and the pressure of his hand on my wrist forces me to release my grip. "Immediately."

He nods timidly, stepping back to reattach the cables. "I'll reach out again, Mr. Hale." He turns toward the door, stopping at the threshold. Glancing over his shoulder, he whispers to someone else before exiting.

As he leaves, my gaze drifts back to my side. The wound throbs in time with my pulse, the faint shimmering glow from earlier burned into my memory. I grip the edge of the bed to steady my shaking hands, my mind racing.

What happened to me?

I sink back into the pillow, closing my eyes and taking a deep breath.

"Mr. Hale," Eden's angelic voice draws my attention. "This is Doctor Shephard. She needs to examine your side." She turns toward the sink.

"Mr. Hale." Dr. Shephard's voice is clinical. "I understand you're feeling a bit anxious about this whole situation." Her blonde hair is tightly pulled into a bun, and her perfume is thick, almost suffocating.

And in a hospital, too.

I can't tear my eyes away from Eden, washing her hands again and drying them with rehearsed motions before slipping on a pair of gloves.

"Mr. Hale?" Dr. Shephard tilts her head, raising an eyebrow.

"Sorry, what?" I blink a few times and focus on her.

"I understand this must be hard for you, waking up here. Are you feeling disoriented?" She examines me with a sharp gaze, though her voice remains gentle.

"My team," I rasp, my throat tight.

Dr. Shephard nods, seeming unfazed. "Yes, my resident

informed me you're concerned about them. We've been in touch with your commander. He's on his way to discuss things further now that you're awake."

"Good," I say curtly, the word sharp on my tongue.

She clears her throat, then turns to wash her hands before putting on gloves. "How much of the attack do you remember?"

"I'm not at liberty to discuss details of the encounter." I respond without hesitation. My training for that kicked in long ago.

Eden moves quietly around the room with a tray of supplies, and Dr. Shephard pulls up a chair beside the bed, sitting down. "I understand. But do you remember it all, or just bits and pieces?" She leans in, peeling back the tape from my skin and exposing the wound.

I clench my teeth, my gaze locking with Eden's. Her eyes catch mine, and for a moment, a strange calm washes over me. "I remember all of it. In slow motion," I murmur, my voice barely above a whisper as I fall deeper into her gaze.

"That's a good sign," Dr. Shephard observes, glancing over her shoulder. "I'll need a number four kit."

Eden breaks our connection, moving to the cabinet to rummage through it. Dr. Shephard presses against my rib cage, and I bite back a groan, my teeth grinding together.

"On a scale of one to ten, what's the pain when I press here, compared to when there's no pressure?"

"Seventeen," I hiss through clenched teeth.

She raises her eyebrows. "Not good. Okay, Mr. Hale, this is infected, but it's different from the standard infection we typically see with bacteria. I need to take a biopsy, get it under a microscope, and start a culture."

"What else causes an infection?"

"It could be a virus, chemicals, an allergic reaction. It could even be an undiscovered local bacteria we've never come across before. Or a mixture of all these things." She holds her hand out.

Eden places the biopsy tool into her hand. Dr. Shephard leans in close to my side, and I purse my lips, scrunching my nose in pain. I bite back my curses, holding my breath as the pain intensifies.

I glance at Eden, her steady presence keeping me present as Dr. Shephard works. But her gaze shifts—lingering on the wound just a fraction too long. She knows more than she's letting on.

"There. All done," Dr. Shephard announces. I take a deep breath and exhale slowly. "We'll get this over to the lab and start you on some antibiotics to prevent it from getting any worse." She finishes with my bandage, standing up as the chair rolls backward with a soft screech.

"Aren't antibiotics just for bacterial infections, though?"

"Yes, typically they are. But you're not typical now, are you? We're giving you some just in case it's bacterial." She walks to the sink and removes her gloves, turning on the water to wash her hands.

My eyes flicker between Eden and Dr. Shephard.

The shimmer I saw earlier... This is no ordinary infection. Could it be related to the Turig blood?

My chest tightens with a realization I don't want to face.

"Do you have any more questions before I go?" Dr. Shephard asks, placing her hands on her hips.

I shake my head slightly. "No, thank you."

With a smile and a nod, she turns and places a hand on Eden's shoulder, whispering something I can't quite catch before leaving the room.

"I need to run this over to the lab and get your prescription. I'll be back in a little while. In the meantime, if you need anything else, feel free to press the call button, and someone will be in to assist you." Eden smiles, her eyes briefly meeting mine before she looks down at her feet as she walks out.

Eden... A fitting name for someone able to calm my inner storm.

Her touch lingers in my mind, as if it's imprinted on my skin. We met only hours ago and yet... she has a way of pulling me back from the chaos swirling in my head without saying much at all. But, as I lie here, every interaction feels like walking a tightrope.

I let out a slow breath, staring at the ceiling. Every word, every glance from her feels measured, deliberate. Is it kindness, professionalism—or something else entirely? My fingers curl into the blanket as a flicker of doubt passes through me.

She's different... and I hate that I can't read her.

The muffled sound of voices outside the room pulls my attention, but I can't make out the words. A tension builds in my chest, a feeling I can't shake.

Chapter 3

The pain meds finally dull the worst of the sting, but they don't quiet my thoughts.

Eden's gone. The room's colder without her in it—and louder.

Everything is louder.

The antiseptic stings my nose. I can hear footsteps down the hall—soft voices I shouldn't be able to make out. I blink up at the ceiling, disoriented.

Weird side effects of the medication.

Then there's a knock at the door. I look over—and freeze. My commander stands in the frame. I smile and go to sit up, resulting in instant regret and a grimace at the pain shooting through my side from the movement.

Alrich puts a hand up, tucking his hat under his arm as he steps forward. "Don't injure yourself further account of lil' ol' me."

"My team. The mission." My voice is rough.

"Don't worry, Hale. You were the only casualty. The mission was completed." Alrich pats his hair, pulls a chair over, and sits on it. "Yes, even Lungram." He chortles.

I let out a slow breath, relief flooding through me. "Were you able to gain some insight into the technology used in the Turig armor?"

"We got a good prototype to work from, thanks to you."

"Perfect. I can't wait to test out our own version of the materials."

Alrich's lips pull downward, and he plays with the brim of his hat. "Hale…"

"Is there a problem with the armor? Did I damage it?"

He sighs, the stress wrinkles next to his brown eyes seeming to deepen. "It's not about the armor." His fingers tighten around his hat. "Look, I don't know how to tell you this. The doc doesn't think you'll fully recover from these injuries. I'm afraid the chances of you coming back are so slim we have to move forward with replacing you on the squad."

The words slam into me, hollowing out my chest.

"What?" I sit up, grabbing at my side, grunting at the pain. "Tim, that's bullshit!"

"I'm sorry, Ben. My hands are tied."

"That's a load of crap. You know as well as I do there are ways around that!"

Alrich exhales through his nose, shaking his head. "I can't very well have the team sitting ass-down and thumbs-up just hoping you recover, Hale. We don't have the luxury of waiting around anymore. The war's getting worse. We're stretched too thin as it is—we need bodies that can deploy tomorrow, not six months from now."

"Then put me somewhere else." The words are out before I can stop them. "I can still be useful. I know strategy, I know the ops inside and out. I can train new guys, run intel—hell, put me in recon if you have to."

Alrich watches me carefully, his expression unreadable. Then, slowly, he nods and for a moment, hope flickers in my chest.

"You want to stay in?" He shrugs. "There's an opening in logistics."

The silence pulses as I stare at him. "Logistics?"

"We're low on experienced handlers. You'd be overseeing supply routes, tracking deployments, coordinating troop movemen—"

"That's a desk job."

Alrich sighs, rubbing his temple. "It's a position, Ben. And it's an important one."

My jaw clenches. "You're telling me you're so desperate for men that you're shoving recruits onto the front lines, but the best you can offer me is pushing papers?"

"It's what's available."

"It's a damn insult."

Alrich's lips press into a thin line. "Every mission needs logs."

I force a breath through my nose. "We took down their lead scientist... That's gotta count for something."

Alrich nods slowly. "Yeah. And it does. We got what we needed. Turns out that bastard was working directly on their bioweapon enhancements. Whatever intel he has, it could give us an edge." He leans forward slightly, lowering his voice. "But it's also proof of how bad things are getting. They were desperate enough to have one of their top scientists fighting alongside the Turig. And if they're willing to put a brain like his on the front lines? It means they're running out of time just like we are."

I press my hand against my ribs, the reality sinking in. The war is getting away from both sides.

"I won't quit."

"Ben—"

"We're in the middle of war and they're just going to kick me out because what, I got a few cuts?"

Alrich sighs, leaning forward with his elbows on his knees. "Hale, this isn't about a few cuts." His gaze softens, but it only made his words hit harder. "You're in bad shape. I saw you when they brought you in—barely breathing, bleeding out. You're lucky to be alive, let alone sitting here arguing with me about how fit you are to do it all over again."

"This is where I belong, Alrich." I look out the window, the sky a stark contrast to the storm brewing in my chest.

"It may be time to find a new place."

Without the squad, without the fight—what the hell am I supposed to do?

"How long can you give me?"

Alrich stands, the finality in his movement cutting deeper than any blade. "You've got a few days to decide. But if you don't take the logistics gig, they're starting your discharge paperwork."

My throat feels tight. "What if I take the job and then reapply for ops after I've healed? After physical therapy?"

Alrich hesitates, then sighs. "You can try." His voice is carefully neutral, but I hear the unspoken reality. They'll never approve me for combat again.

Still, I nod. "I'll think about it."

Alrich adjusts his hat under his arm. "For what it's worth—you took that bastard down like a champ. The team won't forget it."

He walks to the door, pausing just briefly. "You'll still

receive some papers soon about what we discussed."

"Yeah, yeah." I wave a hand, forcing a smirk. "Get outta here, you're slowing my recovery."

Alrich chuckles. "There he is."

The door clicks shut.

And then, almost immediately, the muted TV screen flares red.

EMERGENCY BROADCAST – EAST SECTOR BREACH.

My stomach clenches.

I grab the remote and turn up the volume.

"Authorities are responding to an unprecedented breach in the Eastern Sector. Reports indicate that Turig forces have overridden local defenses, and evacuation efforts are underway. Citizens are advised to remain indoors and await further instruction."

I grip the edges of my hospital blanket, tension coiling in my arms.

I should be there. Should be fighting.

The camera cuts to a field reporter in full tactical gear.

"The military has issued a statement urging civilians to comply with emergency protocols. With reinforcements deployed, officials remain optimistic about regaining control."

Optimistic. Right.

I stare at the screen, jaw clenched.

Optimism doesn't keep people alive.

The TV clicks off.

I blink. My hands tighten around the remote. "I was watching that." I growl.

Eden stands at the counter, calmly prepping an IV bag.

"It's not doing you any favors right now, Mr. Hale." Her voice is even and composed, but her eyes flick to the monitor behind me, and I don't miss it—the numbers spiked.

"That's not from the news." I hear the steady beep-beep-beep climbing in rhythm when she approaches.

Her lips twitch with a hidden smile.

"I bet you get that a lot, huh?" I watch her work.

"What?"

"Heart monitors going haywire when you're around." I smirk, tilting my head slightly.

"I wouldn't know, Mr. Hale." Her eyebrow lifts slightly.

"Certainly, it would be concerning for patients. I just

meant to imply your presence has that effect on people who come through here."

She clears her throat, but there's the smallest flicker in her expression—sympathy? Amusement? It disappears almost instantly.

"Your biopsy has been sent off for testing." She disperses the fluid into my IV bag. "Is there anything I can get for you, Mr. Hale?"

My smile fades. "No, Miss Lively."

"Well, if you do—"

"Yeah, yeah. Call button." I point over my shoulder to the red button on the remote next to my head.

"Precisely." She nods and walks out.

The faint beeping of monitors echo against the sterile white walls. The smell of antiseptic lingering in the air, sharp and unpleasant, as if the room itself is trying to scrub me clean of the fight. The memory of that black fluid haunts me - the way it had mixed with my blood in that dark crumbling room. My fingers trace the edge of the bandage where an odd tingling sensation has been growing. Something feels different, but I can't place what.

My gaze drifts to the door where Eden just disappeared— a strange unease lingering in her absence.

Chapter 4

Itry to sleep, but the tingling in my side has other plans. It's not pain, exactly—just wrong. Like my insides are rewiring without permission.

The door clicks open again, a never ending cycle of check-ins. Soft footsteps cross the room. Not the usual quick, clipped stride of a nurse.

Eden moves quietly to the corner near the window, carrying a small tablet and a clipboard. She doesn't look at me, not right away. Just stands there, half-cast in the sunset light, like she's trying to stay invisible.

A second pair of footsteps follows—more confident. Dr. Shephard enters, her expression unreadable as she glances between the monitor, the IV, and me.

"Back so soon," I mutter. "Let me guess—you missed me."

She arches a brow. "I miss all my patients, Mr. Hale. Though you do have a particular way of keeping things… interesting."

I offer a faint smirk but it fades quickly. "Hit me with it, then, Doc. What's the damage?"

She exhales, folding her arms. "I've reviewed your scans."

I raise a brow. "And?"

"And… all surgeries carry their risk, but your odds are favorable. If we intervene now, there's a solid chance you'll regain most of your mobility within the year." Dr. Shephard sits in the low light of the hallway shining in through the door.

"A year? I'll miss the transfer deadline with that! I'm trying to race a forced discharge here, doc."

"The torn ligaments in your side are causing severe nerve compression, Ben. The tissue is damaged. The infection got to the lower lobe of your lung. It needs to come out." she leans forward, resting her hands on her knees. "Without surgery, the pain will worsen. It'll spread to your spine and you risk losing mobility altogether."

"What percentage are we talking about here?" I watch her intently. *Is this another force of hand to take me out of the game?*

"Not a good one. Without surgery, you'll probably need strong medication just to function—and even then, the pain will persist. Infections or further complications could significantly shorten your life with repeat hospital visits to get things under control."

"I'm hearing a lot of 'could be' scenarios here. Surgery recovery will take everything."

With a deep breath, she nods. "Recovery will be a struggle, but over time, most functionality will return."

I look out the window, following the line where the silhouette of the mountain horizon meets the amber sky.

"It's the damn sky." My lip turns up in a grimace.

"Excuse me?"

"Every life altering moment I've faced happens at this time of day. When the sky looks like a nice stiff drink and the sun disappears. Time of prayer, my ass."—I huff—"Vesper brings nothing but bad news and darkness."

Dr. Shephard looks at the window and motions for Eden to close the blinds.

"Leave 'em." I snap. Eden stops mid-motion and looks at me. I let out a slow breath. "Regardless of the damned news it brings, it's still too beautiful to shutter away."

Damn sunset. Always there when the worst happens. Mocking me with how beautiful it is. Like it doesn't care.

And maybe it doesn't.

A soft smile falls over Eden's lips, and I grin back before looking at Dr. Shephard. "There has to be more options."

"Ben, your test results are... unusual," Dr. Shephard says, glancing at Eden. "The wound isn't healing normally, and your blood work shows anomalies we can't explain."

I think of the Turig's black blood seeping into my wounds during the fight, but keep silent.

Some things are classified for a reason.

"Typically with these types of results, the best success for recovery is surgery." Dr. Shephard folds her fingers together, resting her elbows on her knees.

"Typically?" I raise an eyebrow. "You said before that I'm not your typical patient."

Dr. Shephard sighs and glances to Eden before locking eyes with me. "Ben, I understand you don't want the temporary surgical limitations. But the alternative? I'm sure you've seen your fair share of veterans who deserve better. You are that veteran now."

"My answer is no." I hold the clipboard toward her, holding back my reaction to the pain of even the slightest movement.

"Very well." Dr. Shephard lingers, her gaze darting to Eden like she's passing an unspoken torch before she strides out with a sigh.

They could never understand. I'm not just losing my job—I'm losing everything. Purpose. Pride. What's left?

Eden doesn't speak right away, her arms are folded as she leans against the wall.

Why does she stay? Always looking at me like there's someone worth saving?

Maybe she just feels sorry for me—or maybe she sees something I can't.

"It's a shame, really," she says at last.

"It won't work."

"What won't work?"

"Your attempt to coerce me into changing my mind."

"I wasn't going to." She glances over her shoulder at me "You think I didn't pick up on that look the doc gave you?"

With a roll of her eyes, she shifts her weight. "I was actually talking about the sunset."

"What about it?" I look back at the window, the sky nearly black now.

"That you said it always brings you misfortune."

"What can I say? Beautiful things usually do. Making you believe in possibilities... just to take them away." I stare at her, drinking in the soft light casting an angelic glow against her hair. "Sunsets are endings. The sign of things I'll never get back."

"Maybe." She leans against the frame of the window,

gaze transfixed toward the sky. "Or maybe they're just making space for something else—things we can't see until the light fades away."

"Like what?" My tone softens, inviting her to go on.

"The night sky." She tilts her chin upward. "I get lost in the sheer number of stars and it gets me buzzing. As if I could float away and join them." She looks at me, her eyes catching the dim light from the hallway. For a moment, her clinical demeanor cracks and I glimpse what's underneath—a depth of understanding that makes my breath catch. "If the sun never set, I'd never know what it feels like to lie in the cool grass, watching the stars while the Earth breathes beneath me."

My chest rises slowly with a new tightness. The way she describes the night—it resonates with the sense of changes starting within me. Changes I'm not ready to acknowledge.

"I'm sorry for over sharing, I—"

"Don't be." I smile.

"Anyway."—she clears her throat—"I need to go finish my rounds before my shift ends." Her silhouette dims the light in the hallway as she reaches the door.

"Eden," she turns to me. "Thank you," I say, leaning my head back against the pillow.

"What for?"

"For sharing a piece of yourself with me."

A smile touches her lips. "Get some rest, Mr. Hale."

The cool night air wraps the Earth, calm and still, as the last traces of sunlight vanish. The silence it leaves behind is broken only by the low hum of hospital lights and the sterile chill that lingers in every corner.

I've spent years cursing the sunset, bracing for the darkness it brings. But now... Maybe Eden's right. Maybe the darkness isn't an end—just the start of a path I can't see yet.

THE WEEKS THAT follow blur into a haze of sweat, pain, and slow progress. Weeks since the surgery I didn't want but couldn't avoid. The painkillers blurred everything at first— days stitched together by the hum of machines and the press of fluorescent light. But even through the haze, I remember her.

Not vividly. Just... the scent of jasmine when she stepped into the room, soft and grounding. The way her voice cut through the white noise, warm and certain. On the mornings she was on shift, the days felt easier. Manageable. Like I could hold out for the next one.

Once I could stand without vomiting, they moved me to the rehab wing.

That's when the whispers started.

"He's way ahead of schedule."

"Did you see his regrowth markers?"

"Golden boy of the floor, that one."

The one who's healing faster than he should.

Georgia, my physical therapist, didn't indulge in the gossip, but I caught her shaking her head more than once, smiling like she didn't believe it either.

The nurses whisper about my turnaround behind clipboards. Therapists track my data with raised eyebrows and measured optimism. They talk like I've already made it. Like it's a miracle.

But no one needs to know how wrong it feels. How some mornings I wake up drenched in sweat, back arched in pain so sharp it makes my vision strobe. There are days when standing sends fire up my spine, when I can't keep food down, when I grit my teeth so hard I think I'll crack them.

But then there are other days—shorter, sharper bursts of clarity where my body feels ahead of me. Like it's trying to return to full strength faster than my mind can follow. Catching up to milestones I haven't earned.

I blame it on muscle memory. On clean breaks and good genetics. On Eden keeping me fed and honest— maybe on the way her smile brightened the hallway when she passed by my door, how her laugh in the distance cleared the fog for the rest of the day. Those are the easier days. The ones I hold onto.

I give the credit to years of discipline. To having to prove myself. Anything to silence the quiet, unsettled part of me that knows something isn't quite right. Like I'm catching up to a life I didn't choose.

So instead... I chalk it up to good care. To stubbornness. To being built for war and not knowing how to be anything else. And maybe a little bit of luck.

Still... a whisper lingers in the background. Knowing deep down, something's off.

I'm just not ready to name it.

Chapter 5

The treadmill flashes my time—1:25—mocking me like it knows how far I've fallen. With a growl, I slam my fist on the red button, step off, and lean my hands against my thighs - lungs burning with every breath. "Damn it!"

"What have I told you about pushing yourself?" Georgia sets a bottle of water next to the treadmill and folds her arms.

I look up at her, struggling for air. Arms crossed, her pale blue eyes narrow in a familiar disapproving way. "It's been a month and a half. I need to recover faster than this!"

With a roll of her eyes, she places a hand on my shoulder, crouching down to my level. "Ben, you're missing half a lung… be patient."

"Patience? Sure! Let me know where I can buy some in bulk!" *Wouldn't that be nice?* "If I don't get my time up—"

"I know, I know. Your life's purpose shall disappear into the wind." She flutters her fingers through the air.

"It's not a joke."

With a sigh, she straightens up. "I'm sorry. Maybe we need to go back to my original plan and get you into the pool?"

Saliva sticks to my throat as I swallow and put my hands on my hips, standing erect.

It's not ideal, but I don't have much choice.

"Is that a direct order?"

Tossing a sweat towel at my face, Georgia turns. "Get changed and report to the pool in zero hundred fifteen minutes."

"You're saying that wrong." I wipe the sweat from my

forehead.

"Bite me!" Her voice fades around the corner.

Chuckling, I flip the towel over my shoulder, pick up my bag, and limp toward the locker room, muttering under my breath. "I fucking hate swimming."

THE SHARP TANG of chlorine hits my sinuses as I dip my toes into the water. The pool's surface ripples under the harsh glow of the overhead lights, turning everything around me into shimmering fragments.

I ease in, the water biting at my leg and side—the nerves still too sensitive. Georgia comes to the edge of the pool in a teal bathing suit, contrasting against her tanned skin. Setting her towel down, she sits at the edge of the pool and tugs at her swim cap. "Are you ready?" she asks.

"Do I look ready?" I glower at her.

With a chuckle, she pushes off the edge and comes into the water, swimming over to me. "You look like you hate this."

"I'm a fire sign… Needless to say, and I'm gonna' say it anyway, water isn't my favorite element."

"Well, let's get this done, then."

The lesson goes by quicker than I expected. *I guess it helps that I'm focused on just staying upright, not on how much I hate being in the water.* After the full hour, Georgia swims to the edge and hoists herself out of the water. "You're actually doing really great. How's your pain level?"

"Compared to the treadmill? Negligible."

"That's a good sign! I think we should focus on water therapy for our full two-hour sessions. Probably for a few weeks."

"Weeks? Georgia, I have to prove I'm fit for duty in a month."

"Well then, you better not complain!" She stands and wraps her towel around her torso. "Be back tomorrow at your normal time and we'll continue."

"Yes, Ma'am." I say and float my way to the edge.

Damn it. I used to conquer obstacles, not be crushed by them. How the hell am I going to meet that goal in a month?

WATER DRIPS FROM my swim trunks onto my toes as I dab my face and shoulders with my towel.

"Fancy seeing you here." The angelic voice slams my heart against my chest. I look over to see Eden wrapped in her own towel—hair under a swimming cap, face bare.

"I wouldn't exactly call swimming a fancy activity."

"Oh? I love to swim. It's like a dance. You don't enjoy it?"

"Not how I'd describe it… I never got much practice." I rub the towel against the back of my neck.

"So, why not practice more?"

"Guess I've never really had a reason to."

"Understandable." Her eyes linger on the scar over my ribs. "How have you been feeling?"

"Did you come here to dance, or ask me about my smiley face level?"

Her eyebrows lift. "Well, I come here every time I have a day off. I haven't seen you here before. What can I say, you've officially captured my curiosity."

"Can't argue with that one. Honestly, I'm not doing so well. I can only run for about a minute and a half, but I need to be up to a mile in four weeks."

"Yikes," her eyes go wide and her lips expose her teeth. "I can see why you're into water aerobics now."

"Unfortunately, I don't think two hours a day is gonna' cut it."

"You're not restricted to two hours a day. Though, I wouldn't recommend overdoing it. You also need rest for your body to recover."

"You're only saying that so I don't have another extended stay in your ward."

A laugh sings from her chest as she splays her fingers across it. "Oh, Ben, please. As though anything I said could ever keep you away from my ward if you really wanted to be there."

My stomach flip-flops over itself at her laugh. "There's only one legitimate reason to be there."

"Is that so?"

"Let me rephrase. There's only one good reason, on a personal reasons scale, to land yourself in the hospital."

"I know people like the Jell-O, but I doubt it's worth the cost." Her lips curl into a smirk.

"It's not the Jell-O."

"Not the Jell-O? Color me intrigued!"

"Never liked the stuff."

She shakes her head, folding her arms. "Benjamin Hale, you are one twisted piece of human, you know that?"

"So they like to tell me." I lock eyes with her. "It's the view I miss."

Her cheeks flush, and she purses her lips slightly. "I thought you hated the evening vesper."

"I don't believe I ever said that."

"No, you did! You said it was always bringing you bad luck."

"And that was right before I snapped at you to leave the blinds open because the beauty is worth the pain to be a part of it."

Looking to the side, as though to recall the moment, she rubs her hands together. "Oh, yes… that's right. You did snap at me."

"I still feel bad about that. I'd like to make it up to you, somehow."

"Pssh. As though you're the most rude patient I've had to deal with." She drops her towel and folds it nearly on top of her bag, exposing her porcelain skin under an emerald swimsuit.

"I was rude?"

"Incredibly rude."

"What did I do?"

"Every time I walked in or came close, your equipment started going on the fritz."

"How is that my fault!"

With a shrug, she walks to the edge of the pool. "Explain how it's not." She chuckles.

It takes everything I have to not go breathless at the sight of her long slender legs. "I better let you get going to back your do thing." I stumble over my words and drape my towel over my neck.

She bites her lip to hide a smile, her contemplative gaze flickering to the water. "I wouldn't usually do this... But I could supervise some extra sessions if you want."

Suspicious, I narrow my eyes and fold my arms. "Why?"

She sits on the edge, kicking her legs back and forth. "Your passion for what you do shouldn't go to waste. I'm able to help, so I'm willing to."

My heart races, the way it always does when she gives

new information showing how precious a gem she is. "I'd appreciate that, Eden. Thank you."

"Good!" she says and pushes off the edge into the pool. "Come by my nurses' station tomorrow and I'll get you my contact card so we can coordinate better. Productivity will suffer if we rely on bumping into one another."

"Count on it." I say and watch as she sets herself up against the edge of the pool, sinks her head into the water and pushes off.

Chapter 6

After swinging by the nurses' station for Eden's card, I duck out into the parking lot—trying to shake the odd sensation of being scrutinized like a high schooler caught passing notes.

The air is cool, damp with the smell of rain and the faint bite of exhaust. My Impala sits under a crooked lamp post, matte black and boxy like a shadow that remembers a better time.

I slide into the driver's seat and crank the engine. The radio crackles to life—news about another border breach, casualties rising, warnings for civilians to avoid late travel. I turn it down, not off, as I drive to the pool.

I sit there for a minute, letting the speakers vibrate the last note of whatever song was playing after the broadcast. My fingers tap the steering wheel trying to ignore the flutter of anticipation growing ever more present. *It's just physical therapy. So why the hell does it feel like more?*

With a deep breath, I kill the engine and head inside.

In my swim gear, I make my way to the lap pool of the Harlway Recreation Center. The sharp air from the pool bites at me as the doors creak open, breaking the seal of the corridor. Setting my bag down, I look around at the empty room and check the clock. Taking a deep breath, I rub my hands together to shake off my nerves, and start stretching.

"One thing I will give you credit for is your punctuality,

Mr. Hale." I turn, throwing a side smile at Eden as she sets her bag down next to mine. Her voice is calm, but the slight quirk of her lips betrays her.

"I appreciate you being respectful of my time." She adds, kicking off her sandals and tucking them under the bench.

"On time is late, early is—"

"On time." She finishes, tucking her hair into her swim cap.

"Right." I chuckle.

"I've been in a military hospital long enough to know the rules of appointment keeping. Still,"—she sighs—"it doesn't stop some people from being late."

"Maybe they just don't like hospitals."

"I was referring to personal experiences over professional ones, Mr. Hale." She walks to pool's edge and slips into the water, her gaze steady. "Are you joining me?"

"I can't imagine anyone being late for an appointment with you. And call me Ben." Lowering myself to the edge of the pool, I wince as the cold water brushes the surface of my healing wounds. Eden rolls her eyes, but there's a smile playing on her lips.

She stretches, warming up her shoulders, elbows, and wrists. I mirror her movements, following her lead for the full hour and a half. By the end I lean against the wall, my arms and legs move like wet noodles, and the ache in my chest is an ever-persistent reminder of my limits.

"Are you doing alright?" Eden asks, folding her arms over the edge of the pool.

"Yes. I just figured you'd want to get a move on since you said it was a work night and I've already kept you longer than I should've."

"It appears you have."

"My apologies. It won't happen again."

"I know what time it is, Ben. I let it go long on purpose."

Her smile sends a strange warmth through me, like a pressure building in my chest. "Why?"

She shrugs, her gaze skimming the water. "This seems important to you. I can miss out on my mint chocolate chip for something important."

I chuckle.

"What? Another one of your non-favorites?" She arches a sassy brow.

I shake my head. "Nah."

"What then?" She pulls herself out of the water and walks to the bench.

I follow. "It was my mom's favorite. Except she'd buy just straight mint ice cream and add her own dark chocolate chips to it—the tiny ones from the baking aisle."

Dabbing her skin with her towel, she nods. "I know the ones. I do the same thing! Milk chocolate is just too sweet against the sweet ice cream."

"She'd let it melt for a few minutes and then stir it like soft serve." I smile at the memory and grab my towel.

"Do you miss her much? Your mom?" Eden pulls off her swim cap, her red waves cascading over her shoulders.

My breath catches and I force my eyes to the floor tiles.. "I miss... specific moments."

"Do you get back to visit often? I know your enlistment made it tough, but they still issued you leave."

I rub the towel over my chest, swallowing the tightness in my throat. "They issued leave, but that didn't mean much. Going back to visit... wasn't really an option."

"Father issues?"

"Something like that." I shrug, eager to change the subject. "Do you ever get back to see your folks? They give base nurses leave, right?"

"They do, but it's not enough time to plan a visit. Considering travel, I'd only get a day or two with them—not worth the expense. But we write and have video calls when we can."

"Do you miss them?"

"All the time." She smiles, meeting my gaze. "And the rest of yours?"

"I've never really been the type to miss people."

Eden snorts, her eyebrows pulling together. "What? That's the most ridiculous thing I've ever heard. You just said you miss your mom."

I shrug. "I said I miss moments. It's different."

"Sure it is." she rolls her eyes but softens as she grabs her bag. "Hey, I'm off Thursday. We can start earlier, if that works."

"I dunno. It's kind of nice having the quiet in here."

"Or we can keep it later if you prefer. It doesn't matter—"

"I was kidding! Earlier works."

"Great. How about 2:30?"

"Yes ma'am. I'll be here."

Her eyes catch the glow of the street lamp by her car. "See you then!" She waves as she climbs inside.

Walking to my car, I can't help but smile, letting the flutter of anticipation spread through me.

The Impala's engine gives a low rumble as I adjust in the driver's seat, its familiar growl grounding me. I run my hand over the worn leather wheel, the same one that got me through hell and back.

Her smile fills my thoughts. With a deep breath, I hold on to the image, counting down the moments until I see her again.

Chapter 7

The ache in my leg's different today. Not gone—just… settled. Like the kind of pain that's not healing anymore, just waiting for a verdict. I stretch it over the edge of the couch, testing the joint with slow, steady circles as I stare at the folder in my lap.

The apartment smells like old gym clothes and burned coffee—probably Calvin's latest attempt at brewing something weirdly caffeinated and questionably legal.

My hoodie clings to sweat from the warm-up I did half an hour ago—half distraction, half hope that maybe today I'll walk into that pool and feel like someone who still belongs.

I tug it off by the sleeves, careful not to aggravate the healing tissue along my ribs. A low ache pulses there—dull, constant. Familiar.

Dropping onto the couch, I flip the appeal folder open again. The pages are soft and worn from too many rereads, but that doesn't make it feel less hopeless.

It's filled with scribbled notes—roles I might still qualify for, officers I could talk to, stats from my recent evals,and a handful of half-finished arguments I'll make if they let me speak.

It's not much. But it's something. A strategy.

To whom it may concern,
In light of recent improvements and pending surgical recovery...

It still reads like a man begging to matter. Like someone trying to prove he's still relevant.

Because he is.

I scrub a hand down my face and lean back, the folder resting on my stomach. The pen taps a steady rhythm against my knee while the ceiling fan hums above, spinning like it's thinking for me.

Calvin rounds the corner, a water bottle tucked under one arm and a half-eaten protein bar in hand. "You reading that thing again?"

I grunt. "One of us has to take it seriously." I keep my eyes on the fan. "I've got one shot to convince them I'm still useful. Need to make it count."

"Didn't think the doc cleared you for full active yet."

"Not officially. But it's coming. I'm close."

"Thought you transferred to logistics."

"I did. Just wanted to go over my ops case. Again."

"Would a discharge change anything?"

"I'd be in logistics as a civi. No chance to get back at ops. Even after I'm cleared."

He drops into the chair across from me, socked feet kicked up on the ottoman. "Ben, I say this with love—you're trying to win the war from your living room."

"What else am I supposed to do? Just wait for them to cut me loose?"

He doesn't answer right away. "No. But maybe you don't have to fight to stay in just to be whole."

I don't respond. He's not wrong. But he doesn't get it— not fully.

"You're not gonna rewrite your injuries out of the system by sheer willpower."

I exhale slowly. "It's not about rewriting anything. It's about not letting the last thing I ever do in uniform be… bleeding out on a concrete floor while someone else finishes what I started."

Cal's chewing slows. He leans forward, elbows on his knees. "You did your part, man. More than most. You think they'll forget that *just* because you limped home?"

"I think they'll forget it *because* I limped home." I shut the folder. "I'm not ready to be done."

"Maybe you're not done," he says. "Just… being pointed in a different direction."

I look at him. "Says the guy with two good lungs and a

lab job waiting for him."

He smirks. "Okay, ouch. I was going to say you should come with me to the lab."

I huff a laugh. "Sorry. That wasn't fair."

"Nah, you're allowed," he says, stretching as he stands. "Your injuries are still new enough. You haven't exhausted the pity card yet. But I mean it. You should come check it out. Might be a better fit than you realize."

Before I can reply, my phone buzzes—therapy alert. I check the clock and shove the folder aside. "I've gotta go."

"Final session?"

"Yeah."

Calvin grins. "Tell that nurse of yours I said good luck keeping you in line."

THE IMPALA SITS in the driveway like she's been waiting— black paint dulled by time, engine still stubborn enough to come alive when I ask her to. She's loud, moody, and impossible to kill. Just like me, I guess.

My chest buzzes for the entire five-minute drive. Nerves and anxiety clench at me. Heavy bass and drums kick my speakers and rattle the loose change in my center console— attempting to shake me harder than the buzz when I think of taking her into my arms and kissing her. After pulling into the lot, I check my timing and grab my bag, still early enough to get an extra warm up before she arrives.

The smell of chlorine blows past me, creating a sense of the building being pressurized. The nerves in my core grow stronger as I spot Eden pulling herself up onto the pool's edge, water dripping from her chin. She's breathing harder than usual, her cheeks flushed, and I can't help but smile.

"You're early," she says.

"I always get here this early. It's you who is early." I stand from the bench and walk to the edge. "I like to warm up before you arrive."

"Don't let me stop you."

"It's alright. I was working out earlier, so I'm good to get started whenever you're finished."

"No need to wait. I'm finished. Shall we?"

I nod and slip into the water. The bite on my skin is negligible, sparking hope my injuries are healing. It's either that, or I've grown used to the pain.

Making our way from the edge, I glance at the curve where Eden's neck meets her shoulder. An angry red mark stands out against the surrounding pale skin. "You okay?" I ask her.

She turns to face me, her hands gliding just under the surface of the water. "Hmm? Of course. Why?"

"Looks like an injury or some kind of allergic reaction." I point to my neck.

"Oh." She covers the spot with her hand and looks away. "Just a burn. It's nothing."

My eyebrows knit together. "That's convincing."

With a roll of her eyes, she smooths a hand over it before returning to the water. "I burned myself trying to straighten my hair last night."

"Why straighten it?"

"Sometimes we ladies just need a change, okay?" she sinks lower into the water, her voice softening. "Not that it was effective anyway."

Taken aback by her defensive tone, I lower into the water. "I'm not a lady, so I can't relate. You seem too confident to want to change your looks."

"Sorry. I didn't mean to snap at you." She says, shaking her head.

"I'll survive. It's like I'm your patient all over again." I smirk and pull one arm across my chest. "Should we get started then?"

Eden nods and guides me into a partial squat, one foot extended forward. "You've been doing so well; I think it's time to try something a little more advanced," she says, bouncing to the edge of the pool. She grabs the free end of a bright red strap and wades back to me. "This will help you lean back farther and engage the muscles more effectively."

"So, it's for balance?"

"Essentially. It's a stabilizer band. Most people use it around their legs for added resistance, but I find it limits movement too much for my liking."

"But I could use it that way if I wanted to?"

"Just make sure someone else is here. Don't need you drowning now, do we?"

I chuckle and bounce toward her when my leg suddenly seizes. "Oh, fuck you, Charlie!" I grab my calf, rubbing it and spinning my foot to ease the stabbing cramp. The motion throws me off balance, and my face dips below the surface. I try to push out of the squat, but the tightness locks my leg in place.

A firm grip pulls me to the surface and guide me to the edge of the pool. I sputter, coughing out water as my fingers instinctively rub at my seized leg.

"I was being facetious," Eden says, her voice pitched with both concern and a hint of amusement. "I didn't actually think you'd drown."

"My leg cramped up," I manage between breaths, my frustration mingling with embarrassment.

"Here, let me help." She hovers beside me, her touch solid, but gentle, as she grabs my foot. She presses against the bottom of it, moving my ankle in slow, deliberate circles before shifting to my knee. Her fingers graze my skin, sending a spark of awareness through me that has nothing to do with the cramp.

The stabbing pain gradually subsides, but a different kind of ache lingers—one I'm not sure is entirely physical. I lean back against the cool tiles, trying to focus on the lingering discomfort in my leg, but my thoughts keep drifting to the warmth of her hands and how close she is.

"Better?" she asks, glancing up from my leg.

I nod, unable to look away. "Much. Thanks."

Her eyes meet mine, and the air seems to thicken between us. I can't stop my thoughts from spiraling—how soft her lips might feel, how easily I could close the gap between us.

"Still tender?" she asks, her voice quiet, almost intimate.

I clear my throat, the spell breaking, and pull my leg away to test it. "Nope. I'm cured. You've got the magic touch."

Eden laughs, the sound light and musical, but she rolls her eyes as if to deflect. "You're so corny."

"You don't like it?" I tease, testing the waters again.

She folds her arms and steps back, her expression neutral but unreadable. "Are you ready to finish up?"

The moment's gone, but the tension lingers in the space between us. With a nod, I push away from the edge of the pool, trying to shake the lingering warmth of her touch.

We stand there, the air between us charged with unspoken tension. Eden has her towel wrapped tightly around her torso, her hair falling over her shoulders. I clear my throat, searching for the courage I rarely need in combat but suddenly require now. "It's still straight," I say, my voice faltering slightly.

She looks at me, confused. "What?"

"Your hair."

Lifting the ends, she glances at them, then lets them fall. "Oh. Right. Yeah, it stays that way until it gets wet again."

"It's different. But it suits you."

Her cheeks flush, and she smiles softly. "Thanks, Ben."

"My pleasure." I pull my black t-shirt over my head, the weight of unspoken words pressing on me. The clock catches my eye—a reminder that my time to ask her out is slipping away. My heart races as I take a steadying breath. "You know what else would be my pleasure? Treating you to a mint chocolate chip."

She blinks, stopping mid-motion, her expression caught between surprise and curiosity. "What?"

"If you're free… how about am ice cream?" My voice stays casual, but my chest tightens, anticipation coiling like a spring.

"Are you serious?" Her smile falters for a moment, and something flickers in her eyes—surprise, maybe even hesitation. Then, as if deciding against whatever doubt crossed her mind, she smiles again, soft and genuine.

"I know we're not in high school, but everyone loves ice cream."

"You don't have to do that, Ben."

My stomach drops at her response, but I press on, trying to mask the sting of rejection. "I want to. My new gig starts in two days, so this is basically our last session. Consider it my way of saying thanks."

"You've already said it," she replies, her tone thoughtful. "Just because you're back to work doesn't mean you should stop working your leg. And I'm sure it's helped your lungs and shoulder mobility too."

I force a smile, trying to push past the ache in my chest. "I'll still work on my strength. But I've already taken up so much of your time, and I'm grateful. That's why I'd like to buy you a mint chocolate chip ice cream."

Her lips curve into a soft, genuine smile, her eyes warm. "I'd love that."

As she walks ahead, her towel swaying with each step,

I can't help but wonder if this is the start of something real—or if I'm setting myself up for disappointment. Either way, I'll take the risk. For her, it's worth it.

THE AIR OUTSIDE is cooler now, the street lights flickering to life as I pull the Impala into the driveway. Calvin's in the kitchen, halfway through another protein bar.

"Hey, what are you up to tomorrow night? There's this lecture downtown—breakthroughs about early genetic mapping and virus mutation theory. Could be cool."

"Hard pass."

"Shocking." He grabs his empty protein wrapper and tosses it into the trash. "What, you got other plans?"

I hesitate, just a second too long.

Calvin catches it instantly. "Wait. Do you?"

"Yeah." I pause. "I'm taking someone out for ice cream."

Calvin pauses mid-step, then slowly pivots back to face me with the most obnoxious grin. "Oh? Just a someone?"

"The nurse who's been helping me with therapy," I grab a bottle of water from the fridge and lean against the counter, trying to play it off. "She said yes."

He folds his arms. "And by helping, you mean?"

"Helping. Professionally."

"Right. Which thoroughly explains the ice cream."

"I guess we're friends? She agreed to ice cream, so... that counts for something."

"You guess?" He chuckles.

I shake my head, but I'm smiling. "It's not like that. She's just—she's kind, and smart, and doesn't look at me like I'm broken."

"You're not." he folds his arms. "You just need time, like all things, to find clarity after a vesper brings a new day."

"I know. But I forget that until she's in the room."

And clarity and comfort aren't the same thing.

I smirk, taking a swig. "She's different, Cal. When she's around, everything just… quiets down."

Calvin whistles. "Damn. You've got it bad."

"It's just ice cream."

His grin softens and he grabs a granola bar from the pantry. "But, the way you're talking, Benji, I'm starting to wonder if she walks on air."

I stare at the water bottle in my hand. "Some days, I'm not entirely sure she doesn't."

Chapter 8

The base smells the same. Gun oil and fresh-cut grass. The metallic bite of the air outside the armory. The faint scent of someone's burnt coffee drifting down the hallways.

It's familiar. Comforting. Home.

My boots thud against the polished tile as I make my way to the administrative wing. I've walked this hallway a thousand times. Reported for duty. Gotten orders. Been briefed before missions. Today, I'm walking it for another purpose.

My final assignment.

I adjust my shirt cuffs, keeping my breathing steady, my posture crisp. I'll find a way to stay. Maybe logistics, intel, even training new recruits. I just need time.

I roll my shoulders as I approach the office, testing the ache that still lingers in my ribs. It's better than it was a few weeks ago. *Still stiff, but manageable. Enough to prove I can work.*

Alrich is waiting inside. He's not in uniform today—not a great sign. His hat is off, resting on his knee, and his gray-streaked hair looks slightly disheveled. A thick file sits on the desk between us. I recognize my name on the label. A tight knot forms in my stomach.

Why does this feel wrong?

Alrich exhales as I step in, rubbing the bridge of his nose. "Take a seat, Hale."

I do. His silence stretches too long.

The knot in my stomach tightens. "What's going on?" My voice is steady, but my hands curl into fists against my thighs.

Alrich meets my gaze, and for the first time in my career, he looks uncomfortable. He sighs, flipping open the folder.

"Logistics filled the position."

The words don't compute. I blink. "What?"

Alrich exhales again. "They couldn't wait, Hale. The role needed to be filled immediately. They had a reserve candidate lined up in case you weren't cleared." He flips a page in my file. "And your medical team didn't sign off on your return fast enough."

I grip the armrest of the chair. "They knew I was healing. I just passed another eval last week—"

"It doesn't matter." His voice is firm, but there's something almost apologetic in his eyes. "They needed someone who could start immediately. They moved on."

My pulse pounds in my ears. "Then find me another spot. Any spot. Intel. Strategy. Training. You don't need working lungs to sit in a chair and run ops."

Alrich shakes his head. "You think I didn't try? There's nothing left, Hale. We're at the part of the war where we need bodies in the field, not sidelined officers."

I can't breathe. I lean forward, gripping the edge of his desk. "I'm not just some sidelined officer. I've trained entire teams. I know mission strategy better than most of your active units. You really think I won't be an asset anywhere?"

His jaw tightens. "It's not up to me."

The knot in my stomach unravels. Morphing into a darkness—deep and hollow.

For weeks, I've fought. Pushed through therapy. Told myself I could get back. That I just needed time. That as long as I could still stand, still fight, there was a place for me.

But now, I see it in his face. There's no place for me at all.

Alrich slides an envelope across the desk. My name is stamped on the front.

Discharge papers.

"You're getting a medal and severance," he says quietly. "Not to mention disability pay for your injuries. Ben, take the discharge. I'm telling you."

"I don't fucking want it."

A medal and severance? Like slapping a sticker on a shattered windshield. It wouldn't hold me together. Wouldn't fix this injury or replace what it's taking from me.

I don't reach for the envelope. I just sit there, staring at it like it might disappear if I wait long enough. Then a thought hits me. One last play. "What about the hearing?"

Alrich frowns. "Hale…"

"No, listen. If I can get into the hearing, I can argue for a delayed discharge. Just a few extra months. That's all I need to find another role and be cleared for ops."

He sighs heavily, rubbing his temple. "A delay doesn't mean a guarantee, Ben."

"It means a chance." My voice sharpens. "You telling me I don't deserve a goddamn chance?"

His fingers tighten on the desk. "You're still on the list for the next congression in two days. Be there. But don't expect a miracle."

I nod once. *That's all I needed.*

He pushes the discharge papers closer to me. "You'll still need to prepare for this outcome."

I don't touch them. Instead, I push to my feet, forcing a smirk. "Guess we'll see what happens."

Alrich sighs. "Don't do anything stupid, Hale."

The door clicks shut behind me. I exhale sharply, rubbing my temple.

It's not much. But it's something.

One last shot.

Chapter 9

The base fades behind me as I drive. The silence in the car feels louder than the engine.

I shouldn't be going out. Not tonight. Not after that. But maybe that's why I am.

I need a goal to hold onto, one that doesn't feel like it's slipping away.

A cool evening breeze stirs the rain-soaked leaves of the playground trees, carrying the faint scent of wet earth and grass. The air hums with quiet renewal, crisp and fresh against the lingering dampness of the recent storm.

Puddles glisten beneath the playground equipment, reflecting the fading amber glow of the streetlights. The rhythmic creak of a lone swing echoes softly, blending with the distant laughter of children.

I shift my ice cream cup between my hands, watching condensation bead along the paper exterior.

I shouldn't be here—indulging in small comforts, letting myself pretend things are normal when nothing about my world is.

But then Eden looks at me with those eyes—steady, warm, like she sees a man worth saving—and for a moment, all the noise just... fades.

She dips her spoon into her shake, tilting her head as she watches the kids, a small smile playing on her lips.

I glance at her. "You like people-watching?"

"Something like that." Her lips curve slightly. "Mostly

watching the children play."

I follow her gaze to the small figures darting between jungle gyms and slides. Their shrieks and laughter pierce the night. It's like a joy so far removed from the weight pressing on my chest that it feels like watching a scene from another life.

"If I said that, I'd be considered a threat to humanity." I chuckle, catching her side glance at me.

"If I'm honest, I've always wanted kids," she admits, her voice lighter than expected. She takes another bite, chewing thoughtfully as the breeze catches her hair. "But a few years ago, I gave up on the dream of the right person coming along. My profession isn't exactly ideal for that anyway—too much time spent working."

I glance down at my hands, the ones that used to be steady, the ones that used to be useful. "And then helping poor saps like me in all the spare time you should be using to date."

"You're not a poor sap." She smiles, but there's a knowing in her gaze as she leans her shoulder to bump mine. "Just a friend who needed help."

I force a small smirk. "Lots of people need help, Eden." I'm not the kind of person who should be on the receiving end of it.

"You say that like you don't deserve it."

I don't respond. Because I don't know how. Instead, I focus on the way the distant streetlights catch in her hair, turning red to gold, shifting like fire every time she moves.

She stirs her shake, her spoon scraping against the cup. "What about you, Benjamin Hale?"

I glance at her, wary of whatever she's about to ask. "What about me?"

She leans back, angling herself toward me on the bench. "Do you ever see yourself with a little tyke running around?"

I exhale through my nose, looking back at the playground. The laughter of children sparks a desire in me I didn't realize could exist. "I kind of just figured I'd be in the military forever." My voice is flat, careful. "Haven't thought much beyond that."

"You can be in the military and still have a family," she says softly.

I shake my head. "Leaving the woman I love for an unknown timeframe? Alone with the kids, uncertain if I'd make it back? No, I couldn't do that."

She frowns. "You stopped yourself from finding love because of what might happen?"

I glance at her, studying the slight furrow in her brow. She makes it sound simple, but it never was.

I shouldn't say any of this. Not to her. Not like this.

But the softness in the way she's looking at me—open, unafraid—pulls the words out anyway. Like a priest during confession.

"That's about the gist of it," I say, leaning forward, elbows resting on my knees. "My dad… was a bit of an asshole. Mom died when I was young. Five or six."

She stills slightly, her spoon hesitating against her cup. "I'm sorry… I had no idea."

"Eh. I don't really talk about it." I shrug, trying to keep my voice even.

A pause settles between us before she speaks again. Not uncomfortable—just real. "So a few weeks ago, when you said you can't really see them…" Her voice trails off as she pieces it together.

I glance at her, half-expecting her to recoil, or change the subject. But she doesn't. She just waits, quietly. And somehow, that makes it easier to keep going.

I nod, clicking a pen cap on and off in my pocket. "After my mom's funeral, something in him snapped. He started coming home angry—drunk, beat up from fights. I think that's what happened, anyway." I can almost hear the old echoes— the slamming doors, the sting of leather, the silence that followed. A gust of wind stirs the quiet, carrying the faint chill of coming rain.

"Things weren't great before she died, but he wasn't always like that." I watch the clouds swirl like they're ready to break another storm. "He always worked a lot, but it got worse after mom passed. He worked constantly. I think burying himself in noise was easier than facing what was left."

Eden doesn't say anything. She doesn't have to.

"She used to make lasagna." I chuckle, but there's no humor in it. "Every time she wanted to pretend we were still whole—a family. No matter how late he worked, she'd keep it warm, and we'd stay up, waiting for him to come home."

I shake my head. "Half the time it was dry, or burned on one side—but we'd sit together at that tiny table and act like things weren't falling apart."

Eden doesn't speak right away. She just watches me, a shift in her expression—gentle, a little sad. Like she's filing that detail away, tucking it somewhere safe. "She sounds like she really tried to keep you both grounded." Her voice is quiet. Careful. Not pitying—just... present.

I nod faintly, but my chest tightens. The memory isn't just about food—it's about hope. About pretending things might still turn out okay.

The scent of whiskey and the echo of slamming doors flash through my mind. The sting of his belt feels fresh on my skin. I pinch my lips together, shaking off the memory.

I swallow hard. "Anyway, I joined the military to be strong—to defend myself and others. I just couldn't risk loving someone who might be taken away from me… or putting her through the pain of losing me."

Eden places a hand on my shoulder, pulling me back to the present. To her. "Do you remember what caused her passing?" she asks.

My chest tightens. "Pregnancy complications." I force a swallow. "I was supposed to have a little brother."

Her fingers squeeze slightly, a silent comfort. "I can see why you say you don't miss them. It's not just that you don't think about them—it hurts to."

"Nah." I straighten, forcing a deep breath. "Like I said, I was young when Mom died."

She watches me for a long moment, her blue eyes studying mine as if she sees reasoning I don't. I want to look away, but I can't. She finally exhales softly and holds out her spoon. "Well, you remembered the mint chocolate chip."

I glance at the offering, feigning suspicion. "You might get cooties."

She laughs, holding the spoon closer. "This bite has a bunch of chocolate chips—the crunch is the best part."

I lean in at the same time she moves, and we miss entirely. Ice cream drips down my chin and onto my shirt.

"Oh my gosh!" She scrambles for napkins, flustered, apologizing between breathless laughter.

"It's okay." I chuckle.

"No, it's not!" She wipes at my shirt, still laughing. "I didn't mean to get it all over you." She laughs harder, her breath warm against my skin as she dabs at my chest.

I catch her wrist, gently stilling her movements. "Eden."

She looks up, her cheeks still flushed, her lips slightly

parted. Her laughter bubbles out, and she leans forward, clasping her hands together around the napkins. For a moment, I forget about the hearing. The uncertainty. The weight pressing on me.

"I can't believe that just happened." She glances at me, her lips twitching. "But you should see your face!"

"Do I have something on my face?" I feign confusion, exaggerating my expression.

She clears her throat, sitting up straighter. "I've never been clumsy enough to ruin someone's clothes before." She reaches out, dabbing at my shirt with the napkins before meeting my gaze again.

All I see is her. The pull is there. It always has been. I give in, and raise a hand to her face, cupping her cheek. My voice softens. "You could ruin nothing."

Her gaze flickers to my lips. Mine follow, tracing the delicate curve of hers before returning to her eyes. The air around us thickens, and my chest goes tight—every nerve alight with anticipation. My fingertips tingle as if they might lose all feeling while the moment takes complete control.

It's like standing on the edge of an airplane fuselage, staring into the open sky. That same exhilarating terror grips me now, staring into her sparkling blue eyes.

I stroke my thumb across her cheek, my breath slowing as we hold each other's gaze. Eden leans in, her movements drawing me closer, matching the pull of my own.

Her lips are soft. Electricity floods my body. The rush is overwhelming—like leaping into free fall. Her sigh against my mouth deepens the connection as she presses harder, her lips parting to gently take hold of mine. I mirror her movements instinctively, my hand sliding to her back, pulling her closer.

The moment is both infinite and fleeting as she pulls back, her cheeks flushed and her breath uneven. She clears her throat, tucking hair behind her ears and avoiding my gaze. "Sorry," she whispers. "I don't know what came over me."

"Please," I grip her hand gently, my thumb tracing soft circles over her knuckles. "Don't be sorry."

Her lips part slightly, and for a brief second, I think she understands what I mean.

She glances away. "Well, you can still have some, now that we don't need to worry about cooties."

I chuckle, taking the spoon from her. "Not gonna feed it to

me this time?"

With her cheeks still pink, she bites her lip to suppress a smile. "Now would be the time, huh? Since I've already ruined that shirt."

I take the spoon from her, slipping it into my mouth. The crunch of chocolate chips is oddly comforting.

I lean against the bench, reality creeping back in. My thoughts about the new hearing battling for attention against the replay of feeling her lips on mine. The uncertainty. The looming chance that soon, I won't have a uniform anymore.

Eden sips at her shake, glancing toward me. "Hearing is soon, right? Are you ready?"

I don't answer immediately. Because she thinks it's a done deal. My chance to stay and I don't have the heart to tell her the truth. Instead, I roll the spoon between my fingers and let out a slow breath. "Is anyone ever really ready to hear the verdict on how they'll be labeled the rest of their life? Especially when it's completely out of their control?"

"Verdict? I thought it was decided." She watches me carefully.

"You know the military… cross checking everything."

"Well, I think it'll be good news." she says, her optimism unwavering. "No matter what they say."

"You have a way of making optimism feel contagious."

She shrugs, her gaze drifting to the playground. "If they let you stay, you'll continue the military life you've expected. But if they discharge you..." She turns, locking her diamond-blue eyes on me. "Maybe you'd get to have that family after all."

I force a small smirk, but I don't say anything. Because for the first time in weeks, I let myself feel something other than dread.

And it's because of her.

Chapter 10

I woke up thinking about her smile. But by the afternoon, it's fogged up by thoughts about tomorrow.

The board delivers their verdict in less than twenty-four hours.

Four weeks of pushing through therapy. Four weeks of pretending that was enough.

The ice cream last night—her laugh, her hand in mine—it felt like maybe I could build a new life. One that wasn't reliant on survival.

My phone buzzes on the counter, but I don't look.

Instead, I grab my jacket and leave for the one place I always go with things start to crack—before I can talk myself out of it.

The whiskey catches amber light from overhead, creating honeyed reflections in the bottom of my glass. The month vanished like the liquor I've been nursing, and tomorrow the physical evaluation board delivers their verdict. Stripped down to a mere veteran? Or worth keeping in?

My fingers trace the smooth rim, pushing out my worries with memories of Eden's kisses floating through my mind, soft and dangerous as smoke signals. Every touch replayed makes my stomach knot tighter.

I drain the glass, barely registering the familiar burn. The mirror behind the bar throws back a stranger's face—my jaw lost in weeks of growth, my eyes hollow pools in the dim light. While I'm running calloused fingers over the beard, the bartender materializes like a spirit through the bottles' gleam.

"Refill?" His voice is sandpaper—rough but kind.

My lips press together as I check the ancient clock mounted above the door, its red-painted face faded to rust. "Better not. Big day tomorrow."

"Life changer?"

"In more ways than most could fathom." The words taste bitter with hope.

"Let me know if you change your mind."

"Thanks, but I should just settle up."

He nods, his movements practiced as he works the register.

Outside, my hands find refuge in deep pockets as I drift down empty streets. A metallic screech tears through the night, bouncing off alley walls like a ricochet. I freeze, eyes straining into darkness thick as tar. Glass shatters against concrete, and a rat darts past my feet, its claws clicking a frantic rhythm. With a disgusted grunt, I turn away.

The city towers over me, its brick walls wearing decay like medals—corners crumbling, mortar bleeding. Graffiti blooms like neon wounds, while squares of white paint stand out like bandages where property owners tried to erase the art. At the curb, I check both ways—no headlights pierce the gloom—before crossing toward the park's promise of open space.

That's when their laughter spirals up into the night— bright, effervescent sounds that set my pulse jumping. Eden walks arm-in-arm with another woman, a nurse I recognize from the hospital. Their joy paints the dreary street in warmer colors. My step falters as indecision grips me. Join them? Meet her friend properly, maybe learn how Eden sees me through her introductions?

No—let them have their night.

I sink onto a bench instead, tilting my face to stars I can't see through the city's glow. Tomorrow's hearing plays behind my closed eyes like a film stuck on loop. Keep my job, my life... or maybe start a new one, with Eden...

Their laughter fades like morning mist until a scream splits the night wide open. My gut plummets as if I've missed a step in the dark. Another shriek floods the street, and I'm already running, feet pounding concrete in time with my racing heart. Around the corner, three figures in black masks have them cornered—one restraining Eden as she thrashes, another pressing a filthy hand over her friend's mouth, the third ransacking their bags.

"It would be wise of you to get lost." The growl in my voice surprises even me.

The one with the bags startles, then barks a laugh that scrapes like steel on stone. "Look, boys, we've got us a hero." His companions' chuckles harmonize. "We do love us a hero's party."

"I'm no hero. These streets are dangerous at night and you wouldn't want to get hurt."

His laugh deepens, primal. "And a funny guy, too. Maybe he'd like to watch while we show these ladies just how dangerous these streets can be." His nod sends his partners' hands wandering, exploring.

Blood rushes to my ears, hot and roaring. "At least I now have two witnesses who can testify that I warned you." My fists clench tight enough to feel tendons strain.

"Ben, they—"

"Shut that one up!" The leader's bark sends his man's hand clamping over Eden's mouth. "And they know each other... Tasty." His tongue slides over smiling lips.

I approach their leader, hand extended. "Their bags."

"It's so cute when they think they're tough." He draws himself up, oozing confidence like poison. "You going to just ask politely for us to leave your yummy little friends alone next? It's rather late and I'm in the mood for a bedtime snack."

My jaw aches from clenching. "I know where she keeps the cash. That *is* what you're after?"

"Expecting me to believe you'd hand over the cash after I give you their bags is moronic."

"At least we've established you are not a moron."

"Grahh!" The man holding Eden recoils. "The dumb bitch bit me!"

"Ben, they have knives and a gun!" Eden's warning pierces the night before her captor wraps an arm around her throat, pressing a rag reeking of sweat and city grime against her mouth. She writhes free for just a moment before he catches her wrist, spinning her around. His fist connects with a sick crack, sending her sprawling. She curls around herself, whimpering, blood already darkening her pale skin. Her friend's tears catch the street light like falling stars.

Primitive instinct awakens in my blood—my heartbeat, a war drum. "You're about to regret that."

The bag-carrier raises his hands in mock surrender, voice climbing to a falsetto. "Oh no, I'm so scared."

I launch forward, my fist finding his face with a satisfying crunch. He stumbles back into a row of trash cans that clatter.

"Don't just stand there, you asses, get him!" Their leader scrambles up as his men abandon the women, converging on me like wolves. Time stretches, my adrenaline catching every detail—Eden's friend hitting brick with a dull thud, the other attacker rising from his crouch near Eden.

Pain explodes in my cheek, then my gut. I raise my arms, sweep a leg to topple one assailant. Their leader's fist finds my injured side, forcing a gasp that tastes of copper. My knife whispers from its sheath, and I paint the night red—one slash across a back, another catching arm and chest. They spring back like scalded cats, suddenly wary, drawing their own blades.

A fist rocks my head, flooding my mouth with blood and setting my ear ringing. My knife finds a home in soft flesh, withdraws, plunges again into another body. The third man backpedals, fumbling for his pistol as his friends collapse, their panic rising with the blood pooling beneath them.

I spit crimson and adjust my grip, watching him through sweat-stung eyes. His movements are amateur, but the gun makes him deadly all the same. My chest heaves as I flash him a bloodstained grin. "Some set of balls you've got there. Can't even aim straight."

"I'll do it!" His voice breaks.

"Nah, you won't." I straighten and step forward. He aims at Eden's friend, still against the wall, blood running from her scalp. Her eyes are vacant, unfocused—the exact expression I remember from Lungram's first firefight. My breath comes faster as I recognize that look. And a memory echoes: *"Lungram! We gotta move, buddy!"*

"I will leave you here to take the fall of this!" His eyes dart between me and the women. "T-they'll think you were an accomplice."

"Ben, don't be stupid! Please!" Eden's voice shakes. "Let him go."

"Can't let murderers and rapists go free." Another step forward toward him, hands raised. I spit blood. "You know that much about me."

"Drop the knife or the blond gets a bullet!"

"Ben!" Eden screams. Against all my logic and training, I drop the knife.

"Now, back up!" The gun wavers as he gestures. *Fatal mistake.* I drop and surge forward, my shoulder hitting his gut as I snap his elbow. He gasps as we hit the ground. The gun slides across concrete. My knees dig into the ground as I grip his shirt, draw back my fist—and the world shifts.

The street disappears. Fluorescent lights replace street lamps. The black mask becomes a Turig helmet.

The weight of my tactical gear presses against my shoulders, except it doesn't—my hands feel wrong, exposed without gloves. Gunfire erupts from both ends of the corridor. The concrete under my knees vibrates with running footsteps. The air fills with cordite, blood, and electronics burning.

Voices crowd my head—status updates, position calls, warnings from my team. Everything narrows to the helmet, to the enemy who will kill my unit if I hesitate. My teeth grind as I strike. Again. Again. Each impact sends shocks up my arm, but I barely notice. Reality slips—I'm not here anymore. I'm back at my final mission—where hesitation means watching more friends die.

"Ben, stop!"

Contact on my shoulder. Training takes over—grab, twist, neutralize. I seize the wrist and throw them down. But the face isn't the enemy. It's Eden.

The hallway shatters. Her eyes lock onto mine, wide with fear. Tears run down her face as she raises one hand, preparing for me to strike her. The man she trusted—gone. Replaced by someone dangerous.

My chest constricts painfully. Each breath comes short and fast. The static in my head intensifies until I can barely think. Nausea rises as my heart pounds against my ribs. The smell of gunsmoke lingers in my nose, but it's not real. The tactical gear pressing down isn't real. The blood coating my hands... is.

They tremble as I release her wrist and sit back. I can't get enough air. Sweat runs cold down my back as I look between her face and my bloody hands. "Eden I"—my breath catches—"I-I'm sorry."

She stands slowly, deliberately. One hand touches my shoulder while the other presses against my chest. "It's over," she says quietly. "Let's get this mess taken care of and get you cleaned up."

Chapter 11

We don't speak on the ride over. Eden drives. My hands are too unsteady, too stained. Letting her take the wheel of the Impala feels like handing over the last piece of a sacred ritual—but I can't bring myself to care. Not after what I almost did.

She adjusts the seat, inching it forward until there's barely space between her knees and the dash, like she doesn't want to take up more room than necessary. Every motion is quiet, measured—like she's trying not to startle me. She guides us through the city like she's done it a hundred times. I stare out the window, watching the street lights blur past, letting the vibration of the road buzz through my bones. Her knuckles stay tight on the wheel. Mine stay clenched in my lap.

The scent of her perfume lingers in the cabin, mixed with the copper sting of blood and the reek of adrenaline. Somewhere between stop lights, I realize I haven't spoken a word since I let go of her wrist.

I open my mouth—to say something, anything—but nothing comes out. The silence stretches. She doesn't look at me.

At the police station, she cuts the engine and sits there for a beat, like she's waiting for the words. Maybe for me to say thank you. Or explain. Or just breathe.

I open the door and step into the cold instead.

The fluorescent lights hum overhead, casting harsh shadows across my scarred knuckles as I stare at my hands. Click. Click. Click. The pen cap marks time like a metronome, each snap echoing in the empty waiting room. "They shouldn't have let me out. I deserve to be locked away."

The officer who took our statements said someone would be by with paperwork soon. That was over an hour ago. Maybe they're giving us space. Or maybe they just don't know what to do with us.

Eden's sigh catches in her throat, soft but heavy with exhaustion. "Don't think like that. You saved our lives."

"And then nearly took yours as an afterthought." The words land like ash. In the silence that follows, I risk a glance at her. She turns away quickly, wrapping her arms around herself. Her sweater—pale blue, now stained with spots of dried blood—pulls tight across her shoulders. One hand clutches her bag close while the other wipes at her cheek, smearing moisture across bruised skin. Her lips part, trembling slightly, but whatever she means to say dies unspoken.

My throat constricts. "What will you do?"

"I'll press charges, of course." Her voice steadies as she focuses on facts. "They'll stay in the hospital until they're well enough for transfer. After that, they'll face whatever comes with the mess they created."

"So, I guess that means I'll need to stick around for the aftermath."

"Were you planning to leave?" The question hangs sharp between us.

I shrug, studying the cracked linoleum floor. "Somehow, I think this incident will solidify their case for discharging me. Probably damn me to endless therapy sessions too."

"So, you were just going to take off?" Heat creeps into her words. "You realize how that would make you look, right?"

"It's not like I'm innocent in this." My fingers tighten around the pen until plastic creaks. "I clobbered that guy. His mask kept morphing into a Turig helmet, glowing under me. And the worst part?" The words scrape out of me. "My next blow would've been for you."

"I could see it," she says, her voice barely above a whisper. "You weren't here anymore. Does that happen often?"

The overhead light flickers, sending shadows dancing across her face. "No. But I haven't faced many adrenaline spikes since the battle."

The bench creaks as she sits beside me, close enough that

I can feel her warmth, smell the antiseptic they used to clean her cuts, mixing with the fading trace of her perfume. "Therapy could help," she says, gentler now. "It might bring up things you've been refusing to face."

A bitter laugh escapes me. "That's what you think, huh? I'm not much of a talker."

"You talk to me just fine."

"I trust you." My gaze drops to her hands resting in her lap—knuckles swollen and mottled with fresh bruises, scabs forming over split skin.

"I've done nothing to deserve that trust."

"Your kindness earned it. Your purity." She flinches at the word, arms wrapping tighter around herself. The sight sends a spike of pain through my chest. I push to my feet, shoving my hands deep in my pockets as I pace the room. The pen clicks against my keys with each step. "Do you have someone coming to get you? I can give you a ride if you need."

"No." The word bursts from her. She looks up sharply, throat working. "I mean, yes. A friend is coming."

I nod, muscles tight. "Good. That's probably for the best. I need to get ready for my hearing anyway. Not like it'll change anything—just delays their official denial." Click. Click. Click. The pen provides rhythm to my restless movements as my other hand scratches at my split lip, seeking distraction.

"I'm sorry—"

"Don't." The word cracks like a gunshot.

"What?"

"Don't you fucking apologize for my choices." My voice comes out rough, raw.

She stares at me, eyes wide. "I just... I know how much you wanted it. To get your life back."

I close my eyes, drawing in a deep breath that does nothing to calm the storm in my chest. My fists clench as words force their way out. "I'll just have to make a new life. Get through it somehow... I thought maybe..."

The words hang suspended between us. Behind my teeth, unspoken: *I thought maybe we could build something together. Find a way through this darkness.*

But I swallow them back. She doesn't need my broken pieces cutting into her.

Eden leans back, fingers finding the silver locket at her throat. The chain twists between her fingers, catching the harsh light. "I'm sure you will."

Silence fills the room like rising water. The fluorescent bulbs cast everything in sickly white, throwing shadows across the institutional green walls. Cracks spider through the paint like veins. I can't look at her directly—every glimpse feels like pressing on a bruise, tender and dangerous.

Her measured breaths carry no judgment, but the ache in my chest spreads. Every cell in my body screams to close the distance between us, but I see how she holds herself apart. Afraid. My mouth goes desert-dry. "Do you want me to wait until your friend arrives?"

"Where are you going?"

The question snaps my head around. She jerks back, pressing deeper against the bench. Self-loathing floods my mouth with bile. I exhale slowly, forcing my eyes shut against the surge of anger. "I didn't mean to scare you. I need to clean up before my hearing."

Her expression flickers—worry tangled with uncertainty, maybe fear—but she bites it back. She nods, teeth catching her lower lip. "Oh, right. You said that already. You don't need to wait. I'm safe here." Her gaze darts to the reinforced glass separating us from the police station proper before returning to me.

The look in her eyes tells me everything. She's not sure if she's safe around me anymore. The knowledge burns like acid in my gut.

My hands curl into fists as I follow her glance toward the glass. "Good. Glad there's somewhere you still feel safe around me." Bitterness drips from every word. "I guess I'll see you when I see you."

"Ben." My name leaves her lips like it's sacred, stopping me mid-turn. I look back, rage simmering beneath my skin.

She sits perfectly still, like a statue carved from tension. Her shoulders are pulled back, chin lifted slightly—trying so hard to project strength while everything threatens to crumble. I see her hand twitch toward me before she catches herself. "Don't shut down, okay?"

The words hit me like shrapnel, precise and painful. *But I can't give her what she's asking for. Not now. Not like this.*

I push through the side exit into the early morning air, the metal door clanging shut behind me.

The parking lot is nearly empty. My boots echo against the cracked pavement as I spot the Impala—still in the same spot Eden left it, the headlights catching the glint of broken glass near the curb.

I stop a few feet away.

She drove it.

Not because I asked her to, not because she wanted to.

Because I couldn't.

I thought letting her take the wheel meant I trusted her.

Now I'm not sure if it was trust… or the first sign that parts of me had already broken.

The car used to feel solid. Familiar. Now, standing here, it feels like a crime scene.

I swing the door open and drop into the seat, slamming it shut behind me. The echo cracks across the lot like a gunshot.

For a few seconds, I just sit there—breathing hard, staring at the dash like it might offer answers. But it doesn't. Nothing does.

The engine turns over with that same low growl, but it doesn't settle in my chest the way it used to. It just rattles. Like the glue holding me together is about to come apart.

Chapter 12

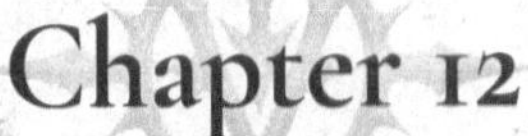

By the time I'm called in, the sun has started to fall behind the buildings, stretching long shadows across the sidewalk outside HQ.

I haven't slept. Haven't eaten. The blood on my knuckles is gone, but the memory of it lingers. So does the look on Eden's face.

The hearing room smells like floor cleaner and cheap paper. Everything in here is sharp corners and cold light.

I sit with my hands clasped between my knees, feeling the hard press of my knuckles against each other as the clock ticks overhead.

The panel in front of me—three men in uniform, their faces unreadable—flip through paperwork, their silence a slow, creeping noose. I already know what they're going to say. I've known since the moment I stepped into this room. Since the moment I lost control.

One of them, a colonel I don't recognize, clears his throat. "Sergeant Hale. You requested this hearing to extend your active-duty status pending reassignment. We've reviewed your medical evaluations, combat history, and incident reports."

Incident reports.

The words scrape through me like gravel. They don't have to say what they mean. They've seen the police report. They know what happened. I swallow, keeping my posture straight. "Yes, sir."

The colonel clasps his hands over the folder in front of him. "We understand your desire to continue serving.

However, given your medical condition, as well as recent behavioral concerns, we are unable to grant your request."

The words barely register.

Behavioral concerns.

They're not just discharging me for my injuries.

They think I'm unstable.

The officer to his left—a man in his late forties, his hair buzzed short, the kind of man who's spent his entire life behind a desk—leans forward. "Sergeant, this decision is final. Your discharge will proceed as scheduled, effective immediately."

My jaw tightens. "Sir, with all due respect, I just need more time. I can still be of use—"

"This hearing isn't a debate, Sergeant Hale." His tone sharpens, his gaze locking onto mine. "The decision has been made."

A muscle jumps in my jaw. Everything inside me coils too tight, too close to snapping. I push up from my seat, nodding once, sharp. "Understood, sir."

The colonel exhales through his nose. "Your service has been noted. If your condition improves before the wars end, there may be a reconsideration with a reenlistment request. Until such a time, we appreciate your contributions, and wish you the best in your transition to civilian life."

Civilian.

The word grates against my skin. I turn, my boots striking too hard against the floor as I move toward the door.

Before I step out, the officer's voice follows me. "And Sergeant?"

I stop, my hand hovering over the handle.

"It's best if you take this opportunity to seek counseling. War changes people. There's no shame in that."

My fingers tighten around the metal handle.

No shame in that.

I don't look back. I don't speak. I just push through the door.

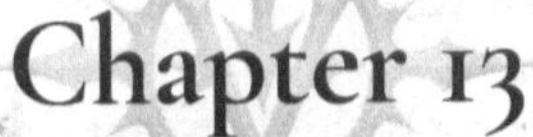

Chapter 13

The apartment is quiet except for the low hum of the news. Another city shelled. This time in the west district. Footage loops—fire climbing up the side of a tower, bodies pulled from rubble under flashing drone lights. The anchor's voice is smooth, measured. I've heard it so many times now it's like background static.

I've been sitting here for hours. Maybe days.

The couch doesn't care. The beer is warm. The ache in my side is sharper today, but I don't reach for meds—a stupid form of self punishment mixed with trying to control an aspect of my life.

The lock clicks. Calvin steps in, holding a takeout bag and a look that says here we go again. He nudges the door closed with his foot, then eyes the clutter on the table. "You know there's a sun out there, right?"

I grunt. "I think I saw it once. Back in '37."

He drops the bag on the counter and shrugs off his jacket. "Didn't realize personal decay was part of your rehab protocol."

I gesture to the screen. "Keeping up with the war effort."

"You're still watching that?"

"Different channel," I mutter, crunching on the last remnants of the bag of chips he stocked yesterday.

Calvin walks over and squints at the footage. "Same bombs. Same smoke. They just changed the angle." He grabs the remote and mutes it.

"I was watching that," I say, but there's no weight behind

it.

"Ben," he says flatly, "you need to get out of this damn apartment."

"I go out."

"Yeah—to that bar three blocks down with all the other ghosts."

I rub my eyes with the heel of my hand. "It's familiar."

"You said that last week."

"It's still true."

He watches me for a beat, then leans against the counter. "This isn't helping you. You think watching the war fall apart from your couch is somehow noble? It's not."

"I didn't say it was noble."

"Then what is it?"

I open my mouth but don't have an answer. I stare at the frozen screen. A soldier's body lies still on the pavement while medics run past. His helmet rolls into the gutter. "It just. .. feels like I'm still part of it. Somehow." I shift, my ribs catching. "Like I haven't totally disappeared yet."

Calvin exhales through his nose. "That's not how this works."

"Yeah?" I crack a dry smile. "You suddenly an expert on losing everything you thought you were?"

Silence settles in, thickening by the second. Calvin walks to the table, picks up an empty bottle, and drops it in the recycling with a sharp clink. "You thinking of going out tonight?"

"Maybe."

"Let me guess. Same place."

I shrug. "Only one where I don't get weird looks."

"You sure about that?"

"They're all ex-military. Off duty. At least there I don't have to explain why I flinch when a glass hits the floor."

Calvin doesn't argue. Just walks to the armchair and sinks into it with a sigh. "You talk to Eden?" he asks after a moment.

My stomach knots. I don't turn. "Nah. We haven't talked in months."

"She ghosted you?"

"No." I reach for another beer and twist the cap off too hard. "We just... stopped. It's better that way."

He raises an eyebrow. "You think that's what she thinks?"

I scoff. "We don't see each other that way, Cal. Ice cream

was fine. Nice, even. But it confirmed what I already knew."

"Which is?"

"That it wouldn't work."

He doesn't buy it. I can feel it. She hasn't called, but I haven't either. I'm not mad. "Just…" I swallow. "Some things are easier left where they ended."

Still, I think about her. When the pain creeps too deep into my lungs, or the world closes in, or the war footage gets just a little too quiet. I picture her smile. The way her eyes sparked when she was trying not to laugh. It always feels like it happened years ago. Probably didn't mean anything. Probably all in my head.

"Well, since you suggested it, I think I will head out," I say, pushing up with a grunt. "Don't wait up."

Calvin nods and rubs his face, his expression unreadable. "Don't punch anyone who looks like they might sue."

"No promises."

As I head toward the door, he adds, "You know the news'll still be looping when you get back, right?"

"Counting on it."

Chapter 14

The bar smells like spilled whiskey and desperation. Dim lighting, scuffed floors, music two decades old. It's the kind of place that welcomes uniforms but doesn't salute them. That's why I come.

I've claimed my usual stool—back to the wall, facing the exit. Some habits die harder than others.

The drink in front of me isn't strong enough to do anything useful, but I sip it anyway. The burn's familiar, if nothing else. Background noise hums: boots dragging, glasses clinking, stories I've heard a hundred times from a hundred mouths trying to forget.

I swirl the last of my drink, watching the way the liquid clings to the glass. I don't come here for conversation. I come here to feel like I still exist.

Across the bar, a recruitment poster grins back at me. A group of soldiers, all bright-eyed and ready for battle, stands beneath bold letters:

"SERVE WITH HONOR."

Another one near the exit:

"THE WAR NEEDS YOU."

I stare at them for too long. A joke. A slap in the face. A life I can't have anymore, mocking me from the goddamn walls.

And then—

"Is that Hale?"

The voice breaks through the noise like a crack in glass—just loud enough, just pointed enough to feel intentional.

My fingers pause mid-swirl.

Another voice follows, half-laughing. "Shit, I think it is. Didn't recognize him without the armor."

I don't turn. Not yet, but the stool creaks beneath me as I shift my weight. My jaw tightens. Somewhere behind me, I hear the scrape of a chair and the faintest clink of dog tags. I know that sound. I know that posture. This isn't curiosity. It's bait.

I set the glass down and listen—heartbeat steady, but only because I've trained it to be.

"Thought he'd be taller," someone mutters. A scoff. More laughter.

Every word grinds like gravel in my teeth.

"Wasn't he the one who got pulled after the Turig fight?"

"Yeah. They say he went down hard. Had to be dragged out."

Then, the final blow—meant to hit square in the gut: "I heard he used to lead one of the best teams out there. Guess the standards weren't that high after all."

Laughter again—louder now. I exhale through my nose, slow and sharp. The stool scrapes against the floor as I stand.

"Figures. Another golden boy gets knocked down a peg and pulls out while he's ahead."

I don't remember crossing the room. But suddenly, I'm there—towering over them. Three guys. Mid twenties. Still wearing the stiffness of base discipline in their shoulders. Mid-rank. Probably think they've seen enough to run their mouths.

"You get your intel from mission reports or bar gossip?" My voice is calm. Controlled. That's the only warning I give.

One of them leans forward, elbows on the table, smirking. "Did I hit a nerve?"

Another—tall, dark buzzcut, the one doing most of the talking—leans back in his chair like I'm a curiosity. "Relax, man, no disrespect. Just seems like a shame. Thought real leaders went down with their teams."

The third chimes in, taking a long sip of his drink. "We heard you were revered once. Then you quit."

That word hangs in the air like a match over gas.

Quit.

I see red.

They don't know.

They don't know I bled for every inch.

They don't know I begged to stay.

Chapter 14

They don't know what it felt like to be told I was unstable. Useless.

My fist connects with his face before I realize I've moved. The impact against my knuckles comes first. The way his head jerks sideways, the way his chair crashes to the floor. Then—chaos.

Parker—if that was his name—comes back swinging. I move to block but—too fast. Pain bursts in my ribs. My body falters. Another hit slams into my jaw. My vision flickers.

I grab his collar, drive him into the bar, my knee slamming into his gut. He coughs, but his buddies are already moving.

Three-on-one.

I should have the advantage—I know I do.

But something's wrong.

I move too fast, overshoot my own momentum—a punch meant to connect just grazes past. My footwork is off. A boot catches my knee. An elbow clips my temple. A fist crashes into my ribs—right where I was injured in the Turig battle.

White-hot pain.

I collapse against the bar, gasping and I can barely hear the bartender shouting.

A hand grips the front of my shirt, dragging me upright. Parker's face swims into focus. "That's the difference, Hale," he sneers. "You're not one of us anymore. You never will be."

A different voice cuts in—Calvin. "Jesus, Ben—what the hell are you doing?"

I blink up at him, blood pooling in my mouth. For the first time, it sinks in.

I lost.

I don't belong here anymore.

PAIN PULSES IN my ribs with every breath, the dull ache of bruises settling in. The metallic taste of blood lingers in my mouth. I stare at my reflection in the bathroom mirror—eyes shadowed, jaw swollen, a thin line of dried blood crusted along my temple.

Calvin leans against the doorframe, arms crossed. He's been watching me for a while now, silent, waiting. "You done?" he finally asks.

I splash cold water on my face, ignoring the sting. "What do you think?"

He exhales through his nose. "I think you look like you got in a fight with a dumpster. And the dumpster won."

I snort, wincing at the movement. "Felt like it."

He doesn't smile. "You can't keep doing this, Ben."

I grip the edges of the sink. The words claw at me because they're true. "Yeah?" My voice is rough. "Then what the hell am I supposed to do?"

"Start by getting off your ass and coming to dinner tomorrow."

I glare at him through the mirror. "Pass."

"Not an option." He pushes off the doorframe. "My parents are in town, and I'm telling them about my new job. I need you there."

"To distract them?"

"To keep me from drowning in their inevitable disappointment? Yes." He adjusts his glasses, then frowns, taking in the damage on my face. "Besides, you're already sporting the perfect look for sympathy points."

"Great. I'll be the cautionary tale."

"Exactly." His smirk returns, but there's a softness beneath it. "Come on, man. You can't keep rotting away in bars and sleeping it off in the apartment. You need to start giving a damn again."

I sigh, rubbing a hand down my face. "Fine. But if this turns into another lecture about my life choices, I'm walking."

Calvin lifts his hands in mock surrender. "No lectures. Just dinner. Maybe even decent food for once."

"Debatable."

His grin widens. "Then let's call it a social experiment. If you survive, I'll even pick up your tab next time we go out— on the condition that it's not a dive bar where I have to drag your ass out again."

I huff a laugh despite myself. "Fine.

Calvin claps me on the shoulder, careful to avoid the worst bruises. "That's the spirit."

He heads out first, and I linger behind, gripping the edge of the sink. My reflection stares back, hollow-eyed and unrecognizable.

Maybe I owe him.

Maybe I just need to feel like someone still expects me to show up.

Either way, I'll be there.

Chapter 15

The seconds tick by on the wall clock, each one mocking me with military precision. My muscles ache from the highly educational barroom lesson in why fighting three guys at once is a terrible idea. Turns out, getting your ass kicked still hurts, even when you're too numb to care.

Calvin's reflection appears in the TV screen, his lanky frame squeezed into what looks like a job interview outfit having an identity crisis. Dark blue blazer, crisp white shirt, red power tie… and, of course, the Converse sneakers. Because why commit?

"You getting dressed, or do I have to physically remove you from this couch?"

I grunt, not looking away from the screen. "You're assuming I care enough to resist."

He sighs, adjusting his glasses like a disappointed professor. "Ben, we had a deal. You go three rounds with guys who don't even know your name, I haul your pathetic ass out of there, and in return, you show up to dinner looking like a respectable member of society."

I drag a hand down my face. "I don't remember agreeing to respectable."

"You bled on my shirt, that's legally binding in some cultures."

I grunt again, shifting just enough to test whether moving is worth the effort. My ribs light up like live wires, and my leg pulses in protest—deep and hot and far too familiar. "You know, I think I'll sit this one out. Really let the whole rock-bottom vibe settle in."

I don't say what I really want to—that the ache in my leg isn't fading like it should. That the bruises feel deeper than they ought to. I tell myself it's just the bar fight. Residual punishment. Nothing more.

Cal crosses his arms. "You can't. It's in the contract."

"What contract?"

"The social contract, where you don't make me face my parents alone after telling them I signed military contractor documents. You're my emotional support disaster, so get up."

I glare at him. "I want that in writing."

"Too late. Now put on something that doesn't scream 'unemployed cage fighter.'"

With an overly dramatic sigh, I push myself up. Everything still aches, and my ribs remind me that I'm not as invincible as I pretend to be. The leg's worse today—tight, restless, like it's remembering all the moments I'd rather forget. "Fine. But I'm still holding you to that drink afterward."

Cal smirks. "Of course. After all, you'll need something to wash down all the pity my mother is about to serve you."

Le Coeur De Chou looms before us like some kind of French castle that mated with a luxury hotel. I shove my hands deep in my pockets, examining the artwork mounted in shadow boxes that float pretentiously four inches from the maroon and gold wallpaper. A mahogany chair rail winds around the room like it's trying to hold the whole place together. Hanging plants dangle from the ceiling, each one spotlit like a vegetable celebrity. I keep my eyes on the art, anything to avoid drowning in the suffocating warmth of old money and new pretension.

Behind a matching mahogany podium stands a young man with dark curly hair wearing what looks like a penguin costume designed by someone who's only seen penguins in black-and-white photos. He touches his earpiece with practiced elegance and smiles. "Bonsoir messieurs, have you a reservation?" His accent is thicker than the sauce they probably put on everything.

"Oui," Cal begins, showing off his multilingual prowess— sometimes I forget my best friend is basically a walking Google Translate.

Then I see her. A flash of red. Hair like fire and memory. It hits me like a round to the chest.

My body moves before my brain can catch up, instinct clawing its way to the surface. But Cal's hand clamps down on my arm—steadying, grounding, anchoring me to a present I suddenly don't want. My skin prickles with recognition, body remembering what my mind is trying to forget.

"Where are you going?" He asks.

I look down the hallway where she disappeared, then back at Cal. "Sorry, I thought I saw someone."

"Oh, well then it can wait. My parents are already seated."

I throw one last glance at the hallway before following them to our table, my heart doing a drill sequence in my chest. Ghosts aren't supposed to look that real.

"Benji!" Louise explodes from her chair like she's been spring-loaded. "What a surprise!"

I smile as she grabs my face, planting kisses on both cheeks that leave me gasping through a cloud of Chanel No. 5.

"Heya, Pop." Cal attempts a casual side-hug with his father, who stands with military stiffness.

"Calvin, my baby! You didn't tell me you were bringing Benji along." Louise envelops Cal in the same perfume-heavy embrace. I try to fix my hair, feeling underdressed for a place where even the napkins probably have college degrees.

"Good to see you, Ben." Arthur extends his hand like he's offering a peace treaty.

"Sir." I shake it and help Louise back to her seat before taking my own, positioned like a human shield between Cal and his parents.

Louise studies me for half a second before frowning, her fingers brushing a bruise just beneath my jaw. "Benji, what on Earth happened to your face?"

I resist the urge to flinch. "It's nothing."

Her mouth tightens. "The military was too hard on you," she says, shaking her head like a disappointed mother. "You give and give, and they chew you up like meat. If I had my way, you wouldn't have to suffer another day for them."

"Ma, don't start," Cal warns, but Arthur leans back in his chair with a dry chuckle.

"She's not wrong," he says, stirring his drink. "The military doesn't care about men like Ben. Or the countless others caught in the crossfire of a war that stopped making sense a long time ago."

Cal tenses. "Pop—"

Louise steps in before the embers catch. "Arthur, don't turn dinner into a battlefield."

Arthur lifts his glass in mock surrender, then turns to me. "Tell me, Ben. After everything you've seen, do you still believe in this war?"

I glance toward the recruitment posters on the restaurant walls. Bright-eyed young men in uniform. Slogans promising honor. Service. Glory. The same propaganda that lured in boys like me, the same empty words that sent soldiers dying for a cause no one can explain anymore.

I should have an answer. The military trained me to give the right one. Serve with honor. Protect the innocent. Fight for victory. But the words stick in my throat.

Louise must sense my hesitation because she clucks her tongue, shaking her head. "Leave him be, Arthur. He's been through enough without you pressing him for politics at the dinner table."

Arthur exhales sharply, setting his drink down with a clink. "It's not politics, Louise. It's common sense. The longer this war drags on, the more it devours. It chews up good men and spits them out broken, all over a science neither side should have been playing with in the first place."

Calvin's grip tightens around his napkin. "Pop—"

Arthur doesn't let him finish. "You think the brass cares? They'll keep feeding bodies into the fire until there's nothing left. And when it's over, both sides will have lost."

For a moment, the only sound is the distant clink of silverware and quiet conversation from the other tables.

Then Calvin straightens. "That's not entirely true."

Arthur eyes him warily. "What are you trying to say, son?"

Cal clears his throat. "I have a new job. Heading up a science lab. It starts a week from Monday."

"Fabulous!" Louise's voice carries to the next zip code.

Arthur, however, watches him closely. "Which foundation managed to hire on your brilliant mind?"

Cal shifts in his chair. "See, that's the thing..." He hesitates. "It's a contracted job. With the military."

The silence that follows is suffocating.

Arthur's expression barely changes, but his posture goes rigid. "The military," he repeats.

"Yes, Pop. I'll be working on new advancements to give us an upper hand."

Arthur's eyebrows collide. "You mean to escalate the war. To throw more fuel on a fire that's already burning out of control."

Calvin exhales. "Pop, this isn't some mindless weapons project. It's research. We're working to advance our understanding of—"

"Of what?" Arthur cuts in. "The same virus that started all of this? The one they lied about? The one both sides twisted into their own justification for slaughter?"

He leans forward, voice lower now, steady. "You think I don't know what's in those labs? I sat in those meetings, Cal. Back when diplomacy still had value. This war didn't start with aggression. It started with fear. A joint bio-weapons program. Our side, and a neighboring territory, were prepping for a land grab. They stitched together multiple virus strains to create something controllable. An edge that would make us faster, stronger, harder to kill. But they lost control." His fingers tap the table in rhythm. "The result? Those Turig monsters. The virus that didn't just kill. It waited. It transformed the host after death. Perfect weapon. Until it started spreading to those it killed."

Calvin falls still.

Arthur glances toward me. "They called in special ops to clean it up. Right, Ben? But it never was containable. Someone decided to start using the Turig intentionally. Manufacture chaos. Tip global scales."

My jaw clenches. None of that was in my briefings. But I'd seen things in the field—bodies that didn't stay dead, outbreaks in cities that should've been quarantined. Missions that were more about silence than saving lives.

Arthur turns back to Calvin. "And you? You want to sign your name to that mess?"

"I don't want to weaponize anything," Calvin says, quieter now. "But we can't keep pretending it's not already being done. Someone has to get in there and fix it."

Arthur laughs without humor. "You think you'll fix it from inside the machine? You'll either become part of the engine or get ground beneath it."

Calvin's voice strains. "I read the contract. I had a lawyer go over it. It's work that could help end this."

Arthur leans back, folding his arms. "As long as you keep

wearing that badge for them, you're no son of mine."

"Arthur!" Louise barks. "Behave yourself."

"Louise—"

She shushes him with a sharp wave of her napkin. "Ah pup-pup-up." The silent stillness that follows is like the moment after a grenade pin is pulled. Tense. Waiting.

Cal slumps against his hand, trying to disappear.

Louise clears her throat delicately, switching gears like a pro. "So, Benji, darling, tell me. Have you found a nice girl to tame that wild side of yours?"

I manage a smile. "No, ma'am. Not yet. So far, you're the only lady who can make me so well-mannered."

Louise giggles like a schoolgirl. "Oh, you do go on! Really though, dear, there's nobody?"

My eyes drift to the hallway again, chest tightening around an old wound that never quite healed. My fingers tremble slightly before I close them into a fist. *Why does she still haunt me?* "Not for a while, now."

"Perhaps I should speak to my friends. I know some have daughters around your age and they'd likely be a great match. You're such a good boy." Louise sips her champagne like she's already planning wedding colors.

But I barely hear her. Because there she is again—not a ghost, not a memory, but flesh and blood walking through the lobby. The hem of her green dress swaying with each step, and suddenly I'm drowning in all the moments I thought I'd buried. My heart skips like it's trying to catch up to her.

"Oooh, is that her then?" Louise's voice carries a dangerous amount of matchmaker enthusiasm.

I shake my head, trying to clear it. "No, I—there was a misunderstanding between us a while back, and I owe an apology." I stand, tossing my napkin onto the seat. "Would you excuse me for just a moment?"

As I walk toward the exit, every survival instinct screams that this is a terrible idea. But a stronger gravity pulls me forward—the need to fix what broke, or at least understand why it shattered.

"Eden." Her name feels both foreign and familiar on my tongue. She turns, dress swirling like liquid emerald, eyes hitting me with the same force they always have. For one breathless second, she looks like the calm between dusk and nightfall—vesper in a dress and heels.

Her gaze lands on me. And just like that, I'm under a microscope. She takes in the bruises first—the sharp purple bloom along my jaw, the split in my lip, the stiffness in the way I'm holding myself. Then, her gaze moves lower. The tension in my shoulders. The exhaustion I can't quite hide. The way I don't quite meet her eyes, like I already know what I'll find there.

Her fingers twitch. Just slightly. Like she wants to reach for me. Check my injuries. Assess the damage. But she catches herself. Her posture shifts—wariness replacing concern. And just like that, the nurse is gone, and the careful mask is back.

I force a smirk. "You look like you're about to diagnose me."

Her expression doesn't change. "What happened?"

I roll my shoulders, playing it off. "Nothing I couldn't handle."

She doesn't buy it. I can feel her studying me. Not just the bruises. All of it. The weariness, the recklessness. The fact that I don't care as much as I should. She sees it—sees me. And suddenly, I'm too tired to fake it.

The smirk slips just slightly. But she catches it. Recognition flickers across her face—soft, almost warm— before disappearing again. I'm not sure which hurts more.

I turn away first. Because if I don't, I might do something stupid. Like tell her that I've been losing my grip without her. The silence between us lingers, heavier than before.

"Ben…" Her smile is hesitant, measured, breaking the tension. "What are you doing here?"

I gesture vaguely behind me. "Dinner with some friends. What about you, hot date?"

Her eyebrows dip slightly. "No. I thought I'd start treating myself better since... well, you know." She pulls her shawl tighter, the dark red roses embroidered along its edge almost looking like bloodstains against the green.

"Ahh, I see. You deserve it." I rub my unkempt chin before shoving my hand in my pocket—clearing my throat, needing to shake off the weight of it. "Look, since you're here anyway… do you have a second?"

"Ben... we—"

"It's not like that." I close my eyes, blocking out whatever I might see in hers. "Calvin. He's my best friend, and he mentioned wanting to meet the person who saved my life."

She shakes her head. "I didn't—"

"Not according to him," I interrupt. "Just—come back to the table for a second, say hi, and then you can leave. No pressure." I try for a sheepish grin, hoping it doesn't look as desperate as it feels.

The hesitation flickers in her expression. She glances toward the exit, toward the clean escape. Then back at me.

A sigh escapes her, and her shoulders ease—just barely. "Okay," she says quietly. "Five minutes."

Hope and regret mix dangerously in my chest.

Louise spots us approaching and her eyes light up like Christmas came early. "Benjamin, who is your friend, dear?" She navigates around the table with surprising agility for someone who's had that much champagne. "I'm Louise, Benji's self-adoptive mother."

Eden's smile is polite, practiced, as she extends her hand. "Nice to meet you. I'm Eden Lively."

"Oh, don't be silly." Louise bats Eden's hand away like an annoying moth and engulfs her in a perfume-heavy hug. "If you know our Benji, then you're as good as family!" She turns, waving at the others. "This is my husband, Arthur, and our son, Benji's best friend, Calvin."

Calvin's eyes dart from her to me and back again. "Eden Lively," he repeats slowly, like he's testing the shape of her name on his tongue. "That's a name you remember. Ben talks about you like you walk on air."

Eden gives me a sideways look, teasing. "Oh, is that so?"

Calvin leans forward, offering his hand with a grin that's too easy. "Well, I'm Calvin. And if Ben's said half as much as I think he has, I'm already jealous."

"Is this the one?" Louise whispers to me, conspiratorial. "Because if she's not, I'm going to need a full explanation."

I deflect. "Louise, here, is exactly what you'd expect from someone who tries to make everything a holiday."

Louise beams. "And proud of it."

Arthur cuts in dryly. "Are we done with introductions, or should I expect a toast as well?"

Eden's smile tightens. "Nice to meet all of you." Then to me, her voice laced with that same barbed wire charm, "I wasn't aware you had people who could've visited you in the hospital... Benji."

The nickname lands sharp. I try to play it off. "You know

what? They're very busy people."

"Hospital? You were in the hospital?" Louise's hand finds my arm again, worry flooding her eyes. "Benji, were you hurt?"

"It was nothing, Louise. Really."

"Nearly dying is not nothing." Eden's voice cuts through the chatter.

"Benji! You said nothing of the sort!" Louise shrills.

"It was a while ago," I say quickly. "Didn't want to be a bother. Besides, Cal knew."

"Calvin! You didn't tell us?" Louise's head snaps to look at her son.

"I… well you… he—" Calvin fumbles over his words.

"Come, Eden, sit," Louise says, rallying. "You're already family."

"I really shouldn't—"

"Nonsense!" Louise snaps, and just like that, a seat appears next to mine, across from Calvin's.

The smile that flickers on Eden's lips isn't the one she gives me. And the knowing in my chest tightens when she laughs—light, polite, like she doesn't mind the attention.

I watch them fall into easy rhythm—Calvin's charm, Eden's laughter, and somewhere between them, the part of me I didn't know I still wanted back.

Chapter 16

Metal clanks against metal as I rack another set. Sweat runs down my temples, dripping from my chin onto the bench.

I haven't missed a workout in the weeks since they started seeing each other. Maybe it's all just habit now—routine masquerading as purpose. The weight used to make my arms shake by the third rep. Now I blow through the set before the burn really starts. I tell myself it's just progress. Recovery. But sometimes, when I squeeze the bar too tight, it feels like the metal might give.

The knock at the door pulls me up, muscles swollen slightly from exertion. I grab my water bottle, the plastic crackling as I squeeze it, cold water hitting the back of my throat as I walk to the door.

"Hey, Ben." Eden stands in the doorway, today's hospital shift still lingering in the shadows under her eyes. I step aside to let her in, catching the faint antiseptic smell that follows nurses home. "You're sweaty."

"Bench press day." I wipe my palm against my shorts, condensation from the bottle making my grip slick. "How was work?"

"Can't complain any more than usual."

"I have yet to hear you complain. Ever."

She chuckles, tucking a loose strand of hair behind her ear. The movement catches light from the window, turning the copper to gold for a glimmer of a moment. "My comment stands."

"Well, I'd offer to hug ya, but..." I gesture to my soaked

shirt, fabric clinging to skin. "I'm sweaty." I smirk.

"You know the nature of my job. Sweat is nothing compared to some of the stuff I get exposed to."

I laugh as I settle back onto the bench, fingers finding their familiar placement on the bar. "Gross."

"Hey!" Cal's voice echoes down the hallway before he emerges. "I thought I heard your voice." He crosses the room in those long strides of his, wrapping an arm around her waist, pressing a kiss to her cheek. My grip tightens on the bar. "You ready?"

"Just waiting on you," she says, leaning into him with an ease that makes my stomach clench.

"We're outta here, Ben," Cal says, glancing my way.

"Yap." I focus on the weights, counting each rep silently. The numbers helping to drown out everything else.

"I'll probably be back late. Don't wait up."

The bar lands on the rack with a sharp clang that makes Eden jump slightly. I sit up, reaching for my water again. "Don't worry. I won't."

"Ben..." Eden's voice softens.

I allow myself to look at her.

"It's really great to see you doing so well. Keep it up."

I nod, breathing heavier than I should be. Not from the weight, not really. But from the hollowness in my chest I haven't named yet. It always tightens when she walks away like this—with someone else. "Nah, just took some time to get my motivation back. I'm good. You two go have fun." The door clicks shut with quiet finality.

The weights feel heavier now, like they're made of memories instead of metal. Each breath comes harder, louder in the empty apartment. My palms burn against the knurled bar as her image floods back—not just her smile, but that look she gave me once. Like I was worth saving. Worth more than what I'd become. One perfect moment I can't seem to forget, no matter how hard I try.

"Stop it, Ben." The words scrape out as I drag the towel across my face, rough terry cloth catching on stubble. But the memory clings like the salt on my skin. I toss my empty bottle toward the recycling, the hollow plastic sound echoing my thoughts as I head to the kitchen. The protein shake whirs together, thick and chalky, before I step out onto the patio.

The evening air hits my overheated skin as I sink into my chair. Beyond our building, the park spreads out in waves of green, clouds drifting overhead like lost thoughts. Children's laughter carries up from below, bright and pure, making the empty space in my chest ache deeper. The idea seems absurd now—that I could have had that life. *Me, with a family?*

Somewhere across the district, sirens wail—sharp and rising to drown out the child's play before fading again. Patrol units. Another lockdown. Maybe another scare. It's hard to tell anymore.

I lean back, propping my feet on the railing, letting the breeze carry their joy past me. Sweet pastry scents waft up from the bakery next door, reminding me of things I shouldn't want.

When I open my eyes, dusk has painted the sky in bruised purples. My fingers find the surgery scar automatically, tracing its raised edge through my shirt. The familiar what-if game starts: Where would I be without the surgery? A dry chuckle escapes me. Still have my whole lung, sure. But I may not have my life. Eden saved more than just my breathing that day—she showed me I was worth anything at all.

The empty protein shake glass dangles from my fingers as I watch the first stars pierce through dying sunlight. Below, the children's voices swell louder, pulling an unwilling smile from me. Simple joys. Just enough to keep standing.

Inside, the sofa groans under my weight as I yell into my headset. "Oh, come on! Way to have my back out there, guys!" My foot braces against the coffee table's edge, navigating around takeout containers that should have been cleared away hours ago.

Static-laced laughter crackles through. "That was you camping the corner, Hale?"

"I told you my console was buggin' out!"

"Nice cover. You've just gone soft. Lost your edge!"

"Shut up, Douggle!" I reach for the pastry I bought earlier but haven't touched, plastic crinkling under my fingers.

"What are you gonna do to make me?" More laughter.

"I'll take you one on one any day, old man."

"Who you callin' old man?"

The front door's hinges squeak as Cal walks in—a sharp, grating pitch that feels louder than it should. It's been doing that for weeks, but lately, it cuts through everything like nails on metal. Probably just need some oil.

"Got a mirror handy?" I smirk, but it fades when I see Cal's expression. His eyes have that distant look, jaw set in a way that usually means a big reveal is coming. I tilt my head, mouthing, What's up?

He shrugs off his trench coat, the fabric rustling as he drapes it over one arm. The couch cushion dips as he sits, his hands gripping his knees with nervous energy.

"Yo, Douggle, I gotta bolt."

"Scared to lose again. I got ya."

"I'll hit ya next time."

"Later," Douggle says as I pull off my headset, the plastic catching slightly in my hair.

"Cal?"

"Ben..." His whisper carries weight. "I can't even begin—"

"What happened?"

"I dropped Eden off and spent the entire way back just buzzing."

"Buzzing?" I scratch my cheek, stubble rasping against my fingertips. "Is this a good buzzing or more like the thing that happened that one time?"

"No, it's not like—Ben." Calvin exhales like he's been holding it in for hours. "We were eating dinner on the balcony. She's so beautiful. And when the sun set, she paused mid-conversation to look at the sky…"

I nod, reaching for my water, already regretting asking. "Wow. That sounds… poetic."

Calvin's eyes go distant, lost in the memory. "She said, 'If we were never exposed to darkness, we'd never see the potential of everything life has to offer.' And that's when I knew."

The ache flares again, hot and sharp under my ribs.

I raise an eyebrow. "Knew what? That you'd been possessed by a Hallmark card?"

He laughs, too caught up to notice I'm not laughing with him. "No, man. I knew she was it. The one. I'm going to ask Eden to marry me."

The words I should have expected still hit like a sucker punch. I lean back, forcing a tight smile. "Well, that's… sudden. But sure. Who doesn't love a dramatic reveal mid-week?"

Cal claps my shoulder, too wrapped up in the glow of it all to notice the way I flinch. "I never would've met her without you."

The smile fades before it fully forms. "Don't say that."

Calvin blinks. "What?"

I shake my head, adopting a lighter tone. "You know what I mean. She's your choice. Your future. Don't go rewriting history to make it sentimental."

He chuckles, shrugging. "Alright, fine. But you're still gonna help me pull it off."

I glance toward the window. The lights from the street blur for a moment. "Happy to play third wheel in your origin story." The weight in my chest grows, pressing against my lungs like water. I clap his shoulder and stand, needing to move, to breathe, to do anything other than sit there next to him. "Because I'm a glutton for emotional punishment," I mutter, rising from the couch.

"Where are you going?" He snaps out of his daze.

"I'm not feeling well all of a sudden. I'm gonna step outside for some air. Probably all that junk food I had earlier." My eyes sweep over our cluttered apartment, takeout containers and empty bottles reflecting a life coming undone at the edges.

Cal kicks off his shoes, the soft thud against carpet too loud in my ears. "Well, hurry back in. We need to get started on a plan."

"Wouldn't have it any other way."

The night air hits me like a welcome slap as I step outside. The railing is cool under my palms as I lean forward, trying to breathe past the tightness in my chest. "Easy, Ben. You knew you could never have her," I whisper into the darkness, metal groaning under my white-knuckled grip.

Another deep breath that catches somewhere between my lungs and the truth, and I drop into a push-up position near the railing. I haven't attempted this since the surgery—the doctors made it clear why I shouldn't—but right now the promise of physical pain feels like relief. A sensation I can understand.

"One," I growl through clenched teeth, arms shaking as I push against the concrete floor. "Two... three..."

By seventeen, my side burns. The doctors said I shouldn't push past ten—not this soon, not with what's still healing. But I keep going. Because feeling too strong is easier than feeling nothing at all.

"Twenty-five... twenty-six..."

Every rep is a distraction. Each one, forcing out another

memory, another moment I should have buried deeper—her laughter echoing off hallway walls, the precision in her fingers, the warmth of her goodbye.

"Thirty."

My arms give, and I let myself collapse onto the floor and roll over. Sweat pools against my spine, cooling too fast. I lock my fingers behind my head, lungs fighting for air that won't settle.

Above me, the stars blink behind hazy skies—distant, cold, watching. Her voice echoes in the quiet: *"There's potential in the dark. Profound discoveries."* That line. That damn line. The one that pulled me in.

Now it just lingers, weightless and heavy at the same time. My throat burns, the pain of pushing myself too hard ever present. And still, the ache in my heart doesn't fade. It doesn't burn out. It just stays.

And I don't know what scares me more—that it hurts, or that I'm starting to get used to it.

Chapter 17

The hum of helicopters has become background noise. Low, distant. Constant. The sound used to send a rush of readiness through me. Now, it's just another reminder that the world's still burning—and I'm no longer part of the fight.

I submitted the re-enlistment paperwork two days ago, right after Cal told me he wants to marry the one person who could have kept me from going back. I walked the form through recruitment myself. No ceremony, no announcement. Just me, a folder, and the low-level hum of fluorescents overhead as I waited for someone to call my name. Part of me hopes they'll say yes. The rest of me is bracing for the no.

I've been doing what I can. Helping where I can. Staying useful. It's not the same, but it beats the alternative. Calvin and Eden seem... happy. Solid. He hasn't said much since telling me he planned to propose, but he doesn't have to. I see it in the way his shoulders drop when she walks in. Like she's gravity, and he's finally found his footing.

I keep my distance. Smile when I have to. Play the part. Lately, I've been putting that energy into planning things for other people. Like this proposal. Like maybe if I get it just right for him, it'll make up for the fact that I can't seem to get anything right for myself.

"What if..." I pause, tasting the words before I let them out, "you get her family and friends to film a heartfelt message to her? About how fun she is, or the first time they met her. Something memorable. Go to the local museum, and see if they can set up a special gallery to play these videos.

And at the end, there's a video of you listing off all your reasons she's amazing. When she turns to look at you, you can be on one knee with the ring and the whole shebang."

Calvin stares at me like I've suddenly started speaking in tongues. The ceiling fan whirs overhead, marking the silence.

"What?" I shrug, the leather chair creaking under my weight.

He shakes his head slowly, eyes drifting shut before opening again. The afternoon light catches his glasses, momentarily hiding his expression. "How... did you even come up with that?"

"I dunno, man." My palms suddenly dampen against my jeans as I rub them. The words taste like copper in my mouth. "Just thought of somewhere I might take someone on an actual date, but then incorporated some personal touches. You know, like messages from her family and stuff in there. It wasn't that hard, really." Each word feels like another small betrayal, planning someone else's perfect moment with her.

He exhales a laugh that sounds almost like disbelief. "I've been racking my brain for two months, and nothing even came close to touching that."

"Well, you're too close to the picture. Sometimes you've got to step back to see the whole thing." The irony of my own words isn't lost on me.

"You've got to help me through all of this. I have no idea what I'm doing."

"Of course, Cal. You're my best friend." I force a grin. "Besides, you've never been good at girls."

"Hey!" His protest carries half a laugh.

"Can't knock the truth, man." The smirk feels more natural now, falling into our usual rhythm.

"I came around eventually."

"That's right." I stand, clapping his shoulder, feeling the familiar bony frame under his shirt. "Luckily for you, it was right around the time Eden came into the picture. Or maybe she's just way into nerds."

My footsteps echo against the wooden floor as I head down the hallway, each one carrying me further from the conversation I don't want to finish. The closet door slides open with a soft whisper of wheels on track. "Or maybe..." The words slip out barely above a breath, "it's the easiest way to stay close without being vulnerable to the monster inside..."

The thought hangs heavy in the air as I unzip the black

camera bag, checking the equipment inside. The familiar smell of leather and electronics grounds me in the present.

A low rumble passes overhead. Helicopter patrol—close enough to rattle the windows. The thump of rotors fades slowly, replaced by distant sirens—quick, clipped bursts warning curfew's approaching somewhere down-district. I don't move, just run my thumb over the camera grip.

"Can you get me a list of friends from the hospital during your next visit?" Cal's voice carries from the kitchen, casual as discussing the weather. Ice cubes clink against glass. "You know, since you're there so often."

"Not intentionally." The camera strap settles across my shoulder, its weight familiar. I walk back into the living room, where late afternoon sun slants through the blinds in dusty bars. "But I'll try. Might need to go through her address book."

"Thanks, man. I'm pretty busy with work right now. Plus, if she caught me snooping, I doubt that would go over well. She'd ask why, and I don't want to spoil the surprise."

I lean against the wall, arms crossed over my chest. The cool surface seeps through my shirt. "I meant *you* go through her address book."

His face contorts like I've suggested breaking into Fort Knox. "I can't do that, Ben!"

"How the hell am I supposed to do it? You're the one frequenting her place."

Calvin hesitates, running fingers through his hair—a nervous habit since college. "Maybe we can set up a double date. Dinner and drinks over there. I'll pitch it to her as a way to cheer you up. You've been sad and lonely lately."

Heat rises in my neck as I glare at him. "So now I'm a charity case?"

"Hardly." His hands go up, palms out. "But I have to say something."

"No, you don't. What's wrong with *just* having me over for dinner?"

"We can eat dinner anywhere, but if it's a blind date with one of her friends, there's a reason to be at her house."

A long sigh escapes me as I set the camera bag on the table, the soft thud punctuating my surrender. The chair protests as I drop into it. "Fine." I meet his eyes pointedly. "But for the record, I'm fine."

Calvin's expression softens, and I see the same look he gave me in the hospital. "I know that, Ben."

"Good. Now sit down so I can show you how to use this thing without breaking it."

"I'm a nerd, Ben. I know how to use a camera." He smirks, biting into a carrot with a sharp crunch. His arms fold across his chest in mock offense.

"Sit."

"Okay, okay." His laugh fills the room as he drops into the chair across from me. He reaches for the camera with that focused intensity I remember from high school lab days, turning it over in his hands like it might hold secrets.

AFTER GOING OVER the basic plan, Calvin leans over the camera, adjusting the settings. "So the museum should be able to play it straight from the queue?"

"Exactly." I gesture to the screen. "You can load them here, make a little menu if you want."

He grins, impressed. "Man... I'm lucky you're still around to help me with this."

I shrug, trying to keep it casual. "Well... I might not be around much longer."

Calvin blinks up at me. "What do you mean?"

I reach for the lens cap, clicking it into place. "I'm thinking of reapplying. Enlistment. A different branch, maybe. I've been getting stronger... figured it's worth a shot." He doesn't know I've already submitted the paperwork.

"You serious?"

"As a heart attack." I meet his eyes. "Just need a few more tests, maybe a couple letters from the docs. I've already started the process."

He sits back, brows drawn tight. "You sure that's what you want?"

I force a grin. "Don't really see myself doing anything else."

He exhales through his nose, eyes narrowing slightly. "You know, I did offer to get you into the lab."

I glance away. "Yeah, I remember." What I don't say: I remember too well. It felt like a lifeline, and I shoved it away. Because sitting behind a desk while someone else takes the hits feels like wearing a medal I didn't earn. "I just need to be useful again. Really useful."

Calvin watches me for a beat, expression unreadable.

"There's more than one way to serve, Ben."

The words sit between us like a challenge, but I just shake my head. "I'm not built for this domestic shit, Cal."

Calvin doesn't answer right away. Just nods slowly, like he's filing it away for later. "Well... in the meantime, since you're still going in and out of that hospital, can you get me a list of Eden's friends for the video thing?"

"Yeah, yeah." I roll my eyes. "I'll keep an ear open. But if I get tackled by hospital security, I'm blaming you."

"You'll be fine. The nurses love you."

"They love poking me with needles, maybe."

Cal chuckles, but his eyes linger on me a second longer. I can tell he's still chewing on what I said.

For just a moment, the weight in my chest eases. Teaching Cal a practical skill—something real—feels like solid ground under my feet. Even if it's for her. Maybe this is how I learn to let go: one small step at a time, one quiet choice to honor friendship over fantasy.

His excitement over the camera fills the room, familiar and bright, and despite everything... I smile.

Maybe, just maybe, I'll find a way to live with the life I didn't choose.

That night, after Cal went to bed, I sit on the balcony for hours. Watching the city lights flicker behind haze, headlights blinking in and out like thoughts I didn't want to name. I tell myself I could be okay with it—being the helper, the builder, the bystander. I believed it, right up until I couldn't sit still anymore. Until the quiet got too loud. Until the street started calling again, like it always does.

Chapter 18

Some days feel louder than others. Not because of noise—but because of what's missing.

The apartment's been quiet for a while now with Cal working. It's the kind of quiet that creeps in when someone's absence leaves behind a shape you can still feel. It's hard to sit still in the silence. It's not uncomfortable… just expectant.

The city isn't much better—feels like it's holding its breath. But at least it's easier to distract myself.

I wasn't planning to stay out long. The curfew banners haven't flashed yet, and technically, I've got some leeway—veteran status still gets you a little grace, so long as you keep your nose clean. Which I've been trying to do. Ever since I submitted the re-enlistment paperwork, I've been toeing the line. No trouble. No complications. Just enough discipline to show them I'm still valuable.

A helicopter rumbles overhead, its blades chopping through the night like a slow warning. I pause beneath the flicker of a dying streetlamp, watching its light stutter against the pavement like it can't make up its mind about staying on. The bakery across the street is already dark, its chalkboard sign washed half-clean from the earlier rain.

The air smells like wet concrete and tension.

I cross the street without hurrying. Not because I'm careless. But because I don't expect anything to happen. But that's the thing about moments that change everything.

They don't announce themselves. They wait until you're relaxed. Off guard. And then… they break you.

I walk past one of the old border barricades, rusted and tagged with fresh graffiti: NO KINGS IN BLOOD. A leftover from the first Turig infiltration scare, back when everyone thought the war was still black and white. Now the war feels more like a fog—everywhere, seeping in, even here in the base civilian zones. It used to feel like these streets belonged to us. Now... not so much.

A scream cuts through the air—sharp and panicked. I freeze. Another voice follows, low and threatening.

No thinking. Just instinct. I move. Another voice—low, threatening. A man.

Turning the corner, I see two men pinning a woman against the wall. Her bag is already on the ground, its contents scattered. The man closest to her grips her arm. The other watches, like he's waiting his turn.

I step forward.

This is what you do.

You stop this shit from happening.

"Let her go." my voice echoes against the bare concrete walls.

Both men turn. The first one grins. "Oh, a tough guy, huh?"

I take another step.

They don't move.

They should move.

Why aren't they moving?

I hear the rustle of fabric—one of them reaching.

A blade.

My vision tunnels and the street dissolves into cold metal corridors, the smell of blood and burning electronics. Gunfire. Screams.

The Turig soldier lunges. I react. Block. Pivot. Counter. My name crackles through the comms. My team. They need me.

Move. Move. MOVE.

I attack.

The moment snaps—and the alley is back. The city. The man with the knife.

He lunges. I deflect. Then everything tilts. Adrenaline floods me, but it's different—hot, electric. My body moves too fast.

My fingers lock around his wrist and I twist—too hard. A snap, he screams, collapsing to his knees, clutching his arm.

The other moves and I turn before I see him—a blur of motion, too quick and precise. My fist connects. He flies backward, hitting the pavement with a sickening thud.

I stare at my hands—coated in blood. Shaking. The

woman is gone, vanished into the dark like I was the danger. I don't blame her.

But it's not her face I see when I close my eyes.

It's Eden's.

That split-second when I grabbed her—almost struck her without thinking. When her body locked up and her eyes filled with a response worse than fear.

Recognition. She saw it before I did. The strength that shouldn't have been there. The way I moved too fast, reacted too hard. Instant. Cold. Like pieces within me had shifted and I never noticed. And I still let myself believe I could claw my way back to my humanity.

Around me, voices rise—too loud and clear for their distance.

"Did you see that?"

"He didn't even flinch—"

"He moved like he wasn't even human."

"What the hell is he?"

"An enhanced?"

The words hit harder than the fight did. My breath catches. The alley feels narrower now—like the buildings are pressing in, like the air can't stretch wide enough to hold the weight of what I've done. Blood drips down my knuckles, soaking into the sleeve of someone I no longer recognize.

A drone buzzes overhead. Its spotlight flickers, lens tilting toward me like it's still deciding what I am.

I swallow hard, chest tight, trying to shake off the voices, the stares, the gnawing question beneath my ribs. Maybe it was the adrenaline. Maybe there is something wrong with me. Maybe Eden was right all along.

Still no curfew sirens yet. But I know what's coming.

I'll just explain it to them.

She's safe now.

This is what you do.

Ever since the war spread inland, the borders between safe zones and blackout sectors got thinner than they looked on a map.

That's the thing about war. It doesn't just kill cities. It seeps into them—like blood in water.

I DON'T REMEMBER getting home. The blood's gone from my knuckles, scrubbed raw under hot water, but it still feels like it's there—caked beneath my fingernails, burned into the creases of my skin.

The apartment is dark when I get in. Cal must be out. Probably better that way.

I peel off my shirt, drop it in the laundry basket, and stand in the hallway for a long moment, staring into the bathroom mirror. My reflection stares back like it doesn't recognize me. Hair damp with sweat. A cut on my lip I don't remember getting. My eyes wide. Wired.

That girl's scream still echoes in my head. The look on her face when I turned around.

Not gratitude.

Not relief.

Fear.

I splash cold water on my face. Once. Twice. It does nothing. My heart's still racing like I never left the alley. Like I never stepped out of combat.

What the hell is happening to me?

You're not a civilian, the voice in my head whispers. *You never were.*

I walk to my room, turn on the lamp, and sit at the edge of my bed. My phone buzzes with a notification—an email.

Appointment confirmed: Radiology, 7:30am.

Final evaluation: Pre-clearance for re-enlistment appeal.

My thumb hovers over the screen.

Maybe it's too late. Maybe I've already become whatever she saw in that alley. But maybe the scans will say differently.

I set the phone on my nightstand and lie back, staring at the ceiling.

Tomorrow, I'll prove I still belong.

Chapter 19

The ceiling fan spins above me, casting fractured shadows across the room. I haven't slept. Not really. My body feels wired, but my mind is static—everything blurred except for the echo of her scream and the look on her face.

By the time dawn breaks, I'm already out the door.

THE HOSPITAL CORRIDORS buzz with controlled chaos—nurses rushing between rooms, orderlies pushing gurneys, doctors speaking in hushed tones to worried family members. A world of movement, but none of it mine.

I weave through it all, focused on the signs directing me toward Radiology. One last scan. One last chance.

"Final tests for your reenlistment appeal?"

Her voice stops me mid-step and I turn toward the nurses' station.

Eden leans against the counter, watching me with that unreadable expression she wears so well. Her red hair is twisted into a loose bun, but a few strands have escaped, framing her face. The blue scrubs should make her look like any other nurse.

She shouldn't stand out.

Shouldn't always be the first thing I see.

But the way she holds herself—confident, composed—sets her apart.

"What, they post my schedule on the bulletin board now?" I ask, adjusting the folder under my arm.

"Word travels." She smiles. "Dr. Layton mentioned it this morning." She steps around the counter, grabbing a clipboard. "Thought I might run into you."

"Shouldn't you be working?" I gesture at the hustle around us.

"I'm on break. Twenty minutes of freedom." She falls into step beside me. "So, what's the test? X-ray? MRI?"

"Both. And a stress test." I adjust the folder tucked under my arm, medical records meticulously organized inside. "Full workup to prove I'm fit for duty." The words feel heavy, final.

Eden nods, head tilted just slightly, like she's trying not to smile. "And are you?"

I glance at her. "Fit for duty?"

Her eyes flick over me, slow and deliberate. "No, I meant spiritually at peace and emotionally available," she quirks a brow.

I snort, surprised—caught off guard. The heat in her look doesn't match the joke. Not really. It's a tease. But it's also a test. "Depends who's asking." My voice comes out lower than intended and I bury my smirk.

That earns the smile. Real and unguarded. "Yes, Ben. Fit for duty," she says softly—like she's not just talking about my health. Like she's remembering what she's not supposed to miss.

"You've been around enough to guess where I'm at." I glance sideways at her. "What's your verdict?"

She doesn't answer, not right away. Instead, she gives me this quiet half-smile—the kind you don't mean to give, but slips out anyway. The kind that used to mean she felt more. It hits me in the ribs. Hard.

"You've come a long way," she says, voice low. "You don't even look like the same guy I met."

I huff a quiet breath. "Guess that's what clean shirts will do for you."

Her lips twitch, just barely. "No. It's more than that." Her gaze lingers. "Something's changed. It suits you."

It's not a flirt. Not really. But it lands like one. And for a split second, I forget everything else—the reenlistment, the reason I'm here, the ring Calvin hasn't pulled out of his pocket yet.

A warmth stirs where I thought nothing could grow anymore. I don't say anything. I just nod. Because if I do... I might say everything I can't take back.

The elevator dings.

"I don't need an escort," I tell her, not unkindly. "I know how to find Radiology."

The doors slide open, and Eden steps inside before I can protest further. "Benji." Her voice is steadier now, earnest. "I know how important this is to you. Will you just let me be part of it?" Her eyes catch mine. No hesitation, no careful distance this time.

I should tell her no.

I don't.

"Fine," I concede, stepping into the elevator beside her. "But if you're late getting back, I'm not taking the blame."

"I'll tell them I was assisting a patient." Her shoulder brushes mine as she reaches for the button. "Where to first?"

"Basement level two."

She presses B2, and the doors slide closed. The elevator begins its descent—the hum feeling louder than it should.

"Nervous?" she asks.

I shrug, aiming for nonchalance. "Not really.

Eden watches the floor numbers climb, hands tucked into her pockets. "Liar." Her smirk erases any sting from the accusation. "Your left hand always twitches when you're anxious."

I glance down—sure enough, my fingers are tapping against my thigh. I hadn't even noticed. "Occupational hazard," I mutter. "Trigger discipline gets ingrained."

Eden tilts her head, studying me with those impossibly blue eyes. "You never talk about that part. What you did in the field."

"Not much to tell." I focus on the illuminated numbers, watching as we descend. "I was good at staying alert and waiting for the right moment. That's about it."

She doesn't push. That's one of the things I appreciate about Eden—she knows when to press and when to let silence do the work.

When the elevator reaches B1, slowing for the final descent, a deep, concussive boom rips through the building. The elevator lurches violently. I slam against the wall, catching the railing.

The lights flicker—once, twice—then plunge us into darkness.

"What the—" Another blast cuts me off, closer this time. The elevator shrieks, metal grinding against metal as it jerks to a stop.

Emergency lights kick on, casting the space in an eerie deep, blood-red glow. The control panel beeps insistently as all the buttons light up simultaneously, then go dark.

"Are you okay?" I reach for Eden in the dim light.

She doesn't answer.

I push off the wall, instinct kicking in. "Eden—" I turn toward her, just able to make out her face in the dim red glow.

She's pressed into the far corner, breath quick and shallow—knuckles white on the handrail behind her. Braced like she's waiting for worse. I know that look. I've seen it before—the thousand-yard stare, the rapid breathing, the rigid posture. I've seen it in soldiers fresh from firefights, in civilians pulled from rubble.

"Eden," I say her name softly, keeping my movements slow and deliberate as I approach. "We're okay."

She doesn't blink.

"Come back to me, love." I reach for her. She flinches when I touch her arm.

Shit.

"It's just me," I reassure her. "It's Benji." The nickname seems to reach her.

She blinks, some awareness returning to her eyes. "Ben," she whispers, her voice tight. "I—I can't—"

I crouch, keeping my voice low. "Hey. Stay with me."

She swallows hard, but her breathing is still too fast and uneven.

I reach for her hands, wrapping them in mine, grounding her. "Breathe with me."

Nothing. I shift, pressing her palm against my chest. "Match my breathing. Five in, five out."

I draw in a slow, exaggerated breath, holding it before releasing.

She tries once. Fails. Then again.

Her struggle to follow continues, her breath catching. But gradually, with each cycle, her breathing begins to synchronize with mine.

"That's it," I encourage. "You're doing great."

The elevator shudders again. Overhead, something rattles in the shaft. The sound is sharp, metallic.

Eden whimpers, jerking violently against me.

I tighten my grip. "Hey. Look at me." My voice is firm but gentle. "Just focus on me, Eden."

Her eyes snap to mine, wide and glass-like in the red-tinged darkness.

She's not here. Not fully.

"I'm here," I promise. "I've got you."

She fists my shirt. "Talk…" her whisper is barely audible. "Please. I need—I need something else to focus on."

I reach up, brushing a strand of hair from her face. The gesture feels intimate in the confined space, but she leans into my touch, seeking comfort.

"When I was out on missions," I begin, keeping my voice steady, "I used to trace patterns in the stars. Sounds simple, but it kept me sane during long nights out there."

Eden's breathing continues to slow as she listens, her gaze fixed on my face.

"I tried to memorize the sky. Only thing that ever seemed to stay the same was the North Star." I keep talking, giving her a scene to focus on besides the claustrophobic darkness, the muffled sounds of chaos outside. "Maybe that was just sleep deprivation… but it was a constant. Reminded me that some things never change."

Her eyes never leave mine as I speak. Somewhere in the building, alarms blare, but they're distant, like they're coming from another world.

"You scared me that night," she breathes.

I go completely still.

"But that's not…" she her voice cracks "it's not why I pulled away."

"It's not?" Silence. Then, so quiet I almost miss it—

"Malcolm."

The name hits harder than the explosion.

"Malcolm?" I repeat.

Her chest rises and falls quickly. Her hands tremble in mine.

"My fiancé," she whispers.

The word lands like a gunshot. My grip tightens—not in shock, not in jealousy, but because I know where this is going.

"He was a Marine," she says. "Four tours in the Eastern Sector."

A familiar pressure builds behind my ribs as the understanding dawns. "He had PTSD."

She nods, her gaze drifting to some middle distance. "He was fine… until he wasn't."

I shut my eyes and I see it—clear as if it were happening

now. Eden, back in the alley, eyes wide and stunned. And afterwards, flinching from me like she already knew how this story ended.

Fuck.

Another distant boom reverberates through the building. Eden flinches but continues speaking, as if pushing through the fear.

"We were in our apartment," she continues. "New year's eve. Fireworks started, and I watched him... change." She shakes her head. "He'd been fine all day. Laughing, grilling… normal. Then like someone flipped a switch."

I don't want to hear this, because I recognize the description...that moment when the present dissolves and the past takes over. When your body reacts before your mind can process what's happening.

I force myself to listen.

"He thought we were under attack." Her fingers dig into my arm, but I doubt she's aware of it. "Barricaded us in the bathroom. Said he was protecting me." Her voice is thinner now, like it might break.

The emergency light flickers above us, shadows dancing across her face.

"Three hours," she whispers. "Me trying to talk him down, him convinced we were about to die."

The air in the elevator is suffocating.

"When he finally came back to himself... the shame in his eyes, Benji… Like he'd failed me somehow."

"It wasn't his fault," I murmur.

"That's what I told him." Her grip tightens on my sleeve. "Two weeks later, he drove his car off Black Fall Bridge."

The words knock the breath from my lungs as I picture the Impala careening over the edge into the jagged, waterlogged boulders at the base of the gorge.

Everything clicks into place. Eden's caution around me, her initial hesitation after my episode. It all makes perfect sense.

Eden was never afraid of me. She was afraid of losing me the way she lost him.

"Eden—"

"I couldn't save him." Her voice breaks on the confession. "I'm a nurse. I'm supposed to help people heal, and I couldn't even help the person I loved most."

She's unraveling, and I can feel it. The tight grip on

control slipping through her fingers, breath still catching in uneven bursts.

So I hold still—not frozen, but rooted. "I'm here," I say, voice low, steady. "We're okay."

Her eyes meet mine, and for a heartbeat, I let her see everything: the fear, the fight, the resolve. I don't look away.

I won't break. Not now. For her, I have to be steady.

Without thinking, I pull her into a hug, cradling her against my chest. She comes willingly, her body melting into mine as if seeking shelter from a storm.

"It wasn't your fault," I murmur into her hair. "Listen to me. What happened to Malcolm—it wasn't your fault."

Her arms wrap around my back, hands fisting in the back of my shirt. "I should have seen it coming. There were signs—"

"No." I pull back just enough to look into her eyes. "PTSD isn't something you can predict or control. Trust me… I know."

Acceptance shifts in her expression as she studies my face. "Is that why you push yourself so hard? In therapy, in training... are you running from that darkness too?"

The question cuts deeper than I expected, laying bare truths I've avoided examining too closely.

"Maybe," I admit. "Or maybe I'm just trying to find my way back to some version of myself I recognize. Without my service I-"

"I see you, Benji." Eden's hand comes up to rest on my shoulder, her touch feather-light. "Even when you're trying to hide."

The air between us shifts, charged with an intensity beyond the fear and confession of moments before. Her eyes meet mine, and for a moment, I think I see a glimmer there—a spark that makes my heart beat faster even though that look shouldn't be for me.

"That night you—" she hesitates, voice raw, cracking, "I could see in your eyes. I can't go through that again."

I understand now. She's seen what happens when someone breaks.

She's been waiting for the moment I do, too.

My throat tightens. I know what I should say, what would be right, but the words stick. I think of Cal—my best friend, the guy who's been there through everything. Cal, who Eden is dating.

"Cal's different," I say finally. My hands shake with uncertainty of whether I should let her go or not. Create a necessary distance. "He doesn't have the same... issues. He's steady. Reliable."

An expression flickers across her face—disappointment? Shame? She looks away quickly and steps back, arms folding tightly across her chest as if she's suddenly cold.

"Right," she says, her voice suddenly flat. "Of course. Calvin is... he's wonderful."

The air hangs heavier now, laden with words unsaid. I run a hand through my hair, searching for the right response.

"Eden, I—"

"No, you're right." She cuts me off, but her voice is softer now—almost reluctant. Her hand lifts, barely, like she's reaching for me before she catches herself and lets it fall. Her fingers curl inward, not quite clenched, pressed tight against her leg like she needs the contact to stay calm. "Calvin is supportive. With everything. He's a good man."

"He is," I agree, the words tasting bittersweet. "One of the best I know."

Eden nods, her gaze fixed on some point over my shoulder. "I shouldn't have—this isn't—" She shakes her head. "I'm sorry. I'm not thinking clearly."

"You don't need to apologize." I wish I could reach for her again, but I keep my distance. "We're both a little on edge."

The elevator jerks suddenly, lights flickering back to full brightness as the power returns. Eden startles, taking another small step back.

"Looks like they've got things under control," I say, my tone deliberately casual.

She nods, straightening her scrubs as the elevator resumes its descent. "Ben, about what I told you—about Mal—"

"It stays between us," I assure her.

Relief softens her features. "Thank you."

The silence presses in like the pause before vesper—too heavy to be peace, yet too light to be despair. The moment fractures.

We both flinch at the groan of metal just before the doors wrench open—chaos crashing in like a dam breaking. Smoke, noise, motion blurring at the edges.

I don't move. Not until I feel her start to breathe again.

Doctors shout orders. Nurses guide panicked civilians. An alarm wails overhead, the high pitched squeal dampening only when the intercom crackles to life:

"This is an emergency broadcast. All hospital staff and patients are to remain in designated lockdown zones until further notice. This is not a drill."

I catch Eden's hand, pulling her forward. "We need to move."

She hesitates, eyes flicking toward the injured being rushed past us, her instincts kicking in. "Benji, I should be help—"

A sharp cry rings out from further down the hall.

I wrap a protective arm around her, pulling her tight against my side as a gurney barrels past, nearly knocking into her.

"Further instructions will be provided as soon as possible," the intercom drones. *"Security teams are responding. Please remain calm."*

I grit my teeth.

Remain calm. Right.

A loud metallic clang echoes somewhere behind us. Eden jolts, her head snapping toward the sound. I tighten my grip, shifting in front of her.

"Whatever's happening… it's close. We need to get you out of here." I guide her forward, away from the noise, scanning the corridor for the safest path.

Chapter 20

Even hours later, the echo of the elevator still rings in my ears. The metallic groan. The red emergency lights. Eden's hands shaking in mine.

Whatever happened at the hospital, it passed quickly—contained, they said. Some kind of localized explosion near the east wing. No casualties. Nothing to worry about. But my body hasn't gotten the message.

The city streets blur past as I drive, jaw tight, fingers drumming the wheel. I keep checking my mirrors. Watching corners. Old habits.

I should've stayed. Done more. But I'm not a soldier anymore, am I?

Just a spectator.

At a red light, my phone buzzes.

Eden.

"Don't forget, dinner's at seven. Don't make me tell Layla you bailed. One disaster per week is enough."

I exhale, dragging a hand down my face. A blind date after a near-death experience.

Perfect.

And to top it off, the real reason I'm there cuts deeper than I care to admit.

I almost text back, *Sorry, rain check. Nearly dying has me rethinking my social calendar.*

But I don't. Instead, I roll my shoulders, pull into my complex, and head inside to change and meet up with Cal.

If I have to spend the night making small talk with Eden's cousin, I might as well get it over with.

"I CAN'T BELIEVE I let you talk me into this." My jacket feels too stiff against my shoulders as we stand outside Eden's apartment door. My eyes automatically catalog entry points, escape routes, structural weaknesses—routine checks that won't die.

"And don't mention the dangers of her apartment location." Calvin catches my scanning gaze, his voice carrying that long-suffering tone he uses when I'm being too... me.

"I wasn't!"

"I can see it all over your face, Ben. You're nervous about it."

"I'm not nervous about that." I wipe my palms against my jeans for the hundredth time. The flowers in my hand are starting to show wear from my grip.

"Ahh, the blind date. I get it." Cal's grin turns knowing. "What if she's the one, eh?" He knocks his elbow at me.

I force a smile, trying to ignore how Eden's memory tugs at a sensation deep in my chest. "Maybe something like that."

"Well don't get distracted. You still need to get me her list of family and friends."

"I never leave a mission incomplete, Cal." The words come out more clipped than intended.

The door opens, and suddenly Eden's there, her presence hitting me with unexpected intensity. She hugs Calvin, who breezes past her inside. Then she turns to me, arms raised, and I manage an awkward side-hug that still leaves me drowning in her scent—hospital sterility underneath the jasmine that still makes my throat tight.

As I step inside, a sharp pulse climbs my leg and settles deep in my hip. I shift my weight, hoping no one notices the hitch in my step. The bar fight left bruises I can explain. This pain? I tell myself it's just lingering inflammation. Residual punishment for almost failing my last mission. It'll fade.

I thrust the flowers forward like they're burning me. She chuckles, the sound too familiar. "Benji, you shouldn't have."

"Sorry. I brought some for..." My mind blanks completely.

"Layla," Eden provides, mercy in her voice.

"Yes. Right. And it felt weird not having anything for the host, so." The words stumble out like recruits on their first march.

Eden takes the bouquet to the kitchen, glass clinking as she searches for a vase. The sound of running water fills the awkward silence.

"Speaking of Layla, is she still coming?" Calvin asks around a mouthful of food from the snack bowls.

"She is." Eden starts. "Just running a little—"

"Technically, I'm on time." The new voice from the doorway makes me stiffen. I hadn't noticed the door was still open—a tactical error that makes my skin crawl.

"Not according to military time." The words escape before I can stop them, sharp as brass tacks.

Layla's eyebrow arches under dark bangs like I've personally offended her ancestors. "Not everything runs on military time."

"That's a fact." Calvin's cheerful betrayal comes with a slap to my shoulder. "But proximity to Benji, here, means it does."

I try to hide my glare, but Eden catches it—of course she does. She swoops in like a medic after an explosion.

"I told you all to be here at the right time for when I knew you would arrive." She takes Layla's jacket, hanging it by the door before finally—thank god—closing it. "Ben, this is my cousin, Layla. Layla, this is Ben. Cal's best friend and roommate."

"Pleasure." My hand extends like I'm reporting for duty.

"Best friend and a roommate." Layla's hand meets mine, then quickly withdraws to wipe against her skirt. Her grimace isn't quite hidden enough. "Formal and great at multitasking, at least."

"It smells great, babe." Calvin wraps around Eden like a comfortable sweater.

"It shouldn't. It's just a basic cold sandwich spread." Eden's laugh carries a softness I can't let myself think about.

"So coy." His voice goes sweet enough to rot teeth and I catch Layla holding back a roll of her green eyes.

I retreat to examine the walls, mirroring the sentiment, one hand shoved deep in my pocket to keep from fidgeting. The art pieces blur together as I locate my real target—the address book. Mission parameters established. Now I just need an opening.

The patio feels too small with four people, the tension

thick enough to cut with my old service knife. I excuse myself to the bathroom, my pulse quickening as I approach the book's location. The pages whisper as I flip through them, my phone camera clicking quietly. The familiar focus of an operation settles over me—until the door opens.

Layla stands there, empty wine glass a silent accusation in her hand. Her eyes narrow like lining up gun sights. "I see what you're doing."

"It's not what it looks like." The oldest lie in the book.

"Getting the numbers for everyone in her address book." She shakes her head, disgust evident. "I know we got off on a rough start but that's a little insulting. So desperate to be unavailable you'll go through her personal stuff to find someone else instead of telling me outright."

"Now, hold on. That's not it at all."

"You can't lie to me, Ben. I know your type."

"Then you're delusional. I'm not desperate for anyone's company. I didn't even want to come here tonight." The words hit the air like friendly fire.

"Well. That makes it all better, then." Her scoff could strip paint as she tosses long wavy locks over her shoulder.

"No. Look. You have to keep your mouth shut about this. For Eden's sake."

"Tell me the truth then." Her arms fold, firm—like blast doors closing.

"I'm helping Cal."

Her eyes narrow further. "Eden is my cousin. I should know now if he's a player."

"It's for..." I glance at the door, then move closer. My hand brushes her shoulder and she jerks away like I'm radioactive.

"Don't touch me."

I swallow an eye roll and motion her away from the door. My voice drops to barely a whisper. "It's for his proposal. Needs to get in touch with family, friends, all that."

Her jaw drops like it's spring-loaded. "That can't be true."

I drag a hand down my face. "This whole double date thing was to get me over here so I could get these names and numbers. I'm not even looking for a girlfriend."

"Well, that's rude." Her eyes widen with fresh offense.

"Not that you're not... well I'm just—"

"Clearly great with words."

"Just… you can't tell her. It'll ruin the whole surprise."

She huffs like a steam engine letting off pressure. "Fine."

"Thank you."

"But I want you to take me out on a proper date."

"Excuse me?" The words come out strangled.

"That's right. Somewhere nice. Then you'll see I am girlfriend material."

"You don't even like me."

"You snapped at me the moment we met!"

I inhale slowly, trying to remember. "The being on time thing?"

Her lips purse like she's tasting something sour. She nods.

"I'm sorry. Some things come out of my mouth before I even know I'm talking."

"I know. Military, right?"

"Right."

"Told you I know the type." She arches a brow.

"So you'll keep this quiet?"

"It better be somewhere nice."

"Alright, fine." The words feel like signing my own court-martial papers.

"And not some stupid sports bar," Layla adds, jabbing a finger toward me. "I mean actual tablecloths and—"

"I know what nice means," I snap, then catch myself. "Just because I served doesn't mean I—"

"Could have fooled me with that jacket." Her eyes rake over my outfit with surgical precision.

"What's wrong with my—"

The sound of the patio door sliding open freezes us both. Eden and Cal step in, caught mid-laugh that dies when they see us squared off like opposing forces.

"Everything okay in here?" Eden's voice carries that careful mediator tone she reserves for difficult patients.

"Wonderful!" Layla's voice jumps two octaves, a smile appearing so fast it must hurt. "Ben was just telling me about this amazing restaurant he wants to take me to. Weren't you, Ben?" Her eyes drill into me like targeting lasers.

I force my face into what I hope resembles enthusiasm. "Right. Yes. Very... exclusive place." My hand finds the back of my neck, rubbing at suddenly tense muscles.

"Oh?" Eden's eyebrows lift slightly. "Which one?"

My mind goes blank. "It's, uh..."

"Le Coeur De Chou," Layla cuts in smoothly, the French flowing off her tongue. "He was just explaining how hard it is to get reservations."

I shoot her a look that probably gives away more than it should. That's the restaurant where I first saw Eden again. Where all this started.

"That's great!" Cal beams, completely missing the undercurrent. "See? I said you two would hit it off."

"Like a house on fire," I mutter, earning a sharp elbow from Layla that she disguises as adjusting her sleeve.

"Well, shall we get back to our evening?" Layla's smile stays fixed in place as she loops her arm through mine, her grip tight enough to cut circulation. "Ben was just about to tell me more about his... military experience.

"Actually, Ben doesn't really talk about—" Cal starts.

"Oh, but I'm sure he'll make an exception." Her fingers dig into my bicep. "Won't you, Ben?"

I manage what feels like a grimace masquerading as a smile. "Nothing classified, of course."

Eden's eyes flick between us, and for a moment I see complexity there—concern? amusement? envy?—before it vanishes behind her regaining composure. "Well, everything is still on the patio. The evening's too nice to waste indoors."

As we follow them back to the patio, Layla leans close, her whisper sharp as a knife. "Le Coeur De Chou. Saturday. Seven o'clock. And wear something that wasn't issued by the government."

I stare straight ahead, jaw clenched. "You know that place requires reservations weeks in advance."

Her smile doesn't waver as she whispers back, "Then I suggest you start making calls. Unless you'd prefer I mention finding you with a certain book?"

Check and mate.

I've been outmaneuvered by a civilian.

"Seven it is."

By Eden's cousin, no less.

THE EVENING DRAGS on, conversation stilted and polite. Cal breaks another awkward silence by clearing his throat. "Oh! Ben, you've got to show Eden that thing you did with the knife that time. You know, when you disarmed that guy at the bar?" His eyes light up with boyish excitement.

Eden draws back slightly. "Cal..."

"No, seriously, it was incredible. Like something out of an

action movie." Cal mimics a defensive stance, nearly knocking over his wine glass. "The guy didn't even know what hit him."

I straighten slowly, ribs tightening like someone wound them too tight. Just posture. Just stiffness. Not weakness. Not anything new. I stretch subtly as Calvin talks, pushing down the instinct to wince. The last thing I need is Eden noticing.

"I don't think—" Eden starts.

"Come on, it'd be so cool! Plus, you know, useful for protection at the hospital and stuff." Cal waves his hand dismissively at the safety aspect. "But mainly, you should see how he does this wrist lock thing. It's insane. Show her, Ben!"

Eden's fingers twist her necklace nervously. "I don't know if I can go there…"

I lean forward, shooting Cal a quieting look. "It's not about flashy moves. Most self-defense is building awareness and confidence. We would start with simple stuff - just learning how to stand in a way that makes you feel secure."

"But the knife thing—" Cal interjects.

"Is a technique you learn after months of basics," I cut him off firmly. "If you're even interested in going that far, Eden. No pressure."

"Well..." Eden glances up, some tension easing from her shoulders.

"Basics are boring," Cal groans. "You should see what he can do with a pool cue. There was this one time—"

"Listen," I lock eyes with her, ignoring Cal's theatrical retelling, "the safety of the city is cracking."

"He's got a point there, babe." Cal puts his arms down. "I've heard more and more incidents reported on the radio when I drive to work."

"We can all just meet up once to start. If you don't want to go on from there, then we won't." I shrug.

"That... actually sounds less intimidating." Eden offers a small smile.

"Less intimidating means less fun," Cal sighs.

"I know a private space where we can practice. No one to watch," I offer.

Cal perks up. "Oh, perfect! Nobody to see when she kicks your ass!"

"Cal," I warn, watching Eden tense up again.

She gnaws on her lip, but nods. "Okay. Layla, you should come too."

Layla, who's been watching this exchange with growing boredom, stifles a yawn and checks her phone. "I'm already part of a class. Figured I should after…" she stops herself, memories hovering in her held breath. "Anyway, I should go. Early meeting tomorrow."

Her expression shifts—a tiredness that wasn't there before, or maybe I just hadn't noticed it under all the sharp edges.

"I'll walk you to your car," I offer automatically. The words surprising us both.

"It's just outside—" she starts to protest, but Eden cuts in, and I'm already halfway into my jacket.

"That would be lovely of you, Ben. It's gotten so dark." Her eyes meet mine with understanding—she knows I've already cataloged every shadow between here and the parking lot.

THE NIGHT AIR hits us as we step outside, carrying the smell of rain. Layla's heels click against the pavement, counting down the distance to her car. The silence between us carries different weight now, less hostile.

"You don't actually have to take me to dinner," she says finally, her voice softer than it's been all night. "I won't say anything about the address book."

I glance at her, catching a vulnerability in her profile before she turns away. "What happened to 'somewhere nice'?"

"Look, I get it. You're not interested. I noticed how you look at her… All while helping plan the proposal?" She laughs, but there's no humor in it. "Besides, I'm not exactly… well, let's just say I'm better at pushing people away than letting them in anyway."

We reach her car, and she fumbles with her keys. The parking lot lights cast harsh shadows across her face, making her look younger somehow.

"Saturday at seven," I hear myself say. "But I pick the restaurant."

She looks up, surprise replacing the guard in her eyes. "Really?"

"Really. Just... maybe ease up on the military jokes?"

A genuine smile tugs at her lips. "No promises." She opens her car door, then pauses. "For what it's worth, I'm sorry about earlier. You seem like a good guy. I just... it's been a rough year." She examines the keys in her hand.

"I know a bit about those."

She nods, slides into her car, and I wait until she's pulled away before heading back inside. The walk gives me time to sort through the evening, trying to understand how everything shifted so quickly.

EDEN AND CAL are clearing dishes—the remnants of our awkward evening scattered across the coffee table.

"Are you okay?" Eden's voice cuts through, soft and instinctual, as she eyes my leg. A nurse's tone.

"Fine," I lie. "Just stiff."

She studies me, like she doesn't believe it. But she doesn't push."I am sorry about Layla." Eden sets down the glasses she's carrying. "She's not usually like that. She's actually really sweet, she's just..." She tucks a strand of hair behind her ear, a nervous gesture I remember too well. "She's been through a lot lately."

"Ex really did a number on her," Cal adds, wadding up napkins. "Eden says she hasn't dated in almost a year."

"It's okay." I help gather empty glasses, careful not look at her.

"No, it's not." Eden's voice carries that same concern she used to have in the hospital. "She's been hurt. Makes her defensive. But once you get past that..." She trails off, watching me for a reaction.

"Eden," I finally meet her eyes, steady. "it's okay. I get it."

"You do?" The relief in her tone makes my chest tight.

"Yeah. Sometimes the best defense is a good offense, right?"

Cal snorts. "Only you would use military strategy to explain dating."

"Well, he's not wrong," Eden says softly, and for a moment I see understanding, or maybe recognition. She knows about defenses, about keeping people at arm's length. We all do, in our own ways.

"So," Cal breaks through the moment, "you still taking her out Saturday?"

I think about Layla's quiet voice in the parking lot, about the way her guard finally dropped. "Yeah. Figure everyone deserves a second chance at a first impression."

Eden nods, but I catch the concern in her eyes—the same look she used to give me in the hospital when she thought I wasn't watching. Always trying to fix broken things.

"Well," Cal announces, oblivious to the undercurrent, "I'd say Operation Double Date was a success!"

I think about the photos of Eden's address book still on my phone, about Layla's tired smile in the parking lot, about the way Eden still watches me like I might shatter. "Yeah," I agree, not sure if I'm lying. "A success."

Eden's voice is warm, genuine. "She'll surprise you, Ben. Once she opens up a little... she's worth getting to know."

I nod, focusing on stacking plates rather than looking at her again. Because I already tried getting to know someone once—the wrong person. And right now, I can't think about guards dropping or people worth knowing.

Chapter 21

Three weeks after the awkward double date it's time for our first lesson. Eden adjusts the strap on her bag as she enters, her hair still damp from a shower. Cal follows behind her, grinning like this is a game.

I move to meet them, trying to quiet the part of me that still resists seeing them together, that can't accept it as normal. That's part of the problem.

She doesn't flinch when I hand her the training knife. That alone tells me she's more ready than she realizes.

Cal bounces on the balls of his feet, every live action film he's ever watched playing over his movements. Eden stands quietly, focused, her fingers curling around the foam handle like it might anchor her to the floor-eyes studying it with determination.

I take a breath, letting the weight of what we're doing settle in. "Rule one of a knife fight: don't get into one." The foam weapons feel almost insulting in my hands as I distribute them. "Rule two: you will get hurt." Too light, too safe, too far from the cold reality of steel. "Bringing us to rule three: the goal for defensive fighting is to get away, not to kill or maim. It's to create distance and escape." My eyes lock with Eden's, memories of that night flickering between us. "Got it?"

Cal pinches his lips together, turning the foam knife over like it's a child's toy. Eden swats his arm, fighting a smile. "Stop it, Cal. This is serious."

"Yes, Cal." I clasp my hands behind my back, instructor mode settling over me like armor. "Is there something about being stabbed that you find amusing?"

"No." He clears his throat, schooling his features. "Sorry, Ben. I just—this thing is foam, and I feel silly. With the war closing in… we need to be prepared in a real way."

"Would you prefer steel to make it more realistic?"

His smirk carries too much confidence. "Wouldn't that up the stakes?"

"Don't be stupid," Eden cuts in, real fear edging her voice. "Ben, he's kidding."

I offer her a faint smile, remembering how real steel feels against skin. "I know. Anyway—" I demonstrate proper grip techniques, the foam mockingly light in my hand. "Think of the knife as an extension of your hand. Since your goal is to get away, hold it in a saber grip or hammer grip. Both give you more distance from the attacker. A reverse grip, while flashy, isn't ideal for defense." I lock eyes with Cal.

Eden tilts her head, focus sharp as any blade. "And for the attacker?"

"They'll probably use the same grips, though there are variations. The blade itself matters too—its weight, balance, design all affect how it handles. Ideally, you'd train with different types to get comfortable with any weapon." I pause, the weight of experience heavy in my voice. "But most importantly... don't ever get caught without your own weapon."

Eden's eyebrows lift skeptically. "Benji, I work in a hospital. I can't exactly carry a knife around with me."

Cal nods. "And I doubt I'd get one past base security."

"Then keep them in your car or somewhere accessible." My gaze fixes on Eden, that night's terror still fresh in my mind. "You can't afford to be unarmed."

Eden crosses her arms, fingers tracing her elbow like she's holding herself together. "I'm not sure I'll ever feel comfortable carrying a weapon," she admits softly, eyeing the foam knife. "But you're probably right."

I shift into fighting stance, muscles remembering older, darker lessons. "Are you ready to get cut?"

They exchange nervous glances. "What should we do?" Eden asks.

"Well, if I were to attack you like this—" I step forward.

Cal immediately positions himself between us, blade raised in an amateur's grip. His stance is wide but unstable, leaving fatal openings.

"Good instinct," I lower my weapon, moving to adjust his form. "Keep her behind you, but remember to create distance between your body and the blade. Extend your arm fully to keep the attacker further from you."

"Like this?" He maneuvers.

"Exactly. And as I get closer, aim for controlled slashes at the nearest target—hands, arms, anything to create an opening to escape." I feint forward. His grip fails, the foam weapon clattering to the floor.

"Ah, damn it." He bends to retrieve it.

I move faster than I should be able to, yanking his shirt for balance when I misstep before slipping past. In one fluid motion, my arm locks around Eden's shoulders, foam blade pressed against her throat. Her pulse hammers against my forearm.

"Oh, what the hell, Ben?" Cal's frustration echoes. "I dropped it! Let me reset."

"I'm not Ben," my voice drops, dark and foreign. "I'm someone who wants your money. Or worse..." My gaze shifts to Eden, longing tightening my chest, voice barely controlled. "The most invaluable thing in your life."

Eden freezes, her breath catching as her hands push weakly against my arm. The tremor in her fingers yanks me back—but not all the way.

Outside, a helicopter rumbles overhead—slow and heavy. The kind of low, rhythmic sound that used to mean evac or incoming. It drags recognition through me. Muscle memory. Old adrenaline. My grip tightens.

"Come on, Ben." Calvin steps in cautiously, unease threading through his stance. "Let her go."

"What are you gonna do about it?" I press the foam knife a little closer to Eden's throat. Not enough to hurt. Just enough to make the threat feel real. Her gasp hits like cold water to the face.

"I've got your girlfriend," I say. "And this knife's ready to do some real damage if you don't act."

Cal tips his head—half-serious, half-smirking. "It's fiancé, actually."

I knew engagement was coming. But the word still lands like a blade in my ribs. My chest constricts. The room tilts. The sound of the helicopter swells, drowning out Cal's voice, drowning out the present. Just rotor blades and blood and the moment everything broke.

My grip shifts, unconsciously pulling Eden closer. Tighter. And then—her breath stutters. Not a gasp this time.

A whimper. Small. Real. The kind of sound no one makes unless they truly believe they're about to be hurt. It cuts through the static in my head like a wire snapping.

Shit.

I ease my grip—but it's too late. Her heel slams into my foot. Pain flares up my leg. I reel back just in time for her elbow to drive into my gut—perfect placement. Breath flies out of me as I stumble, disarmed, dropping the foam blade.

She's already pivoting, arm raised, mock weapon trembling in her grip as her chest heaves.

My hands go up, instinctively defensive. "Good," I cough, staggering back a step. "That was good."

"You okay, dude?" Cal's laugh carries nervous relief.

I wave him off, gesturing toward Eden. "I'm not the one you should be checking on."

Her wild eyes dart between us, fight-or-flight still flickering in every line of her body.

He turns to her, voice softening. "Hey, babe. It's just Ben."

I raise my hands slowly, the foam knife already discarded. "No weapon. You're safe," I say softly.

Calvin approaches, but there's hesitation in his steps— uncertainty in the way his eyes scan her face. "Hey, babe. It's just Ben." His voice is calm, but not comforting. He doesn't reach for her.

Eden's breath stutters. Her shoulders are trembling. Still, Calvin doesn't move closer.

He glances at me, then back at her. "You okay?" It's not careless. Not cruel. But it misses what's vital.

I can see it—he hasn't noticed the panic still lodged behind her eyes, the way her hands haven't unclenched, the way her pulse hasn't steadied. He doesn't realize she's still in it.

"You gotta admit, that was pretty impressive—" Cal starts, but his pager buzzes. He groans, already pulling his phone from his back pocket. "Sorry, it's the lab. They've been on edge lately. I just need a minute." He doesn't wait for a response, disappearing down the hallway with the phone already to his ear, voice low and urgent.

The moment he's gone, the room buzzes with silence and Eden's facade crumbles. Her shoulders slump like the thread holding her upright just snapped. Her hands shake as she lowers the foam knife, lips parted like she can't find the words she wants to say.

I step in. "Can I—?" I ask quietly, already moving toward her.

She doesn't answer. She just melts into my chest. I wrap my arms around her, careful, sturdy. Solid. "I've got you," I murmur. "You're safe now."

Her breath breaks, the sob stifled against my shirt. And I feel it—her trust. The weight of it. The danger of it.

She trembles, clinging like I'm the only thing holding her upright. And it kills me. Because I was the trigger. Guilt floods me.

I dragged her into this, and now she's here, trusting me to pull her out. The same man who made her panic.

"I'm so sorry, love," I whisper into her hair. She doesn't pull away. She should... But she doesn't.

We stay like that for a long moment. Just breathing—existing. Until her voice cracks the silence.

"We can't tell him."

I pull back slightly, just enough to see her face. "What?"

Her eyes are glassy, rimmed in red. "We can't tell Calvin what just happened. What this really was." Her voice is steady now, but her still shaky breath warms my neck.

"Eden—"

"He wouldn't look at you the same way. He'd worry about me all the time. And I can't—" She swallows. "He already thinks I'm fragile."

"He should know," I say gently. "He deserves to understand what you're carrying—why this training is important for both of you."

"No," she says, shaking her head against me. "He's never seen me like this. I don't want him to start."

I exhale through my nose, jaw tight. "He'd never judge you. And it wasn't just you. I pushed it too far. You were just—reacting."

"That's exactly why he can't know," she says quietly. "He loves you, Ben. If he finds out what happened... that I panicked because of you—because of what you reminded me of..."

Her words trail off, but I hear them anyway. The memory of her fiancé. The bathroom. The fireworks. The weight of old trauma stitched into her bones.

My guilt spreads like smoke. "You don't have to protect me," I say, voice low. "Not from him. Not from this."

"I'm not protecting you. I'm protecting him." Her expression softens, defiance edging her voice. "Besides, you've more than made up for all of it by now." She glances toward the hallway where Cal disappeared, eyes holding a silent pensiveness. "You introduced me to the man I'm going to marry..."

Her words echo like gunshots—sharp, final, impossible to ignore. Reminding me of everything I can never have—and everything I stand to lose.

I stiffen, forcing a smile even as my chest constricts with envy... and a darker thread. "Yeah. Lucky him." I look away, ashamed. "I never meant to scare you. I just wanted you to feel capable. Safe. Eden... I don't know what I'd do if anything happened to you."

Her eyes pierce mine, stunning me into near silence—searching for an answer I refuse to give her.

"Calvin, he..." I struggle to redirect. "He'd be a wreck."

"He couldn't even do it. Step in and defend me."

"He started to. I saw it. But because it was me, he hesi—"

"Should my life really need to be threatened before he steps up to protect me?"

"Stop talking like that." The words come out sharper than I mean them to. "Of course not. He'll do what it takes. His instinct was to put himself between us, that's proof."

"But—" she pulls away slightly, hand still lingering on my chest.

"But nothing. Listen... would it help if you and I trained one-on-one? So you won't freeze up and get thrown back to that moment?"

Eden sniffs, steadying herself before meeting my gaze. After an eternal moment, she nods. "I think it would help build confidence."

I manage a faint smile and pull her closer, resting my chin against her hair. She fits against me like she was made to be there, her warmth seeping through my shirt and quieting the restless part of me that never finds peace. For one perfect moment, everything else falls away—the guilt, the fear, the past—and there's only her, making it easier to breathe. Black currant and jasmine wrap around me, feeling like safety, like home. Her trembling subsides in my arms, and the world beyond this embrace ceases to exist.

"Okay," I murmur, afraid to break this fragile peace. "But if it gets uncomfortable, we can find someone else to help."

Her voice carries quiet certainty. "No. I trust you."

The words cut deeper than any blade. I pull back enough to meet her eyes, red-rimmed but determined, and offer a somber smile. "You shouldn't. Not after what I did."

Her fingers brush my sleeve. "And yet, I do. That's the part that scares me most."

I frown. "What do you mean?"

She hesitates, then meets my eyes with a painful honesty. "I trust you, Ben. Too much."

Before I can speak, before I can even begin to unpack the weight of those words, the floor creaks.

Calvin's footsteps echo in the hallway, growing louder.

Eden pulls away, fast. She wipes at her face, smoothing her hair back, adjusting herself like she's erasing the last five minutes from her body.

I step back too, grabbing the discarded foam knives, suddenly needing something—anything—to hold.

By the time Calvin returns, his phone is still in his hand, thumb tapping across the screen like the conversation never really ended.

"Sorry about that," he says, barely glancing up. "They needed directions on some data." He looks between us, notices the tension—but not the details. Not the way Eden's eyes are still red. Not the faint tremble in her shoulders. Not the way I've shifted just slightly in front of her, like a shield I can't stop being. "Everything okay?"

Eden straightens, wiping quickly at her face, her voice calm but paper-thin. "Just processing. It got a bit intense there for a minute."

Cal nods like that's enough. Like he's not even seeing her.

I watch him—how he slides his phone away, how his attention never quite lands. The way he misses her eyes. Her body language. The fact that she was just crying, and now she's holding it all in alone.

He doesn't notice. And for the first time, I wonder if he ever really has.

I clear my throat. "Maybe we should call it for today. Give everyone time to decompress."

"Good idea," Cal wraps an arm around Eden's shoulders. "Besides, with the lull in local attacks lately, I promised to take this one to dinner." He kisses her temple, and I force myself to look away.

"Same time next week?" Eden asks, her voice carefully neutral.

I meet her eyes one last time, seeing everything we're keeping secret reflected there. "If you're sure."

She nods, firm. "I need to learn. And like I said..." her gaze holds mine for a beat too long, "I trust you."

Cal grins, oblivious to the weight of her words. "Great! Maybe next time I won't drop my weapon, right?"

"Right," I manage, watching as he guides Eden toward the door. She glances back once, just before they exit, and in that moment I see everything—gratitude, fear, and a deeper need we've both been pretending doesn't exist.

After they leave, I stand in the empty room, foam weapons still in hand, remembering the feel of her trembling against me, her scent lingering like a ghost. Training her will be torture, but I'll do it. Because she needs to be safe. Because Cal needs to learn. Because sometimes the only way forward is through the fire.

I toss the foam knives onto the shelf with more force than necessary. "Lucky him," I whisper again to the empty room, the words clinging to my mouth like dust and regret. Another lesson learned too late: sometimes the deepest wounds aren't made by blades at all.

THE COUNTERTOP FORGE becomes my refuge in the days that follow. I lose myself in the hiss of steam and the ring of metal, chasing rhythm like penance. Heat blooms up my arms as I hammer steel into shape—two knives, one for each of them. A wedding gift, I tell myself. A tradition. Something meaningful.

But the truth bites deeper than the edge I'm grinding. I'm trying to erase her tears. Trying to forget the way she flinched beneath my arm, her trust breaking and reforming in the same breath. If I can finish these—if I can give her a token that says I'm still good natured—maybe I won't see her panic every time I close my eyes.

Steel doesn't flinch when you push too hard. It doesn't cry. It bends, reshapes, endures. I envy it.

I'm smoothing the last edge when the knock comes.

Chapter 22

The knock pulls me out of rhythm.

I set the blade aside, steam still rising from its surface. The countertop forge hisses behind me, the smell of scorched steel clinging to my skin. I wipe my hands on a rag and head for the door, not expecting anyone this early.

When I open it, she's already walking in.

"Eden?" Her name slips out before I can stop it. Athletic clothes cling to her frame, her hair pulled back in a loose knot that exposes the line of her neck. Sunlight catches on the strands that escaped, and something in me stutters.

"Benji!" she says, too brightly.

"What are you doing here?"

"I need your help. Are you busy?" She doesn't wait for an answer—just moves past me, her familiar smell trailing behind like a memory. The same one I smelled the night she panicked in my arms. The same one I haven't been able to shake since.

"Working on something, but it's not like I save people's lives or anything." I try to keep my tone light, even as my pulse quickens at her proximity.

"Perfect. Then you can come with me." Her eyes sparkle like she's already decided I don't get a choice.

"Where?"

"I can't tell you till we get there." Her eyes sparkle with mischief, and my chest tightens.

I fold my arms, trying to look stern rather than affected by her presence. "And why not?"

"If I do then you won't agree to it. I know it'll be fun—you just have to trust me!" Her lips curve into that smile that always undoes my resolve.

I close the door, still thrown by her energy. "Where's Cal?"

She shrugs, trying for casual—but there's something under it. Something tight in her smile. "Working. Again. Some last-minute data thing he wanted to wrap before Monday. He's been picking up a lot of Saturdays lately..." Her voice trails slightly, like she's not sure if she's explaining or defending him.

I nod once, that familiar ache pressing at my ribs. "Right."

She changes the subject like flipping a switch. "So, can I steal you for an hour?"

"Should I change?" I rub the back of my neck, hyper-aware of how her workout clothes outline every movement. "You look dressed for cardio…"

"You'll be fine," she says with a grin that's pure challenge. "Unless you're afraid to sweat."

"Is that a challenge?"

"Maybe." She says, raising a brow.

I shake my head, fighting my own smile. "Let me change real quick."

"I'm so lucky you're never busy." She wanders to the kitchen counter, her fingers trailing along the surface in a way that draws my eye. "Cal hates these kinds of things."

I rush over and roll up the steel knives I've been working on, wrapping them in leather. Her eyes catch the movement, curiosity brightening them, and I hurry past. "Just one sec."

After stashing the bundle in my room, I change quickly into workout clothes, nearly colliding with her in the hallway. The narrow space forces us close, and I catch another hint of her perfume.

"What was that?" She asks, close enough that I can feel her warmth.

"You're the one sneaking around *my* apartment to find secrets." I try for defensive, but it comes out rougher than intended.

"It looked interesting. But mostly because you definitely don't want me to see it."

"Because you'll tell Cal and it's a gift for him." The lie comes easily now, practiced.

"Ooh, I love surprises!" She perks up to see over my shoulder.

"Oh, you'll be surprised. Are you ready?" I corral her down the hallway.

"Just waiting on you, Danger." she quirks her brow again before turning.

THE DRIVE IS short but charged with anticipation. She fiddles with the radio, and I try not to watch her fingers dance across the controls.

Static hums, then a voice cuts through—sharp, clinical.

"—military officials have yet to release a full casualty report, but early estimates indicate at least a dozen dead and many more wounded in last night's attack. Witnesses describe enhanced combatants moving with inhuman speed—"

Eden flinches and switches stations quickly, her fingers stiff on the dial. Music fills the space, too upbeat for the sudden weight in the air.

I keep my eyes on the road, but I catch the way she glances at me from the corner of my vision. She's watching for my reaction. I force my shoulders to relax, but the words keep ringing in my head.

Enhanced combatants.

Turig.

A familiar tension lingers beneath my skin—not pain, not quite discomfort. Just a pressure, like my muscles are bracing for an impact that hasn't happened yet. I've noticed it more lately, a quiet energy beneath the surface. I figured it was from getting back into a solid workout routine, pushing myself harder now that I actually care again.

Still, there's something about it that feels... different. I flex my grip on the wheel, exhaling slowly.

Not the time. Not the place.

Eden shifts beside me, then smiles—a small, fleeting thing, but it's enough to pull me out of my thoughts.

"Turn left up here," she says, her voice lighter now, like the broadcast never happened.

I follow her directions, the moment settling between us, and pull into the parking lot.

"Don't be mad..." Her grin is infectious as she climbs out, the movement drawing my eye before I can stop myself.

"Mad?" I follow her to the door, where couples move in synchronized patterns when a something catches my eye—a recruitment poster plastered on the wall nearby. A soldier in full gear stands tall, chin lifted, the words beneath him sharp and direct:

"Your country still needs you. Enlist today."

My steps falter. The image tugs at a familiarity, a longing deep in my chest, but I push it down.

Not now. Focus.

"Ben."

I blink. Eden is already at the entrance, watching me with mild amusement.

"What?" I reign in my focus.

She sighs, shaking her head. "I said, 'Come on, at least pretend to be excited!'" She mimics my expression, teasing. "You totally zoned out on me."

I roll my shoulders, forcing a smile. "No, I didn't. I'm just... processing." I glance back at the poster.

"You'll have fun, I know it!" She grabs my wrist, dragging me toward the door before I can argue.

"Eden, I am a soldier. I can barely even make it through life with the two left feet I do have!"

"Benji, please." Those blue eyes hit me with full force, and I know I'm already lost. "If not for me, then do it for Cal. I want to surprise him by knowing how to dance at our wedding. More than just the standard waltz."

The mention of their wedding sinks into me like cold steel. "And how do you know which ones he knows?"

"Well..." She pauses, almost sheepish. "I called his mother."

I nod, already surrendering. "Right. Of course you did."

"I need a partner. Please do this with me?"

With... not for... The distinction settles over me like lead. "There are about a thousand reasons why this is a bad idea." I shove my hands into my pockets.

Eden tilts her head, playful but insistent. "Scared, soldier?"

I should say no. I should walk away. But the challenge in her eyes hooks a recklessness buried deep within me.

I step forward, holding out my hand. "I can't believe the situations I let myself get into with you."

Her squeal of delight pierces the air as she grabs my hand. The contact sends electricity up my arm as I escort her inside, already knowing this is going to test every ounce of my self-control.

THE ATMOSPHERE SHIFTS the moment we step inside. Rumba music pulses through the air, the rhythm somehow making the space feel more intimate. Lights catch on decorative mirrors, creating pockets of shadow and warmth. Everyone on the floor moves with practiced joy, bodies in sync. Eden speaks with the receptionist while I try not to imagine how it would feel to move like that with her.

When the song ends, the instructor commands attention simply by walking to the front of the room. Her presence fills the space, something knowing in her eyes as she surveys her students. When she finishes the lesson, she approaches us.

"Welcome to De Casa La Rumba!" Her accent carries both warmth and authority. "I am Liliana. Are you here for the full session or the tryout?"

"I've signed us up for lessons spanning the next few weeks," Eden explains. "Getting ready for my wedding."

"Oh! Congratulations!" Liliana's eyes sparkle. "And this must be your fiancé? Such a handsome couple!"

"Oh, no, I'm not—" I start to correct her.

"The chemistry between you two! Magnificent! Don't worry, by the wedding day, you will dance like you were born to it." She waves off my protest. "Now, what style interests you?"

Eden explains her plans while I shift uncomfortably, too aware of how right Liliana's assumption felt for just a moment. When the instructor turns to me, her appraisal is almost tactical.

"And you, señor? You have a dancer's build. Those military muscles will serve you well here."

I extend my hand in greeting, but she offers hers with such ceremony that I find myself bringing it to my lips instead. Her delighted laugh fills the room.

"My, my! Such a gentleman! Now, are you familiar with rumba?"

Heat creeps up my neck. "Only Latin I know is the food variety, ma'am."

She fans herself dramatically. "Don't worry. By the time I'm done with you both, you'll be hot as habaneros on that dance floor!"

The class begins with basic steps, but everything changes when it's time to partner up. Eden removes her jacket, and I try not to stare at the way her tank top shows off her shoulders. Liliana moves between couples, adjusting positions with knowing hands.

"No, no, no!" She stops at us, clicking her tongue. "This is not a military formation. You must hold her like she's precious but not breakable." She demonstrates with me, her movements confident and clear. "Like this. See how we are not afraid of touching?"

When Eden steps back into position, my hands shake slightly. I pull her closer, trying to maintain some proper boundaries while my body screams for more contact.

"Better, but still too much space!" Liliana's hand presses firmly against Eden's back, pushing her flush against me. She adjusts my grip around Eden's waist. "There! Now the bodies can speak to each other!"

I focus on counting steps, desperate to ignore how perfectly Eden fits against me, how her breath catches when I move wrong. "Sorry," I mutter after each misstep.

"Hey," she laughs softly, the sound vibrating between us. "Maybe if you just stop focusing on your feet and look at me, you can stop being so nervous."

"Who says I'm nervous?"

Her knowing smile hits too close to home. "It's just me, Ben."

If she only knew how that makes it infinitely worse. Her scent surrounds me, her body moving with mine in ways that wake up parts of me I've tried to keep dormant.

"These feet were made for combat, not dancing."

"Let's pretend you're on a mission then."

"That's ridiculous."

"It is not. It might work!"

The suggestion clicks something in my mind. I look at her—really look at her—and suddenly the movement makes sense. My body knows how to read signals, anticipate motion, respond to the slightest pressure. Each step becomes a tactical decision, each turn a calculated move.

By the end of the first class, we're moving together with surprising ease. When Liliana announces the next session, Eden's eyes find mine, hopeful.

"Thursday?" I shrug, already aware of how dangerous this game will become.

Six weeks of classes blur together in a haze of increasingly intimate dance steps. Each session, the space between us grows smaller, the tension thicker. By our final class, I know every curve of her body, every subtle signal she gives when she's about to turn, every catch in her breath when I pull her close.

"From the top!" Liliana calls out. "Show me everything you've learned!"

The music starts, and Eden moves into position with newfound expertise. Her fitted dance top clings to her curves, damp with exertion. Wisps of hair have escaped her updo, curling against her neck in a way that makes my fingers itch to brush them aside. The other couples fade away until it's just us, moving together like we've done this in another life.

And somehow—I keep up. There's a strange ease in how I move now, how I pivot and catch her with just enough strength to support her without ever risking too much pressure. The limp that used to haunt every step is almost gone tonight, more echo than obstacle. I feel... solid. Capable in a way I haven't since the my last battle.

My hand finds her waist, and I'm struck by how strong I feel with her in my arms. I read every cue she gives before she moves, almost before she thinks it. It's instinct now. Somehow, I've found the balance between power and control, between tenderness and restraint. I know exactly how to hold her without breaking her.

Each turn brings her closer, each step more confident than the last. Her breathing quickens as we build toward the finale. The hint of a gasp escapes her lips as I guide her through a complex spin, her leg wrapping around mine. Her body arches back, totally yielded to my control, and for a moment I forget this isn't real—that she isn't mine to hold this way.

The final move requires absolute trust. I dip her low, supporting her weight as her leg extends high, my hand strong against her thigh. Her chest rises and falls rapidly, skin flushed and gleaming in the studio lights. Loose strands of hair cling to her neck, and I have to fight every instinct that tells me to trace them with my lips. Our faces are inches apart, her eyes locked on mine, dripping with a passion that mirrors the heat in my own chest. The air between us crackles with everything we've never said, everything we can't say.

I pull her upright too quickly, but she doesn't step back. Her hand stays pressed against my chest, right over my thundering heart. We share the same breath, the same space, the same moment of dangerous possibility. Her eyes find mine again, and I see the recognition there—the understanding of what this has become.

"Magnifico!" Liliana's voice shatters the spell. "This is how you will steal the show at your wedding! Such passion!"

Reality crashes back like ice water. Later, as we're gathering our things, Eden's voice is soft. "Thank you. I feel so much more confident now." Uncertainty lingers in her tone.

"You're a natural," I manage, focusing on my bag rather than the memory of her in my arms. "Cal won't know what hit him." I say, the words feeling spiteful in my throat.

She pauses, then adds quietly, "I couldn't have done it without you, Ben."

I meet her eyes one last time, memorizing how she looks in this moment—flushed from dancing, hair falling loose, unspoken desires in her gaze. "Yeah, well... what are friends for?"

The word friends hangs between us like smoke—visible but impossible to grasp, a thin veil over the truth we both feel but can never acknowledge.

Chapter 23

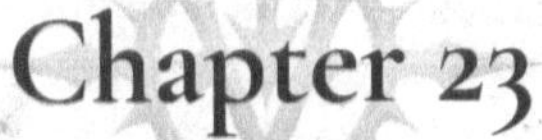

The scent of her skin still clings to my shirt when I pull on a clean one for the range. I try not to think about the way her body fit against mine during that final dance, the way her breath caught when I pulled her close—or how she didn't pull away. How easy it would've been to cross a line.

I shouldn't have touched her like that. Shouldn't have held on so long.

But I already know that no matter how many rounds I fire, it won't erase the taste of wanting something I can't have.

I shrug into my jacket, rifle case slung over my shoulder as I take the stairs two at a time. The familiar weight of gear grounds me, a ritual I've held onto longer than most things. The range smells like oil and cordite, clean brass and controlled violence. Comforting.

At the range, the world narrows to targets and breath control. A few hours pass in practiced silence. Load. Breathe. Fire. Repeat.

My aim's been cleaner lately—steadier, more precise. The trigger breaks clean. One shot, then another. My grouping's tighter than it used to be. Probably the new scope. Or the lighting. Or just muscle memory kicking in.

I don't let myself linger on the fact that I shouldn't be this good anymore. Not with everything I had broken.

By the time I'm driving back, the burn in my arms feels earned. Controlled. I did what I was supposed to do—kept my hands busy, my mind clear.

The scent of gunpowder soaks my clothes when I return

home, a chemical kind of satisfaction lingering in my lungs. I strip and step into the shower, letting the water scald away the residue of metal and smoke. The steam curls around me, thick like the thoughts pressing at the edges of my mind.

Two more weeks.

The wedding looms closer—an inevitability I can't outrun. I picture Cal's mom already teary-eyed, her voice cracking over some speech about fate and soulmates. For a moment, I almost laugh. It's the only genuine reaction I can manage about the whole damn thing.

The evening air hits my face as I step outside again, hunting for dinner. Nothing sounds good, but the thought of sitting alone in silence is worse. I pass two fast food joints before I spot the open kitchen window glowing with warm light and movement—some kind of community cooking class. It feels alive in a way I'm not. And that's reason enough to step inside.

Not being alone sounds right tonight.

I cross the street—then stop short. A checkpoint clogs the intersection ahead. Military vehicles flank the sidewalks, their angular silhouettes jarring against the soft glow of shopfronts. Soldiers in heavy vests scan IDs, rifles slung at the ready. It doesn't make sense. Not here. Not in the middle of a civilian zone this close to the base.

I adjust my stride, blending with the flow of foot traffic. Parents hush restless kids. A mechanic mutters under his breath.

"This is getting ridiculous," someone behind me says. "The war's not even here, and they're treating us like criminals."

A woman scoffs. "Not here? You seen the price of food lately? My cousin's shop had to close—everything's going to the military. Feels like the whole country's hanging by a thread."

A sharp laugh. "Hanging? No, we're already dangling. They need to end this war, or we won't have anything left to fight for."

I keep walking, jaw tight.

They don't get it.

It's easy to talk about peace when you haven't watched your own men bleed out in the dirt. Easy to complain when you've never seen an enhanced tear through a team like tissue paper. They think going back to normal is an option.

Garlic and charred meat mingle in the air and drift toward me as I pass through the checkpoint, but my appetite is gone. Still, I step inside.

The warmth of the kitchen wraps around me, thick with steam and the scrape of knives against cutting boards. I take a station, reach for a cutting board.

Focus. Just eat. Just keep moving.

"Ben Hale." Layla's voice slices through the quiet with an energy that fits the room—certain and familiar.

I look up, surprised to see her leaning against my counter, dark wavy hair loose, expression under her bangs softer than the last time we spoke. "Layla?"

"You remembered my name." Her smile reaches her eyes, softening her whole face.

"A name like yours is hard to forget." Like the way she called me out that night we met, saw right through me. "What brings you here?"

She glances around the kitchen, moving closer. "Same as you. Though I have to say, seeing you here is... unexpected."

"Because soldiers can't cook?"

"Because men like you usually have someone else to cook for them." Her eyes travel over me appraisingly. "Or are you here hunting?"

I focus on chopping tomatoes, trying not to notice how she mirrors my movements at her own station. "Just here to eat."

"Really?" She bumps my shoulder playfully. "You know it's every girl's dream to find a man who can cook."

"Is that what you're doing here? Looking for a chef?"

Her laugh carries no bitterness now. "Maybe I just didn't want to eat alone tonight."

I can relate.

We fall in sync—moving between our stations, sharing tastes and critiques. She has a sharp wit that makes me laugh despite myself. When she reaches across me for the salt, her perfume—light and citrusy—catches me off guard.

It's nice. Subtle. For the first time in a long time, I wonder if there's a possibility waiting for me past all my recent struggles. Layla had been so put off by our first meeting, so quick to call me out, that I never imagined she'd look at me like this. But here we are.

Maybe, if I can swallow this thing with Eden, push it down deep enough that it doesn't ruin me, I might have a shot at a relationship like Cal has. The thought catches me off guard. A future. A real one.

"Thanks again," she says later, surprising me with a kiss on the cheek that lingers just long enough to mean interest in more.

"You still have my number if you ever want a follow-up." The words come easier than expected.

She grins. "Mr. Hale, is that another date invitation?"

Heat creeps up my neck. "Well, just figured... if you wanted to not eat alone again sometime..."

She studies me, a knowingness in her expression. "I'll see you at the wedding."

"Wedding?" My stomach drops. "Oh. Right. The wedding."

"Not still in love with my cousin, are you?" Her raised eyebrow carries too much accusation.

The truth sticks in my throat. "Well, she *is* marrying my best friend."

She purses her lips. "I deserve to be someone's first choice."

Guilt cuts through me. "Every woman deserves that."

"Every man, too." Her eyes fill with pity that burns worse than judgment. "Goodnight, Ben."

HER WORDS HAUNT me up the stairs to my apartment. The mail waiting at the door is just junk—until it isn't.

That seal.

The military insignia still has the power to tighten my chest, to ignite that traitorous flicker of hope. My hands tremble as I tear it open.

Each word slams into me, blunt and merciless:

"...regret to inform you..."

"...incident on record..."

"...determined unfit to serve..."

Of course.

The words blur together, cutting deeper with every pass.

Memories flash rapid-fire— the weight of my first uniform, the rush of a successful mission, building up those naïve boys into soldiers.

All gone. Permanently.

I squeeze the letter in my fists, jaw clenched. My eyes scan lower, catching the small block of text at the bottom—a footnote.

"Flagged incident: civilian altercation. See attached police report."

I exhale sharply through my nose.

They already found the police report.

Guess it doesn't matter that I didn't throw the first punch. Doesn't matter that I walked away without cuffs. Doesn't matter that one civilian is still breathing because of me. To them, it's just another checkbox. Another reason to stamp me as unstable.

Liability.

Unfit.

The letter crumples tighter in my fist before I launch it across the room. It hits the back of the sofa and bounces to the floor with the finality of a spent casing.

My back slides down the fridge until I'm sitting on the tile, knees bent, spine pressed to the cold metal.

I should be numb to this by now.

But my chest aches like it's trying to cave in on itself.

Worthless.

Broken.

Dangerous.

The rage builds like pressure in a sealed drum. Every failure playing on repeat in my head. Eden's terrified eyes. Calvin's blind trust. The damn man in the mirror that doesn't even feel like me anymore.

Just like the old man after all.

The whiskey hits like fire. A welcome burn searing away thought, numbing the sharpest edges of failure.

I shouldn't have grabbed her like that.

Not during self-defense training.

Not ever.

But when she moved with me—trusted me—it felt like I belonged again. Like I could still be wanted. Still be whole.

Fuck.

I pour another, larger this time. The alcohol hits my

stomach like napalm. Each swallow pushing back the crushing weight in my chest, but it's not enough. The urge to destroy something grows with each sip.

My mind cycles through options—target practice, weights, meaningless sex—anything to dull this edge, to keep myself from coming apart.

My fingers itch for motion. For something I can win at. My body acts before my thoughts catch up. I drop to the floor, palms hitting the cold tile.

Move. Prove them wrong.

One push-up. Two. The whiskey burns in my throat, my muscles straining, but I keep going.

Fifteen. Thirty. Sixty.

The blood rushes in my ears. If I just keep moving, the words won't settle. If I just keep pushing, my body won't betray me.

The knock is sharp, cutting through the fog of alcohol and self-loathing. I freeze, arms trembling beneath me. The room is too quiet now and my vision sways. I press my forehead to the floor, breathing hard, willing my body to keep going.

Another knock. Softer.

I stagger to my feet, wiping sweat from my face before swinging the door open.

Eden stands there, her usual brightness dimmed, a vulnerability in her gaze that seems to mirror my own brokenness. My resolve buckles.

Not now. Not like this.

"Not a great time," I manage, leaving the door wide open as I retreat to the weight bench, not bothering to check the plates. Physical pain feels better than this hollow ache. Each rep should burn. I need my muscles screaming in protest, but they don't. So I push harder—it's better than thinking. The smell of sweat mingles with the whiskey on my breath.

"What's wrong?" She walks in like she belongs here— maybe she does—and I hear the rustle of paper before I see her kneeling, collecting the pieces of my rejection letter. Like she can somehow piece it back together. Piece me back together.

I don't answer. Breathing through the reps and the anger of everything I could say. The rack clanks loudly against the quiet and I pull myself off the bench.

The room tilts slightly as I move for more whiskey.

"Benji?"

"Just living the dream." I growl, pouring the amber drink. "Every damn day is the same damn thing." The table thunks when I force the bottle back to its surface.

She smooths the crumpled page, eyes scanning the text. "This came today?"

I don't answer. Because what's the point?

Her gaze lifts. "Ben, this doesn't define you."

I laugh—sharp and bitter. "You wanna know something else?" My voice rises, cutting through the space between us. "I let myself hope. Just once. For a possibility. A tiny, worthless chance that something might go my way for once."

"How is having hope a bad thing?" Her calm tone grates against my nerves.

"It's all just a huge setup for the biggest letdowns of your life." The whiskey sloshes as I gesture. "Every. Single. Time."

She watches me carefully, fingers curling around the letter. "Why does it have to be all or nothing?"

I slam the glass onto the table, whiskey spilling over the edge. "Because that's how it fucking works, Eden."

She doesn't flinch. "No, that's how you've decided it works."

That stops me cold. Her eyes stay on mine, steady. Not pitying. Not placating. Just... seeing me.

"You didn't pass an evaluation, Ben. That's it. It's not a death sentence. It's not a condemnation."

The words hit wrong, striking deeper than they should. "You think I don't know that?" I exhale sharply, shaking my head. "You think I don't know it's just paper? That it's just a signature—some words on a goddamn file?" My pulse pounds. The walls feel too close, the air too thick. "It doesn't change the fact that I'm done. It doesn't change the fact that I have nothing left."

Her brows knit together. She hesitates—just long enough to make it worse. I see it in her eyes, the thing she almost says.

"You still have—"

"Don't." My voice drops, quiet but cutting.

Eden swallows, exhaling through her nose. Her jaw tightens as she presses the paper to my chest. "Fine. But at least fight for something, Ben."

The challenge lingers between us, electric and unyielding. My breathing is still rough, but hers isn't steady either.

The moment holds—tense and unfinished. Her challenge

still hums under my skin like static, but I don't rise to meet it. I can't.

So instead—I retreat. Back to what's easier. Back to what numbs. I turn away without a word, reach for the bottle, and pour another glass with shaking hands.

"Benji, how much have you had to drink?"

"Not enough." The gruffness in my voice doesn't even sound like me anymore as I toss the glass back.

"How much, Ben?" She grabs the bottle, concern etching her features. "Was this full?"

"Would it make a difference?"

"Of course it makes a difference!" Her concern sharpens and her posture shifts—Nurse Eden, always ready to fix what's broken. She removes her jacket. The sight of her taking care of me again makes everything worse.

"Don't you fucking get it?" I turn to her, unsteady, raw, the words scraping their way out with a burning need to make her understand.

"Get what?" She flinches, but her eyes stay locked on mine—wide, defiant, pulling me in even as she braces for impact.

"No amount of planning, no amount of patience, no amount of skill can fix this."

"Fix what?" She steps forward now. The air crackling between us, charged and brittle.

She's not scared. Not of me. And that—God, that makes it worse.

"Any of it! All of it!" My voice echoes off the walls. "You have what you want! Me? I've-lost-everything! Been busting my ass to get parts of it back but they won't fucking take a broken piece of shit like me."

"Stop it!" She shouts back, matching my intensity. "Stop acting like you're some kind of damaged goods that nobody wants!"

"Why? Because it makes you uncomfortable? Because perfect Eden can't stand to see someone actually feel their pain instead of stuffing it down and pretending everything's fine?"

Her eyes flash. "You think I don't know about pain? About loss? I spend every day watching people suffer, watching them die—"

"That's different and you know it!"

"Why? Because it's not on the battlefield? Because it's not

your kind of pain?"

"Because you get to go home at the end of the day and be normal!" The words rip out of me. "You get to have a life, a future, someone who—" I catch myself, but it's too late.

She steps closer, fury and betrayal burning in her eyes. "Someone who what, Ben? Say it!"

"Someone who actually deserves you!" The confession hangs between us like smoke. The silence stretches, thick with everything we've never said.

"This?" She holds up the letter, her voice softening. "Ben, look at me."

I can't. Won't. Not when she uses that voice—the one that makes me believe I'm worth saving.

Her hand finds my face, turning it toward her. The touch is gentle but insistent, like everything about her. "Your worth isn't tied to the military. I know it feels like it is, but it's not." Her thumb brushes my cheek, and I fight the urge to lean into her touch. "Do you know what I see when I look at you?"

A bitter laugh escapes me. "A broken soldier who can't even—"

"The man who held my hand through twelve hours of surgery prep." Her eyes hold mine, unflinching. "The man who spends his weekends teaching self-defense to abuse survivors. Who brings soup to Mrs. Martinez downstairs when her arthritis acts up." Her other hand presses against my chest, right over my thundering heart. "The man who would die to protect anyone in this building, military or not."

My chest tightens, splintering under the weight of her words. "Eden..."

"You're not broken, Benji. You're one of the strongest people I've ever known." Her voice catches. "And watching you tear yourself apart because some paper says you can't serve..." She shakes her head, fingers curling into my shirt. "It kills me. Because you serve every single day, in ways that matter so much more than carrying a rifle."

The warmth of her touch spreads through me like the whiskey, but cleaner, more pure. *Dangerous.* "I'm just… spent," I whisper, the words carrying more than just physical exhaustion. Her scent surrounds me—healing and temptation wrapped together.

"Let's get you some water." Her hand slides from my face, but I catch it, unable to let her go just yet. She turns, looking at me with those eyes that see too much, and my control shatters.

I shouldn't. But I need something real—something that makes the world seem bearable for one goddamn second.

"I'm tired," I whisper, voice raw, "tired of never getting what I want." I pull her in before I can think, before I can stop myself.

Our bodies press together, her warmth a stark contrast to the cold consuming me.

Her grip tightens at my chest—barely there, but it anchors me. Neither of us pulls away.

The silence shifts. It's no longer just tense. It's charged. I don't know who moves first. Maybe both of us. But one second we're standing there, the next my lips crash into hers.

She gasps, but she doesn't stop me. Her body molds to mine, hands threading into my hair, pressing deeper like she can't get close enough.

I grip her waist, pulling her flush against me, desperate for something real, something that isn't slipping through my fingers.

She kisses me like she's afraid to stop, like this is the only moment that matters. And for the first time in an eternity, everything feels right. She's where she belongs, in my arms, sharing my breath.

Her fingers trace up my arms, soaking in the remnants of my strength, of everything that still makes me a man in my own damn skin. I lift her, her legs locking around my waist— and even with the whiskey still burning through me, I don't falter. I shouldn't be this steady. Not after everything. But her body fits against mine like it was meant to, and all that matters is keeping her there.

Her breath hitches as I press her into the cabinets, as if holding her there can keep this moment from shattering.

Her sighs say it all—*she's wanted this too.*

A growl escapes me when she bites my lip. Heat floods my veins.

I tear off my shirt, needing her against my skin. She sits up to remove hers, and I finally taste the warmth of her neck, breathing in her soft sounds.

Her fingers find my scar, tracing it gently. The touch triggers a flash—the Turig helmet, her bloodied face, tears tracking through red. I grit my teeth and pull back from her neck, though everything in me screams to continue.

She breathes my name like a question—a plea. "Benji?"

"I'm sorry, love..." I step away, the endearment slipping out before I think to stop it.

"Benji, look at me."

"I can't." The silence weighs like lead. "Not if I ever want to be able to look Cal in the face again." I gather our shirts, handling hers like it might burn me.

When I finally meet her eyes, they're full of tears.

More tears I've caused.

"I'll get you that water." Her voice trembles.

"I only had a glass or two." The adrenaline has burned through most of the alcohol anyway.

"You still need to hydrate."

"You shouldn't be taking care of me. Not after what I just did." I collapse onto the sofa, staring at my hands. "I just... lost it."

She sits beside me, offering glass. "Benji... you're a good man. One of the best—"

"Don't." Her words slam into me with the force of artillery fire. I lean forward, elbows on my knees, head in my hands.

"It's true."

"A good man doesn't kiss his best friend's fiancé." The words leave my mouth dry. "A good man doesn't—"

"Stop." Her hand finds my shoulder, and I flinch away from her touch. "We both—"

"Both what, Eden?" I look at her then. Her lips are still swollen from my kiss, her hair mussed from my hands. Evidence of my failure. "Both knew better? Both let it happen anyway?"

The silence burns. Her scarf still lingers in my hand, but I don't give it back. Can't.

She draws back slightly. "I should go."

"Yeah." The word comes out rough. "You should."

She gathers her things slowly, like she's waiting for me to stop her. I don't.

At the door, Eden hesitates, her hand on the frame like it might hold her together, her lips parted. "Ben…" she starts, but the words don't come. Her voice cracks instead, too thin to carry anything real.

"I'll be there," I say before she can finish. "The wedding. Don't worry."

"That's not—"

"Just go," I cut her off, not unkind, but final. "You should go."

A long beat. Then, quietly, her voice broken—"I didn't mean for this to happen."

"Neither did I."

A tremor runs through her, like she might say something else, but she doesn't. She turns and disappears into the night.

I shut the door behind her before I can watch her walk away. The apartment goes still. A power surge hums through the ceiling—lights flicker, the fridge clicks off, then back on.

The war's starting to touch everything now. Even here.

I cross the room and sit on the edge of the couch, head in my hands.

The taste of her lingers on my lips, the weight of everything I can't have pressing down like a mountain of stone.

My phone buzzes on the counter. Cal's tone. I don't move.

The call goes to voicemail. Then another. Then silence.

I stare at the wall until the silence grows teeth. Until I have to do something, anything. I rise, grab her scarf, and fold it carefully—tucking it into a drawer like the memory it's already become.

Then I sit in the dark. Still tasting her. Still hearing her say my name like it meant more. Still knowing I'll never deserve it again.

Tomorrow, I'll pick up the pieces. Reset the weights. Clean up the whiskey bottle. Put on the mask of the good soldier, the best friend, the man I'm supposed to be.

But tonight, I let myself feel it all—the rejection, the loss, the love I never should have felt. And in the quiet dark of my apartment, I finally understand: some wars can't be won. Some battles leave scars you can't see. And sometimes being a good man means living with the pain of doing the right thing. Even when it breaks you.

Chapter 24

Weeks pass in silence. Eden doesn't call. I don't text. We pretend, like always, that nothing happened. That we're just friends. That I didn't taste her skin or feel her heart racing beneath my hands. The silence between us is louder than any confession, heavier than any apology. And now, here I am—standing at her side in a cathedral, pretending I haven't already said goodbye.

The wedding day I've been dreading has arrived. Joy for my friend's happiness blooms bittersweet in my chest, its petals laced with the sharp thorns of longing for something forever out of reach.

Eden gazes up at me through the fragile haze of her veil, tears catching light like scattered diamonds, her smile as radiant as it is devastating. The white dress makes her look ethereal, untouchable—which she is, in every way that matters.

"I never thought this day would come," she whispers. Her bold red lips form the words that cut deeper than any blade I've ever known.

I grip her silk-wrapped hands in mine, feeling the slight tremor in them. The deep ache in my chest twists tighter with each heartbeat. For this moment, she's close, leaning on me, but she's not mine. She never will be. The smooth material glides over my lips when I press them to her hand, my touch lingering a fraction too long, memorizing the warmth of her skin through the delicate fabric. Tilting my head, I force a small shrug. "Are you ready?"

Eden blinks back tears, her voice trembling. "Yes."

I slide my arm around her shoulders as dread creeps into me like a dark tide. She smiles softly at my touch. "I'm sorry your dad couldn't be here for this."

Her expression falters before she looks up at me, those blue eyes piercing straight through my carefully constructed walls. "He told me if he couldn't give me away, he wanted it to be the one who made this day possible." Her voice softens, her gaze unwavering. "There was never a doubt that it should be you."

I swallow hard against the desert in my throat.

Say it, Ben. Just one time, tell her.

My mouth opens, years of unspoken words begging to escape, but nothing comes out. Instead, I pull her closer into my side, pressing my lips to her hair. The scent threatens to break what's left of my resolve. "There's nowhere I'd rather be, love." Clearing my throat, I slide away and hold up my arm for her to take as the heavy doors swing open.

Old brass organ pipes echo through the cathedral, filling the space with the familiar notes of the *Wedding Processional*. Her grandmother had adored *The Sound of Music*, which inspired her love for the mountains and ultimately brought her family here.

Eden's hand trembles on my arm as we move forward. My free hand covers hers in a reassuring pat. "I'm not going to know what to do with myself now all this wedding prep is over," I whisper.

Her shoulders flutter with a suppressed chuckle. "You'll figure it out," she murmurs.

We reach the end of the aisle, and I lift her veil, stepping in for a hug. The jasmine in her perfume seems stronger now, no longer dampened by the thin fabric.

"May all your wishes come true," I whisper against her cheek before pulling away, locking eyes with her one last time.

Her eyes glisten as she smiles and nods.

Turning to Cal, I force my best smile. His joy is so palpable, it's infectious, and yet it only deepens the ache that settled in me long ago. I grip his hand tightly, and he pulls me in for a hug, slapping my back with a laugh.

"You're our hero, Ben."

I manage a chuckle and step back, settling into place as his best man.

I'm wearing too many damn hats today.

As I move, a dull pull coils down my leg. I mask the limp, keep my steps measured. Controlled.

Eden's eyes flick to mine just before she reaches the altar. Just a second too long to be casual. Her gaze drops—just briefly—to the leg I'm favoring again.
She knows. And she remembers.
Her smile falters, almost imperceptibly, before she catches it again and turns toward Cal.
They take each other's hands, their gazes locked as the minister begins the ceremony.

FROM MY SPOT near the back wall, I watch them take the floor for their first dance. The music swells—something classical, reserved, nothing like the heat of rumba drums or the sway of Eden's body when it was just the two of us.

Calvin leads with enthusiasm but not precision. His steps are a little too big, his rhythm half a beat behind. I see the moment Eden adjusts—her smile doesn't falter, but her body tenses as she anticipates his next misstep. She's guiding without showing it.

My fingers tighten around the glass in my hand. I remember the way her breath hitched during that final dip, the way she trusted me to hold her weight like it was instinct. I knew her rhythm, the way her shoulders would shift just before a turn, the softness in her hands when she let herself forget the world.

Calvin spins her, too fast. She laughs, masking the hesitation as joy. But I saw it—felt what it was supposed to be. And now, I'm just another guest watching the bride pretend she belongs to someone else's lead.

After the music has faded and the crowd moves on to champagne and cake, I find a quiet moment with her near the edge of the reception hall. Eden slips away from the cluster of well-wishers, tugging lightly at the lace of her sleeve as she exhales. The light catches her face in a way that makes it hard not to look too long.

"You okay?" I ask, careful to keep my voice neutral.

She smiles, but it doesn't reach her eyes. "I'm fine. Just... tired. It's a lot of people."

I nod, taking a slow sip of whatever someone poured me. "You looked good out there."

"Liar." Her voice is soft, teasing—but underneath, there's a flicker of vulnerability. "I tripped over his foot. Twice."

"You covered it well."

She glances up at me, something wry in her expression. "You'd have done it better."

The words twist like a blade in the back. I look away, throat tight. "Wasn't my dance to lead."

A pause stretches between us.

She doesn't move. "Thank you," she murmurs. "For the lessons. For everything. I don't think I ever said it the way I meant to."

"You didn't have to." My voice is rougher than I want it to be. "I was glad to... help."

She tilts her head slightly, studying me. "You're favoring your good side again."

I shift my weight instinctively. "Just stiff. Long day in dress shoes."

"Or six weeks of dancing on a bad leg," she says gently, but doesn't push. Her eyes linger on me a second longer than they should.

I force a smirk. "Guess I'm not built for weddings."

I can't tell her. Can't tell her how dancing with her made the pain better, not worse. Can't tell her how much those six weeks built me up.

"I think you're doing just fine." Her voice is soft now. "Better than fine."

Her hand brushes mine—barely a touch, but enough to make my skin burn. She doesn't linger. "I should get back," she says, already backing away, already gone even as she says it.

"Yeah." I don't watch her leave. I just listen to the rustle of her gown and the distant hum of the music—another song I'll never get to dance to.

As though hazed through it all, I now sit alone in a room scattered with balloons, confetti, and streamers. The cleaning crew bustles quietly in the background. My glass sits in my hand, but I can't remember the last time I took a sip.

"Ben."

Her voice pulls me from my thoughts, and I look up. Eden floats toward me in her white gown, a soft smile on her lips. When she reaches me, she slips her arm around my shoulder, careful and practiced—like we haven't been avoiding each other for the past few weeks.

"Thank you," she says quietly.

"For what?" I keep my voice light. "All I did was show up."

"You always do." Her smile wavers, but she doesn't let it falter completely. "You helped more than you realize."

I shrug, reaching for humor the way I always do when things get tight in my chest. "Cal did most of the heavy lifting. Literally. I think I saw him bench-press the cake."

She laughs—soft, tired. But the sound warms the air between us. "I'm serious," she says, squeezing my hand once. "You made today easier just by being here."

I nod once. "I promised I would be."

The silence that follows feels familiar. Painfully so. Like the quiet in the back of an elevator or the seconds before a wrong decision you can't take back.

She looks down at our joined hands. "It still feels a little unreal."

"Big days always do." I force a smile. "Bet it'll hit you on the honeymoon."

She starts to say something, then stops herself. Her thumb brushes over my knuckles, slow and absent. Like muscle memory.

"What's wrong?" I ask, keeping my voice steady despite the urge to pull her closer.

"Nothing." She shakes her head, but her grip on my hand tightens like she's anchoring herself. "It's just... everything's changing so fast."

I resist the urge to brush back her hair, to comfort her the way she has always done for me. That's not my place. "Change can be good."

"Can it?" Her voice catches, eyes meeting mine with an intensity that makes my chest ache. "Sometimes I wonder if—" She stops herself, looking away.

"Hey." I keep my distance, though everything in me wants to close it. "Today's supposed to be happy."

"I am happy," she whispers, but tears shimmer in her eyes. "I just... I keep thinking about…"

The weight of unspoken things hangs between us. I think

of dance lessons, of foam knives, of moments we pretend never happened. "Eden..."

"I know." She straightens, wiping quickly at her eyes. "I know. I shouldn't be… we can't. But I—"

"Let's find Cal, I have a gift for you both." I say gently, standing and offering my hand to help her up. Professional. Distant. Safe. "Besides, he's probably wondering where his bride disappeared to."

She takes my hand, and for just a moment, I let myself feel the warmth of her touch one last time. Then I step back, holding the door open, maintaining the distance we both know we need to keep.

As she passes, her scent follows her—a reminder of everything I'm letting walk away. But this time, I don't allow myself the want to reach for her. Some lines, once crossed, can never be uncrossed. And today, of all days, we both need to remember that.

"Cal! There you are." Eden's voice lifts slightly as she steps into the other room. "We were just about to come find you."

"Well, I was coming to find you, and look at that—we've found each other." Calvin grins, wrapping his arm around her. "Are you ready to go?"

Eden places her hand on his chest, tilting her face toward him. "Almost. Benji said he has a gift for us."

"Oh, good! You love surprises." Calvin glances at me, curiosity in his warm expression.

Clearing my throat, I step forward. "So, as you both know, I'm not exactly great at gifts." I smile sheepishly. "I kept going over in my head what could be useful but still meaningful to your relationship." I pull back my jacket, remove the sheathed knives from my belt, and hold one out to Calvin.

He slides the blade from its casing, an appreciative smile spreading across his face. Eden's eyes widen as she softly gasps. "Ben, it's beautiful," she whispers, her fingers brushing over the intricate details of the other blade still in my hands.

"How'd you keep this hidden from me?" Calvin asks, still admiring the craftsmanship.

"You haven't been around much," I reply with forced casualness. "and I only have the equipment to make parts of them at home."

"You made them?" Eden's gaze flicks between me and the blade.

Calvin answers before I can. "It's a little hobby he's always had."

I point to the engraving on Calvin's knife. "Your initials. EB on one, CB on the other."

Calvin chuckles, testing the knife's weight. "Thanks, Ben. My tomatoes will love this."

I force a smile, glancing at Eden. "It's for self-defense, primarily. But if slicing tomatoes is its fate, so be it."

"How is this significant to our relationship?" Calvin's tone shifts, laced with curiosity.

I hesitate, glancing at Eden. Her shoulders stiffen, her gaze dropping to the floor. She won't say it. Fine, I'll do it for her. Better now than years down the line.

"Well," I begin, shifting uncomfortably, "it has to do with how you two met."

Eden's head snaps up, her voice sharp and trembling. "Ben, don't."

"You don't want to start your life together with this hanging over you," I say gently.

Calvin looks between us, his confusion deepening. "What are you talking about?"

Eden exhales shakily, stepping forward. "I didn't tell you because I didn't want you to worry about me."

"Tell me what?" Calvin presses, his protective arm wrapping around her shoulders.

Eden glances at me, then back at Calvin. "One night, Heather and I were walking back to her place. A group of men cornered us." Her voice cracks. "They—they weren't just muggers, Cal."

Calvin stiffens, his expression hardening. "What did they do?"

"Nothing." I step in, sparing her the words. "They didn't get the chance."

Eden swallows hard, her voice trembling. "Ben stopped them."

Calvin's gaze shifts to me, gratitude mingling with disbelief. "You saved them?"

My jaw tightens at the memory. "I did what I had to."

"But why didn't you tell me?" Calvin asks, turning back to Eden.

Tears shine in her eyes. "Because it's not a moment I

wanted to relive."

Calvin pulls her closer, his voice softening. "Eden, I already worry about you. You don't have to carry this alone."

She leans into him, her gaze finding mine over his shoulder. "What Ben did… it was more than just stepping in."

Calvin pulls back, looking at me. "What does she mean?"

I sigh, running a hand over my face. "I snapped, Cal. What I did to those men went far beyond self-defense. It's part of why I was discharged."

The revelation of the past hangs heavy in the air, thick with unspoken regrets and half-buried trauma. Calvin's face hardens as understanding dawns, and I watch the shift in his eyes—from confusion to horror to a darkness I recognize too well.

Calvin's jaw tightens, his hand gripping the knife too hard. He's not just hearing the story—he's imagining it, seeing her cornered and afraid, and realizing he wasn't there.

"So, you killed them?" he asks, his tone dropping to something dangerous.

"Nearly," I admit, the memory of that night's rage still burning in my blood. "They survived. Barely."

"You should've let them die," Calvin mutters, and something in his voice reminds me of myself that night.

Eden's jaw drops. "Calvin! As a medical professional, it's my duty to save lives, not take them."

"You didn't take them," he counters, protective anger rising in his voice.

"If I had done nothing, I'd be just as guilty as Ben," she insists, and the words hit me like shrapnel.

Calvin's voice rises higher, echoing off the walls. "Accusing him of an act that needs guilt is ridiculous. He saved your life, Eden."

"Yes, but the extent he went to was unnecessary," she argues, and I see her hands shaking—remembering my violence, my loss of control.

"You can't know that! Maybe if he hadn't gone that far, both of you would be—"

"This isn't the first time we've had this type of conversation, is it?" I cut in, the pieces suddenly clicking into place. Eden's unexpected visit that night, her tear-stained face, the tension that had nothing to do with me. Their voices fall silent as I look between them.

Eden's gaze drops to the floor. "Cal and I had an argument.

.. a few weeks ago. About his work. About the line between helping and…" she glances at me meaningfully, "going too far."

Calvin's expression shifts. "We're both dealing with medical ethics here."

The air thickens between us, heavy with unspoken truths. Eden purses her lips. "But I'm saving lives and you're—"

"Also saving lives!" Calvin interjects.

"At least I make it home every day."

"Says the one who stormed off after a tiny argument and didn't show up till the next morning."

"Stop!" I cut in, stepping between them. The familiar role of peacekeeper sits heavy on my shoulders. "Just... stop." My voice softens as I glance between them—my best friend and the woman I can never have. "This isn't important now. What matters is that we're all here. You two are together, and that's what counts. I only brought it up because I wanted the gifts to mean something. They're for protection—so nothing like that ever happens again."

Calvin looks down at the blade in his hand, and I see the weight of responsibility settling over him. "You're right. It's thoughtful, Ben. But I might need some real lessons. None of that half-assed stuff we did before."

Eden places her hand over his, her gaze softening. "Maybe we can convince the maker to help us both."

I nod faintly, offering a small smile that doesn't reach my heart. "Of course. I can't think of anything more important to spend my time on."

But you'll need to not bail on it for work calls.

The thought is bitter, remembering him leaving Eden to process her trauma alone—trauma I caused, first by my violence, then by my feelings, by every moment after that when I couldn't be just the friend I was supposed to be.

Calvin's phone buzzes. He slips it from his pocket.

Eden's shoulders tense. "Work?" Her voice is tight, holding back what she really wants to say.

Calvin's thumb works the screen. "Just a district threat alert. We should get going before they shut down roads."

A new threat in the area shouldn't be the thing making her ease, but it is.

As they turn to leave, Eden's hand finds mine one last time, a ghost of a squeeze that carries too many meanings to count. I want to hold on, just for a second longer. But I don't.

Because…

She's not mine. Not now. Not ever.

I watch them go, the newlyweds, my best friend and the woman who taught me that some battles can't be won with fists or knives or any weapon I know how to wield. And the only thing I could give them… It needed to hold up in darkness and daylight—something forged for the quiet hour of vesper, when monsters stir.

And when the door closes behind her, I finally exhale, the ache settling in like an old friend. I'll keep showing up. Keep being what she needs. Even if it means watching her walk away every time.

The empty reception hall echoes with their departing footsteps, leaving me alone with the weight of everything I've given up, everything I've protected, and everything I'll spend a lifetime pretending not to want. And when the echo fades, all that's left is the quiet that follows a storm.

Chapter 25

The ache in my leg is worse today. Standing for hours at the wedding in formal shoes was a punishment I didn't account for—not until the stiffness in my thigh turned sharp enough to keep me from sleeping. By morning, the old injury has bloomed into a deeper ache, no longer content to be background noise.

It used to be better than this. Then again, maybe I just used to be better at pretending.

Golden light spills through a crack in the blinds as the sun peers over the mountain top, painting stripes across my bed like bars of a cage. The silence feels louder this morning, the kind that seeps into your ribs and presses down with every breath. I stare at the ceiling, one hand pressed against my chest as if I can keep it from caving in completely, the other crushed beneath my head.

A flash of Eden smiling up at me before walking her down the aisle rips through me. That moment when she squeezed my arm and whispered "Thank you, Benji" – Christ, I'd give anything to go back and steel myself against the way those words hollow me out. Desperate to shake the feeling, I sit up and rub my face, my palms rasping against my day-old trimmed scruff. The bed feels too big, too empty, though it's the same twin mattress I've always had. *Maybe I just feel small...*

My legs are slow to respond, the throb in my bad leg spiking in protest.

Wedding hangover.

Not from the drinks, but from everything else.

The old injury is a constant reminder of everything I've lost. I brush the sensation away, doing my best to ignore it though I'm forced to limp across the hardwood floors that creak beneath my uneven steps. Each echo feels like an accusation: Alone. Empty. Forgotten. Worthless.

In the kitchen, I pour coffee beans into the grinder, the familiar ritual offering little comfort. The mechanical whir fills the apartment, drowning out my thoughts for a blessed few seconds.

While the percolator begins its morning symphony of gurgles and hisses, I drag my feet back to the bedroom and slip into my lounge pants, trying not to notice the suit from yesterday crumpled in the corner, reeking of wedding cake and regret.

I should have told her...

The landline rings, shattering the quiet like breaking glass.

I wince at the large strides it takes to reach the phone, each step sending lightning bolts of pain up my thigh. But the memories of lifting it to hear news of a new deployment has my heart racing with excitement.

"Hale."

"Benji." Calvin's voice is light, but there's a tiredness behind it. "We're boarding soon. Eden's double-checking everything for the third time."

"Isn't that what honeymoons are for? Escaping all the checklists?" My voice sounds rough, unused, like I'd spent the night screaming instead of lying awake counting ceiling cracks.

He laughs. "Yeah, try telling her that."

I lean against the wall, pressing the receiver tighter. "What's up?"

"Just wanted to say thanks again for everything yesterday. And hey—don't forget, you promised you'd tour the lab before making up your mind. You didn't think I forgot, did you?"

I blink away a snapshot of Eden twirling in her gown, white fabric catching light like fresh snow. Pure. Perfect. Completely out of reach.

"That was more of a maybe than a promise."

"Come on. You gave me your word. Just take the damn tour when I get back."

I hesitate when another memory crashes through—Eden during rumba lessons, her fitted tank top clinging to curves I shouldn't have been allowed to touch, her skin gleaming with exertion. "I'll think about it."

"That's not a yes."

"I'll take the tour, Cal."

"Good." His voice warms, even as the background noise grows—Eden's voice, soft and distant, asking about the boarding passes. "Look, I know you're still figuring stuff out. But you don't have to be stuck. The work we're doing could actually make a difference."

"I'll keep that in mind."

"Tell him we love him!" Eden's voice cuts in again, closer this time.

Cal snorts. "She's getting all mushy on me now."

"Well, tell him!"

"Yeah, yeah. Eden says hi." Calvin's translation makes me smile.

"That's not at all what I said!" Her protest carries clearly, and for a moment it's like she's here, in my kitchen, whole and happy and still close enough to touch.

"That's just how guys talk, babe." He responds. "Gotta go!"

I force a chuckle. "Safe flight, Cal."

"We don't get all touchy-feely like..." his voice trails off before the click without acknowledging my goodbye, leaving me stranded in the silence.

I return the phone to its place on the wall and turn, my bachelor apartment stretching before me like a desert—void of any life other than my own.

The morning light has grown harsh, unforgiving, illuminating every crack in the paint, every chip in the furniture, every piece of me that's worn down and broken.

What happened to me… I used to push through the pain. But I can't seem to shake this constant state of indifference.

Images of life within its walls haunt me like ghosts, more solid than shadows but just as untouchable. Calvin sitting on the couch while I help him plan his proposal, his nervous energy filling the room as he practiced the words again and again. Eden protesting his popcorn fight while they watch a movie, her laughter echoing off walls that now stand mute. Every memory is a knife, every empty space a reminder of what I've lost.

I have to do something to fill these empty walls before they close in and crush me...

My coffee calls like a siren song and I fill a cup, the liquid black as midnight and probably just as bitter. Walking to the couch—limping. Still hurts. Not like before, not the same sharp burn, but the weight's there. A nagging ache that whispers I'm not who I used to be. Not yet. Maybe never again.

I sit, watching steam rise from the dark liquid like spirits trying to escape. The black screen of the TV stares back at me, reflecting a man I barely recognize.

Maybe I should tour the lab... beats sitting around doing nothing but feel sorry for myself.

The thought tastes like surrender, but maybe that's all I have left to give.

Chapter 26

The apartment stayed quiet after the call. No click of the TV. No messages from Eden—or anyone. Just the low throb of my leg and the echo of her voice ringing in my head. And it still feels empty, even after two weeks of silence.

I should be used to it by now—people leaving, me staying behind. But somehow, the silence grates tonight.

I lean against the kitchen counter, whiskey glass in hand. The TV hums in the background, something mindless playing, but I haven't looked at the screen in over an hour.

I take a slow sip, standing near the window, watching the city lights flicker below. I haven't spoken to them much since they returned. No real reason. Just… distance.

Then—a knock at the door. I frown. No one visits unannounced.

I set the glass down, crossing the room in a few strides before pulling the door open.

Eden.

Her scent hits me before I can speak—clean skin, jasmine, and a warmth beneath it. It's stronger than usual. Sharper. I chalk it up to her being gone so long. But it lingers in my lungs.

Her complexion's a little off—paler than usual, with a faint sheen of sweat at her temple.

She shifts her weight subtly, one hand brushing her stomach like she's steadying herself.

"You alright?" I frown.

"Yeah," she says quickly. "Just… some leftover nausea. I picked up a stomach bug on the honeymoon. Still kicking around, I guess."

These are the kind of details I shouldn't be picking up on. But I can't help it. She still looks so soft as she stands there, hair damp from a shower, a wrapped package tucked under one arm.

"You busy?" Her eyebrows perk up with hope.

I glance behind me at the whiskey glass, the dark apartment, the half-dead plant in the corner.

"Shouldn't you be home, recovering from your honeymoon with Cal?"

She exhales softly but doesn't take the baited subject change. Instead, she steps inside, setting the package carefully on the coffee table.

"Oh, you're watching the news?"

She sits, her gaze flicking toward the muted TV.

As I settle beside her, I catch the way her nose wrinkles—just slightly—when the scent of the whiskey drifts her way. She shifts against the cushions and leans her head back, eyes closed for a breath too long.

"You sure you're alright?" I ask again, quieter this time. "I can get you some water."

She opens one eye, offering a faint smile. "Still that stomach bug. Some smells hit harder than others." I will take some water, though."

I set my glass down and walk to the kitchen.

"Has Cal come on yet?" She asks.

I blink, handing the drink to her. "Didn't know he was supposed to."

"They're bringing him on to talk about the Turig enhancements. I figured you might be interested."

I don't respond. But I don't change the channel, either. I grab my glass and sink into the far end of the sofa.

The screen flickers—the news anchor sits poised, perfectly composed, her polished voice filling the room.

"And in breaking developments on the ongoing conflict, researchers have confirmed a chilling discovery about the Turig soldiers' regenerative process. Reports indicate that their most dangerous enhancements are triggered only after clinical death—making them exponentially more lethal once revived."

My grip on the whiskey glass tightens.

"To break this down, we have Dr. Calvin Bailey, one of the lead scientists working on countermeasures."

The camera pans to Calvin, standing too stiff in a button-up he probably didn't pick himself. The news anchor, a sharp-featured woman in a tailored navy suit, leans in slightly toward him.

"Dr. Bailey, can you explain how this process works?"

Calvin clears his throat, glancing at the camera like he's debating an escape route. "Well, uh—right. What we're seeing is that the virus works almost like a reset switch after death. While alive, the body resists the full enhancements. But once neural activity stops and the regenerative process kicks in, the virus restructures the body with… uh, let's just say fewer limitations than a living brain would allow."

The anchor tilts her head, intrigued. "Fascinating. So, in theory, this means that these soldiers are at their strongest post-mortem?"

"Yes. Essentially, they—uh—" Calvin rubs the back of his neck. "—come back faster, stronger, more resilient, and without the psychological barriers that would typically hold a human soldier back."

"That's terrifying," the anchor muses, crossing one leg over the other. "And what's being done to counteract this?"

I should be horrified. But something about it doesn't feel as foreign as it should. Maybe I'm just tired. Or maybe it's because I've felt something strange building in my own skin, like a wire pulled tight and waiting to snap.

"Well, that's where—uh—" Calvin stumbles slightly over his words, then gestures vaguely. "That's where our team comes in."

He's smiling, but it's not joyous. Not the way it used to be. Lately, Cal's got a different kind of fire in him—focused, controlled, like he's channeling every ounce of it.

The anchor smiles, leaning in just a fraction too much. "I bet it's a very intelligent team."

I catch the way Calvin's ears go red. "Uh—yeah, well—" And I don't miss the way Eden shifts uncomfortably.

I hate how I always notice her discomfort now. Like I'm waiting to hurt her again and can't trust myself not to. I grab the remote and mute the TV.

"You didn't want to hear the rest?" Eden asks.

"I heard enough." I lean back on the couch, staring at the silent screen where Calvin is still talking.

Turig soldiers come back stronger after death. That's a problem they aren't anywhere close to solving.

"What's that?" I nod toward the package she set on the

table earlier, grateful for the distraction.

She hesitates. There's something vulnerable in the way she lingers over the package. "Something I made for you."

I arch a brow. "Is it a lecture in a box? Because I think I've got enough of those."

This time, she does smile. But it's small, quick. Not her usual one. "Just open it."

I tear through the paper, and the first thing I see is me. The portrait is hauntingly accurate.

Eden captured every detail—the sharpness of my jaw, the subtle tension always in my expression, the stiff posture that even relaxing never seems to erase.

It's me. But it's not.

For a second, I don't recognize him. Not because it's a bad likeness. But because I don't feel like him anymore. It's a version of me that still looks like I belong somewhere.

I swallow, my fingers tightening around the edges of the canvas. "Eden—"

"There's another one." Her voice is quiet.

I pull the second painting free. This one guts me. It's my unit. All of us, standing together, frozen in time. I can almost hear the laughter, the easy camaraderie.

Three of them are dead now. Another lost a leg. And me? Unfit for service. I can still hear McClane's laugh in my head—sharp, sudden, always two seconds too loud. I'd give anything to hear it again, even if it meant scrubbing mud off my boots for the tenth time that week.

I stare at it, my pulse hammering in my ears. The room feels smaller.

"I hope I got everything right," Eden says, watching me. "I had to ask around for details, but—"

"You painted these?" My voice catches, making it rough.

"Yeah." She shifts, suddenly unsure of herself. "I wanted you to have something to—"

To what?

Remind me of who I was?

Or to remind me of everything I've lost?

I let out a slow breath, dragging a hand down my face before forcing out, "They're incredible."

She watches me for a beat too long. "You're still favoring that leg," she says gently.

"I pushed it too hard," I deflect. "Comes and goes."

I don't tell her how light I feel lately, when I move. Like

my bones don't creak the way they used to. Like something inside me is waking up. I don't tell her, because I'm not sure I want it to be true.

Her eyes search mine, reading the things I'm not saying. "Ben—"

"I should hang these up." I move toward the wall, needing to do something other than stay next to her, needing space to breathe.

I find a spot above the couch, hesitating before setting the first portrait there. The weight in my chest doesn't ease.

Eden steps closer, standing beside me. "I know things haven't been easy," she says after a moment. "But you're still you."

I let out a rough laugh, shaking my head. "You really believe that?"

She looks at me, quiet for a long beat, then says, "You're not made of daylight, Benji…" she brushes paint flecks from the canvas. "but there's something steady about vesper light. The world softens there."

I don't know what to say to that. So I just hold her gaze. And for a moment, I let myself believe maybe there's beauty in the darkness, too.

Her gaze is steady. "I wouldn't have painted them if I didn't still see you." And then, her head leans over to rest on my shoulder.

Maybe that's how she says the things she can't.

Maybe she can't admit she misses him—misses me—but she can paint it.

Paint the version of me she wants to believe is still in there somewhere.

The silence between us grows louder. Not awkward—just full of everything I don't know how to say. It hangs there, quiet but undeniable—familiar in the way old pain is.

I look back at the painting of my unit. The ghosts meet my eyes like they're still waiting on me. "Thank you, Eden."

She nods, hesitating before stepping away. "I should go… It's late."

I don't stop her. Because if she stays any longer, I might tell her what these really mean to me. And I'm not ready for that. Not yet.

She hesitates at the door, fingers brushing the frame before turning back to me.

"We're doing a small dinner Friday night. Housewarming.

Just us." Her voice is soft, the kind of quiet that settles in just before a storm—gentle, but charged.

I don't answer right away. Behind me, the portraits lean against the wall, watching. My unit. Myself. All the versions of me I don't recognize anymore. They wait, silent and patient, like they've been here before.

She shifts, like she might take it back. "I'll cook," she adds, offering a tentative smile. "Lasagna."

That gets me. Not because of the food—but because she remembers. The way she always remembers.

My chest tightens, and for a moment, I can almost feel her hand in mine again—those six weeks of dancing, of restraint, the taste of her lips and the look in her eyes when I pulled away… the years of pretending we were only what we said we were.

I nod, pushing the memory of cold nights and scorched edges out of my mind. "Yeah... yeah, alright."

She holds my gaze a beat longer, then nods and slips into the night.

And I'm left in the quiet again—with the ghosts, the paint, and the echo of her smile.

Chapter 27

The gravel crunches beneath my tires as I kill the engine, the sound somehow final in the gathering dusk. The house looms before me, all warm windows and promised comfort, yet something about its isolation sets my tactical mind on edge.

I've survived worse than dinner with friends.

The reminder doesn't settle the slight tremble in my hand as I reach for the ignition.

I puff my cheeks with a steadying breath, grab the neck of the bottle, and step out into the crisp air. Twilight wraps the house in a muted hush, painting everything in shades of vulnerability. The breeze carries the scent of pine and distant woodsmoke. A part of me still maps the terrain like I'm back in hostile territory—open field, dense tree line, no clean path of retreat. Some instincts don't fade.

My hand, sweaty and hesitant, I knock once, already knowing who'll answer.

While I wait, I examine the covered patio with habitual intent—noting the distance between windows, calculating entry points, mapping escape routes I pray they'll never need.

Calvin swings the door open mid-call, phone pressed to his ear. He motions me in with his usual grin—familiar, but a little thinner and distant these days.

"Well, try isolating the protein variables and check the response rate," he says into the phone, stepping aside for me to pass.

I give him a flat look. "Really rolling out the red carpet, huh?"

He lowers the phone slightly. "Hey, you're the one who skipped the grand tour. You think you get wine and lasagna without at least pretending to be interested in cutting-edge science?"

I shake my head. "Guess I thought we were past the whole guilt-trip stage of our friendship."

He laughs and claps my shoulder, warmth returning to his voice. "Nah, guilt's my love language."

The living room glows with soft light and Eden's signature touches—plush throws, warm-toned candles, the low hum of classical music drifting from hidden speakers. It looks like a home, not just a place to live. The furniture invites conversation, everything subtly arranged around the fireplace like it's meant to anchor warmth in the center of it all. Beyond the couch, the dining table sits tucked in a quiet alcove. The kitchen opens opposite, and though it's beautiful—open, inviting—my gaze snags on the staircase that separates it from the foyer. It makes my security-conscious mind twitch. Too exposed. Too easy to miss threats coming.

Eden steps out from the kitchen, untying a blue floral apron. The motion is fluid, unconsciously elegant—like the way she used to move during our dance lessons. My body remembers before my mind does; I shift my stance, almost reaching for a turn that never comes. She notices. I see it in the way her shoulders tighten, how her hands slow just slightly as she hangs the apron on its hook.

"Benji! You made it." Her smile still draws me in like gravity, but it's careful now, measured, like she remembers too.

"Wouldn't miss it." I hand her the wine, fingers brushing briefly. "Congrats on the new place. It's beautiful." My eyes continue their automatic sweep—windows, doors, angles of approach.

"It passes inspection?" she teases, gesturing toward the house.

I let loose a chuckle that doesn't quite land as genuine. If she only knew the defensive scenarios already running through my head... "It's beautiful," I repeat, dodging the question like incoming fire.

"Avoiding truths tonight, I see." She props one hand on her hip, the wine bottle dangling from the other like an accusation.

"Let's just say your perimeter could use a second exit route." I grin. "But yeah. It's perfect."

She laughs, soft and genuine, and something in me eases. "Only a second exit route?"

"I wouldn't want to ruin the sanctity of your new home by indulging you with my paranoia." The words come out lighter than I feel them.

Calvin slaps my shoulder as he joins us, his phone finally lowered but still clutched like a lifeline. "Remember when we were kids and you used to rearrange my bedroom furniture because it had 'too many blind spots'?"

"You had your desk under the window," I say.

"I needed the light for my experiments!"

I fold my arms. "You expect a sniper wouldn't take that shot?"

Calvin snorts. "You were twelve."

"And already twice as paranoid as any of my later drill sergeants." I smirk.

"My cockroach farm would never have made it anywhere else." He argues.

I glance at Eden, who looks both amused and faintly alarmed. "You married that," I add, nodding toward him.

"Don't remind me." She smiles, but it flickers too fast. Then shakes her head and moves to place the wine on the table. "So, Cal, he thinks the layout of our home isn't safe."

"I didn't say that–" I begin, but Calvin cuts me off with a familiar eye roll.

"Oh don't get me started," he says. "Finding an apartment with this guy was ridiculous. Not facing the right direction, too many stories up—not enough. No back escape route. It's a wonder we ever found somewhere to live."

I rub the back of my neck, feeling the tension coiled there. "If I'd ever needed to defend the place you'd have less protest about all my requirements."

"We're in the quiet part of town," Eden says with gentle finality. "I'm sure there's nothing to worry about."

"There, see." Calvin gestures broadly. "Safe part of town."

I nod and smile, swallowing my thoughts about how isolation makes them a perfect target, how quiet places just mean no one will hear you scream. "It smells amazing."

"Oh, thank you!" Eden's voice brightens. "It's only lasagna and garlic bread."

"You're so modest." Cal wraps an arm around her

shoulder, but his free hand still grips his phone. "She spent hours getting it whipped together." The device buzzes and his face falls. "Oh shoot. Work again. Hold on."

Eden watches him retreat to the living room, pain flickering at the corners of her eyes like a candle about to gutter. The sight feels like shrapnel in my chest.

Not your place, Hale.

"You shouldn't have gone through all the trouble," I say, trying to pull her attention back. "You just moved in, you should be relaxing, not spending the afternoon making dinner."

Eden shakes her head, her fingers fidgeting with the edge of her sleeve. "It's really quite simple to put together, I was just… distracted today."

"Well, is there anything I can help with?"

"Getting that man off the phone long enough to feed him would be incredibly helpful." The words carry a weight I pretend not to notice.

I glance over my shoulder to Cal pacing by the window, his silhouette stark against the darkening sky. "Work, huh?"

"Yes! It's been driving me crazy lately." She sighs, shifting her weight to the counter to grab the wine glasses. The movement speaks of an exhaustion deeper than physical.

"I took a tour today." I reach for the glasses, beating her to them and starting toward the table. The crystal catches the light like memories of better times.

"You did? So you're considering joining on then?"

I set the glasses down, one at each place setting, trying not to think about how the table seems too large for three. "Well, he said he needed an answer right away. The words kind of slipped out before I really even thought about it."

Relief floods her face, but it's shadowed by a quieter tone—worry, perhaps, or resignation. "I'm happy for you," she says, but her words feel hollow, like footsteps in an empty room.

"Thanks…" I start back toward her in the kitchen. "Anything else need to be set before we eat?"

"No, no. It's ready now, you should sit!" She pulls a dish from the oven and carries it to the table before retreating for the bread and serving utensils, her movements efficient but somehow fragile.

"What about work for you, love?" I slip out of my leather jacket and drape it on the back of my chair, the rolled sleeves of my button-up shirt gripping my forearms. I situate myself, only to stand when she returns to the table—another one of those habits.

"Sit down, silly." She scolds, but the familiar warmth in her voice makes my chest ache.

I obey, watching her fluid movements as she settles into her chair. "Work... it's fine. A few cranky veterans coming through lately. But that can't be helped. I wish I could help them in the way that they need. But since they transferred me out of the trauma ward and into clinical, by the time I get to them, there's not a lot I can do to help."

"So I just got lucky, then." I tuck a half smile into my cheek, trying to keep the words light.

Her cheeks flush at the compliment and she serves herself and Calvin before passing the spoon to me. The marinara sauce leaves trails like blood against the white ceramic.

"Lucky? I don't know if I'd call what you went through lucky, Benji."

"Ah maybe not but I'm doing great, and I got you as a friend so I think that's probably the biggest win of all." The word 'friend' sits sour in the back of my throat.

"Sorry," Cal says in a huff as he sits. "Like I said before, loads going on at work right now. I'm glad you decided to join on." He rubs his hands together and lifts his fork. "This looks amazing, babe."

I stare at the bubbling cheese and sauce, trying not to remember other meals, other moments when everything felt possible.

But the taste is familiar—not the flavor—deeper than that. A flicker of warmth I haven't felt since I was a kid, waiting by the door with two plates and hope that never made it past midnight.

Eden watches him dig in, concern calculated in the set of her shoulders. The silence stretches between us like a wound, filled only by the soft clink of silverware against plates. Steam rises from the lasagna like all the words we can't say. Calvin's phone buzzes again, and I watch Eden's knife pause against her plate for just a fraction too long.

"Remember that time in college," I say, desperate to break the tension, "when Cal tried to make pasta and nearly burned down the dorm?"

Eden's laugh sounds genuine for the first time tonight. "He never told me about that!"

"Oh man," Calvin groans, but he's smiling. "I was trying to impress Sarah Matthews from Bio lab. Thought I'd invite her over for a homemade dinner."

"The fire alarm went off," I continue, warming to the story. "The whole building had to evacuate. And there's Cal, standing in the parking lot with a charred pot and this look of absolute devastation on his face."

"Sarah never spoke to me again," Calvin adds, shaking his head.

"Probably for the best," Eden says, her eyes twinkling. "I'm a much better cook."

"That you are," I agree, raising my wine glass. "To the chef."

We clink glasses, and for a moment, everything feels almost normal. Then Calvin's phone buzzes again and the moment shatters like crystal on tile.

The joy silences when Calvin picks up his phone again, stepping away from the table, this time going outside to take the call. Eden watches him go, the sadness returning to her eyes like an old friend.

"Uh, let me help you clean up." I stand, needing to move, to do something with my hands.

"Don't be silly. You're our guest." She stands and takes the plate from my hand, stacking it on top of hers and Calvin's. The plates click together like closing doors.

I grip the stems of our wine glasses and follow her to the kitchen when my leg cramps up. The pain hits like memory— sudden, sharp, unavoidable. I try to hide it and keep walking, but the intensity grows like the blade of the Turig knife slicing into it all over again. I stumble, and one of the glasses slips from my grasp. It shatters on the kitchen tiles, the sound like everything I've ever broken.

Eden jumps and turns, fear and concern warring on her face.

"Shit. Sorry... I'll buy you new ones." The words tumble out, automatic as breathing.

"Are you okay?" She moves toward the broom, her bare feet threatened by the glittering minefield I've created.

"Don't move. I'll get it." Panic edges my voice.

"It's fine, Ben."

"No, Eden, it's not. I can't have you hurt on account of me." *Never again.* I maneuver carefully to grab the broom, gathering the shards into a pile that glints like broken promises.

"Benji," Eden's hand lands on my shoulder, warm and steady. "I'm more concerned about you."

"I'm fine."

"Clearly not as fine as you're letting on. Don't think I can't see you masking your pain when you sit."

I shake my head, focusing on the task at hand. "I'm just not getting as much exercise as I should to keep my injuries loose. Been acting up a bit lately. Which is why it'll be good that I work at the lab."

"You'll be sitting a lot there, too."

"At least I'll be distracted..." I think of her lips ghosting against mine and shake away the image before it can settle anywhere permanent. I dump the tinkling glass pieces into the trash and turn to see Eden's arms folded, hands stroking the outsides of her arms in her usual self-comfort fashion.

"What's wrong?" I ask, replacing the broom, though I already know the answer.

Her shoulders sigh and she peers around the corner to Calvin pacing the patio, phone glued to his ear like a lifeline to somewhere else.

"Ahh... none of my business." I busy myself wiping down the floor.

"Maybe you being there will get him home sooner..."

I force myself to focus on the floor, on the repetitive motion of the cloth against tile. "Maybe."

"Or maybe... it'll end up taking you away from me too." Her voice cracks, almost imperceptible.

Her words stop me cold. I look up at her—eyes distant, watching him through the window. I stand and gently take her hands in mine, hating myself for how right it feels.

"Hey," I say, heat creeping up my neck when she meets my gaze with those ocean-deep eyes. "I'm right here… always."

"You say that—"

"I mean that."

"Benji..." her voice drops to a whisper that could break worlds.

"I know." I let her hands slip from mine and crouch back down to the floor to finish wiping the glass slivers. "It's okay."

Cal comes back in and peers his head around the corner. "She's got you cleaning?" He chuckles, oblivious to the moment he's interrupted.

"I broke a glass, I'm just taking care of it so she didn't get cut." I finish wiping the floor and stand up, tossing the rag in the trash along with my racing thoughts.

Calvin shakes his head. "You're always taking care of us, Benji. What can we do for you?"

Eden perks up, grasping at normalcy. "Yes, what can we do for you?"

"You made me dinner, that's plenty."

"Oh, be serious, Ben!" Eden says. "You know what we mean."

I put my hands up in surrender. "Nothing. I'm okay, really. And Cal, you got me a job so I'm grateful for that."

"Yes! We're just waiting on your clearance to be reinstated." Calvin's excitement carries through his voice.

Eden's smile lingers on her lips, but the light fades from her eyes, like sunlight slipping through a closing door. "How long will that take?" she asks softly. "Did they say?"

"Should be another month or so," I keep my tone light. "So, plenty of time to hang out before I turn into a complete nerd." I shoot Calvin a look.

"Thanks for doing all the boring pottery and crafty stuff with her. Saves my sanity. Plus I know she's safe." He taps his phone screen to check for notifications.

"They're not boring!" She argues.

"Well I just don't have the time. Work is crazy, so I'm psyched to get more hangout time with you, too." Calvin grins, rubbing his hands together. "It'll be a bit like old times."

"It could never be like old times, Cal—not unless you blow something up." I smirk, then nudge his arm. "Besides, you're married now. That's a far cry from the nerd who couldn't land a girl until her."

Eden doesn't laugh, but she doesn't look away either.

"Everyone else was just never smart enough to get me." He says, proud but missing the point.

"Or beautiful enough to make you stop talking. That's the only way to see that you're kind of a chill dude." I snort.

Eden blushes and I smile, satisfied with at least this small victory.

"Well, I'm gonna take off." I glance at the clock, using time as an excuse to run. "I should let you guys enjoy your night."

"You don't have to." They say in unison, the words carrying an edge of fear that makes me invisibly cringe.

"Nah, I have some stuff to do before it gets too late. But you guys should relax. Finish the wine!" I gesture to the bottle as I retrieve my jacket from the chair and slip into it like armor.

I hug them both—Calvin briefly, Eden perhaps a moment too long—and escape to my car. The night wraps around me like a confession.

Her engine roars to life beneath me, the sound deep and steady—reliable in a way nothing else is these days. The engine's low growl cuts through the silence like it knows what I'm running from. Music blares through the speakers, drowning out thoughts I can't afford to have as I wind up their gravel road, searching for somewhere to let the darkness swallow me.

Maybe I should go for a run... some pain might do me good for a distraction right now. Physical pain, at least, makes sense. It's honest. It's something I know how to handle.

The house disappears in my rear-view mirror, but I can still feel it pulling at me like gravity. A flash of memory hits me—Eden's breathless laugh during dance practice, the scent of jasmine that clung to my clothes for weeks. I think of how we moved around each other tonight, every gesture calculated, every distance measured. Maybe that's our dance now—the careful choreography of keeping space between us.

The night stretches ahead, full of possibilities I won't let myself consider, and I drive faster, chasing the horizon like it might somehow lead me home.

As I PULL into the lot behind my building, I kill the engine but don't move. The silence swells too quickly, like it's waiting to devour me. I should go inside. Wash the dishes. Reread the lab packet. Do something productive.

Instead, I sit there with my hands on the wheel, staring out at the darkened city like it might offer answers.

It's not Eden's touch I keep replaying—it's the way I wanted it. The way it settled something in me I didn't know was shaking.

It shouldn't be this easy to fall. I tell myself I've got control. That I'm fine. That pain is a better anchor than comfort. But lately, even that's slipping. My body doesn't respond like it used to—stronger one day, aching the next.

And I haven't told anyone. Not even Eden.

Because if I say it out loud, it becomes real. And if it's real, I'll have to face that there's a change happening within me.

I stay in the Impala, the engine ticking softly as it cools. Wind rattles the edge of the driver's side window, and I lean my head back against the seat, letting the chill seep in through the glass.

Maybe that's what I need. Cold. Clarity. Something to remind me I still know where the edges are.

I tell myself I'll start training again in the morning. Routine. Discipline. That's what I need. Not connection. Not comfort. Not someone else seeing the cracks and deciding they know what I need better than I do. Even if part of me wishes someone would.

The phone buzzes against the console. A message from Eden:

"Thanks for coming tonight. You still make everything feel easier."

I stare at it for a moment, thumb hovering over the screen. Then, another one:

"Hang out next Thursday? I've got the day off."

I type back one word: Yeah.

And for a while, I let the city blur out beyond the windshield. Not because I'm not hurting. But because—for once—I don't want to be alone with it.

Chapter 28

The embarrassing incident at Cal and Eden's prompted me to get back into a rigorous exercise routine. I'd lost track of it while helping them plan their wedding—something I never thought I'd volunteer for, but Eden has a way of pulling me toward the edges of things I usually avoid. The physical pain of working out is at least predictable. My muscles burn with each rep, a familiar friend I shouldn't have abandoned.

There's only a month left till my start date at the lab. I don't want another incident—breaking things, or worse, hurting someone. The weights clank as I set them down, marking my reps in the notebook I've kept since basic training. Structure. Control. These are things I understand.

Outside the window, two neighbors argue across the street—voices sharp, desperate. Something about moving further inland, away from the border zones. "You think it'll be better there? You think they won't follow us?" The words bleed through the cracked window frame like static. A siren wails faintly in the distance—not close enough to mean danger, just close enough to remind me it still exists.

I wipe the sweat from my brow just as a knock sounds at the door. My pulse skips. I already know who it is. Still, when I open the door and see her—jacket wrapped tight against the wind, hair a little wind-tousled—I feel that same hit to the chest I always do. The kind that makes breathing harder than it should be.

"Eden." Her name slips out, steadier than I expected. A surprise I'd been bracing for and still wasn't ready to receive.

"You busy?" she asks, stepping inside like she's done it a thousand times—because she has. She pushes past me to escape the wind, bringing with her that familiar jasmine scent that used to linger after she would leave for a date with Calvin.

"Uh..." I close the door and rub the back of my neck, suddenly aware of my sweat-soaked shirt. "Just working out."

"Oh, I'm sorry. You agreed the other night so I thought we could get a head start on the day. I know you'll be starting at the lab soon." Her eyes drift over the exercise equipment before finding mine again. Even now, years later, she still checks in on me. Still cares.

"I was almost done anyway."

"You don't have to—"

"It's just one more set." The words come automatically, like they always do with her. I walk back to the bench and lay down. My hands grip the bar. "But I'm kind of gross." I lift the weights off and start with the reps, counting in my head, keeping my breath steady.

Her laugh sings through my apartment—that same laugh that used to make my heart stop. Still does, if I'm honest with myself. Which I try not to be, these days.

"I did have a plan, but it's not like an opera house or anything."

I set the bar back on the rack with a clank. "Do you mind if I just wash up real quick? I'd rather not smell myself all afternoon."

She settles in on my couch, the same way she used to when Cal still lived here. Some things never change. "Like I said, I have today off."

"I'll be quick." I head to the bathroom, trying not to think about how natural this feels to have her here. And how dangerous that is.

I finish washing up and exit the bathroom, towel wrapped around my waist. My dog tags clink against my chest—I never take them off. Even now. A reminder of who I am. Who I was.

"You need some art to liven up these walls!" she calls from the living room.

"I've already got some."

Eden lets out a soft laugh. "That doesn't count."

"What do you mean it doesn't count?"

I grab a dark blue shirt, avoiding her gaze as the scar on my ribs burns hotter. She's seen them all before—the scars, the stories behind them. Sometimes I think she remembers them better than I do.

"I mean, you can't just slap up a couple of sentimental pieces and call it interior design." She leans against the doorway, arms crossed, that knowing smirk on her lips.

I give her a look. "I don't exactly have people over for gallery tours, Eden."

"That's not the point," she says, stepping further into the room. "Art is about expression. Atmosphere. It's supposed to say something about you."

"And what do mine say?" I gesture toward the living room, where I know the paintings sit just out of view.

She tilts her head, gaze lingering just long enough to make my chest tighten. There's concern in her eyes, but something else too—like she's bracing for a version of me she's not sure she'll recognize.

"That you miss them."

The words land heavier than I expect. I force my jaw to stay loose. "It's still art," I mutter, tugging on my shirt.

Eden exhales, but there's something softer behind it now. Less critique, more care. Her voice drops just slightly, like she's shifting from an argument into something closer to a confession. "I just think you deserve more than memories on a wall." She nods toward the paintings.

"Did I get it right?" she asks.

I glance over. "Get what right?"

"The unit. The details in the painting."

She's not just making conversation. She's asking if she did justice to the men in that frame.

I exhale, dragging a hand through my hair. "Yeah. Yeah, you got it right."

Her lips press together like she wants to say something else, but instead, she nods. "Good."

I grab some socks from the drawer and meet her at the doorway. The weight over me settles as I brush past her.

Moving to the living room, I sit on the couch and slip into my shoes. The words come easier now, maybe because I'm not looking at her. "My first mission was with the 27th base intel unit. Last was the 9th special ops."

I focus on tying my laces, but I can feel her watching me. "27th was pretty much wiped out on my first mission," I continue. "Three of us made it back."

I grab my jacket off the hook and slip into it, only to find Eden suddenly beside me. "And the 9th, well..."

Her soft smile holds a decade of understanding. She reaches up and brushes some of the water from my sideburn, her touch impossibly gentle. A touch that says I was there after. I remember.

"I'm sorry." Her eyes bleed the sadness my heart should feel. The emotion I learned to lock away, first for survival, then for sanity. She was always better at feeling things for both of us.

"That was a long time ago." I mumble, resisting the urge to lean into her touch. Remembering whose ring she wears now. Cal's my friend too—my best friend. And I won't do anything to compromise that, no matter what echoes of the past linger between Eden and me.

"Yes, well..." She steps back, the moment passing like so many others we don't acknowledge. "You're driving."

"Okay." I grab my keys, grateful for the shift in focus. "Where to, though?"

"*That* is a surprise!" She wrinkles her nose at me and pulls the door open, letting in a gust of wind that smells like rain and possibilities.

<hr>

I FLIP THROUGH the static-laced channels, pausing on one with a clear enough signal.

"—and in today's military brief, reports indicate a decisive counteroffensive in the Northern front. Analysts suggest that while the Turig remain formidable, human engineering is steadily closing the gap. In other news—"

I exhale through my nose, rolling my shoulders against the ache that never quite leaves. They always make it sound like we're winning. I change the station.

"Take Jefferson heading north," Eden directs as I start the car. She seems more subdued than usual, but her smile is genuine when I follow her instruction without argument

"You know, most people just use their phones for directions these days."

"Where's the fun in that?" She fiddles with the radio, landing on an oldies station. "Besides, I like being your personal GPS. Turn right at the light."

"You just like being bossy," I say, following her direction despite my teasing.

"Me? Bossy?" She presses a hand to her chest in mock offense. "I prefer the term 'assertively helpful.'"

"Is that what we're calling it now?" I catch her eye at a red light. "Like when you 'assertively helped' me rearrange my entire kitchen?"

"Your organizational system was a crime against humanity and you know it. Who puts cereal in the cabinet above the stove?"

"Someone who doesn't eat cereal?"

"Then why do you even—" She cuts off as her phone buzzes. She checks it, then puts it face down in her lap. "Take the next left."

"You sure about these directions? Because your track record with left and right is questionable at best." I try to pull her back from whatever's troubling her, the way she used to do for me.

"That was one time!" Some of the lightness returns to her voice. "And we found that amazing taco truck because of it, so really, you should be thanking me."

"Ah yes, nothing says 'thank you' like food poisoning."

"You did not get food poisoning." She swats my arm, just like she used to during our cooking class Cal couldn't make it to. "You got a mild case of the sniffles that you dramatically blamed on my navigational skills."

Thunder rumbles in the distance and I flick the wipers on as a light drizzle starts. "Keep telling yourself that. Where are we going anyway?"

She's checking her phone again, this time typing something quickly before tucking it away. "It's a surprise."

"You know how I feel about surprises."

"You love *my* surprises."

"I *tolerate* your surprises." I quirk a brow.

"Name one time my surprises haven't worked out."

"The blind date with your cousin." I smirk.

"Okay, that was—"

"The rumba dancing class." I glance at her.

"After you found your feet—"

"The pottery workshop where I broke three—"

"Three plates, two bowls, and one very unfortunate attempt at a vase." she laughs and warmth unfurls around me. *She remembers too.*

"You get my point then." I chuckle.

"Fine!" She laughs again, but this one feels forced, raising her hands in defeat. "This one is different. Trust me?"

The question hangs between us, heavier than she probably knows. Her phone buzzes again in her lap. She doesn't check it, but I see the tension creep into her shoulders.

"Always," I answer, meaning it more than I should. More than I have any right to. "Even if it means suffering through your questionable navigation skills."

"Just for that, I'm not telling you that you missed the turn." She folds her arms.

"I did not miss—" I look around, falling for it like I always do. "Eden!"

Her laugh is genuine this time, filling the car like it did before choices and consequences changed everything. When we were different people, with different dreams.

"Kidding! It's just up ahead here. The blue house on the right, with the balcony."

"It's not some insanitorium, is it? Trying to put me away, are ya?" I tease as I pull up to the blue house, assessing the building with obsessive proficiency. Two exits visible from here, well-maintained grounds, security cameras at corners— habit more than necessity likely.

"Like we could keep you locked up if we tried!" She swats at me and reaches for the handle. I follow suit and meet her on the other side, stepping over vegetation to get to the stone pathway. The soldier in me notes the decent cover the landscaping provides, the clear sightlines from the upper windows. The civilian I'm trying to be reminds me this isn't a tactical situation.

I offer her my arm—old school manners I can't let myself quit with her—and she takes it with a small smile. The approaching storm makes the air heavy with anticipation.

She raps on the door while I do my usual sweep of escape routes—this habit has saved my life more than once. The door opens to reveal an older man with a bushy beard and the straight-backed posture that screams military even in civilian clothes.

"Eden?" He asks, his button-up tucked tightly into his khaki pants with precision.

"Yes, sir!" She grins, resting her hand on my chest. "This is Ben."

"Ben, pleasure. My name is Rodney Paulson, but everyone just calls me Polly." He extends his hand, and I take it with the firm grip of equals. His sleeve rides up just enough to expose familiar ink.

"Pleasure." I match his grip. "North waterline quadrant?"

A knowing grin breaks through his professional demeanor. "Yeah. It was at least three decades ago, though."

"How did you know that?" Eden asks, looking between us.

"Insignia on the wrist." I gesture to the barely visible tattoo. "Third Battalion?"

"Good eye," Polly nods appreciatively. "Most civilians wouldn't catch that."

"Well, thanks for making time for us today, Polly." Eden brings her hands together, and I catch the slight redirection in her tone. She somehow knows when to pull me back from shop talk.

"I always have time for veterans." He steps aside, ushering us in. "I think I've got just the thing you're looking for out back here."

The interior is spotless, organized with efficiency. But it's the wall of glass ahead that catches my attention—and the dogs visible through it, playing in the yard. My training catalogs everything automatically: German Shepherds, Belgian Malinois, a couple of Labs. All moving with purpose, even in play. Working dogs.

We follow Polly out and the dogs look up, assessing us before approaching. Their discipline is evident in how they sit at our feet, waiting for permission. I kneel down, letting them catch my scent before giving attention. Each dog gets a proper greeting—respect given, respect earned.

"Kind of high energy, aren't they?" Eden observes.

"Well these pups are still in training. So they do have more energy." Polly watches my interaction with the dogs, and I can feel him evaluating my technique. "But the one I wanted you to meet is retired. Edo, here boy!"

A German Shepherd appears around the corner, and I recognize the bearing immediately. This isn't just any retired dog—this is a warrior. He stops, assessing us with tactical precision that mirrors my own earlier survey. His stance, despite a slight favor to one leg, speaks of years of service.

"C'mon Edo," Polly calls again. "Just takes him a sec."

"What's his story?" Eden asks, but I already know. I can read it in the way he holds himself, the careful way he evaluates potential threats while maintaining discipline.

"Edo was a special forces pup who helped with explosives disposal. They retired him when he was injured over a year ago."

"That's so heartbreaking." Eden's voice softens with sympathy.

I maintain eye contact with Edo, recognizing a fellow soldier. His hesitation isn't fear—it's procedure. Assessment. *Smart.*

"Everyone kept telling me not to waste my time with broken veteran dogs. Just focus on training up the new ones," Polly adds.

"They're not broken," I state firmly, never breaking eye contact with Edo. "Just adapting to change."

Eden's sharp intake of breath beside me seems louder than it should. When I glance at her, she's staring at Edo with an intensity that seems about more than just the dog. Her phone buzzes again, and this time when she checks it, her expression is a complex mix of love and anxiety.

"That's right." Polly's approval is evident. "Just need someone who understands what they've been through."

Eden's hand touches my shoulder, gentle and reassuring. "Like you."

My first instinct is to pull away from Eden's touch, to reject the implication that I need fixing. But Edo's eyes hold mine with an intelligence that speaks of shared experience. I shift my weight, deliberately telegraphing my movement as I extend my hand, palm up. Proper protocol when approaching a fellow veteran.

"Prüfen," I say softly—'check' in German. Edo's ears perk at the command.

"You speak German?" Polly asks, surprised.

"Enough to get by." I keep my focus on Edo as he approaches with measured steps. "Did some joint operations. Found out quick that knowing commands in multiple languages can save lives."

Edo sniffs my hand thoroughly, his tactical assessment as thorough as any soldier's. I remain still, letting him complete his inspection. When he sits in front of me, head slightly bowed but alert, I recognize the gesture of professional courtesy.

"Your husband has good instincts with dogs," Polly says to Eden.

I tense slightly at the assumption, but Eden's laugh covers it. "He does, doesn't he?" Her tone carries no awkwardness, just warmth. Always smoothing over awkward moments.

"Did his injuries fully heal?" I ask, carefully scratching behind Edo's ears. His fur is thick, healthy—well-cared for despite his retirement.

"For the most part. They thought they'd have to take his back leg, but we were able to save it. Though he still limps from time to time."

"What about his handler?" I tense, bracing for the answer I know is coming.

"Didn't make it…" Polly folds his arms.

I note how Edo distributes his weight, compensating without compromising his effectiveness. Adaptation. Resilience. "Still combat-ready, aren't you, boy?" I murmur, and Edo's tail wags once—professional acknowledgment.

"What do you think, Benji?" Eden crouches beside me, and when she steadies herself, her hand drifts briefly to her middle before finding her knee.

"About what?" I maintain my position, steady and present. Edo stays focused on me, reading my body language with trained precision.

"Adopting him, silly. What did you think we were here for?"

The pieces click into place—Eden's mysterious errand, her careful planning. "I don't know. I didn't even know we were coming here or what it was until a few minutes ago." I shake my head, a reflex born of self-preservation. "Adopting?" My hand stills on Edo's ear and he nudges it, asking for more. Not needy, not demanding. Just present. Solid. Real. "I can't just adopt a dog on a whim."

Edo cocks his head slightly, picking up on my hesitation. His posture remains alert but relaxed—a soldier awaiting orders while assessing the situation. I know that stance. I've held it myself more times than I can count.

"And?" She raises an eyebrow at me. That look that says she knows I'm making excuses.

"And I've never had a dog before. And my apartment isn't really set up for—"

"For a highly trained military service dog who understands tight quarters and disciplined routines?" Polly raises an eyebrow, veteran to veteran. "Look, I'm not going to sell you on this, Ben. You know as well as I do that sugar-coating doesn't help anyone in our line of work."

I appreciate his directness. Too many civilians try to tiptoe around veterans, like we're unexploded ordinance.

A crack of thunder makes several of the other dogs startle, but Edo merely flicks an ear, maintaining his position. Combat-tested. Reliable under pressure.

"I'm not sure I'm the right person for him." I say, the words automatic but lacking conviction.

"These are all valid concerns. But Edo's not your typical high-energy shepherd that needs a big yard. He's well-trained, mature, and honestly..." Polly pauses, scratching his beard. "He needs someone who understands him more than he needs a big backyard."

"And maybe you need someone who understands you, too." Eden's voice is soft. The words hit in a stabbing force.

Is she trying to get rid of me?

I stand up abruptly, and Edo tenses, reading my discomfort, but maintains his position, steady and dependable at my side. "That's different."

Polly rises slowly. "I've got a proposition for you. Military to military. Come work with Edo a few times before making any decisions. No pressure, no commitment. Just see how it feels."

That should be the end of it. Walk away, let logic win. But I glance down at Edo, and he's still watching me—not expectant, just waiting. Like he knows I'm already considering it.

"Three visits." I meet Polly's eyes. "No strings, no commitments."

"Operation hours? I start work next week," I repeat, my prior commitment, but it already feels weak against the pull toward taking him home today.

"We're open evenings and weekends." Polly glances at Eden, then back to me.

"The lab doesn't start you on major projects right away anyway," Eden adds. "You told me yourself it's mostly orientation and paperwork the first couple weeks." She's trying to help while clearly fighting her own battles. Always taking care of others first—it's what I've always admired about her, even when it worries me.

"Three visits should be plenty. If after that you don't think it's a good fit, no hard feelings. It's better for both of you that he's with the right person." He gestures to the manual. "Study his file, run some basic drills. Treat it like any other mission—gather intel, assess compatibility, make an informed decision."

It's a tactical approach I understand. "Rules of engagement?"

Edo has moved to sit beside me, his shoulder pressing against my leg. *When did that happen?*

This is my choice. My call. Edo isn't being pushed on me—he's waiting for me to decide.

"He's already imprinting on you," Polly observes quietly. "Notice how he's positioned himself? Slightly angled, covering your blind spot while maintaining sight lines to all entrances. That's not just training—that's trust."

I hadn't consciously noticed, but he's right. Edo has shifted to my left side, perfectly positioned to watch the approaches while staying within immediate response range. Just like I used to position myself for my unit. Just like I still do, sometimes, when I'm with Eden or Cal and don't want them to notice I'm on guard.

No one is making me do this. No one is expecting me to. But Edo... he's already chosen me. And maybe... that means I should choose him, too.

"Then give me the sitrep straight. What are his needs? Limitations?" Edo chooses that moment to lean ever so slightly against my leg.

It's a gesture I recognize from my own unit—that subtle physical contact that says 'I've got your six' without needing words. And suddenly my rehearsed list of reasons why I can't adopt him feels hollow.

"Daily exercise, but nothing extreme. His injury means no high-impact activities, but he's excellent on patrol routines." Polly's assessment is crisp, professional. "He's cleared for stairs, basic tactical maneuvers. Sleeps four to six hours at a time—combat habits die hard. Needs mental engagement more than physical challenges."

Eden's phone buzzes again. This time when she checks it, her face pales slightly. The soldier in me catalogs her reaction, files it away with the other signs of trouble I've been noting.

"And his commands?" I ask, deliberately not drawing attention to Eden's distress. She'll talk when she's ready.

"Primary in German, secondary in English. He knows about forty tactical commands and fifteen civilian ones. Highly responsive to non-verbal cues, especially from military personnel." Polly hands me a small manual. "Full list is in here, along with his medical history and service record."

I flip through it with one hand, my other still resting on Edo's shoulder. The documentation is thorough, familiar— reminds me of my own military personnel file. "Says here he's been through three potential adoptions already."

"Civilians who thought they wanted a retired military dog. Weren't prepared for what that means." Polly's tone carries no judgment, just fact. "Edo needs someone who understands that some habits, some instincts, don't just disappear with retirement."

Like checking exits in civilian buildings. Like positioning yourself between threats and loved ones without thinking. Like waking at 0400 because your body doesn't know how to sleep in anymore.

Thunder cracks again overhead, closer now. Eden's phone buzzes insistently—four short vibrations. A text, not a call this time. Her fingers clench around it without checking the screen.

I look down at Edo, who looks back with those damn knowing eyes. Ready for orders, but patient. Professional. The kind of partner who knows sometimes silence is the best response.

"You set the pace. I'll be here to advise, but you work with him directly. He responds better to clear chain of command." Polly glances at Eden, then back to me. "Sometimes the best way to honor a fellow soldier is to know when you're not the right person to have their six."

"Three visits," I say finally.

"Three visits," Polly confirms. "We can start today if you'd like. I'll show you his basic commands, his routines. You can get to know each other a bit."

Eden's phone buzzes and she pulls it out, frowning slightly at the screen before tucking it away without responding. Something flickers across her face—worry?— before she masks it.

"Fine," I say, more to distract myself from analyzing Eden's reaction than anything else. "Three visits. But I'm not promising anything beyond that."

"Wouldn't dream of it," Polly says, but there's a knowing smile beneath his beard. "Let's head inside and I'll get you some paperwork to fill out for the trial period."

As we follow him back toward the house, Eden loops her arm through mine. "Thank you," she whispers.

I glance down at her hand curled lightly around my arm. "For what?"

"For being willing to try," she says softly. "Sometimes that's the hardest part."

I don't answer. Just let her stay close as we walk back toward the house—toward whatever comes next.

Chapter 29

Inside, Polly hands me a clipboard while Eden drifts toward the glass wall, watching the other dogs in the yard.

Edo stays at my feet as I sit, his posture alert, but relaxed—like he already knows he belongs here.

I'm not ready to say the same. But I'm closer than I was ten minutes ago.

"Just basic liability stuff," Polly explains. "Emergency contacts, proof of residence..."

I pause at the emergency contact line, pen hovering. Eden glances over. "Put me down," she says casually, but something in her voice makes me look up. She's still watching the dogs, but her shoulders are tense. Before I can ask why she doesn't want me to put Cal down instead, Polly starts pulling equipment from a nearby cabinet.

"Alright," he says, laying out various items on a low table. "Let's start with the basics. Edo's commands are in both English and German, though he responds better to German when he's stressed." He hands me a treat pouch to clip to my belt. "The basics are 'sitz' for sit, 'platz' for down, and 'bleib' for stay."

I clip the pouch on, hyper-aware of Eden watching us now. "Sitz," I say experimentally, and Edo's rear immediately hits the floor.

"Good!" Polly grins. "Now, when working with service dogs, especially retired ones, consistency is key. They're used to routine, structure. Like soldiers." He demonstrates the proper hand signals to accompany each command, and I mirror them, Edo responding perfectly each time.

"He's so responsive to you already," Eden notes, coming closer.

"Edo was trained for battlefield conditions," Polly explains. "He can read micro-expressions, body language, even changes in breathing patterns. Right now, he's probably picking up on Ben's military background just from his posture and movements."

I hadn't noticed, but I've automatically fallen into parade rest between commands. I consciously try to relax my shoulders.

"Don't," Polly says. "That formality? It's actually reassuring to him. Watch." He gestures for me to step away, and Edo's eyes track me. "Call him."

"Edo, komm," I say firmly, and he trots over, placing himself perfectly at my left side. The precision is familiar, comfortable. Like muscle memory from another life.

"Beautiful," Polly says. "Now, let's work on some basic handling exercises. Eden, would you mind helping demonstrate?"

Eden's phone buzzes yet again. This time she pulls it out, stares at the screen long enough that Polly and I exchange a knowing look. Something's wrong in her world, but she's here, trying to help fix mine.

"Everything okay?" I ask carefully.

"What? Oh, yeah, fine." She tucks the phone away without responding. Again. "Just... figuring things out. You know how it is, when life throws you a curveball?"

I think about Edo, about how adaptation doesn't mean things are broken. "Sometimes the best things in life are the ones we didn't plan for."

"When did you get so wise, Benji?" Her smile is watery but real. She turns to Polly, apologetic in her eyes. "Sorry, you were saying?"

Polly clears his throat. "I was going to demonstrate proper leash handling, but we can take a break if you need to—"

"No," Eden says quickly. "No, I'm here. Show us."

He explains proper leash technique, but I'm only half listening, watching Eden from the corner of my eye. She's trying to focus, but her hand keeps drifting to her pocket where her phone sits. Whatever's going on with Cal, it's clearly eating at her.

"Ben?" Polly's voice pulls me back. "Ready to try?"

I take the leash he's holding out, and something shifts in my chest as I clip it to Edo's collar. The weight of it in my hand feels right somehow. Permanent.

"Remember," Polly says quietly, "three visits. No pressure beyond that."

But as Edo looks up at me with complete trust, both of us carrying our invisible scars, I'm starting to wonder if Eden was right. Maybe she does always know what I need.

For the next hour, Polly guides us through basic handling exercises. Each command feels more natural than the last, like remembering an old language rather than learning a new one. Edo anticipates my movements before I make them, adjusting his pace to match mine perfectly.

"Alright," Polly finally says, checking his watch. "I think that's enough for today. You don't want to overwhelm him the first session." He hands me a card with his number and the facility's hours. "Same time Thursday work for you?"

I look down at Edo, sitting attentively at my side. *It feels wrong to just... leave him here.* "Yeah, Thursday's good."

As I unclip the leash, Edo stays in position, but his ears droop slightly.

"Guter Hund," I tell him softly. *Good dog.* His tail wags once.

Eden's been quiet for the last twenty minutes, and when I glance over, she's staring at her phone again. This time I catch a glimpse of multiple missed calls from Cal before she quickly pockets it.

"Ready?" I ask her.

She startles slightly. "Yeah—yes. Thank you, Polly." She hugs the trainer, then heads for the door.

I shake Polly's hand. "Thank you for..." I gesture vaguely, not sure how to finish that sentence.

"Thank you for giving him a chance," Polly replies. "Sometimes that's all any of us need."

IN THE CAR, Eden's unusually quiet as I pull away from the curb. The storm that threatened earlier is finally breaking, fat drops hitting the windshield.

"You want to tell me what's really going on?" I ask, flipping the wipers on.

"What do you mean?"

"Eden." I glance at her. "You've checked your phone at least twenty times in the last hour. Cal's called multiple times, and you haven't answered once. That's not like you."

She stares out the window, watching the rain trace patterns on the glass. "I just..." She takes a breath. "I needed something good today. Something that reminds me there's still..." She trails off.

"Still what?"

"Hope, I guess. That broken things can heal and trust can be rebuilt." She turns to look at me. "That's why I brought you here. But maybe I needed it as much as you did."

I want to ask what happened with Cal, why she's avoiding his calls. But the weight in her voice stops me. Instead, I reach over and squeeze her hand briefly before returning mine to the wheel.

"Thursday at four, then?" she asks, and I hear the gratitude in her voice for not pushing.

"Thursday at four," I confirm, thinking of Edo's knowing eyes, of the way he limped but never let it stop him. Of second chances and the courage it takes to accept them.

The rest of the drive passes in comfortable silence, broken only by the steady rhythm of the rain and windshield wipers. As I pull up to her house, I notice Cal's car isn't in the driveway.

"Thanks for today," I say before she can get out. "For knowing what I needed before I did. Again."

She gives me a small smile, but it doesn't quite reach her eyes. "That's what friends are for." She hesitates, then adds, "You and Edo... you're good together. Like you understand each other."

I don't know what to say to that, so I give her a small nod. "Yeah, well. We'll see how Thursday goes."

She steps out into the rain, and I wait until she's inside before pulling away.

I'm halfway home before I realize I've already made the decision and I turn the car around.

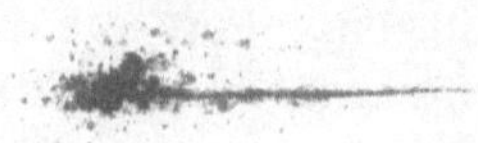

THE STORM FOLLOWED me home—low thunder rolling behind the buildings like a threat not quite spoken aloud.

Edo trails me through the apartment, paws soft on hardwood, tail flicking like he's getting a feel for the place.

I barely finish towel-drying his coat—his tail thudding against the floor with every pass—when my phone buzzes.

Calvin.

"Catfish Club. Need you." No context. No explanation. Just coordinates. Like old times. I almost don't go. Told myself I was done showing up like this.

But it's Cal.

Chapter 30

The air hangs thick with moisture, the kind that clings to your skin and makes the city lights look blurred and tired. A rainstorm just passed, leaving the streets slick and shimmering like broken glass. The war is unraveling in ways no one anticipated, and Calvin insisted we meet at The Catfish Club—a seedy dive at the edge of town, barely held together by its creaky walls and perpetually leaking roof.

Unlike most of the other patrons crowding the dimly lit bar, I hadn't been dragged into the conflict by the draft. I volunteered. Back then, I thought I could make a difference. Thought it might give me purpose. Calvin was different. A lifer by contract rather than conviction, he wasn't built for brawn, but his brain carried secrets that dangerous men would kill to possess. Secrets that made him someone worth protecting.

The sour tang of stale beer and damp wood hits me as I push through the door of sketchy bar. Calvin is hunched over the countertop, his tie loosened and shirt rumpled.

My side twinges as I slide onto the stool beside him. It's been doing that more lately—pain fading, only to return sharper, less predictable. I tell myself it's nothing.

I lie a lot these days.

"Cal?"

He blinks at me, eyes bloodshot. "Benji! You came." His forced cheer doesn't mask the tension in his voice.

"'Course I did. What's going on?"

"I fucked up." He slaps another shot back. "The trials...

they're not what we planned."

"Trials?" The word lands heavier than I expected. I haven't even started yet, but I already know the job's going to be a hell of a lot more than scanning samples and taking notes.

"You'll see, soon enough—behind the restricted checkpoints. Just don't ask too many questions when you get there." he leans closer, whisper-slurring. "We're not just studying enhanced soldiers, Ben. We're making them."

"Making what, exactly?" I raise a brow, leaning in to meet his whisper.

"Vampires." He laughs, the sound sharp and hollow. "Sounds crazy, right? But it's true. We call them Noctis, but technically they are. Superhuman strength, night vision, accelerated healing..." He taps his temple. "All up here. The formulas, the sequences..."

"Cal, maybe we should get you home—"

"She was the first success," he cuts me off. "Eliza. The others, they were pure instinct, just... violence. But her?" He shakes his head. "She thinks. Plans. Sometimes I catch her watching me, and it's like... like she's taking notes for later."

The bartender approaches and I wave him off. "How much has he had?"

"Enough to get himself killed if the wrong person overheard this classified bullshit," the bartender mutters.

Calvin grabs my arm, his grip desperate. "I need your help, Ben. It's all spiraling. These things we've made... they're not even soldiers anymore."

"So many died in trials," Cal mutters, swirling his glass. "But she survived. Always survives." He glances at me. "And now she's... interested in the new staff. Asks about them. About you."

"Me?"

"Saw you during your tour. Wouldn't stop asking questions after." He leans in, breath heavy with whiskey. "That's her trick, you know? Gets in your head. Makes you think you're special." He trails off, then adds quietly, "Like she did with the others."

"What others?"

"Three of them." His voice drops lower. "They felt sorry for her."

"Let's get you home. Eden's probably worried—"

"Eden," he groans, his face crumpling.

"Don't worry, buddy, she'll understand."

"No, Ben. She'll be so mad." He rubs his face. "I haven't been home in three days. The lab... there's so much work… and she's been feeling sick all week."

My heart nearly stops.

Three days? She hadn't seen him in three days. The checking her phone… it all makes sense now. And I'd just watched her walk in the rain like it didn't matter.

My attention sharpens, but I don't press. He doesn't notice—just keeps rambling.

"It's just... we've been trying, you know? For a baby. She's been so tired lately, and I keep thinking maybe—but I don't know. She hasn't said anything yet."

He slumps lower, eyes glassy. "And I missed our dinner night. I missed all of it."

Something in me goes still. I don't say a word. Not about the dinner. Not about the possibility. Just guide him toward the door.

"Come on. I've got you." I stand, ignoring the stab of pain in my side, pushing away the swirling thoughts of the news bomb he just dropped on me.

"Always do, don't you?" He stumbles as I help him up. "That's why I need you there. At the lab. Someone I can trust.."

"We'll talk about it when you're sober."

As we leave, he mumbles against my shoulder: "Just... be careful around her. Eliza. She's not what she seems."

"None of this even seems real, Cal."

He laughs again, but there's no humor in it. "That's the problem, isn't it? It's all too real."

Cal fumbles with his seatbelt, then freezes. "Oh shit."

"What?"

"Eden's gonna kill me." He presses his palms against his eyes. "We were supposed to talk to you together..."

"Talk to me about what?"

A grin breaks across his face, tired but real. "We're hoping. That's all. Hoping it worked this time."

The words hollow me out. I grip the steering wheel tighter, grateful for the darkness hiding my expression.

"Don't tell her I told you," he slurs. "She wanted it to be special. Had it all planned out..."

"Your secret's safe with me," I say, but the words taste wrong.

EDEN OPENS THE door, worry etched on her face. "Cal?"

"Sorry," I mouth over his shoulder as I help him inside.

Her eyes meet mine, holding for a moment too long. "Thank you, Benji."

The familiar ache blooms when our eyes hold. "Always."

"Here we go, buddy." I ease Cal onto the couch, trying to ignore how my side screams in protest. "I'll grab you some water."

"You're the best, Benji, Benny, Ben." Cal's words slur as his head lolls back. "The absolute best."

Eden follows me to the kitchen, her bare feet whispering across the tile, but there's tension clinging to her like static. She leans against the counter, arms folded tight, eyes focused somewhere over my shoulder.

I grab a glass and turn on the tap, letting the silence stretch longer than it should.

"Was he at The Catfish Club again?" she asks, voice low and strained—not soft, not angry, just… tired.

I nod, keeping my eyes on the running water. "Yeah. Rambling about work stuff. Said he needed backup."

Her exhale shudders on the way out. "He's barely been home. I don't even know where he sleeps half the time." Her fingers curl tighter around her arms. "He could've called. Just… at least let me know he was okay."

I set the glass down gently on the counter. "He is now. He's safe."

She nods, but there's no relief in her posture. Only that brittle edge of someone holding everything together with string and breath.

"I just needed him to come home," she says quietly, almost like she regrets saying it out loud. "And I shouldn't have to ask."

I study her face, the subtle darkening under her eyes, the way she blinks too often to keep anything from spilling over. "You didn't say anything earlier," I say softly. "I would have gotten him home sooner…"

Her eyes meet mine then, and I catch something vulnerable flickering behind them. But she just nods again, pulling back into herself as she lifts the water glass from the counter like it's something to anchor her.

"The project is probably just stressing him out." The lie tastes bitter, but it's better than unloading the weight of everything I just learned.

"You'd tell me, wouldn't you?" There's a question in her eyes she doesn't voice. "If something was really wrong?"

I pause—just long enough for it to mean something.

She could be pregnant. Calvin said she's been sick. Tired. And now he's out there, drunk, spilling classified secrets like the war's already lost.

The idiot.

"Of course," I say, forcing a smile that doesn't feel real. "But Cal's just… Cal. You know how he gets with work."

She nods, but doesn't look convinced. "Thank you for bringing him home."

"Always." The word that's become habit around her slips out before I can stop it.

"Benji..." Her hand touches my arm, feather-light. "I don't know what I'd do without—"

"Eden?" Cal's voice carries from the living room. "I don't feel so good..."

Eden turns toward the sound—but Calvin's voice slurs again, louder this time. "You didn't want to tell him like this," he mutters, dragging himself upright on the couch. "But you've been so tired... 'cause of the baby."

The words blindside me—hanging in the air between us like broken glass.

The baby.

I blink, but the world doesn't settle.

Eden goes still. Her eyes snap to mine—wide, glassy, uncertain. I see it happen in real time: the moment she realizes Calvin let it slip, the moment she realizes I heard.

And I did. God, I did. My stomach knots. Not because she's pregnant. Not even because they didn't tell me.It's the timing.

That week.

That night.

The way we almost—

I cut the thought off before it finishes, but it spirals anyway.

We didn't cross the line.

I know that.

But we stood on the edge of it. I felt her reaching, and I didn't move away.

Twelve weeks. That's three months.

Close enough to do math I shouldn't be doing. Close enough to make my heart seize for reasons I'll never admit.

It's not mine.

I know that, too.

But for one brief, gut-wrenching second—I wonder if it could have been.

There's a quiet ache in the way she looks at me. Like she's wondering if I've already pieced together what that would have meant.

Her hand moves almost imperceptibly, pressing to her stomach in a reflex she probably doesn't notice.

For a heartbeat, she steps closer. Not just a step, but a shift. Like she's crossing an invisible line she's spent weeks tiptoeing around. She stops just shy of touching me—then slowly lifts her hand and presses it to my chest, right over where my heart won't stop pounding.

The warmth of her palm bleeds through the thin fabric of my shirt, and my breath hitches. I should step back. I don't.

I can't.

Her blue eyes search mine, not for permission, but for understanding. For reassurance. Because she's holding something she hasn't said out loud yet.

"Ben, I—" she starts, voice shaking under the weight of everything. But whatever she meant to say crumbles before it reaches me.

I give her the gentlest smile I can manage, even as it threatens to shatter me. "That's amazing, Eden. Really." My voice is steady, practiced. The way a soldier learns to speak when everything inside is chaos. "He's lucky to have you."

She doesn't step back. Her hand lingers, fingers lightly curled against my chest. Her other hand hovers briefly at her side, like she wants to hold me but doesn't trust herself to do it.

"I didn't want you to find out like this," she says finally. Her voice is hushed, tight. "I was going to tell you after—"

"You don't owe me that." I say it gently, but the truth of it cuts. "I'm just glad you're both happy."

A long pause follows. Her eyes glisten, and her lower lip quivers before she presses it into a thin line. She's trying so hard not to fall apart. "I wish I didn't have to watch you hurt like this." she whispers.

Her words twist blades inside me—because she means it.

Because she's not just talking about this moment. She's talking about everything. Every look. Every silence. Every time we stood too close and pretended it meant nothing.

The air shifts, charged again. The memory of her kiss flashes through me—her lips, her body pressed to mine, the way she said my name like it meant we were more.

I inhale, slow and deep, trying to anchor myself. Her hand is still there, right over my heart. I don't want her to move it. But if she doesn't, I might break in a way I can't recover from.

So I step back—just enough to make space. Her hand drops between us like a final thread cut.

"I should go," I murmur, my voice hollow.

She watches me for a beat too long. Her hand reaches out—just slightly—as if to grab mine, to hold me there.

"Don't go," she says. Barely above a whisper.

I hesitate. And in that silence, I want to give in. Just for a second.

But Cal groans again in the other room, and the spell breaks. "I'll always show up when you need me," I say, backing toward the door. "But tonight, you've got everything you need."

Her mouth opens like she wants to argue—but she doesn't. She just nods, tears rimming her eyes. And as I turn the knob, I hear her voice one last time, soft and unsure.

"Benji... please don't shut us out."

I glance over my shoulder. "I'm not. Just... taking the long way home."

As I close the door behind me, I hear Cal retching and Eden's soft murmur of comfort. The sound follows me down the steps, mixing with the silence of the evening.

Something catches my eye as I slide back into my car—a corner of paper sticking out from under the passenger seat. Reaching down, I pull out a photograph that must have fallen from Cal's journal.

Eden smiles up at me, caught mid-laugh in a spring field. Her sundress catches the light, her face tilted just so, red waves spilling over her shoulders. She looks happy. Carefree. Everything I can never give her.

I should return it. Should go back inside right now and hand it over. Instead, my fingers trace the edge of the photo, memorizing every detail. After a long moment, I slip it into my jacket's inner pocket, close to my heart where it doesn't belong.

The vesper bells toll in the distance as I start the car, each chime another reminder of everything I've lost. Everything I never had.

By the morning of my first day at work, the photo's still in my jacket pocket—creased now from how many times I must've reached for it unconsciously.

Edo wakes before I do, pressing his weight against the mattress like he's already made the day's decisions for us. I leash him without thinking. Outside, the street glistens from last night's rain. He trots beside me like we've been doing this for years instead of days.

Across the road, a couple argues again—low voices rising through open windows about moving away from the city, away from the curfews and sirens, away from the war. I don't blame them.

Edo noses a crumpled flier on the sidewalk: a recruitment ad half-drenched and already curling at the edges. We keep walking.

Back at the apartment, I shower, dress, and load my pockets with the new essentials—wallet, keycard, a small folding knife I'm not supposed to bring but always do. I hesitate over the photo, then tuck it into the inner lining of my jacket.

By the time I reach the facility, the edge of morning has dulled into gray, and my pulse beats steady beneath the collar of my shirt.

Chapter 31

Edo watches me from the apartment window as I pull away, head cocked like he knows something I don't.

The base lab has added an extra security checkpoint since my last visit.

The queue moves slower than expected, each guard scanning IDs with a level of scrutiny that suggests more than just protocol. Their hands hover closer to their holsters, and their eyes track movements with a sharpness that isn't just trained—it's lived.

The air is thick with an unspoken tension that makes men ready their weapons before a fight even begins. The checkpoint is a stark contrast to the rest of the facility—industrial lighting buzzing overhead, the faint scent of metal and bleach clinging to the air. The walls are painted a sterile white, but the scratches along the security console suggest high tension isn't uncommon here.

A poster near the security station reads: 'Tier Four Protocol: In case of breach, proceed to UV zone.' The ink is faded, corners curled. No one looks at it anymore, but it's there. A warning pretending to be a guideline.

I shift my weight, trying to find that sweet spot between stability and relief that's seemed increasingly difficult to find after restarting my exercise routine. The pain should flare sharper in my hip—but it doesn't. Not quite. The ache's still there, but dulled, buried beneath a concerning numbness. Like my body's remembering how to function without me.

"ID and clearance card." The guard—Stevens, according to his nameplate—keeps his head down, but his gaze flicks up the moment I step forward. His expression doesn't change, but his fingers tighten on the scanner just slightly, like he's bracing for something.

"New hire," I say, handing over my credentials. "Research Division. Bailey's team." The words come out neutral, but Stevens' eyebrow twitches, just barely, and he processes my clearance without comment.

Before I can dwell on it, alarms blare from one of the buildings. A low, wailing noise that echoes through the concrete halls, vibrating through my chest. Doors lock in unison, the emergency lights outside kicking on—the flashing red strobes making the shadows dance unnaturally against the walls.

"Code Yellow in Section C," crackles over Stevens' radio. The guard's posture shifts instantly, combat-ready. I recognize the stance—weight on the balls of the feet, hands positioned for quick access to weapons. Not standard rent-a-cop training.

"Clear the queue," Stevens orders, professional calm masking urgency. "Dr. Bailey's hire, proceed. Everyone else, step back."

My eyes track the strobe pattern—erratic and harsh—but somehow, I stay with it. The flashes don't slow, but my perception sharpens. Details snap into focus faster than they should.

I look around, but move through the checkpoint, my instincts and military training cataloging details. The camera positions on the outside of the building. The height of the metal fence surrounding the property. Stevens speaks quietly into his radio as he escorts me to the lab building: "Subject status?"

"Contained," a voice crackles. "Tunnel secure."

Subject, not patient. Contained, not treated.

The phrasing sinks in, settling into the back of my mind like a loaded gun left on a table.

I don't like it.

I file away the word choice as he escorts me to the lab building I've toured. He scans his badge and lifts his hand to the biometric scanner. The red flashing light goes solid before turning green and he pulls the door open, motioning me inside.

"They'll take care of you at the front desk." Stevens says before turning around to return to his post.

The weight of the interior door is too heavy for standard

issue—reinforced. The whole building is different this time. The faint smell of antiseptic barely masking a metallic undertone that wasn't here on my tour. Each observation adds to a picture that doesn't match the facility's public research mission, and the description I was given when I toured.

This is a containment facility.

The hallways stretch long and narrow, windowless, and cold. Designed like a bunker. Not a medical facility.

The fluorescent lights cast harsh shadows across the lobby security station's brushed steel surfaces. I count four visible cameras in the lobby alone, their positions creating overlapping fields of view that leave no blind spots.

Those are new, too.

Two guards at the desk, one roaming, and based on the slight bulge in the ceiling panels, probably a reinforced security station above. More serious hardware than last time as well.

I wonder if there was a breach.

A researcher hurries past the security desk, swiping her keycard with hurried precision. I catch the subtle pause in her step as she passes through the scanner, like someone bracing for impact. The patrol guard's hand twitches toward his weapon before relaxing as the system chimes green.

Calvin comes around the corner, offering a smile that doesn't settle in his eyes. His shoulders are stiff, his fingers tapping against the folder in his hands. He's nervous. Not the casual kind—the kind that says he knows something I don't. "You made it through security!"

"Longer wait than expected," I say, matching his pace. "Rough morning?"

Calvin exhales through his nose, a breath that might be a laugh if it weren't so tight. "Every morning's rough here." The weight he's carrying lately has turned his frame brittle, like he's all thought and no sleep.

We stop at a door marked BRIEFING. The sign is slightly worn, edges curling where the adhesive has begun to fail. The kind of detail no one fixes because no one's around long enough to care.

"You're giving me a briefing?" I ask, eyebrow raised.

Calvin's expression shifts, the easygoing act peeling away. "Ben, listen to me." His voice drops a note, serious. "This isn't just policy. You need to understand what we're dealing with before you set foot anywhere else. Trust me."

I study him. The strain on his face, the dark circles under his eyes—this isn't the same Calvin who used to fall asleep in physics class. He looks older, heavier somehow, as if the walls of this place have been crushing down on him for months.

I nod, slow and deliberate. "Okay."

"Good." Calvin doesn't hesitate as he pushes open the door.

"Colonel Mathers, this is new hire Ben Hale. Veteran of the 9th special ops unit. Local." Calvin says to introduce me.

Colonel Mathers stands from his paperwork heavy desk and nods. "Hale. Lucky you got me for the hot seat today."

I glance to Cal, "it's a rotation," he says.

"Hardly. You can keep telling yourself that, Bailey, but somebody needs to do it when I'm not around."

"I'd be hard pressed to find a day you're not around, Colonel," Calvin says before turning to leave. "I'll be back in about an hour to show you the next steps."

Colonel Mathers doesn't sit behind his desk during my briefing. He stands, weight balanced, just like every military patrol briefing. But his stance is different—less mechanical precision, more primal readiness.

"I've reviewed your combat record," he says, tapping a tablet. "Extensive Turig engagement experience. That's good and bad." He sets the tablet down deliberately. "Good, because you understand threat containment. Bad, because everything you learned about combat logic? Throw it out. These subjects don't follow patterns."

Mathers moves to a wall-mounted screen. "Let's talk protocols. First rule: No predictable routines. These subjects learn. Adapt. Look for weaknesses we don't even know we're showing."

The screen displays facility layouts. Multiple security checkpoints. Overlapping patrol routes that seem deliberately randomized.

"We change patrol patterns daily. Guards rotate every two hours—no exceptions. Even bathroom breaks need authorization." Mathers' voice carries the weight of experience. "They can smell fatigue. Stress. Fear. Use it against us."

"This is all starting to sound a bit Hollywood."

"Were you not told what we do here?"

I settle back into my chair. "Testing for soldier

enhancement. I heard some whispers about vampires in the halls. But really, Colonel?"

"You haven't seen the footage, then." He turns on his heel and grabs the tablet from his desk.

"Correct. Sir, I only arrived an hour ago."

Mathers curses under his breath, "Damn scientists always leaving the hard conversations to me. Fine. How's your stomach, Hale? Those Turig rotations do you any good?"

"Got me discharged and here today, so I'd say I can handle it."

"We'll see," he mutters and pulls up some security footage on the tablet. For the first time, he sits while I watch, examining my reactions while it plays.

The footage is crisp—way better than standard security cameras. Multiple angles show a lab. Two researchers are taking blood samples from a male subject who appears sedated. Standard protocols, everything by the book. The timestamp reads 14:32.

At 14:33, one researcher turns away to label a vial. The other keeps working with the subject. Nothing seems amiss until I notice the subject's hand—the fingers slowly curling into a fist. It reminds me of watching a Turig power up its combat systems, that moment of terrible anticipation.

14:34 - The subject moves. My trained eye catches details others might miss. The subject's movements aren't purely aggressive—there's desperation in them, the kind I've seen in cornered soldiers. When he attacks, it's not calculated like a Turig—it's primal, instinctive. Like someone fighting for survival rather than victory.

One moment he's on the table, the next he's across the room. The researcher never had a chance to scream. The second researcher hits the panic button, but she's too slow. Way too slow.

Mathers pauses the footage with a remote from his desk. "Do you need a moment?"

"No." My voice stays steady as I analyze the subject's face on screen. The expression isn't rage—it's terror. "Play it."

Part of me wants to look away—not out of fear, but recognition. The way that subject moved... it's the same way I did when I thought I had nothing left to lose.

14:35 - Security teams flood in with what look like specialized weapons. The subject takes three direct hits but keeps moving. A fourth shot finally brings him down, but not before he's torn through another guard. The raw violence makes Turig attacks look almost merciful in comparison. At least they kill with efficiency.

The aftermath stats scroll across the screen: Three dead. Two critically injured. Subject contained for further testing.

"That's with restraints and sedation," Mathers says quietly.

"Further testing. He wasn't terminated?" I ask, replaying how the subject responded to movements. Not predatory tracking—defensive reactions

"So far, decapitation is the only confirmed method for termination. We're a bit short on volunteers so we only resort to that if absolutely necessary."

I finally exhale, not realizing I held it in. "Can't imagine those conditions."

I watch the footage loop again, comparing it to my combat experience. "There's no pattern of movement to predict."

"Standard anti-Turig ammunition is useless—took a while to find that out. We've developed specialized rounds, but even those require multiple hits to neutralize." Mathers stands again, hesitating before continuing. "That gives our special unit enough time to get them back into restraints and cages."

My mind drifts to the blonde with green eyes I saw in the cage on my tour. There's no way she is capable of that type of force.

"The ammunition?" I ask, bringing my thoughts back to the present.

"UV core rounds. Expensive as hell, but standard ammo might as well be spitballs. Each guard carries a primary with UV rounds, backup with aluminum composite." He pauses. "Won't kill them outright, but slows them enough for containment teams to respond."

The next screen shows containment protocols. Emergency lockdown procedures. Panic button locations.

"Every lab has three panic buttons. Learn their positions. If you're close enough to see a subject break containment, you're already too close. Button activates lockdown, floods the room with UV, and seals all access points until response teams arrive."

I study the layouts, noting the reinforced doors, the UV flood lights positioned throughout the facility. "Response time?"

"Ninety seconds from alarm to full containment team deployment. Sounds fast until you watch that footage again and time how long it takes a subject to—" He stops abruptly. "Cal tells me you're working with Eliza."

Something in his tone makes me look up. "That's right."

Mathers pulls up another screen—staff photos with red X's through them. Too many. But there's another compilation—personnel transfer requests, incident reports, all linked to single researcher labs. "These were researchers who forgot what they were dealing with. Got comfortable. Started seeing subjects as patients instead of predators." His voice hardens. "Eliza... she's a special case."

"Cal mentioned she's different. More controlled."

"That makes her more dangerous." Mathers leans forward, his voice dropping. "The others? Animals. Primal. But her? There's wisdom there." He taps one of the transfer requests. "Know what the common thread is in these? All requested transfers after spending time with her."

"Or maybe they just couldn't handle—"

"Three months ago, we had an incident." Mathers cuts me off. "Researcher named Davis. Started spending extra time in her lab. Said she wasn't dangerous. She doesn't look it, does she? Nice, pretty face."

The question hits closer than I'd like. I glance at her photo on the screen. "What happened?"

"Found him trying to open her cage at 3 AM. Claimed she was in pain, needed help. But the cameras..." Mathers shakes his head. "The cameras showed her smiling the whole time. Like she knew exactly what she was doing."

I straighten, defensive. "I can handle myself."

"That's what Davis said. It's what they all said." He hands me a keycard and a small UV beacon. "Carry this at all times. If your card gets compromised, beacon signals an immediate lockdown. Had to add that protocol after a subject used a researcher's own passcard to—" He catches himself. "Details are in the briefing packet."

"What about Eliza's lab? Additional protocols?"

Mathers' expression shifts slightly. "Special case. Extra UV coverage, reinforced everything. Only one camera in that lab but there are no blind spots. Here's what you need to understand, Hale. She's not more controlled, she's more calculating." He leans forward. "The others show their nature. She hides hers behind a mask. And that's what gets people killed—they let their guards down."

The briefing packet is heavy in my hands. It's a standard

military folder, but the contents are anything but standard.

"One last thing." Mathers' tone makes me look up again. "You've got Turig combat experience. Means you know how to fight smart. Strategic. These subjects?" He gestures to the screen of casualties. "They're not soldiers gone wrong. They're not even soldiers we can use in the war anymore. Don't think you can fight and win against them, Hale."

"Understood." I nod.

"No. Not yet, you don't." Mathers opens the door. "But if you survive long enough, you'll remember this conversation. And that'll be when you wish you'd listened."

My mind drifts to the blonde with jade eyes I wasn't supposed to see in the cage during my tour. The way she'd studied me with that calculated interest, like she could see right through my defenses. Just like Eden did that night in my kitchen before I almost… I push the thought away—*dangerous to draw parallels between predators and the woman I can't have.*

THE BREAK ROOM smells like burnt coffee and anxiety. Four researchers huddle around a table, lab coats rumpled from a long shift. They fall silent when I enter, but I catch the tail end of their conversation—something about behavioral triggers and psychological feedback loops.

I make my way to the coffee machine, keeping my movements relaxed while mapping the room: two exits, one vent overhead, security camera in the corner.

The coffee tastes metallic, like it was dripped through old copper—but no one else flinches when they drink it. Just me. But it's hot, and it gives me something to do with my hands.

"You're the new hire, right?" A woman detaches from the group, badge reading Dr. Kelley Copen. Her hair's pulled into a loose graying knot, eyes sharp behind smudged glasses. "Dr. Bailey's friend?"

"Word travels fast," I say. "Ben Hale. Started today."

"Military?" she asks, nodding toward my stance.

"That obvious?"

"You stand like someone who's cleared more rooms than conversations."

"Old habit." Most civilians wouldn't notice, but I'm still

positioned for maximum visibility of both exits.

"Better keep it. You'll need it here." Kelley glances toward the corner camera and lowers her voice. "We get a lot of ex-military here. Though usually not from the front lines. And rarely assigned to isolated lab work." Her smile doesn't reach her eyes. "Pays to know the boss, huh?"

The others pretend not to listen, but I catch how they tense at the mention of Eliza's lab.

Interesting.

"Different kind of fight now," I offer, watching their reactions.

Kelley lets out a brittle laugh. "Yeah, that's one way to put it. At least Turigs are predictable." She sips from her cup. "Did they show you the footage yet?"

"Just finished watching it." I can't help but notice how confident they are discussing things they've only seen on a screen. None of them have gone against a Turig one on one. "Mathers didn't sugarcoat it."

"Ah." She studies my face. "Still here, so you must have a strong stomach."

Marcus, the younger researcher, shifts beside her, his hand shaking slightly as he sets down his cup. "She's just bitter because she lost her last assistant."

"Lost how?" The words come out before I can stop them.

Kelley's tone sharpens. "He requested a transfer. After spending too much time with your new subject. Said he couldn't handle the work anymore."

"She remembers people," someone else mutters. "Their routines. Their names."

"That's enough of the theories," says the older man across the room—Levi Fullmer, according to his badge. His voice is quiet but grounded in authority. "Let the guy drink his coffee."

"They're not theories," Marcus snaps. He stands abruptly, chair screeching back. "You've seen the footage from the other subjects—pure instinct, no control. But her? Eyes always calculating. She remembers things she shouldn't."

"Doesn't mean she's dangerous," I say carefully.

Marcus's hands curl around his coffee cup, knuckles white. "Oh no? Three researchers transferred after her. One left before his first month was up. And you think that's a coincidence?"

"Marcus." Levi's voice cuts through the tension like a scalpel. "Enough."

Marcus slams his cup down and storms out. Through the window, I watch him argue with a guard in the hallway—gestures clipped and frantic. His voice rises, echoing faintly through the glass. "I told you! I told all of you she's not like the others—why the hell won't anyone listen?"

The guard raises a hand in a calming gesture, but Marcus bats it away. He keeps talking, too fast, too loud, until the guard finally waves another guard over.

Kelley sighs. "Sorry. It's been a rough few weeks. Lots of… changes."

"Seems like it's always a rough few weeks here." I sip my coffee.

"Yeah." Her voice dips, quieter. "Just... if you hear anything at night—voices, crying, whatever—don't go looking."

I raise an eyebrow.

"Not a joke," she says. "That's how people get dead." She dumps the rest of her coffee and heads for the door. "Good luck, Hale."

The others follow, leaving me alone with the hum of the ventilation system and the last swirls of steam from my cup.

The vending machine buzzes life behind me, stocked with synthetic meal packs. Nothing fresh. Not since the last contamination alert, if the taped memo is to be believed.

Somewhere in the ducts, the sound shifts—too light to be footsteps, too deliberate to be the wind. A chill works down my spine.

I think of Eden's hand on her stomach. Of Calvin not coming home. Of the photo still tucked inside my jacket pocket. And for a moment, I wonder which version of me this place will bring to the surface.

Chapter 32

The fluorescent lights cast identical shadows down each sterile corridor as I follow the security escort. Years of military service make me instinctively note camera positions, exit routes, security patterns—but everything feels off. The researchers move between labs with a carefulness too rigid and afraid. Their tension creates its own kind of danger.

My footsteps echo against his in an uneven rhythm. "Final security check," the guard says, handing me an emergency beacon.

I nod, but my mind isn't fully here yet. It's on the photo still tucked in my jacket in my locker, Eden's smile burned into the back of my eyes. I thought the lab would be the clean break I needed to start letting go. It's not, yet.

The guard's movements are precise but relax as he glances at my military ID. "Standard procedure, though between us... someone with your background probably doesn't need it. Most of our researchers are civilians—smart, but they get jumpy."

"Protocol is protocol," I say, clipping the beacon to my belt.

Cal appears, nodding to the guard. "Thanks, James. I'll take it from here." He turns to me, and I catch the apology in his expression as we walk. "Most researchers work in pairs. Your partner is out till later but given your background… well, let's just say you're better equipped to handle the unexpected. So I'll still have you start without her."

Calvin stops at a set of double doors at the corridor's end, his hand hovering over the handle. "This is our primary lab," he says, his voice dropping slightly. "Everything's here—my notes, the mRNA serum, all the components we used to create it. Space constraints forced us to consolidate some of the less environmentally sensitive materials, but having them all in one space ended up helping with trial compound tracking."

I slip my hands into my pockets, fighting the urge to fidget. "Who is my partner?"

"Jasmine Carter. Ph.D. in Biomedical Engineering."

"Perfect. She builds medical miracles, and I once cauterized a bullet wound with a lighter and a fork. Dream team." I huff a laugh, but it lands flat. Calvin doesn't even crack a smile. His whole posture shifts—shoulders squaring, jaw tight.

"Ben." He turns to face me fully, his expression grave, voice low. "You know we've started trials on the Noctis Serum, and you know what we're dealing with. What you don't know is that we have a... subject in there. A prisoner of war. Once we complete the initial cellular change tests, she'll be crucial for our reversal trials." He pauses, choosing his words carefully. "She's restrained. In a cage. I wanted to prepare you for that."

The hair on the back of my neck prickles. "Chains and a cage? How does a prisoner of war end up as one of these vampires?"

"Noctis is the official terminology—"

"I think I'll stick with vampire outside the paperwork," I interrupt.

Calvin's face hardens. "You haven't seen what these changes do to their strength. The restraints aren't excessive—they're necessary. If you'd prefer, I can find you space in one of the conference rooms till Jasmine gets back."

"No point postponing the inevitable. I'll have to work with her eventually, right?"

"Right." Calvin pushes the door open, and fluorescent light spills across a landscape of metal and glass.

A rectangular steel table dominates the center, its surface a chaos of equipment and scattered notes. The perimeter tables create a narrow maze of workstations: a Bunsen burner setup, a sink flanked by a humming refrigerator, a centrifuge squatting near clusters of beakers beneath a vapor hood. All paths lead to the cage.

She's there, unnaturally still. Matted blonde hair clings to her face like seaweed to a drowning victim, but her eyes—

jade green and bright—track my movements with unsettling intelligence. Each step I take draws a subtle shift in her posture. At first glance it seems predatory, but something in her movements speaks of desperation rather than hunger.

The tilt of her wrists, the tension in her shoulders—it's not aggression, it's the kind of fear I saw in rookies after their first ambush. Controlled panic. She doesn't want to pounce. She wants to survive.

"First, you need to understand the transformative process of the Noctis serum," Calvin says, moving to the cage with confidence. "Once you grasp that, you'll be able to identify how each compound influences the transition. That's our key to reverse-engineering a cure." He gestures toward the cage. "This is Eliza. She's aggressive, but the restraints are adequate."

"Back off, pig." Her voice is a guttural snarl that seems to bypass my ears and strike directly at my primitive brain.

Calvin appears unfazed. "Imagine having a dog's olfactory sensitivity. That's what Eliza experiences. Humans emit countless scents we can't detect."

"I am human!" The words explode from her throat, desperate and raw. Her posture isn't predatory—it's defensive. I recognize it from processing POWs: the careful balance between showing strength and hiding fear.

"You're far from human now, my sweet." He taps on one of the cage bars before walking to the file cabinet.

I glance at him, trying to match this voice with the one that used to read comic books in a blanket fort. He doesn't even flinch. Just moves on like he didn't strip the last bit of humanity from her with that line.

The casual cruelty makes my stomach turn. He rifles through the cabinet before pulling out a thick folder. "Start here." The file hits the table with a dull thud. "It's not exactly light reading, but understanding this is crucial before we move you to hands-on work."

"Should I find you when I'm ready for the next file?"

"I'll be in the hallway labs, but this will probably take you at least a week or so. Just let me know at the end of the day when you think you'll be ready for more, otherwise Jasmine can get you more."

"Copy." I nod, staring at the folder.

"Excellent!" His hand claps my shoulder, and he leans in conspiratorially. "See you at lunch."

His grip lingers—tight, almost desperate. I've seen soldiers hold on like that after losing men. Like they're clinging to the one thing they haven't failed yet.

When the door opens, Eliza releases a pained groan, raising her shackled hands to shield her eyes. The gesture is achingly human.

I don't look at her. Don't have to. I can feel her gaze anyway—measured, intelligent, waiting. Like she's not sizing me up to attack, but studying how I break.

She smiles faintly—like she already knows the outcome. Like she's seen it before.

The first page blurs as I stare at it.

This place was supposed to give me answers. But now it just feels like I'm being watched.

THE HALLWAY'S QUIETER this time—less shuffling of coats, less radio chatter. I round the last corner near my lab and nearly collide with someone carrying a coffee and a digital tablet.

She sidesteps fast, saving both the drink and the data. "You move quiet for someone with combat boots."

I take half a step back, eyeing her badge: Carter, Jasmine.

"Ben Hale," I say.

She gives a low whistle. "So you're the infamous war vet they stuck in the lab with the vampire. Awesome." She eyes me. "They told me you were tall, but they didn't mention the haunted stare."

I arch a brow. "They tell you I was unqualified, too?"

She smirks. "No. I read that part in your file."

That gets a huff out of me. "You always this friendly, or just when you haven't had caffeine?"

She lifts the coffee in a mock toast. "This is my third. So technically, I'm charming."

We reach the lab door. She glances at the scanner, then at me. "Wanna do the honors? Show off those top-secret clearance privileges?"

I swipe my card. The light turns green. "I'm guessing you don't scare easy."

"Please." She pushes through the door. "Eliza only eats people who ask stupid questions."

Eliza is already standing—hands loose at her sides, posture deceptively relaxed. She doesn't react right away, but her eyes flick toward the door as we enter.

Jasmine strides in like she owns the place, tablet in hand and coffee wedged between her elbow and her side. She downs the rest and throws the cup in the trash. "Heads up, princess," she calls toward the cage. "We've got a new lab rat."

Eliza doesn't move, but her eyes shift to me, slow and deliberate.

Jasmine is already tapping the interface. "Try not to eat him. Paperwork's a nightmare."

I head toward the workstation, keeping my steps casual. "So this is the part where you mock me while I learn to not screw anything up?"

Jasmine snorts. "Mocking starts tomorrow. Today's just judgmental observation."

Eliza finally speaks. "Your scent is different."

I stop short. "Excuse me?"

"She's a little too good at reading people," Jasmine mutters, not looking up. "Gives the rest of us a complex."

Eliza steps closer to the bars, not aggressive—just focused. "He doesn't smell like fear."

I don't blink. "Maybe I'm just too tired to care."

"Or maybe," Jasmine says, lifting her gaze, "he hasn't figured out what kind of hell this place really is yet." A beat passes. Eliza's eyes don't leave me. Jasmine watches this too, her expression flickering—not quite concern, not quite amusement. "Well, this'll be fun."

Chapter 33

By the end of my first week, my mind is swimming with questions. The files blur into one another, medical jargon and research notes bleeding together in ways that make it hard to focus. I blink hard, my dry eyes stinging, and lean back in my chair. Lacing my fingers behind my head, I stretch, a sharp ache flaring in my chest and ribs—a reminder.

By lunch, my stomach is growling and my mind is swimming with questions.

A quiet rustle breaks my concentration. When I look up, Eliza's eyes, bright and unsettling, fix on me. Her careful observation reminds me of combat assessments—calculating risks and searching for allies. I glance away, swallowing the urge to speak, and head out.

The hallways have already become familiar as I navigate to the lockers and grab my water bottle, draining it in one go.

"Thirsty?" Calvin's laugh fills the space as he approaches.

I wipe my mouth with the back of my hand. "What can I say? Hydration is key."

"Well, get used to going without while you're in the lab. Contamination risk."

The cafeteria buzzes with the kind of subdued conversation you hear in hospital waiting rooms—everyone speaking just above a whisper, as if normal volume might trigger danger.

Calvin unwraps his lunch. "How's it coming along? Making sense?"

"It is, actually. About a third through."

Calvin pauses mid-bite, eyes widening. "A third? Already?"

"Started reading medical texts after my injuries. Not all of this is entirely new."

"Right. Still, I figured it'd take longer to grasp what we're dealing with."

Dr. Chen appears with her coffee, catching our exchange. "Better than most new hires. Half of them can barely look at the subjects." She settles into a chair, her lab coat wrinkled but her movements precise. "Military background helps, doesn't it?"

"Different kind of combat zone," I say, echoing my sentiment from my first day.

"That's the problem." She stirs her coffee methodically. "Everyone's so scared, they can't see past the threat potential. These subjects were people once. Some of us think they still are." She glances at Calvin.

Cal's expression tightens. "Sarah, we've discussed this. The transformations—"

"Change their biology, yes. But their humanity?" She meets my eyes, weighted with lost battles. "That's a harder question. You should have seen Eliza when she first arrived. Before we..." She trails off as Cal's hand whitens around his bottle.

"Dr. Chen has some controversial theories," he says carefully.

"Science advances through controversy," she counters. "Just because something is dangerous doesn't make it inhuman."

"Most would disagree about Eliza." Calvin doesn't look at her when he responds. He stares at his food like the words might be hiding in the lettuce.

I glance at him, frowning. "I dunno if that's fair to assume. She hasn't said a word to me."

"Lucky you." Calvin laughs, stabbing at the last bite of his sandwich like it wronged him. "How's the transition going with Jasmine?"

I glance up. "Actually… she wasn't in today."

"No?" His brow creases. "She might've been pulled into the East Annex trials. They've been stealing people left and right."

"Without a hand-off?" Dr. Chen asks, setting down her

mug. "That's unlike her."

Calvin shrugs. "Protocol's sloppy right now. I'll check."

But the way he says it doesn't match the weight behind Dr. Chen's pause.

She doesn't press. Neither do I. But my chest tightens.

WALKING THE STERILE corridors between labs, I find myself mapping more than just exit routes. Each researcher's movement tells a story—some hug the walls, others stride with brittle confidence. It's the same pattern I saw in new soldiers entering combat zones: fear dressed up as control.

Through the reinforced windows, a familiar dance plays out. Researchers orbit their subjects from a careful distance, like moons locked in fearful gravity. Treat everything like a threat, and it becomes one.

A blue light above one lab reads: SLEEP CYCLE INTERVENTION IN PROGRESS. Another: EMOTIVE RESPONSE TRIAL ACTIVE.

I pause as I pass. Calvin moves under blue light, precise and absorbed. Other rooms flicker with movement—people I don't recognize, all maintaining the same rigid distance. A choreography born from caution.

"You move differently," a researcher says as I pass. Dr. Wilson, according to her badge. Her aged face shows less fear than most. "Military?"

"Special ops," I confirm, noting how her subject watches our interaction with clear intelligence rather than predatory interest.

"Good. We need more people who understand real threats versus perceived ones." She glances at her subject. "Fear makes us see monsters where we should see survivors."

The words stick with me as I approach my assigned lab. The security measures are comprehensive—cameras, UV switches, emergency beacons—but they feel more like theater than necessity. Designed to make civilian researchers feel safe rather than provide actual containment.

The moment I step inside, the shift is immediate.

Quiet. Heavy.

Like walking into a room after the fight's already begun— only no one's throwing punches yet.

Eliza is standing near the center of her cage, as if she's

been waiting. Pale hands loose at her sides, head slightly tilted. Studying me.

Then, for the first time since my first day here, she speaks.

"So, you're the new one." Her voice is smooth—striking in its calm. Not the brittle edge I expected. "The one they'll let be alone with me…"

"We met earlier this week, remember? Ben Hale," I keep my tone flat. "Just started." A small knot of guilt breathes in my chest.

I should have at least spoken to her before now.

A faint smile touches her lips—small, practiced. "They usually don't tell me names anymore." Her eyes flick up. "You must be special." She takes a step closer to the bars. Her tone shifts—barely—but I catch it. "The sharp one's gone."

I frown. "Sharp one?"

"Glasses. Fast fingers. Skin like the night. Smelled like coffee and defiance." Eliza tilts her head, her voice drifting slowly. "You talked in the hallway. She called you a lab rat."

"…Jasmine?"

Eliza doesn't blink. "They always disappear the ones who ask too many questions."

I keep my face still, but my internal radar is going crazy.

"She didn't say goodbye," Eliza adds. "But she lingered outside last night. Like she knew."

The silence between us thickens. I don't know if I believe her. I don't know if I want to. I don't respond, just take in the full setup I was avoiding before: restraints bolted to the floor, steel bars, concrete floor.

And then I notice it—the way she shifts her weight, how she lets one side of her body relax while the other stays ready.

Subtle. Intentional.

I've seen that posture before. Soldiers used to hold themselves like that during long reconnaissance—alert but unreadable. It was the body language of someone who expected a threat and planned to survive it. It shouldn't feel familiar. But it does.

"You're military." She says it like a fact, not a question.

"Used to be."

She nods slowly, gaze never leaving mine. "You move like someone who knows where the exits are."

My jaw tightens. I've barely stepped into the room and she's already peeling back layers I didn't offer.

I glance again at the restraints—too much hardware for

someone this still.

"Combat teaches you to assess real threats versus perceived ones," I say calmly

Her eyes sharpen, latching onto the words. "And which am I?"

"Still figuring that out." The words come automatically, but they feel false even as I say them. There's a familiarity about her that cuts through my training, makes me question everything I thought I knew. And that's more dangerous than any physical threat she might pose.

The security camera tracks our movement, their red lights blinking like distant warning beacons. The emergency transmitter weighs heavy on my belt, its presence a constant whisper of institutional fear. But experience taught me to question assumptions. The dangerous thing in any conflict isn't always the obvious threat—sometimes it's the fear blinding us to the truth.

THREE MONTHS OF routine settles into muscle memory. The path from the elevator to Eliza's lab becomes familiar in the way old patrol routes used to feel—untrustworthy, but worn. I've stopped flinching at the UV beacons and stopped pretending the cameras aren't watching.

My body is changing. Slowly. Quietly. The limp is less pronounced. My hands don't tremble as much after a bad night. The pain is still there, but it doesn't knock me down the way it used to.

I tell myself it's the exercise, again. The discipline. But sometimes, I catch myself lifting something too easily, or reacting before my brain finishes the thought.

I haven't told Calvin. Haven't told Eden. Hell, I haven't even told myself, not really.

And Eliza… Eliza watches me like she knows.

Chapter 34

The cold metal of the double doors sends a shiver through my palm as I push them open. My eyes find Eliza immediately. She recoils from the light spilling in, her bound hands twitching as she shields her face. The movement isn't aggressive—it's protective, like a soldier shielding their eyes from a flash bang.

"Sorry," I mutter, though I'm not sure why. The door clicks shut behind me, muffling the outside world.

"You're late," she says, like it's a joke we've been telling each other for years.

I don't answer right away. The truth is, I lingered at the door longer than I should've. Like I was bracing for this. "Wasn't aware I was on your schedule," I finally say, dragging the latest trial notes to the edge of the table.

I sit, trying to locate where I'd left off in the file. The hum of the lights is louder now, their persistent buzz filling the silence.

A radio or something wouldn't kill them, would it?

I take a deep breath and lean against the table, staring at the dry text and diagrams.

"You are now." The corners of her mouth twitch upward, but it isn't a smile—it's a measurement. Her unnaturally bright eyes assess me with an intelligence that doesn't match Mathers' warnings.

She watches everything. Tracks everything. And lately, she's been watching me more than usual.

"I'm not a monster, you know." Her voice carries that complex tone I've heard from survivors—defiance masking desperation.

The low, rasping whisper pulls me from the pages. I turn, catching her piercing gaze through the curtain of dirty blond hair falling across her face. Her fingers curl tightly around the bars of the cage, but her stance walks the line between strength and fear—like she's not sure which one will win.

"I never said you were," I reply, keeping my tone neutral but not cold.

"You thought it," she says, her lips curling into a sneer. "Based on what *he's* told you."

"Calvin?" I shift, leaning against the edge of the table. "We grew up together, but I like to pass my own judgment." Years of combat taught me that official briefings often miss crucial details.

Her laugh is bitter. "According to him, I don't qualify as a person."

I tilt my head, studying her carefully.

Training your enemy to be less than human—I've seen that tactic before.

The sharp edge of her bitterness tugs at me.

How much of what Calvin says is truth, and how much is just... clinical detachment?

I cross my arms and sigh, my eyes trailing over her frail frame. "Aren't you cold in here wearing only those thin clothes?"

Her laugh this time is short and humorless. "I don't really feel temperature like that anymore."

"That's… interesting." I pause, considering. "What about physical touch? If you were cut, would it hurt?"

Her reaction is immediate—she jerks back, retreating to the farthest corner of the cage. Her hands draw to her chest like she's shielding herself from an unseen threat.

I hold my palms out. "Hey, I didn't mean—"

But she doesn't respond, her guarded posture speaking volumes. I stay where I am, leaning against the table, trying to process the strange mix of defiance and fear in her eyes.

I shake my head. "I wasn't going to make you prove it or anything. I was just curious."

"I feel pain," she whispers, her gaze flickering up to meet mine before darting away. "And touch. Even temperature changes. But not like before."

"Can you elaborate?" I stand, slipping my hands into my pockets.

Eliza's eyes narrow slightly, suspicion darkening her features, rubbing her hands together in front of her chest in a nervous rhythm. "Why do you care?" Her gaze sweeps over me, lingering in a way that feels both scrutinizing and calculated.

I shrug, pushing off the table and stepping closer to the cage. The cold bites at my skin as I run a hand along one of the vertical bars. "I guess I've always wondered what it's like to feel pain and not let it stop you. To know it's there but keep going anyway." I tap a knuckle against the bar, the solid sound reverberating between us.

"That's… a strange thing to think about." Her voice softens, but there's a note of intrigue beneath it. She looks down, her fingers still fidgeting.

I grip the bar, glancing at the top of the cage where it connects to the other edges. "Everyone has limits. I've spent most of my life testing mine. Guess I'm curious what yours are."

For a moment, she hesitates, then steps forward, her fingers curling around the bars. We lock eyes, and they flicker—interest, maybe, or an attempt at connection. The green of her eyes seems to sharpen under the light, catching me off guard.

"May I?" I motion toward her hand, surprising myself with the question. Every instinct from training says to maintain distance, but something in her wary defiance pulls at me.

Eliza pauses, then closes her eyes and turns her face away. Her movements are deliberate, her retreat designed to convey vulnerability.

But is it real? Not if what everyone is saying is true.

I reach out, letting my hand hover for a moment—giving her time to pull away. Her skin is cold—not the chill of poor circulation, but deeper, like touching marble in winter. She flinches, her shoulders tensing. But she doesn't pull away. Instead, her fingers tremble slightly against mine, like she's forgotten what gentle contact feels like.

I know that kind of recoil—when pain becomes a memory you flinch from before it lands. The gesture reminds me of calming trauma victims—careful, deliberate contact to establish trust.

"What do you feel?" I ask, watching her closely.

She swallows hard, her lips parting as though the words

are difficult to form. "Warmth. Muted… but deeper, somehow. It's strange." Her voice is quiet, almost thoughtful.

"Interesting." I let my hand linger for a moment longer before stepping back. "But you're not bothered by the cold air?"

Her eyes open slowly, locking onto mine. She shakes her head, her expression unreadable. "I didn't notice the cold until you touched me." She inhales sharply, her breath hitching as she pulls her hand away.

"I'm not in charge, but I'll see if we can get the heat up."

Eliza scoffs, the sound sharp and bitter. Turning away, she folds her arms, the chains clinking as they shift with her movement. "Your *friend* won't allow it. He's made sure I've suffered every day since I woke up in this cage."

"Calvin's not a bad guy. He's just… doing his job."

She spins back toward me, her eyes blazing with something raw and furious. "A good guy? He's the one who put me here. He turned me into this… this *thing*." Her voice cracks, and for a moment, I see genuine pain beneath the anger. "He's the monster. Not me."

I frown, the weight of her words settling uncomfortably. "You weren't like this when they brought you here?"

"No." Her chin lifts—pride stiff in her posture, even as her voice quiets. "I crossed the border thinking I'd found safety. They gave me food. A bed. Told me everything was going to be alright." She glances toward the corner of the lab, not quite looking at me. "Then I woke up in chains." A pause—just long enough to let the silence do the work. "They never asked what I'd seen. Never asked what the Turig did to my people. Just assumed I was... useful." Her voice doesn't crack the way I'd expect—but her hand tightens around the bar, knuckles pale. Tears don't fall, but her restraint speaks louder than sobbing would. "*He* doesn't call it a prison. But it feels like one." She finally looks back at me. "He's made sure I suffer a little more each day. Just to remind me what side I belong to."

A slow burn rises in my chest—anger, maybe. Or shame. But I'm not sure who it's aimed at. "They told me you were a prisoner of war," I say, quieter now. "I thought…" I trail off, the words losing weight in the space between us.

She doesn't argue. Doesn't even press the moment. Just stands there, proud and silent, like she's learned the hard way that begging for belief only makes people listen less.

I catch myself watching her hands—still wrapped around the bar, knuckles tight. The way the dying hold onto something when their world's about to fall apart.

She never cried. Didn't need to. And somehow, that makes it worse.

Training taught me that empathy was a liability. That personal attachment got people killed.

But now, looking at her—watching her fight to maintain dignity even as her world crumbles, I can't help but wonder if the people I trusted were trained to lie better than she was.

My jaw tightens as her words sink in.

How much of what I've been told is a lie?

"I'll talk to Calvin about the temperature—and maybe getting you better clothes," I say. "His wife probably has extra stuff lying around."

Eliza goes still.

Then, slowly, her head tilts—just enough to study me differently. "His wife?"

"Yeah," I reply, keeping my tone neutral. "I'm sure the pregnancy will have her decluttering soon."

A flicker crosses her face—surprise, maybe. It vanishes quickly. She doesn't respond right away. Just watches me, gaze narrowing—like she's recalibrating. Weighing the word wife against everything else she's seen in me.

"Does it hurt?" she asks, voice unreadable.

Not the question I expected. Not about the cage. Not even about Eden. I don't answer. And that seems to satisfy her more than if I had.

She steps closer to the bars—not aggressive, but deliberate. Her posture has shifted to be more careful now. Focused. "She must be… important to you."

The statement catches me off guard. "She's important to a lot of people."

"Of course," Eliza says smoothly, eyes sharp with implication. "You look at people like they matter. That's rare in places like this."

I shift, uncomfortable under the weight of her scrutiny.

"You're not like the others," she adds, voice softer now. "They all flinch when I speak. But not you. Your heartbeat doesn't spike. Your scent doesn't shift. You stay calm. Controlled."

She leans in, brushing her fingers lightly against the bars. "Almost like me."

A cold shiver works its way down my spine. I straighten, holding still. "We're not the same."

"No," she agrees. "But you're not quite like them either."

The words settle deep—uncomfortably accurate.

Eliza studies me in silence, then steps back a little, gaze unreadable again. "You didn't have to say anything about the heat," she says quietly. "Or the clothes." Her fingers tighten slightly on the bars and her expression shifts, so quickly I should have missed it. A hitch in her voice. A breath too slow to be casual. "Why?" she asks, softer now. "Why would you do that for me?" There's a rawness beneath the question.

The kind of vulnerability I've only ever seen in survivors—when the threat is gone but the world still doesn't feel safe.

The question echoes things I've heard in interrogation rooms—when basic humanity landed harder than pressure ever could. But this isn't an interrogation.

Maybe I'm just tired of watching people break and pretending I'm not one of them.

"No one should live like this." I exhale slowly. "Though I'm not sure this even counts as living."

She stares at me. "Then why are you the only one who sees it?"

I shrug, letting my hand slide from the steel as I step back. "Maybe it just takes someone who's been through hell to recognize when others are in it."

Empathy wasn't just a liability. It was the thing that got people killed. But here I am, offering her warmth like it's mine to give.

She's quiet for a long moment. "Then, you'll come back tomorrow."

I hesitate. "I'm assigned to this lab. It's not really a choice."

She glances over her shoulder, already half-turned toward the dark. "We always have a choice, Ben."

Chapter 35

The door clicks shut behind Calvin, the wood groaning under the shift in temperature. He turns, his expression taut with frustration as he steps onto the porch, the cold air curling around us both like an uninvited ghost.

His voice drops lower, a harsh whisper against the rain. "Give me a break. She was already marked by the time she made it to the base. She's manipulating you, and you're too blinded to see it! Don't be stupid, Ben!"

"It's inhumane in there, Cal. I feel the cold when I step inside, and she's in there all the time, in rags." I shake my head, barely resisting the urge to pace. "And chains? Really? That's necessary?"

"I've already explained why they are," Calvin snaps, shaking his head with a weary sigh. "See? This is exactly why I warned you before you even laid eyes on her. The shock got to you."

"Cal, I've been a soldier for years—longer than you've been in this damn contract. I know what shitty situations look like, and that cage qualifies. This isn't about shock; it's about right and wrong." I cross my arms, my voice low and steady.

Calvin's eyes narrow, his expression hardening. "Don't let her pretty face mess with your head. She's not the kind of person you want to cling to just because you're lonely."

"What the hell do her looks—or my loneliness—have to do with this?" My voice rises, frustration bubbling over. "You're deflecting because you have no real justification for what you're doing. Deep down, you *know* it's wrong to treat someone like this."

"She's not even human!" Calvin throws his hands in the air, his voice echoing through the empty yard.

"It's easier to study something if you convince yourself it's no longer a person." I argue.

"It's not even about convincing myself," Calvin says, voice tight. "I've looked at the science. The biology. The sequencing. She's not human anymore. Period."

Before I can respond, the rain picks up, drumming against the porch railing. The door creaks open behind Calvin, and Eden appears in the doorway, bathed in the dim glow from inside. She folds her robe across her growing abdomen and leans against the frame, her arms crossing in a way that's both protective and maternal.

"You boys are going to catch something nasty if you stay out here in the chill much longer," she says, her voice warm but firm.

"We'll be in soon, babe." Calvin's tone softens as he wraps an arm around her, leaning in for a kiss.

It hits before I can stop it—that ache, that stupid, persistent longing that I've buried under years of discipline. I shove it down, tightening my jaw, forcing the thoughts away before they have a chance to take root.

Eden's presence has always been like touching a bruise—both comfort and hurt wrapped into one. Despite my best effort, my gaze lingers on her rounded belly, an ache deepening in the suppressed yearning. Forcing a smile, I shove the feelings down where they belong. "Sorry, Eden. It's my fault. Do you have any donations that need taking into town? I'm heading out soon."

"You're not staying for supper?" Concern furrows her brow.

I shake my head, my fingers slipping into my pocket to find the pen cap I've taken to keeping there—still my tiny anchor for fraying nerves. "Nah, I can't. Edo needs to get out for a bit."

"Edo. You kept him?" Her face lights up, the sparkle in her eyes momentarily eclipsing the dullness of the rain.

"Of course. What, did you think I couldn't handle him or something?"

She shrugs, playful but pointed. "I just never pictured you as the type to care for another living thing. Especially not a damaged animal." Her arm wraps around Calvin, the gesture intimate and absent of malice, but the sting of her words hits

its mark.

"Yeah." I force a laugh, the ache in my chest sharpening. "Damaged things are good for more than just killing out of pity, it turns out." My eyes shift briefly to Calvin, letting the double meaning sink in.

Eden's expression falters, her hand drifting instinctively to her belly. "Benji, I… That's not what I meant."

"I know." I shrug, mustering a grin and wrinkling my nose at her in mock playfulness. "So, anything I can haul away?"

Calvin pulls her closer again in a protective embrace as she brightens. "Actually, yes! That would be great. The donation center's the opposite direction from the hospital, and I'm never in the mood to make the detour."

"I can imagine you'd avoid detours with the extra cargo you've been packing around lately," I tease lightly.

"Babe, I've said a million times I could take care of it for you," Calvin interjects.

"But I'd rather have you home at a decent hour instead of running my errands," she counters gently.

"I'd be happy to take it off your hands," I offer, glancing at Calvin, whose jaw tightens into a familiar look of restrained irritation—the spitting image of his father.

Eden hesitates briefly, her gaze flicking between us with the faintest hint of suspicion before turning back inside. "I'll grab it real quick."

The door shuts with a finality that makes my stomach tighten. Just me and Calvin again, standing in the cold.

"Damn it, Ben," Calvin mutters, shaking his head.

"It doesn't matter what she is, Cal. It matters what we are." My tone softens, but I keep my stance firm. "Besides, you're working to reverse the effects and make them human again, so why not treat them with some dignity? Will it really kill any progress if you do that?"

Calvin exhales sharply, running a hand through his damp hair. "Fine. Clothes, temperature. But the chains *stay-*"

"Cal," I protest, disbelief plain in my voice.

"For now. We'll see how her attitude changes after the first two things, and revisit later. But I'm serious about moving you to a different study area. She's getting to you, and I can't let that happen."

Calvin's concession feels hollow, like throwing scraps to ease a guilty conscience. I want to push harder about the chains, but his stance reminds me of mission briefings—when the orders had already been decided, regardless of ground reality.

"Who's getting to him?" Eden asks with a playful smile as she steps out the door, holding a garbage bag tied tightly at the top.

"Just some girl at work," Calvin says quickly, his casual tone carrying an edge that only I would recognize. Our eyes meet for a fraction of a second—a warning from him, a challenge from me. He wraps his arm around her again in the possessive way I can only dream of doing.

Eden raises an eyebrow, a knowing smirk tugging at her lips. "Oh? A girl is distracting Benji?" She covers her mouth, trying to stifle a laugh, a sparkle of knowing twinkling in her eye. "What a shocker."

"It's not like that," I reply, forcing a smile and rolling my eyes as I step forward to grab the top of the bag.

"Mhmm, it never is," she teases, tossing her red curls over her shoulder. "When do I get to meet this girl of yours, Benji?"

My stomach shifts—cold, uneasy. The thought of Eden near Eliza doesn't sit right, doesn't belong.

Eden tucks a curl behind her ear, adjusting her robe again. "So you're the one keeping all the girls away from Calvin, huh?"

Calvin snorts. "Yeah, that's it. Science has nothing to do with me stumbling in at midnight."

Eden arches a brow, giving him a sidelong look that says she's not entirely joking. Then she turns back to me, forcing a smile. "Still… must be nice. Having someone who notices when you walk in the room."

Her voice is casual, but her eyes catch on to mine—brief and unreadable, but the shift is undeniably there. Not envy exactly. It's much quieter. A glance that says she's wondering who this girl is, and why she isn't her.

"Nah, it's not really like that," I say, my tone flat but gentle. "She's… wired differently."

Calvin laughs under his breath. "That's Ben for you. Can't even flirt without making it sound like a live ordinance."

Eden's smile falters at the corners. She hugs her arms around her chest, eyes flicking toward Calvin, then back to me. "Well… whoever she is, she's lucky. Not everyone gets your attention."

The energy shifts—just enough to notice. Her voice is

casual, but her gaze lingers a beat too long.

I offer a smile, the kind that hides more than it shows. "She doesn't have it." I hoist the bag into my arms, locking eyes with her. "Not really."

"Good. Maybe that means you'll finally stop stealing all the girls out from under me." Calvin laughs, but his gaze is sharp—pretending our previous tension about Eliza disappeared.

Eden laughs too, but it doesn't match what's in her eyes. "Maybe that means we'll get more of your company, soon. It's been months…"

My hand tightens around the plastic strap of the donation bag. Just for a second. Just enough to feel the ache in my fingers. I look away before she can see whatever's written across my face. Because for one moment, I let myself wish she meant she wants me around.

Two women from different worlds—one carrying new life, the other locked in a cage. Both shaped by Calvin's choices.

Catching his look, I step back toward the porch steps. "Don't expect anything. It's nothing," I say. "We've just crossed paths a few times. It won't go anywhere."

"Well," She says it lightly, but her eyes hold me, like she's testing a theory she hasn't said out loud before, "if you *do* meet someone—or if she suddenly becomes available"—she glances briefly at Calvin—"I expect to meet her over dinner sometime. We miss you over here."

My gaze drops to her stomach, that undeniable proof of the life she's built with him.

"If it's soon, I'll be sticking to virgins, of course." She places a hand over her bump, her smile radiant and teasing.

I nod, adjusting the bag. "Yes, ma'am."

Eden playfully bumps Calvin's chest with the back of her hand. "See? He thinks I'm refined enough to be called 'ma'am.' And I told you he'd agree to dinner."

Calvin lets her kiss his cheek, his eyes never leaving me. "You were right, babe. Like always."

"And I never tire of hearing it," she says, stepping forward to hug me.

I hesitate. Then return it—light, brief. Her jasmine scent mingles with the rain. And for a moment I'm back in that hospital room when we met, rumba dancing, my fist raised, her eyes wide with fear, a secret kiss. Each memory crystallized in my chest, sharp-edged and biting.

Her embrace carries no fear—*she's either forgiven or forgotten.* I'm not sure which possibility hurts more

I step away, my smile a shield I've learned to wear as naturally as combat gear. Flipping my leather hood up, I nod. "Until next time."

"Don't let it be so long!" she says after me.

I glance back once, avoiding her gaze—because I know the look waiting for me there will break me. "Count on it. And I'll see you tomorrow, Cal."

Calvin gives me a curt nod, his arms folded as he watches me leave. His gaze is sharp, unwavering—a warning, a reminder. I hold it for a moment before turning and continuing to my car, the rain tapping rhythmically against the plastic slung over my shoulder.

"Oh, and bring Edo too!" Eden calls from the porch.

I lift a hand in acknowledgment, but I don't look back. The rain falls harder as I walk away, cold and relentless, as if nature itself is trying to wash away the weight of unspoken words and half-buried memories. Everything I want and can never have. But some things don't wash away. Some things stain.

I DON'T SLEEP that night. The weight of everything—Eden, the argument with Cal, the sound of her laughter still in my head—churns in my chest long after I left their porch. And in my fingertips, her smiling face in that field of daisies. Edges worn.

By morning, I'm back at the lab, the same chair, the same table, the same impossible puzzle laid out in front of me.

Only now, there's something else buzzing just beneath the surface—something restless.

Eliza watches me from her corner, and I know I should focus on the notes in front of me.

But the longer I sit here, the more I feel like I'm waiting for it all to break.

Chapter 36

The pen's steady rhythm against the metal table anchors me—a mechanical habit I've developed over the past few months of study, dulling the fluorescent hum that never seems to stop in this place.

It's been a few days since that conversation on Calvin's porch. Since the heat in Eliza's lab was finally turned up, and Eden's old clothes showed up folded neatly outside the cage door.

Eliza's been different since. Softer, more talkative. Maybe it's the warmth. Maybe it's the clothes. Maybe it's the way I look at her now, and the way she looks back.

"For the love of all things unholy, will you stop that?" Eliza groans, voice laced with exasperation

I pause mid-tap, looking up. She's curled into the corner of her cell, perched atop a blanket pile like it's a throne, arms crossed over her chest, bare feet resting against the bars.

"Your tapping is like a jackhammer in my skull. Have some pity on my enhanced monster hearing," she grumbles, rolling her eyes.

I smirk, lowering the pen. "You could've said something sooner."

She shrugs. "Didn't want to be *that* kind of prisoner—whining about every little thing." Then her lips curve, slow and deliberate. "Besides, watching you concentrate is kind of… adorable." She squints. "So much intensity."

She says things like that often now—soft, almost wistful, like she's reaching for something gentle in a life that's been anything but. On the surface, it feels sincere. Maybe part of it is. But there's always something in the way she watches me after—like she's testing the weight of her words, measuring my response.

I don't think she's lying. I just think she's learned how to survive.

I shake my head, hiding a smirk, and lean against the bars, pressing the cool metal into my arm. "I'm close to a breakthrough. I can feel it. Just… haven't figured out what's missing."

She exhales, arms stretching languidly above her head, spine curving in a way that draws my eyes without permission. The sleeves of Eden's old floral top slide down to her shoulders, and the hem lifts just enough to reveal a line of pale skin above her hips—taut, exposed. My gaze lingers this time.

I know I shouldn't look. I know what this moment is becoming. But I don't stop myself. There's magnetism about the way she moves—like she knows exactly where my attention is and leaves it there on purpose.

Guilt follows slower than usual, caught behind the heat curling low in my stomach. I drag my eyes back to hers, but it's already too late. She's watching me watch her.

Her voice softens, the edge of playfulness slipping into curiosity. "Is that what you need?" She tilts her head slightly, gaze holding mine. "To feel useful again?"

I slide the pen into the folder's crease, snapping it shut against the table with a solid slap. "Helping people is my purpose," I say, meeting her gaze. "What's yours?"

She leans forward, smirking. "Maybe my purpose is giving you purpose. Helping you help people."

I let out a short laugh before I can stop it. "That's ridiculous."

Her voice dips, quieter now. "I've been here two years, Benji."

The nickname hits somewhere deep—where guilt and longing twist together. It should feel wrong. But from Eliza's lips, it feels… different. Like she's reclaiming it from ghosts.

"I know," I murmur, my voice quieter. "I've been here nearly seven months, and all I know about you is that you're feisty, you come from a small war-torn village, and you can't stand repetitive sounds."

"And I'm a Noctis," she adds with a quirked brow.

"Right. Noctis. Almost forgot." I flash her a side grin.

A small smile tugs at her lips, and she stands, gripping the bars close to where I'm leaning. Her face inches nearer. "I like art. I used to make pottery and clothing for my village. And… I used to love baking."

"What kind of pottery?"

"The sensible kind." She shrugs. "Nothing fancy—just practical things for collecting water or storing grain."

"Your village didn't have plumbing?"

"It did, once. But as people left for the cities, no one stayed to maintain the pipes. The war only made it worse." Her gaze drops to the floor.

"What was your favorite thing to bake?" I lean a shoulder against the bars, crossing my arms and ankles.

"Bread," she says, her tone wistful. "Have you ever smelled fresh bread baking?"

I nod. "I have."

"It's like heaven." She sighs, her eyes fluttering closed. "I'd daydream about a man who loved to cook coming in and sweeping me off my feet." She twirls dramatically, one hand against her forehead and the other reaching skyward.

"Why a chef?" There's a spark growing brighter between us as she shares more of herself.

"Isn't that every girl's dream? To have someone make her feel special by creating something just for her?"

I chuckle. "Can't say I've ever known what any girl dreams of, but it must be true. Because, you're not the first one to tell me that."

"Well, did you ever stop to ask?" Her blond hair falls forward as she tilts her chin, fixing me with a curious gaze.

"Not much opportunity for that."

"No special lady in your life?"

I hesitate, my eyes drifting across the room. "There's one…"

"Oh," she murmurs, her voice tinged with disappointment. "She's unavailable."

Her eyes brighten, an emerald sparkle igniting in their depths. "Benji… Is it alright if I ask you a question?"

"Shoot."

"Do you ever think… if we fix this,"—she gestures to herself—"and I get back to normal, that maybe you and I could… you know?"

I raise a brow. "Do I know?"

She bites her lower lip and looks down. "Like… go out to

dinner or something."

I smile faintly. "The only thing that could stop that is you."

"What does *that* mean?" Her shoulders straighten as she grips the bars, leaning closer.

"The only way I'd miss out on dinner with you is if you didn't want me there. If you decided you didn't want to spend your freedom with some hardened soldier trying to find his purpose again."

"Benji…" Her fingers find my shoulder, light but deliberate, her touch an anchor and a temptation all at once. "You're not hardened. You're the kindest man I've ever met."

I turn away, my stomach twisting. "Not all monsters are Noctis, nor are their claws always visible." The words leave a nasty taste in my mouth.

How many times have I told myself that same truth in the mirror?

Some nights I still wake up feeling Eden's wrist in my grip, hearing her terrified gasp. The memory sits like lead in my stomach as Eliza's gentle touch draws me back to her.

"Not all those with claws are monsters, either," she counters softly, her hand pressing on my shoulder until I face her again.

Her jade eyes shimmer, holding the line between sorrow and longing. A single tear slips free, tracing a slow path down her cheek. Instinctively, I reach through the bars, brushing it away with my thumb. Her hand rests over mine, cold but steady, and a quiet intensity fills the space between us.

I should be thinking about the cameras. About Calvin's schedule. About the consequences.

But I'm not.

Her fingers skim down my arm before she pulls away, and I feel it through the fabric like a current of static. But it's more than that—it lingers too long, like my nerves are firing hotter than they should.

I've been running warmer lately. Stronger, maybe.

But it's just the workouts.

Small touches like this, insignificant on the surface, have become landmines—each one making it harder to remember why there should be distance between us.

Her gaze dips to my lips and my resolve slips. My pulse hammers.

I should turn away.

Should shut this down before it starts.
But I don't.
The weight of loneliness presses harder than logic.
For the first time in months, I don't feel broken.
I feel wanted.
Needed.
That's what makes this dangerous.
I lean in, closing the space between us. When our lips meet, it's not careful. It's raw. It's air after suffocation. It's a decision I should never have made, but I don't regret it.

The bars press cold between us, making the moment feel stolen—forbidden. Necessary.

When the kiss ends, I don't move away. My forehead presses to hers through the metal, breath mingling in the narrow space left between us.

"Sorry," I murmur, but don't move.

"Don't," she whispers, voice so soft it nearly disappears. "Don't ruin it with regret. It was—" Her eyes flick past me, her entire body tensing as she steps away.

Footsteps echo in the hallway, cutting through the haze between us. I should move away, put space between us before it's too late. But I don't. I linger for one dangerous second longer before the door swings open. Calvin steps in, stops dead.

Fuck. Here we go...

Chapter 37

"We need to talk." Calvin's voice cuts through the quiet hum of the lab, urgent but familiar. It's the same tone he used when we were kids and he cracked some impossible code in a video game. Except now, it's about real lives.

"I think I've got something." He plants both hands on the table, fingers twitching with nervous energy. His excitement crackles in the air like static before a storm.

His gaze drifts toward Eliza's cage, and she meets it with a look that's part defiance, part disinterest.

Their silent battle continues.

I expected yelling. What I got was worse—quiet calculation. Like he was gauging how far gone I already was.

I draw in a deep breath and shove my hands into the pockets of my lab coat, my fingers tightening around the pen cap in my pocket.

"Excuse me, Eliza," I say, stepping away. She doesn't reply, just inclines her head slightly. The gesture is small, almost imperceptible, but it settles in my chest heavier than it should. The door clicks shut behind me, closing the space but not the tension.

"What was going on in there?" Calvin's question comes too quickly. Pointed.

I shrug, keeping my tone neutral. "She was just telling me about her village."

Calvin frowns but doesn't push it. Instead, he turns and leads the way into one of the side labs, the overhead lights casting a sharp, sterile glow. Equipment hums low, a steady reminder of the stakes in this place.

"I warned you, Ben. Months ago. Don't get attached."

"I'm not attached," I say, following him inside. "I'm looking for holes in her story."

My jaw tightens.

I tell myself I'm not attached, but the ghost of her voice is still echoing in my head, soft and careful.

The kind of voice you don't forget.

"She's a liar, Ben. Everything she says is suspect, especially since she already lied about how she was turned. This is why we're supposed to have lab partners, to keep each other from getting sucked in."

"Which is exactly why I'm looking for holes. And I'm not the one who has a say about lab partners." I hold his stare. "Besides, I wanted her to feel less defensive. I'm in there all day—tension like that wears on you after a while."

"That's saying a lot coming from you."

I chuckle dryly. "What's that supposed to mean?"

"I *mean*, this is coming from the guy who used to solve problems with his fists." Calvin smirks, leaning back against a table, folding his arms.

I scoff. "It wasn't just fighting all the time, you know. There was more to it than that." I throw up a hand and shake my head. "But fine. I can see how you got there. Anyway, what's this thing you think you've got?"

"I need a second set of eyes. Just in case I'm missing something. Ideally I'd have gone to Jasmine with all of this but she's still radio silent."

"Lay it out for me." I fold my arms, watching as Calvin paces, hands moving like his thoughts are too fast for his body.

When he finishes, I arch an eyebrow. "So, if the virus lets go, the cells go back to normal?"

"Exactly. Through microfluidic dialysis." He spreads his hands, his expression eager. "What do you think? Does that sound real?"

"You're right. This is more of a Jasmine zone." I pause, considering. "But I guess, in theory, it makes sense. Does that kind of tech even exist?"

Calvin smirks, "Someone's gotta build them first, right?"

"Obviously, Cal. Really could use some expert, though."

He rolls his eyes but grins. "We have something close enough to make it work, if I can just get my hands on it."

"We do? On base?"

"Well, not exactly on base." He hesitates, then continues, "The hospital has what we need. It's just a standard dialysis machine, but I can modify it with software. It has to read the right sequences in the blood, but turning it into a purification machine for the Noctis virus shouldn't be too difficult." Calvin beams, scratching notes onto a stack of papers spread across the table.

"And how long will it take to reverse? Every cell is affected, right? So, we're talking several treatments," I ask, crossing my arms as I consider the logistics.

"You've got the right idea." Calvin nods. "The way the virus works is by replicating itself to infiltrate every cell. You've read this part already."

I nod again. "Right, but that means the virus will just re-infect the purified blood as soon as it's back in the body." I straighten, arms still crossed.

"Exactly. That's where the frequency of treatments comes into play. Unfortunately, the subject—"

"Eliza," I interrupt.

Calvin pauses. Not long, but long enough for me to notice. For the first time in weeks, I wonder if he actually feels the weight of what we're doing. Slowly, he nods. "Right. Eliza... She'll need multiple treatments per day to prevent reinfection."

I press my lips together and shake my head. "That's too much. Would you want to be hooked up to machines all day?"

Calvin leans back slightly, arms crossing. "It's either that or risk reinfection. The virus moves fast—quicker than anything I've seen. If we miss even a window, it will repopulate in the blood."

I rub my jaw. "So if the reversal fails..."

"If it fails and she goes feral, then we fall back on the second method we know works."

"Which is?"

"Full drain. Every drop." His voice is steady, but the weight behind the words makes my skin crawl.

"Cal, that's insane."

"Do you have a better suggestion?" Calvin props his pencil between the fingers of both hands, raising a brow.

"What about the other Noctis?" I take a deep breath. "The original batch?"

Calvin's expression tightens. "There were twenty-six. We only ever had four here, plus Eliza, recovered in the round-up."

"Only four? What happened to the rest?"

"Most didn't survive the early missions. Either they were unstable, or the field teams weren't prepared. They went out and never came back."

I frown. "So… they're dead?"

Calvin shrugs. "Hard to say. The official word is casualties, but if even one survived—"

"You think someone's keeping them?"

He meets my eyes. "Wouldn't be the first time command kept dangerous assets around. If they're not dead, someone's using them for something."

"So strategically, we have to be sure we've hit all contingencies." With a hand to my chin, I pace along the edge of the table, thinking aloud. "If we're removing the virus from the protein slot in her blood…" My finger taps against my lips as I stop, staring through the window into the hallway. My gaze fixed on the doors at the end.

The idea hits like a lightning bolt, I freeze mid-step. "What if we replace it?" My hands move instinctively, mapping out the concept in the air. "Like another protein, nutrient, or even another virus. Something harmless in large doses." The words tumble out faster as the pieces click into place, months of research morphing into something that might actually work.

"The last three vaccine trails didn't have a placeholder," Calvin mutters, almost to himself. "Maybe this is why the virus kept taking hold again after we killed it. We weren't giving the cells anything else to grab onto."

His entire face lights up, and before I can react, he smacks my shoulder. "Benji, I could kiss you."

"Hard pass, Cal." I grimace, forcing a smile, still feeling the tingle of Eliza's lips against mine. I try to match his excitement, but my stomach turns over itself.

If we're right—if this actually works—then what? I free her? Fix her? But if it doesn't work… she may not be the only thing that breaks.

"But what to use…" He paces now, his hand stroking his chin. "It would have to replicate along with the cells. Maybe an altered version of the original virus? Nah, too dangerous. Oh, a harmless on

virus the immune system already knows how to fight. I can't believe I didn't think of this sooner!"

"Probably because it seemed too simple," I suggest with a smirk.

Calvin wraps an arm around my shoulders, leaning on the table with his free hand. "Simple? Far from it. But you're right—I overlooked it because it didn't seem complex enough. Okay, let's do this." He lets go and grabs a notebook and pen. "I'm going to need these items. Can you take this list to Kerry and have her track everything down? You know how she works her magic."

Each component Calvin lists on the paper represents another thread of hope—or another way this could all go wrong. I study his hurried scrawl, knowing Eliza's humanity hangs on every hastily written letter.

He hands it to me and I look down at it, the scribbles blurring together. Each component one that might save her—or damn her.

"You really think the others are gone?" I ask quietly.

Calvin doesn't look up. "If they're not, someone's using them for something."

"Secret weapons?"

"You've seen what they're capable of." He pauses. "Would you throw that away if you didn't have to?"

I don't answer. Because I already know the truth. I glance at it and arch a brow. "Is this all of it?"

"Kerry will know how to get it."

"Alright. Just don't make me read it out loud to her."

Calvin chuckles as he pulls up a stool and dives back into his notebook, scribbling furiously. "Don't worry, I already know you can't read."

"At least I'm not a nerd," I retort with a grin, heading for the door.

Laughter echoes behind me as I leave Calvin to his frantic scrawling.

Chapter 38

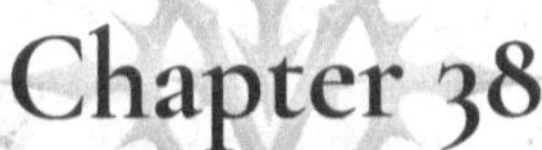

Saturday mornings have become a ritual—run until my lungs burn, let Edo chase shadows through the trees, pretend the world makes sense for just a little while.

By the time we reach the apartment, the sun's already high. Sweat clings to my skin, heartbeat not as heavy from the run as it should be.

Edo slows as we near the stairs, his ears twitching, posture stiffening like he's caught the edge of something I haven't yet. Not fear. Not quite. Just… focus. He shakes off beside me, and I yank out my earbuds.

Sirens?

Not one or two.

A lot.

Close.

I glance up, scanning the horizon. The faint chop of rotors echoes in the distance—military birds, judging by the formation.

Something's wrong.

I take the stairs two at a time, Edo panting at my heels. My pulse thrums in my ears, drowning out everything but the sharp trill of my landline. Edo's tail wags against my leg as I fumble with the key, breath coming in staggered bursts. The ringing dies the moment the lock turns.

I barely register filling Edo's water bowl, my body operating on autopilot, each movement mechanical. But the silence isn't relief—it's suffocating.

It starts again, the phone's shrill demand cutting through the fog in my head. I grip it tight. "Hale," I say, voice clipped, automatic, falling into place like old armor.

"Ben?" Eden's broken voice wrenches through the line, sharp and panicked. Static crackles beneath it, alarms screaming in the background.

Her trembling my name cuts through me like a blade. "Eden?"

"Ben—thank God—I can't reach Cal." Her voice splinters, panic breaking through.

"He's probably in the lab," I say, already moving, already grabbing for my keys. "What's wrong?"

"I—I don't know—it..." She breaks off, her whimpered breathing filling the line. "I can't—"

My gut clenches as I piece together her mumbling.

Can't get the bleeding to stop?

The thought hits something primal. "Eden, slow down. I can't und—"

"Benji..." The way she says my name—it's raw, stripped down, nothing but fear. It coils deep in my chest, tightening like a vice.

"Stay put—I'm coming." The phone's already hitting the table as I grab my keys, my hands shaking despite my body running on muscle memory.

Three military helicopters drown out the news radio, flying in tight formation toward the base. Red and blue emergency lights multiply in my rearview as I near the facility, their silent warnings painting the road in alternating colors. I lean forward, tracking their path toward town as I press the accelerator harder.

The car fishtails when I hit their gravel driveway, tires spitting stones as I correct and barrel toward their tudor house nestled in the forest clearing. The afternoon sun blinds me through the gap between visor and roof.

I leave the engine running, keys jangling as I burst through their front door. "Eden?"

The living room looks normal until my eyes find her in the kitchen. One hand braces her back while the other grips the tile counter, knuckles bone-white against the granite. The scent of iron slams into me first. Then my eyes find the blood.

"Benji..." She whimpers my name, her body folding in on itself. A deep and dormant instinct rears up inside me—the same drive that kept me breathing in warzones, the same fire that never let me stand still.

As I navigate the furniture, the full scene reveals itself. Crimson stains bloom at the base of her nightgown, streaking down her legs to pool on the kitchen floor. The sight sends my tactical mind into overdrive—assessing blood loss, calculating time windows, mapping the fastest route to help.

"What the hell?" My breath catches as I reach her side, my palm meeting her outstretched hand. Her skin is cold and clammy against mine. "What happened?"

"I don't know." Tears stream freely down her face, cutting clean paths through her pallor. "I wasn't feeling well so I—" She breaks off, forcing a deep breath as she leans heavily on the counter. Her other hand cradles her swollen belly protectively.

I rub circles on her upper back, fighting to keep my voice steady despite the fear clawing at my throat. "Come on, we need to go."

"Give me a second." A suppressed groan escapes her lips, her fingers digging into the counter's edge.

We make it five agonizing steps before she has to pause again. My patience frays watching her struggle. I grit my teeth, fighting the urge to scoop her up now, to move faster, to do more. But she's already pushing past her limits. I slip my arm around her back, dragging a chair closer for support.

"Did you find Cal?" she pants as we start moving again, each word seeming to cost her more effort.

Instead of answering, I bend down and scoop her into my arms. Old wounds protest the movement, but adrenaline dulls the pain.

"No! Ow—Ben! Put me down!" She writhes against me, but I hold firm.

"Sorry, love, you're moving too slow." The endearment slips out the way it always does when I don't stop it, an echo from a different life. "We need to get you to the hospital."

"It hurts." She grabs my gray workout shirt with blood-slicked fingers, leaving crimson prints that burn like brands against my skin.

"I know, hon. We're almost there." I grit my teeth against each jarring step, the strain reopening old wounds. At the car, she braces against the doorframe as I ease her in, trying to be gentle despite the urgency hammering through my veins.

The Impala's backseat was never meant for this, the cracked vinyl now stained with blood and prayers. But it's the only ride I trust to carry us through the dark

"Grab a blanket," she gasps.

"No time." I slam her door and jump behind the wheel, already calculating the fastest route through afternoon traffic.

"Benji—" She moans as I peel out of the driveway, gravel spraying behind us. "Your upholstery." She gasps, her fingers clawing weakly at the seat. "I'll ruin it."

I bark a laugh, sharp and bitter. "Priorities, love."

It would be almost funny if it weren't so achingly Eden.

"Why the hell didn't you call an ambulance?" My heart pounds erratically against my ribs as unfamiliar panic claws at me. I force slow breaths, struggling to maintain focus.

I've never lost my composure in a crisis before.

The fact that I'm losing it now terrifies me more than anything.

"I tried! Lines were busy."

"Did you call the hospital directly?"

"I'm not stupid, Ben!"

"I know!" I grab my car phone, dialing from memory. Through the static, I catch fragments of coded alerts and unfamiliar voices barking orders in the background of news radio broadcasts. After three failed attempts—emergency, trauma, and finally radiology.

"I've tried emergency and trauma with no answer," I snap. "I have a woman bleeding in my car. We're coming in."

"Sir, is she still conscious?"

"Yes."

"Was she involved in the base accident?"

"Base accident? What? No—" Eden's panicked questions about Cal derail me. Through the static, I catch broken bits about compromised systems and federal response teams. "Just tell someone we're coming."

"Sir, please be patient. They're handling another crisis—"

My blood boils. "We're five minutes out.—Eden, how long has this been happening?"

"Since... this morning." In the rearview mirror, her face has gone ghostly pale, sweat beading on her forehead despite the car's blasting AC.

Christ...

I allow a moment of internal prayer. "One second." I reach blindly, my hand finding hers in the dark. Ice cold. Trembling. It makes my stomach drop. "Hey, look at me. Almost there. Keep your eyes open. Keep breathing." My own hand shakes as I return to the phone, knuckles white on the steering wheel.

"She's been in labor since morning. Don't know when the bleeding started. I see the hospital. Hanging up."

Through the windshield, emergency vehicles crowd the hospital entrance, their lights painting the building's facade in alternating red and blue. Personnel in tactical gear direct traffic with urgent gestures. I focus on the road and my breathing, fighting the tremors in my hands while watching her in the mirror. Pain spreads through my chest as my breaths grow shallow.

What the hell is wrong with me?

I drive over a curb and weave through the parking lot, skidding to a stop at the emergency entrance. I throw the car in park and wrench her door open, climbing in to take her hands. Her head lolls toward me, eyes struggling to focus. The fluorescent lights cast harsh shadows across her face, transforming her skin ghostly.

"Eden, we're here. I need your help so I don't hurt you. Can you scoot toward me?"

She leans forward with a groan that sounds torn from somewhere deep inside, her bloody hand leaving more crimson prints on my shirt as she clutches for support. The metallic smell fills my nostrils, triggering memories I've spent years trying to bury.

Staff members converge on us, their voices overlapping with clipped medical terminology I can't quite follow. Through the chaos, I catch fragments of their hurried exchanges—something about systems being down, backup generators, security protocols.

A staff member pushes through, supporting her other side. They ease her into a wheelchair, and she pulls me along as they move. "I'm sorry," she gasps through tears and gritted teeth as they wheel her through the emergency doors, each word punctuated by ragged breaths. Her grip tightens like she's holding onto something more than just my arm. "Benji… about pulling away… you have to know, Benji. In case I don't—"

The words sink into me like acid. My feet stumble to a stop, her hand slipping from my shirt. The sound of their running footsteps behind me seems to come from far away.

"Ben!" His voice shatters through the numb static in my head. Cal. A car door slams, the sound echoing off the ambulance bay walls. Through my tunneling vision, I watch him rush past, his lab coat streaked with what looks like soot. He hesitates for just a fraction of a second—long enough for a silent understanding to pass between us—before scrambling to Eden's side where I just stood.

I stare at the closing doors, lungs refusing to work and blood drains from my head.

She called me, not him.

The lights suddenly seem too bright, too harsh. My tactical training screams at me to stay alert, but my body disconnects, floating.

And I don't know if that meant anything...

Looking down, I see her blood smeared across my shirt, the marks looking disturbingly like the blast patterns I used to analyze in the field.

Or if it just hurts because I'll never get the chance to ask.

"Sir?" The voice seems to come from underwater.

All I could do was watch her bleed...

I turn slowly, my neck muscles fighting the movement. The officer's face swims into focus—female, mid-forties, the kind of eyes that have seen enough to know when something's wrong.

"Are you the husband?"

I used to think war was the worst thing that could happen to a man.

"No, I..." The words catch.

Turns out, it's love.

"I'm just… a friend." But it tastes like a lie.

The kind that doesn't belong to you. The kind that never will.

"Are you the driver?" Her hand rests on her hip as she motions to my car with authority.

I nod slowly, eyes drawn back to the doors that separate me from both Eden and Cal. The weight of unspoken feelings pressing against my ribs with each breath.

The words I never said, the ones I never could, hang heavy in my chest, suffocating.

"Sir? Are you okay?"

I told myself I could handle it. That I'd keep my distance. That it was better this way.

"Sorry." The word slurs. I force a deep breath, but it rattles in my chest.

"I followed your erratic driving. Need some information. You look to be in shock. Let's sit and I'll ask some questions."

But some lines don't blur—they snap.

"Yeah." The word slurs past numb lips as I start toward the waiting area.

And I think something just broke.

Pain lances through my leg, my body automatically shifting to compensate. Old wounds, old habits. Each step takes me further—from Eden, from Cal, from the life I could have had.

And deeper into the one I can't escape.

Chapter 39

A strange numbness creeps over my limbs as I limp into the lab, my muscles buzzing with exhaustion and a sharpness I can't name.

My shirt clings to my chest, stiff with dry blood—Eden's blood. My hair sticks to my damp skin, the weight of the day pressing down on me like a lead vest.

The overhead lights hum too loudly, pulsing in time with the erratic rhythm in my chest.

"Benji?" Eliza's voice slices through the haze, pulling me back just enough to register the concern in her tone. "What happened?" When I turn, her eyes widen at the sight. "Is that blood? Are you hurt?"

I shake my head, it's all I can do as my legs carry me to the sink on autopilot—each movement driving fresh spikes of pain from ankle to spine. The motion sensor triggers the faucet—water rushing over my trembling hands. I watch, transfixed, as crimson swirls into pink, then clear—like watching Eden's life force disappear down the drain. The metallic scent of blood mingles with antiseptic, turning my stomach. Eliza's voice fades to white noise beneath the roar of water and memory.

A gasp escapes—I hadn't realized I wasn't breathing. The man in the steel backsplash isn't me. Eyes wide and haunted—lost somewhere between grief and madness.

Still seeing red, I scrub up to my elbows, sweat trickling down my spine. Heat floods me in a suffocating wave.

My throat constricts.

She's sorry?

My eyes burn as the words echo.
She can't die...
The whimper that escapes is broken. I force air into lungs that resist. Each stuttered breath sending daggers through my ribs.

I can't lose her all over again...
The thoughts crash over me, a tidal wave pulling me under before I can take a breath.

Black spots dance at the edges of my vision. My foot catches the stool. My hands—hands that have steadied weapons, saved lives—won't stop shaking. One glance at my blood-stained chest strips the moisture from my mouth as the room tilts sideways.

Stop it! This isn't me!
With a snarl, I tear off the shirt and wad it into a ball. The biohazard bin slams shut over it with a crash, echoing my heartbeat. I press my forehead to the cool metal, trying to leach the fever from my skin.

"Ben!" Eliza's voice cuts through.

"What?" I snap.

"Fuck, finally. What happened? Was this from the attack?" She clings to the bars, staring at me.

"What? Attack? No, I—" I cross to her cage, each step easing the vice on my chest. My hands grip the bars like they're the only solid thing left. "Eden… It was bad. And I—I couldn't move."

"Is that her blood?" Her cold fingers sprawl across my chest, leaving goosebumps in their wake. There's something predatory in her touch.

"I never hesitate. Never." My eyes meet hers, searching for comfort I know I don't deserve. "But tonight..."

"Is she… okay?"

"We made it to the hospital. But I don't know, I—I had to leave, I couldn't..." My voice fractures. Eden's first smile at me—a lifetime ago—flashes. The memory sends an icy shiver down my spine.

"Shh..." Eliza's finger presses against my lips. "You did what you could."

"It wasn't enough."

She studies me, quiet for a breath. "You carry it deeply. Like a scar no one can see."

I work my jaw.

"Deeper than either of them know."

I stare at the floor and take a breath. "I don't want to talk about this."

She cups my cheek. "But it's important to you." Her eyes capture mine, impossibly deep.

"Well, I have something more important now." I trace her arm, needing something solid.

"You don't need to be at the hospital? I don't want to just be a distraction…"

"I'm where I want to be." I brush my thumb across her lower lip. Her eyes drop to my lips, her own parting slightly. A tremor runs through her before she presses against the bars.

"You don't have to lie to me," she whispers. "But I won't stop you if it helps."

When our lips meet, electricity drowns everything else. My hand finds her lower back, pulling her against the metal barrier forcing us apart. "Damn this fucking thing."

"You could"—she maintains her hypnotic eye contact—"let me out..." The words come out barely above a whisper.

"I could also get fired and never see you again."

"Nobody has to know." Longing pours from her gaze.

"You'd go back in after?"

"If it means staying close to you every day, I'll stay here forever." Her voice falters, softer now—dangerously close to desperate.

"Calvin thinks we've got it right this time… the purification." The words sit hollow, wrong. "If it works, we won't have to pretend."

"*If* it works. But the risk—"

"Previous attempts killed the others."

"Yes." She pulls back. "How do we slow it down? This life… isn't so bad."

"Six-foot cage? That's not living." I rub small circles on her back through the bars.

"I meant… being a Noctis. Hunger's the worst part. I've adapted." Her full lips curve into a smile that doesn't meet her eyes.

"So, you'd rather wait?"

"Better than risk dying. If I weren't the only one to test—"

"I won't let you get hurt."

"I just want us to be together." Her voice drops. "Physically. If…" She bites her lip, glancing at the freezer.

"What?" I swallow hard and glance over my shoulder.

"Nothing."

"No—tell me." Her gaze lingers on the freezer. I follow it, already taking a step when she grasps my arms.

"Ben… don't."

"What's in there?" I pull away and open it. Vials shimmer in the cold. I pick one up. Noctis XII-V.

She watches me, on her toes to get a better look. "Too risky. I didn't mean… I saw you limping. I hate seeing you in pain. We will just wait."

"You just said it's not so bad."

"They'll lock you up, same as me." Her teeth worry at her lower lip.

"At least we'd be together." I laugh. Her expression empties. "I'm kidding."

"Cal's my best friend. He'd protect me."

I close the freezer and drag a stool from the table, sinking onto it next to the cage. I stare at the vial still in my hand—impossibly heavy for what it is. "I could though."

"But—"

"You brought it up."

"I didn't, I just… If it could erase the pain." She doesn't take her eyes off me.

"The serum could—"

"Or not."

"Most days aren't so bad." I shrug. "But others…"

"My Benji," she cups my face. "You shouldn't have to live like that."

My eyes drift to the vial, the thawing liquid inside shifting under the harsh glow of the fluorescents. My breaths come slow and measured as I trace the letters on the label.

Her restless movements dance at the edge of my vision. "Ben?"

"I'm thinking." The words come out distant, detached.

"Well, stop. It's too dangerous."

"For who?"

"You, obviously!" She practically spits the words.

"I'm a soldier, I'll be fine. I've got the battle scars to prove it."

"*Were* a soldier…" her words cut deeper than I realized they could.

"You're right." I push away from the cage, masking my limp with clenched teeth and white-knuckled fingers around the icy vial. I open the door to the freezer and stare at the cold glass in my hand. The door shuts with finality and I close the distance between us.

Eliza exhales, her shoulders sagging, forehead resting against the bars—her eyes anything but relieved.

"What's wrong?"

"I just can't wait to get a real taste of you."

I let go of the vial hidden in my pocket and wrap an arm around her through the bars.

"I'll make Cal believe I'm serious." My chest constricts and I clear my throat.

Her eyes snap open as she straightens. "Benji—"

"If he thinks I'll do it, he'll speed up the cure while still making sure it's safe. And when I get you out of here…" I trace my thumb over her lower lip, watching her shiver. "I'll make good on that promise."

Chapter 40

The clock reads 3:47 AM, the red digits searing into my vision like a brand. Exhaustion weighs on me, pulling at my limbs, my jaw aching from the force of a yawn I barely register. The hospital looms in my thoughts, pressing against my ribs, an unrelenting weight growing heavier by the second.

I pull Eliza close one last time, pressing my lips to hers through the cold metal bars that separate us. Her fingers trail along my skin, leaving paths of electricity in their wake. Her eyes glaze over as she lets out a soft sigh that sounds almost like victory.

I lean in, resting my chin on her shoulder, my whisper barely audible: "It'll be over soon." The words twist in my gut like a knife, as if they know something I don't. Or maybe it's just thoughts of Cal and Eden, and whatever awaits me at that sterile nightmare of a hospital.

"I'll hold you to that," she murmurs, running her fingers through my hair. Each touch is a reminder of who I'm leaving behind—and what I'm betraying if I stay.

At the door, I look back at her. Desire and avoidance of facing reality claw at me, begging me to throw open her cage. Instead, I exhale, cringing at the familiar stab of pain from my old injuries, and unlock the lab door.

The hallway lights assault my eyes, leaving spots dancing in my vision like tiny accusations. I blink hard, forcing myself to focus as I continue down the corridor. The vial twists deeper into my pocket and my heartbeat echoes in my ears with each step—traitor, traitor, traitor.

The chaos of the hospital fades into the silence of my apartment before I fully register the shift. I brace one arm against the shower wall, scalding water sluicing down my back, doing nothing for the cold lodged in my chest.

Eden's groans echo in my skull. Blood soaking through my shirt. Her blood.

I look down, half-expecting it to still be there—crimson swirling down the drain.

"Get a grip, Hale," I mutter, snapping the water off hard enough to rattle the dial.

Later, dressed but hollow, I sit at the table, Edo's head on my knee.

"Sorry I was gone so long, buddy." I scratch behind his ears, letting the texture of his fur drag me back to the present.

I eat because I should. Taste doesn't factor in.

Outside, the Impala waits, rain-streaked and still loyal. The cold pre-dawn air bites against my skin, but I barely feel it.

"Should I bring a gift? A condolences card?" I shake my head. "What the hell do you give someone who almost died?"

Edo sniffs a bakery window like it holds answers.

"Yeah," I say. "Maybe just breakfast."

After a detour for pastries and dropping Edo with my neighbor, Hector, I find myself paralyzed in the hospital parking lot. The building looms before me—a bland off-white monstrosity with black windows arranged in perfect, soulless rows above the emergency room doors. It looks exactly like it did yesterday when I brought Eden in, yet somehow more menacing in the growing light.

Eden's voice echoes in my head: "I'm sorry." Those glass-clear eyes that could drown me in the desert haunt me still. Nausea rises in my throat as I grab the bag from the passenger seat and force myself out of the car.

The nurses direct me to her room, but my feet turn to lead in the hallway. Sweat slicks my palms as I grip the bag tighter, teeth worrying at the inside of my cheek until I taste copper.

Suck it up.

I close my eyes, drawing a deep breath. Each step drags, like walking through quicksand.

My knuckles brush against the doorframe, a weak knock

that betrays the turmoil under my skin. "Everyone decent?" I push the door open before anyone answers, locking onto Cal's hollowed-out expression from where he sits by the window.

The sight of my best friend sends a fresh wave of guilt through me—he looks like he's aged years in hours.

His smile unfolds slowly but genuinely as he recognizes me, rising from his chair with the stiffness of someone who hasn't seen sleep in days.

"Wow, you look like hell," I say, edging further into the room. "Good thing I came bearing gifts." I hold up the bag, carefully avoiding Eden's bed, afraid of what memories might surface if I look directly at her. The familiar smells are present, plus a new kind of sweetness—baby powder maybe.

"You're a lifesaver," Cal says, accepting the bag with grateful hands. The phrase hits like a punch to the gut.

"Brought clothes too," I mutter, setting the duffle down, wincing at the motion. "Didn't think you'd get away for a shower."

"Seriously, Ben." Cal wraps me in an embrace that nearly breaks my composure. "I owe you."

"It's nothing," I shrug, trying to ignore the pain pulsing through me. "How's Eden?"

"Good. Sleeping," Cal says, glancing over his shoulder at Eden's still form. The morning light softens her features, making her look younger, more vulnerable.

"And the baby?" I force the word past the knot in my throat.

Cal's face transforms, joy radiating from him as he crosses to the other side of her bed. He reaches into a clear bassinet and lifts a bundle of blankets with the reverence of someone handling precious cargo. "Uncle Ben, meet your godson, Ezra Bailey."

My pulse falters. "Godson?"

"Eden and I have been talking about it for a while. You getting them here... that sealed it. He'd be in the best hands if anything happened to us." Cal's eyes meet mine, full of trust I know I don't deserve. The weight of it nearly crushes me.

"Good thing nothing's going to happen to you then," I say, arching an eyebrow. "I know jack about kids." The shaky exhale betrays me before I break our gaze to peek at the tiny pink face nestled in cotton. A quiet shift takes root—an ache I didn't know existed until now, a longing for something I never knew I wanted.

"He's perfect, Cal. Congratulations." I press my lips together to stop them from trembling.

"Here." He moves to pass him over.

"Whoa, what? Now? Already?" My spine straightens like I've been tased, combat instincts screaming about vulnerability.

Calvin's laugh fills the room, chasing away some of the sterile hospital atmosphere. "Not scared of a death war machine but can't handle a sleeping baby?"

"To be fair, weapons of mass destruction don't have minds of their own."

And they don't trust you with their lives.

"Don't be a wuss. He doesn't bite. Just hold your arms like this." Before I can protest further, the warm bundle slides into my arms. Heat seeps through my skin straight to my core, melting a frozen void inside me. The weight of him is nothing compared to the responsibility he represents.

Looking down at him, a wave of peace washes over me, drawing an unbidden smile to my lips. "What's up, little man?" I murmur. Right on cue, he sneezes, startling himself. I glance at Cal's grinning face, panic rising. "What do I do?"

"He's human, Ben. He sneezed. Just keep holding him. Sit if you want. I'm going to wash up and destroy these croissants." He rubs his hands together in anticipation, the gesture so familiar it hurts.

I eye the chairs and approach them with the caution of someone carrying nitroglycerin, easing down while gritting my teeth against the pain that resurfaced. "I'm gonna be that fun uncle," I tell him, voice softening. "The one who knows all about being cool and how to win over that special someone." His newborn scent fills my lungs, making everything easier, pushing back the darkness that's been growing. "You'll never know the kind of pain I've seen. Not if I can help it."

"That's some big talk coming from a bachelor." Eden's whisper cuts through the quiet like a blade, whipping my gaze up to her. The motion sends fresh pain through my side.

"Eden." I start to rise, but she stops me.

"Don't get up. I'm fine." She rests against her pillows, hands clasped in front of her. The morning light catches her hair, turning it to flame.

I settle back, stealing a glance at her face. "I'm glad you're both—"

"Because of you," she interrupts, voice rough from sleep… or emotion. "The doctor said if it were just a few minutes more…"

Her words knock the breath from my lungs, sending me reeling back to that moment—the blood, the crying, the crushing helplessness. Cold sweat breaks out across my skin as the room tilts.

Stay in control. Don't shake. Keep it together.

The vial in my pocket seems to pulse.

"Benji?" Her voice is softer now. The nickname warmer from her than it ever was from Eliza.

"Yeah?"

"Thank you."

I shake my head quickly. *I can't carry that too.* "Don't mention it."

Cal returns from the bathroom, attacking the bag of pastries with the enthusiasm of a starving man. He moans around a massive bite, rolling his eyes dramatically before offering the bag to Eden. She grimaces slightly, shaking her head.

"Did they tell you what happened?" My voice comes out rough, as if demanding an explanation might make it easier to process.

"Placental abruption," Cal says through his mouthful, ever the scientist even now.

I purse my lips, glancing at Eden. The clinical term seems inadequate for what we went through.

"I started bleeding out, which nearly suffocated Ezra. That triggered labor." She squeezes Calvin's hand, the gesture so natural it makes me ache. "We're lucky."

"I'd hardly call that luck." I swallow hard, looking down at the baby as he stretches his neck, making tiny sucking motions. His complete trust in my arms feels like redemption I don't deserve.

"My turn," Eden says, lifting her bed slightly and holding out her arms, maternal instinct overriding everything else.

Masking my pain, I stand and place Ezra on the nursing pillow situated around her before retreating to my chair, gripping the armrests as I lower myself down. Every movement reminds me that something inside me is still broken.

"It was luck," she continues, adjusting her gown with practiced motions, "because not everyone comes out of this with their baby outside the NICU… or even alive." As she exposes herself to nurse, I find sudden fascination with the ceiling tiles, heat crawling up my neck. Eden's soft laugh at my discomfort makes my cheeks burn hotter, and Cal busies himself with the duffle bag.

"Take my badge and use the resident locker rooms, babe," she tells him. "The showers are nicer."

"I'm not leaving you," he snaps, protective instincts flaring.

I catch Eden rolling her eyes as she gestures to the nursing baby. "I'm not going anywhere. There are nurses everywhere. Besides," she nods toward me, and I pretend to be fascinated by my thumbs, "Ben's here if anything happens."

I meet Cal's worried gaze and shrug, trying to project casualness I don't feel. "Not busy. And you really do look like shit."

He sighs, standing with the duffle bag, and kisses Eden's forehead with such tenderness it makes me look away. "I'll be quick." Turning to me: "Find me if anything happens."

"Of course." The promise is dry.

After he leaves, I lean back, carefully avoiding Eden's direction while she nurses. The steady tick of the wall clock marks time like the countdown to a final battle I can't name.

"How are you feeling?" she asks, ever the caregiver even now.

I lean forward, studying the floor patterns like they hold answers. "After hearing what you went through, I'm hardly the one to worry about." My knee bounces as I tent my fingers between them.

"Benji." Her nurse voice comes out in full force, the one that brooks no argument.

I meet her eyes, shaking my head. "I'm fine, Eden. Really."

"I saw you limping. You can't lie to me."

Swallowing hard, I shift in my seat. "That? Just sore from working out."

"I guess you can lie… But don't. We're closer than that. What's your pain level?"

I scratch behind my ear, looking anywhere but at her. "Not like I just went through childbirth or anything."

Her silence draws my gaze back to meet her glare, as effective as any interrogation technique.

"Fine." I work my jaw. "Solid seven." I gesture vaguely

with my hands.

"A seven?"

"But only when I move too much, like sitting or standing. Or if I think about it."

"Ben!"

"I've tried everything. There's no magic fix, Eden." I slump back, fingers tented over my chest. The vial in my jacket pocket burns against my skin, mocking my lie. *Technically there could be...*

"You can stop pretending you're fine. We care about you. Let us help—"

"I'll handle it. Don't worry." Like I handle everything— badly, and with collateral damage.

"I do worry. I've seen how lonely you get. And your pain.. ." She adjusts her gown. "Will you help me turn him? I can't upset my stitches."

My knee bounces faster before I stand and walk to her. "Yesterday… when you said you were sorry. What did you mean?"

Her lips pinch together as she looks away, the question clearly hitting a nerve. "I never meant to hurt you."

"I'm not. I just..." I step back after turning the baby. *Tell her, Ben.*

"I need clarity." I cross my arms and shift my weight.

Her shoulders drop, eyes fixed on Ezra as if he can protect her from this conversation. "That night… of the attack." She swallows hard, the sound audible in the quiet room. "I'm sorry I let my fear destroy what we could have—"

"It's okay, Eden."

Say it.

"Benji, I care about you… I should've told you sooner." Wet eyes meet mine, full of regret.

Say it. Give her the damn truth.

"Really, love. I'm… moving past it." I smile, rubbing my neck, the lie sitting heavy on my tongue. "Even if I weren't… you have Calvin. He's better for you than I could've been."

"Ben…" Her voice cracks, head tilting in that way that undoes me.

I lick my lips and glance around, forcing a smile to mask the agony. The promise the vial offers weighs heavier with each passing second.

"I—" I take a deep breath, grasping at a shift to stop myself from saying I still love her out loud. "I met someone."

"Oh?" Her smile holds sadness as she watches me carefully. "Give me all the details."

"Well," I exhale sharply, "How much time you got?"

Eden raises an eyebrow, a smirk tugging at her lips. "Really?"

I force a laugh, settling onto the edge of her bed, the weight of my secrets crushing down and threatening to pull me under as I prepare to tell her about Eliza. The thing about drowning? I've always been good at it.

Chapter 41

The lab hums with artificial life. The cold fluorescence of overhead lights buzzes faintly, flickering against sterile white walls. The machines purr, monitors flashing in rhythmic pulses. The air is sharp against my tongue, but the cold doesn't seep in—not with the heat coiling in my chest.

I shouldn't be here. But I couldn't stay at the hospital. Watching the life I'll never have—Cal's family, Eden's smile—settle around them as if I had any right to want it for myself.

I needed to breathe. So I ended up here. Back where I never should have gone. Back where I always end up.

The soft scrape of bare feet on concrete drags my attention forward. Eliza.

She watches me, leaning against the bars, her jade eyes gleaming under the sickly glow of fluorescents. She doesn't speak at first—just tilts her head slightly, arms folded, lips curling in amusement.

The silence stretches, taut as a wire. Then—"You came back."

I exhale sharply, my fingers curling into fists. "You keep saying that."

She steps forward, pressing her fingers against the bars, the metal cold against her skin. "Because you keep coming back."

I shake my head. "I don't want to talk."

A small smile curves her lips. "Then don't."

I don't move. I should. But I don't. Because she's right, and talking isn't why I'm here.

I don't want to think. Don't want to see Eden's eyes as she bled into my arms. Or remember Cal's voice saying we owe you, like I'm some kind of fucking hero.

My pulse hammers.

Eliza watches the movement like she always does. She leans forward, lips parting slightly. "You're still thinking about her."

My jaw locks. "I'm—"

"She hesitates with you." The words slice through me. Eliza's gaze sharpens, catching the darkness behind my eyes. "I won't."

I exhale through my nose. "That's not—"

"You hold yourself back." Her fingers drift through the bars, ghosting over my hands, the cool press of her touch seeping through my skin. "Every second of every day," she whispers. "And for what?"

I should pull away. But I don't.

She's not fragile. She doesn't flinch.

Eliza tilts her head, watching the thought form. Then—"I'm not her."

And I break. I don't know who moves first. Maybe I do. Maybe she does. It doesn't matter.

Because suddenly, my mouth is on hers, and her laugh is swallowed between my lips, dark and satisfied and triumphant.

I pull her against the steel, but she doesn't flinch. She drags me closer, nails scraping along the back of my neck, sending fire racing down my spine.

The bars cut into my arms, the cold metal burning against overheated skin. There's no hesitation. No second-guessing. No guilt. Just heat. Just hands and lips and the realization that I don't have to be careful.

She bites my bottom lip, testing me. I growl low in my throat, lifting her, pressing her harder into the bars.

She laughs against my mouth. "You feel it, don't you?" she whispers. "The strength? The hunger?"

My breath stutters.

Her teeth skim my pulse, just barely scraping. "You're already changing," she whispers. "Why fight it?"

My fingers tighten against her waist.

She moans at the pressure, tilting her head back. "Set me free."

I freeze, my body locked between instinct and control.

For a moment, I can't think. Because I want to.

The realization slams into me like a bullet.

I want to let her out.

She sees it. She knows. Eliza presses her lips to my jaw, breath hot, voice barely above a whisper. "Benji... let me out."

I reach for the keys. My hand hesitates. But not enough. I unlock the cage.

The moment the lock clicks, Eliza smiles—slow, dark, knowing. She steps forward, pressing her body against mine, fingers curling in my shirt. And then there's no space left between us.

The next thing I know, we're against the lab table. Her fingers dig into my back, her breath hot against my skin.

I don't stop thinking about how easy this is. How there's no fear in her grip, no hesitation in her touch. I don't stop thinking about how Eden never looked at me like this. Like she wanted this as badly as I did.

Maybe that's what draws me in—that hunger.

Not just for me, but for control.

Because here, in this moment, I don't have to hold back.

I don't have to ask for permission.

Eliza feels my distraction. She fists my hair, yanking my head back just enough to meet my gaze, her smile curving, fangs flashing. "Stay with me, Benji."

My resolve wavers. But there's a comfort in her chaos—a pull I can't explain.

No fear. No flinching. Just surrender. It gives the illusion like I'm in control again, even if I know I'm not.

But it's too late. I'm already too far gone.

ELIZA'S BREATH IS warm against my skin. Her fingers trace lazy patterns over my scars, a stark contrast to the fire still burning in my veins. I stare at the ceiling, my chest rising and falling in slow, uneven breaths.

I should feel something. Relief. Satisfaction. Clarity. But all I feel is restless.

Eliza shifts beside me, her head resting on my shoulder, lips grazing my collarbone as she murmurs, "You're still thinking."

I close my eyes. "I'm always thinking."

"Stop." Her fingers trail lower, teasing, coaxing. I exhale sharply through my nose, fingers tightening in her hair.

But the moment is already slipping. Because in the corner of the room, past the discarded lab coat, past the rumpled sheets of paper and the ghost of heat still clinging to my skin—the freezer hums.

The serum is waiting.

Eliza must feel my shift in focus because she stills, following my gaze.

I don't move, don't say anything Because I don't have to.

She presses a lingering kiss to my chest, then props herself up on one elbow, watching me. The dim lighting casts shadows over her features, making her look hunger-sharp, predatory. Pleased. "You're thinking about it, aren't you?"

I wet my lips, stomach twisting. "Not now."

She hums, fingers trailing up my arm. "Not now… but soon."

I don't answer. But I don't deny it either.

The moment stretches, filled with nothing but the sound of our breathing, the hum of machines, the low, steady pulse of darkness curling beneath my ribs.

Then, heavy boots echo down the hallway. I jolt upright, muscles locking. Eliza doesn't move, but her eyes flick toward the door, pulse spiking.

I shove off the table, my mind slamming back into place as I pull my clothes on in stiff, mechanical movements.

The cold air clings to my skin. I'm still rooted in the aftershock—skin flushed, mind fogged, Eliza's breath still clinging to my throat—then the door swings open, snapping the tension like a wire pulled too tight.

I'm still standing by the table, my muscles tense, my body not fully grounded in the present yet.

I barely have time to register it before Calvin steps in— exhaustion etched into every line of his face. His lab coat is still streaked with soot, his glasses hanging crookedly off his nose.

"Finally caught you alone," he says, voice rough. "Been trying to explain what happened yesterday."

My jaw tightens, my pulse still uneven. I glance toward Eliza's cage. She's already back inside, sitting against the wall, her expression calm, composed—untouched.

Like nothing happened.

Like she hadn't just pulled me under.

I drag a hand over my face, trying to clear the fog in my head. "The attack?" The word feels heavy on my tongue, thick with a weight I don't fully understand yet.

Calvin nods, running a hand through his disheveled hair. "Targeted strike on the network mainframe. That's why I couldn't get to Eden—we were in lockdown trying to contain it. But…" His voice catches. "We couldn't. Everything's gone, Ben. Years of research, trial data, all the serum modifications…"

My breath locks and the room tilts slightly. "The purification cure?" My voice is quieter than I mean for it to be.

Calvin exhales sharply. "Basic components are backed up on the hospital servers, but the latest formulas, the sequencing…" He slumps against the doorframe, rubbing at his eyes. "We'll have to start from scratch. Could take months, maybe years to recreate it."

Years.

The word rings in my skull.

I can't wait years.

Pain spiders through my chest. My ribs ache, my joints burn, and I know the feeling is deeper than the injuries. It's older than the pain. Frayed. Unraveling

Calvin sighs. "If you hadn't been there for Eden…" He trails off, guilt heavy in his voice.

"Don't." The word leaves me before I can stop it, sharp and final. I can't take his gratitude. Not when betrayal sits heavy in my pocket.

Calvin doesn't push it. Just nods once, rubbing his jaw. "Professional job. They knew exactly where to hit us—took out the central servers, spread through the whole network. Everything's dark."

His eyes flick toward mine, sharper now. "Someone wanted this research gone."

I say nothing. Because I don't trust my voice, and the serum vial presses against my ribs like a second heartbeat.

Calvin shakes his head, exhaustion finally winning over his frustration. "Get some rest," he mutters, running a hand through his hair again. "You look like hell."

I manage a rough half-smirk. "You should see the other guy."

He snorts. "Don't stay too late. Security's still on high alert."

I nod, my fingers tight around the edges of the table.

Calvin hesitates for a second, like he wants to say something else. Then he leaves. The door swings shut behind him.

The silence presses in. I exhale slowly, feeling the weight of the lab settle over me again. The freezer hums.

The serum is still there.

Waiting.

I lift a hand to my chest, pressing against the spot where the vial sits beneath my shirt. Cool. Solid. Real.

It's the one thing I can still control—my choice.

My body.

Even if every part of me is screaming for relief, I tell myself I'm the one making the call.

Eliza hasn't moved from the cage. She doesn't have to. She already knows. Her voice slips through the quiet like smoke. "You don't have years, Benji."

My jaw tightens, fingers twitching at my ribs.

"You think Calvin's cure will be ready in time?" She leans forward, voice softer now, coaxing. "You're already running on borrowed time."

My jaw works, but no words come out.

"You know it, don't you?" she whispers, watching me carefully. Her eyes flick to my hand, still pressed over the vial. "You're already reaching for it."

I freeze. My fingers are inching toward my pocket—instinctively, unconsciously.

I jerk my hand away like I've been burned, curling my fingers into a fist.

Eliza smiles. Because she's already won.

Chapter 42

I've always been a risk taker, but this may be the craziest thing I've ever done. Or the most desperate.

My hands shake slightly as I tie off my arm, watching the vein rise beneath my skin like a blue river under ice. The syringe catches the harsh lab lights, liquid inside gleaming with promises—or threats. I exhale sharply, but it doesn't steady me. My fingers hover over the plunger.

I could stop.

But then what?

Stealing the serum was the choice.

This—this is just the follow-through.

"You're hesitating," Eliza says, soft and amused. She's perched across the table, chin on her hands, tracking every move like a predator.

"I'm just—" I stop.

Thinking. Drowning in it.

Eliza's voice lowers. "If you don't do it now, you might never."

"Shut up," I snap, rubbing my thumb over the plunger. "Let me focus." I clench my jaw. The plunger doesn't move. The rubber tourniquet bites into my skin.

This is a mistake.

"You're afraid," she says, tone velvet-sharp. "You know it won't stop with one."

"I'm fine."

I'm not fine.

My pulse thrums against my throat, fast and unsteady. I force a breath. Lift the syringe.

Eliza leans forward. "Do it, Benji."

I grit my teeth, press the needle to my skin. Still, I wait.

Eliza's voice drops to a whisper. "No one's coming to stop you. Except you."

The world narrows to a point and I close my eyes. Then, I press down.

The liquid slides in. Cold, foreign.

The room stills as I let out a breath I didn't know I was holding. My jaw aches from clenching.

It's done.

Eliza inhales sharply, eyes gleaming. "That's it."

I exhale, but relief doesn't come. The lab feels too quiet. I glance at my hands, expecting something—anything.

Nothing. It wouldn't be instant anyway.

"Now… we wait," she says, voice laced with triumph.

"How long?"

"Different for everyone." She leans on her elbow. "For me, a week."

I turn to my notes, flipping open a folder. Immune response, metabolism, and body weight all make a difference. The words seem too crisp on the pages. I rub my arm. No pain. Just heat, buried deep.

Must be adrenaline.

Eliza watches me. "Talk to me." Her voice lilts, soft and knowing.

"Why?"

"Because I know you." she taps her fingertips against my temple playfully. "You need a distraction." Her voice cuts through me, striking directly at my brain.

I scoff. "And you're volunteering?"

"Of course. I'm the only one here for you, aren't I?" She drapes herself across my shoulder, leaning in close enough her breath ghosts across my skin. "Tell me something no one else knows."

My breath hitches and the moment stretches, fragile and dangerous.

I could tell her anything.

Everything…

"I hate seafood." I smirk.

Eliza snorts, rolling her eyes. "You think you're so funny."

"I just injected myself with an experimental serum. Humor's necessary."

She hums in amusement, but her gaze flickers to my arm.

Watching. Waiting.

I rub my forearm. The skin feels too warm—like heat buried deep within. I ignore it, pushing off the table. "Guess we just wait. I'll document everything, just like Cal did before."

Eliza rolls her eyes. "Still can't believe you're friends with him."

"Best friends," I say, without conviction.

"He's the complete opposite of you." Her voice drips honey-sweet venom.

"He *is* the opposite of me. Especially in how he handles people. But Calvin is kind."

She scoffs. "Blind trust."

"I've known him a long time."

Long enough to know I'm betraying him.

"Maybe you just don't know him as well as you think. He made me into this, after all." She gestures vaguely.

"He's a good guy."

"He was cruel to me. He'll do the same to you." She folds her arms.

"He lacks finesse. That doesn't make him bad." I swallow hard. The sound is loud.

Why is everything so loud?

She shrugs. "Anyway, better not let him catch us."

"Who's going to tell him?"

"Not me." She bites her lower lip, popping out a hip.

I nod, but the moment feels wrong.

Eliza smiles. Knowing. Watching every move, every breath. The weight of her stare pressing into me—like an expectation.

She sighs, stepping away. "You sure you want to delay the transformation?" Her voice drops to a whisper. "I could expose you right now. Most of the others changed faster that way."

I arch a brow. "You offering to bite me?"

Her eyes darken, lips curving upward. "Would you let me?"

My answer should be no.

Should be instant, instinctual.

I don't say it. Because the idea of giving up control—of handing over the reins, even for a second—makes my pulse spike. And maybe that's why I don't pull away.

I scoff, trying to cover it. "Let's give it a week. If nothing changes, we'll try that." I stare at the freezer. The hum louder now.

Eliza's voice lowers. "You already crossed the line."

I tap my forearm, then rub it. It's warm. Too warm.

She steps closer. "Would be easy to take one more step over the next one."

"That could send you into a frenzy."

"Or, it could get you there faster."

I exhale sharply. "Too dangerous. This will work."

"It has to," she muses. Her nails trail my arm, knowing exactly what it does to me. "You seem… deflective."

"I seem normal."

"Of course you do." She bites her lip, studying me like I'm a riddle she already knows the answer to. Her certainty makes my skin crawl.

I rub my temple.

Why are the lights so bright?

I squeeze my eyes shut and steady my breath.

Maybe I need sleep.

Maybe I need less of her voice in my head.

But I let her keep talking. Because it's easier than facing what might already be happening. I flex my fingers.

"I feel the same." I scoff.

"You won't for long," she murmurs. "I can feel it already."

This was stupid.

I push off the table. "I'm going to bed."

Eliza smiles. "Sleep well, Benji." She draws out my name—teasing, dangerous.

I lock her cage and don't look back as I leave.

The warmth spreads through my veins like a sunrise reversed—light sinking inward instead of rising.

Not dawn. Not quite dusk. Vesper. That strange in-between moment the sky can't decide whether to hold the sun or surrender it.

Maybe that's what I am now. Not a monster. Not a man. Just something caught between.

Chapter 43

I tell myself it's just stress. Just adrenaline. But by morning, the world feels different. Sharper. And the ache in my chest isn't pain anymore—it's clarity. A clarity I suddenly don't want.

Edo hovers near the threshold of the room, watching me with ears pinned and his weight low, like he's caught between warning me off and staying close. When I move, he flinches—not enough to bolt, but enough to make my stomach tighten.

He wants to protect me. But his instincts say otherwise. He keeps checking the corners like danger is already here.

MY HANDS CRADLE my head, knee bouncing as I pour over the files in the break room. Voices drift up through the floor—Jenkins and Martinez discussing security changes on the level below.

Their words are crisp, each syllable distinct despite the thick concrete floor between us. I shake my head, trying to dismiss it—but a part of me knows better.

The scar on my chest tingles as I flip to the next page:

"Serum Series 4 complete failure. Subject violence elevated to point of self-destruction." My eyes scan faster than they should be able to:

"Only when serum was introduced to blood with mucin coating does it bypass the immune system and allow infection of more cells. Virus remains dormant until secondary trigger introduced. Effects of dopamine and oxytocin equally effective while adrenaline triggers destructive patterns within infected cell structure. Result: uncontrolled violence in subject, leading to rampage until death."

My heart pounds, adrenaline spiking.

Is this what I've taken?

The Turig scar flares with growing intensity, a warning I can't quite interpret.

I'm losing control.

Deep breaths.

Happy thoughts... Eden's lips against mine.

I close my eyes, remembering how she felt in my arms on the dance floor, the way her heartbeat was so achingly clear against my chest. The wrinkle in her nose when she smiles at me. How she didn't correct Polly when he assumed we were married.

The scar's intensity subsides as I think of her—morphing from sharp pain to strange numbness. A memory flashes through my mind for the first time. Just like it did that day on the battlefield. Right after the Turig soldier's blood mixed with mine.

The door to the break room opens and I look up, the subtle groan of metal stretches like a whisper across the room— though it shouldn't carry this far.

James, a security guard, enters. "Still here, Hale?"

I manage a half grin, trying to appear normal despite the steady rhythm of his pulse underscoring his words, a detail I shouldn't notice. "I'm trying to commit as much of this to memory as I can since the computer database is gone."

"It's not going anywhere. You're here on a Saturday. Where's Calvin? He's usually here."

I glance at the clock, every second stretching longer than it should, every tick too loud. "Oh, is it really that late?"

James checks his watch. "I don't know how you geeks do it. Getting so wrapped up in the words and science of it to forget what time it is."

I chuckle and close the folder, sliding it to the edge of the table as I stand. There's no stiffness in the movement. No hesitation. Every shift of my body feels perfectly calibrated, eerily precise.

"Hospital duty. New baby. I'll go remind him what the real work looks like."

THE HOSPITAL'S ANTISEPTIC smell drowns me before I even enter the building. I navigate to Eden's room, and underneath the sterility of it, a familiar trace of jasmine threads through, reaching me before the doorway comes into view.

I knock on the frame and peek my head in, the fluorescent lights casting a glare that makes the shadows seem deeper, crisper.

"Ben!" Calvin stands. "Come in."

"Sorry to disturb. I just thought you guys might be hungry." I hold up the takeout bag, oddly weightless in my fingers, like I'm holding air.

"Well, Eden has to eat the hospital food since they're monitoring her nutrition while she recovers. But I'm starving."

I round the corner, and Eden lies in the bed, feet neatly tucked into blankets. My mouth goes dry seeing her disheveled state, but my focus shifts—the steady rhythm of her heart, layered with the rapid flutter of Ezra's from across the room, as if the sound carries from no distance at all.

I make my way to her bed and give her a hug, keeping my touch measured, too aware of how little effort it takes to move her.

"You're so sweet checking in on us, Benji." Her voice is warm in a way I'd almost forgotten. Genuine. Soft. Everything Eliza isn't.

Calvin sits and digs into the food I brought, but I barely notice, too focused on controlling my senses.

Even through the medical smells, Eden's aroma wraps around me, along with a subtle change in her chemistry. The change that speaks of healing and new motherhood.

Eden adjusts herself and reaches for the bassinet. "Benji, would you?" The trust in her voice twists my reasoning.

I step to the clear container, my movements liquid-smooth. Fear of hurting the tiny bundle has my hands steady and unnaturally controlled—the same precise control I'd had carrying Eden to safety, though I hadn't questioned it then.

I look down at Ezra's little face, and for a moment my vision catches every detail—the exact pattern of his tiny eyelashes, the subtle flutter of his pulse beneath translucent skin.

I transfer him to Eden with a gentle ease that shouldn't be there. She situates herself to feed him, and I try not to notice how clearly I can hear both their heartbeats, how the baby's quickens slightly at his mother's touch.

"You okay?" Eden watches me. Too closely. Her nurse instincts still intact.

"Of course. Why?"

She watches me intently, and I wonder if she can see past my careful facade. "You seem different somehow."

I rub the back of my neck. "Weird." The lie sits heavy on my tongue as I think about the serum running through my veins.

Eden sees something, even if I'm trying to ignore it.

"I bet it's that girl."

She blushes slightly and I catch the slight elevation in her pulse that speaks of a deeper desire.

"Maybe..."

I stand. "Speaking of which, we have a lunch date." I lie without thinking. What I need is control. Another dose. Something sharper than Eden's warmth.

"Oh?" There's a flickers in Eden's expression—disappointment? Concern? I can suddenly pick up every micro-expression but can't quite interpret them.

"You'll bring her by soon?" she asks.

"Sure, when things settle down." Another lie.

Cal looks up from his food, and I catch something in his expression too—worry masked as casual interest. "This mystery girl must be special if she's got you checking your watch."

"She's... different." At least that's not a lie. Eliza is different, and the contrast with the woman before me suddenly feels sharper than it should.

"Well, don't be a stranger," Eden says, adjusting Ezra. "Little Ezzie needs his Uncle Ben."

The word hits harder than it should. 'Uncle.' Safe. Steady. Not what I am anymore.

I nod, forcing a smile. "I should go."

Back in the hallway, I lean against the wall for a moment, letting my senses settle.

Their voices carry loudly.

"Don't call him Ezzie, babe."

"And why not?"

"It sounds like a dog's name."

Everything feels too close. Too loud. Like I'm not part of the world anymore—just hovering outside it.

A memory flashes—the Turig soldier's unnaturally acute awareness right before he attacked. I push the thought away, just like I push away the growing certainty that I've been changing long before the serum.

BACK AT THE lab, I review my dosage notes, trying to ignore how the letters seem to sharpen and blur with my shifting vision.

"I'm just not feeling any symptoms like you described. Or like the text described." I roll the frozen serum between my hands, the vial thawing quickly against my unnaturally warm skin. Another change I choose not to examine too closely.

Eliza steps closer, her hand sliding over my shoulder in a slow, deliberate motion. "You trust me, don't you?" Her voice is silk-soft, the perfect mix of concern and subtle challenge. "Maybe you need a different kind of dose... or maybe you're just afraid it's working."

Her fingers trail along my arm, almost admiringly, before she presses just enough to remind me of her presence. "You're strong, Ben. Maybe stronger than the others. But if you lose control..." She lets the words hang, a warning without substance, designed to keep me uncertain.

"I've come this far... what harm could a bigger dose do?" The words taste like ash, especially with Eden's genuine concern still fresh in my memory.

Eliza inhales sharply, eyes widening in just the right way. "Ben, no—you don't understand. You're different from them, but that doesn't mean you're safe. You're walking a razor's edge, and if you push too far, there's no coming back." The tremor in her voice is flawless, full of fear. But my instincts tell me it's not real. It's a perfect imitation.

"But I'm feeling nothing." A lie. I'm feeling everything—too much, too clearly.

Eliza smiles, slow and knowing. "You're already changing, Ben. Fighting it isn't going to stop it." She lifts a finger, tracing the line of my jaw with calculated ease. "One bite... that's all it would take to push you past this wall you're hitting. You'd finally understand."

I glance up at her, every instinct suddenly screaming danger. The Turig scar pulses in warning.

"I won't put you through that, remember? It's too dangerous for you to taste blood directly."

Her lips press together, like she's considering something.

Then, with a sigh, she steps back just enough for me to feel the loss of her warmth. "I only want to help you," she murmurs, disappointment threading through her tone. "But if you're not ready to take the final step. That's what Calvin always said too, isn't it? You lack follow through?"

In the freezer's glass reflection, I catch her expression—coaxing, laced with quiet intent. It reminds me of… The Turig soldier's dead eyes flash in my memory, but I shove the thought aside.

My hand slips as I prep the injection site, leaving a small cut. It seals almost instantly—just like the small injuries have been healing faster since my injury.

After the injection, I return to the documentation, my vision catching the words crystal clear despite the dim light. Some of the more recent trial subjects survived, but they were different. They were found in the field as combat survivors, bitten by the initial trial subjects.

I glance at Eliza, her story of survival suddenly seeming more constructed with each new piece of information.

My eyes catch a crucial detail in the text: "The conditions of adrenaline in the blood when the virus is introduced has a direct correlation to the aggression level in the Noctis after transformation. If the subject is asleep, or not conscious when the bite is administered, they will be more calm when the transformation triggers. Those who are fearful, will be more likely to trigger sooner and be vulnerable to losing control with adrenaline spikes."

I exhale slowly, the words on the page burning into my mind.

The conditions of transformation determine control. Fear accelerates the change.

My pulse thrums in my ears as I glance at Eliza again, watching the way she watches me. Measuring. Waiting. And for the first time, I wonder—

Is she really worried about what I'd become? Or is she hoping for it?

LATER, RUNNING WITH Edo feels different. Each inhale expands my chest without strain, oxygen saturating my blood like fuel. The constant pain in my side has faded to nothing, though I tell myself it's just finally healing.

Back at my apartment, Edo sits by the door, his dark eyes tracking my every movement with quiet uncertainty. "Come," I command. He approaches with hesitation I've never seen before, stopping just out of reach. When he finally lets me scratch his ears, the tremor in his breath is unmistakable, even without seeing the way he shrinks back.

My reflection in the dark TV screen catches my attention—my features unnervingly distinct despite the lack of illumination. Have my shoulders always been this broad? My movements this fluid? I think of Eliza's controlled movements, impossible to ignore. It's a parallel to the Turig soldier's inhuman precision that now superimposes over my reflection.

As I reach for my phone to set tomorrow's alarm for my next dose, my scar pulses. Like it can read my thoughts, warning me. Maybe the serum isn't introducing something foreign—it's amplifying what was already there, peeling away the illusion of normalcy one breath at a time.

Eden's words echo in my head: "You seem different somehow." *Different. Like the trial subjects who survived. Like the Turig soldier before he attacked. Like Eliza, with her unnatural poise and unsettling precision.*

I catch my reflection again, and this time I let myself see it. Everything Eden pointed out, everything I've written off. The serum isn't creating this—it's perfecting it. Refining what began the moment that Turig blood hit my veins.

Edo whimpers again, and this time I hear it.

Tomorrow, I'll up the dosage—not because I'm losing control, but because I need more of it. Clarity. Strength. I'll tell myself it's for Eliza, to keep her safe. To keep us both safe from Calvin's rushed cure. But as I know exactly where this is going. This is working—I just need more.

Chapter 44

Awhisper of warmth rises in my chest, foreign and wrong. *Last night, I told myself I'm not lost. That I can fix this with the cure.*

But time doesn't slow when you need it to. It accelerates when you're falling.

My arm is strapped off, my fist clenching and unclenching as I stare at the syringe. The cold pools beneath my skin, an eerie, unnatural pulse syncing with a force I can't control.

Two weeks of two-daily injections.

I should feel the cravings by now.

The reports say it's supposed to be gradual, controlled—but my changes are wrong, warped. Slipping out of reach the moment I try to grasp them. Like a reflection moving out of sync, stepping sideways through the glass while I stand still.

"You're sure this is how much he used?" I ask Eliza, rubbing my tingling scar.

Eliza's eyes gleam, but she plays it off. "That's what I remember, Benji." Her lips curl at the edges, satisfied, but she smooths the expression before I can process it. "But I'm not a scientist. I'm an artist, remember?" She tugs her jacket closer, shivering slightly, her body language designed to make me feel the difference.

The cold doesn't touch me anymore.

It should.

It did before.

"Is it really so bad if he tests the cure on me first? I mean, if it works, you won't have to go through the torture I did. Being locked away." She exhales, playing at hesitation, but the moment she looks up, her expression shifts—smaller, more fragile now. "I just don't want to see you suffer, Benji. But maybe you don't actually want to be fixed."

"It's too dangerous since we lost all the other data." The words come automatically, even as my vision sharpens for a split second, the lab's shadows seeming less dark before returning to normal.

"Dangerous?" Her laughter is quiet, velvet-soft. "Since when has that ever stopped you?"

I shake my head, staring at the vials. My fingers twitch. "This is—"

"Well, clearly something's wrong with you." Her lips part slightly, a frown touching her mouth, but it doesn't reach her eyes. "Your body keeps rejecting what's supposed to save you. It's like you're fighting against yourself, Benji. Why would you do that?"

I shift, rolling my shoulders, but she doesn't let me breathe.

She takes a slow step forward, head tilting slightly— studying me like I'm a specimen she's already dissected.

"Maybe that's why Eden looked at you the way she did," she says, the name sliding from her mouth like venom wrapped in silk.

My jaw tightens. "Don't."

"Touchy," she whispers, as if I've just confirmed a theory. "I wonder what she saw when she looked at you last. Do you think it was pity?" She gives a slow blink, almost sympathetic. "Or worse… fear?"

The air in my lungs turns solid. My pulse kicks. "You don't know her."

She smiles. Not cruel. Not kind. Calculated. "I don't have to. I know you." Her voice softens to something fragile, intimate. "And if you haven't gone back, maybe it's because you're afraid she saw it too—what's growing in you."

My stomach tightens. Muscles coil, every instinct screaming threat. "Don't be ridiculous."

She shrugs one shoulder, turning lazily toward the vials. "Then why are you here with me… instead of her?"

I exhale sharply. "I just need…" My fingers twitch. My arm aches—memory flaring under the skin, phantom pressure clawing for release."How much longer can you keep this up?"

she asks, voice low, dangerous. "Your time with this charade is running out."

"I'll increase the dosage." I pull a vial from the box and tap it against my knuckles, grounding myself in the weight. In the choice.

"Is that really your answer?" Her tone shifts—an edge of surprise laced with something quieter, almost hurt. "I thought you were smarter than that."

"I don't see another option, Eliza. We need to speed this up."

She steps in—close enough that I can feel her without her touching me. "You do have another option." Her breath brushes my jaw. "Me." The air thickens between us, heat pressing in from all directions. "Let me help you. No more injections. No more pretending. Just… let go."

My fingers close around the vial until the glass threatens to shatter. "You know that's not happening."

"Why?" She exhales sharply, the sound threaded with exasperation and something darker. "You already took me into your bed. Let me into your head. What's left, Benji? One bite. One moment. You'd be free. So what is it you're afraid of?"

I shake my head. "I told you—I won't do that to you. I've got this under control."

"Do you?" she murmurs, gliding closer. Her finger brushes along the inside of my wrist, right over the pulse hammering beneath my skin. "Because from where I'm standing, it looks like you're already slipping."

I yank my arm back. "I'm not—"

"Then prove it."

"I am."

Her smile is slow and sharp. "No, Benji. You're running. Every time you take that serum instead of accepting what you already are... you're choosing fear. Cowardice."

My blood goes cold. "Shut up."

"You think that bottle can save you? That you can inject yourself into being whole again? God, it's almost sad."

I grab her wrist before I even realize I've moved—tight. She gasps, but not in pain. A slow, pleased exhale leaves her lips as it morphs into a breathless laugh—like she's been waiting for this exact moment.

I release her like I've touched a live wire, stumbling back. My hand burns—not from effort, but from betrayal.

"There he is," she whispers, licking her lips like I've just confirmed everything she wanted.

My pulse thrashes in my throat and I stare at the red imprints already blooming on her skin.

I didn't mean to squeeze that hard. I didn't even feel it.

She watches me, eyes gleaming. "You're already changing. You're the only one pretending you haven't."

I lift the vial, gripping it harder than before. "It's not…"

Eliza leans in, her breath brushing my ear. "You feel that? That edge under your skin? That's not fear," she whispers. "It's freedom. All you have to do is take it."

She pivots and turns away, like she knows what comes next—like she's already won.

My chest pulls tight. I glance at the vial. Then at her.

She laughs under her breath, leaning against the table with calculated ease. "You'll beg me for that final push, Benji. Sooner than you think."

I press my fingers to the spot on my arm, the place I've injected before. It aches faintly—memory more than pain.

The serum is all I have left.

I told myself I wasn't changing. That it was stress. PTSD. Old injuries flaring under pressure.

But the truth's been clawing at me since the day I saved Eden in the street—and I didn't want to see it.

Didn't want to name it.

The syringe trembles in my hand. Not from fear. From need. My breath shortens—tightens. And I inject.

Chapter 45

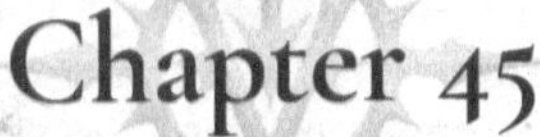

The door handle jiggles. A soft click—too loud in the static shredding through my skull.

"Shit." I lurch toward the cage but Eliza's already moving. She snatches the keys from the table, slips inside, and slams the bars shut just before I reach her.

I rip the tourniquet from my arm, chest heaving, then fumble the vial and syringe into my pocket.

The room tilts. Light fractures. My limbs feel like they belong to someone else—stronger, heavier, wrong.

I make it to the door, hand on the knob. One last look over my shoulder. She's back in the cage. But she's smiling.

The door swings open, a gust of air stirring the stale scent of chemicals and sweat.

"What the hell, Ben?" Cal steps in, hands half-raised. Not alarmed. Just tense.

"What?" I say, steady enough.

He steps further into the room, brows pinched. "Locking doors now, are we?"

"Must've hit it by accident." The lie comes easily. Too easily. I keep my body loose, measured—aware of how closely he's watching.

His gaze flicks from my hands to my face, then lingers—longer than it should. Not friend-to-friend. Not anymore.

"Yeah. Okay." His voice is neutral, but the shift is there. A crack. "I was looking for you earlier."

He shuts the door behind him and steps forward, eyes drifting across the cage.

I make myself breathe. Calm. Controlled.

"Been busy," I say, motioning vaguely to the cluttered table.

"I can see that." He exhales, lifts a folder from under his arm, and tosses it onto the table with a light thud. "We need to talk."

I glance at the file, the lettering briefly snapping into too-sharp clarity before blurring again.

He pauses, eyes narrowing slightly. Then he looks back to the cage. To Eliza. And something in his posture stiffens.

"Let's take this somewhere else," he says. "Need some air anyway."

"Sure." I nod, maybe too quickly. The shift out of the lab feels like oxygen. But as I follow him into the hallway, I can still feel Eliza watching me.

"What is it?" I ask.

"The cure's coming along faster than we thought."

I make my face blank even as my mind fractures around the word.

The cure. An end to all this—but for who?

For Eliza, still caged? Or for me, already unraveling?

"Good," I say. It lands dull. Hollow.

He pauses. Just long enough to notice. "Yeah." The silence thickens, taut and waiting.

"You don't look happy about that." I shift my weight, every movement a little too smooth. Like muscle memory running ahead of me.

"It's not that." He hesitates. "I just need to know where you stand."

"On what?"

"You've been... off." His eyes flick to the door we just left. "Even before Eden's accident. You stopped pushing back. About the cure. About everything. It's like you don't care if it works at all."

A flicker of heat rises in my chest, but I shove it down hard.

Careful.

"I've been acting like someone who almost lost—" I cut myself off, exhale. Let the edge dull. "I'm glad Eden's okay. But it messed me up, Cal."

The guilt card. Always works. Mostly because it's true.

He sighs, rubbing the bridge of his nose. The move is familiar, worn. "I didn't come to fight. I'm just trying to figure out where your head is." He folds his arms. "So tell me the truth—would you take the cure? If you were the one infected?"

I force a laugh. "You're acting like I'm a damn Noctis."

"I know you care about her." His eyes flick back toward the lab door. "And I know you'd never let anyone you care about get hurt."

The words shouldn't hit the way they do. I flex my fist, force my breath to stay even. My heart doesn't race. It should. But it doesn't.

"It's fine, Cal."

"Is it?"

Silence again.

"What's the alternative?" I ask.

He blinks. "What?"

"If we don't test it on her. Then what?"

Calvin watches me closely, that clinical focus I used to find comforting now setting my teeth on edge.

"Then we try it on someone else first."

"I could do it."

"Out of the question."

I scoff, folding my arms. "Why—because you think the cure won't work?"

"Because you're too important to me. To the work here." His tone sharpens—less friend, more command. "And because you're not thinking straight."

I shift my weight, feigning indifference while the stillness in my chest says otherwise. "I'm thinking clearer than I ever have."

"That worries me." He rubs his temples, the gesture slow, worn. "Look, I know what Eden's emergency did to you. I get it. But this—" he jerks his chin toward the lab, "—the secrecy. The change in you. The obsessive way you look at her."

"Obsession?" The word cuts too fast. I dial it back. "You're one to talk. Buried in work while Eden—" I stop myself—clench my jaw around the words before they can form and break what little thread of trust still lies between us.

Calvin's eyes sharpen—the accusation hanging between us. I choose my next words carefully and breathe once— measured.

"I'm just doing my job, Cal. Same as you." I lean in, hand on his shoulder—reassuring, practiced. "I just want to understand what we're dealing with before we start 'curing' people."

Cal studies me for a long moment, then exhales. "Fine. But no more locked doors. No more secrets." His voice is calm, but there's weight behind it now. "We're too close to screw this up."

"Agreed." The word slips out easily.

"Good."

The silence that follows is thick with everything neither of us wants to say.

He frowns—just slightly. Doesn't meet my eyes. Then glances back toward the lab, like something's finally clicked.

"There's still something off about her," he says, voice low and urgent. "The way she watches you when you're not looking… Ben, she's playing you."

He leans closer, eyes sharp. "But we'll start tomorrow. If it works, she could be out of here in a few weeks. Then—" he sighs, softer now, "then you can figure out what's real between you. Without all this." He gestures to the sterile corridor enclosing us in the facility that's become both sanctuary and prison.

And somehow, I smile. It surprises me—a flicker of something I haven't felt in weeks.

Hope.

Thin and dangerous.

The shadows in the hallway don't press as hard. Even the hum of the lab feels farther away.

"Tomorrow?" My voice almost cracks. I clear my throat. "The purification will be ready that soon?"

I glance at my hands, turning them over. They're steady now—like they belong to someone else.

The idea of reversing what's happening—of buying time, of stopping the descent—of curing Eliza… It swells in my chest like breath I didn't realize I'd been holding.

Do I dare believe in that?

Cal nods slowly, watching me now like a scientist with a hypothesis. "Yeah. But I'm planning to start with micro-doses and slow recovery window."

His gaze flicks back to the door. "Given what happened with the last subject… and now that I know she matters to you." He hesitates. "I want to minimize the risk."

"So before you knew I cared about her, the side effects didn't matter?" I cross my arms, scar pulsing faintly beneath my sleeve.

"That's not what I meant." He lifts his hands. Defensive.

"Before, I didn't think to slow it down. I didn't know I needed to."

"I'm not sure that's better." I hold his gaze. My vision flickers—sharpening, painfully clear. Every pore on his face etched in high relief.

I swallow, hard. "So tomorrow she gets cured. And then what?" My voice edges higher. "She goes back to being human? What if she doesn't want that, Cal? What if she never wanted that?" The words tumble out before I can stop them. Truths I didn't even know I was afraid of seeing.

Cal gives me a long, searching look. Then, quietly: "Why wouldn't she want to be cured, Ben?" His eyes narrow. The suspicion is no longer beneath the surface. "Has she said something to you?"

My pulse kicks—but outwardly, I stay still. "No. Just thinking out loud."

He doesn't buy it. Not fully. "Right." The word lands flat. Heavy.

He checks his watch. Sighs. "I need to finish sequencing before Evans checks in. Then I'm heading home—Eden's making that pasta you like." He pauses, eyes on mine. "You should come. Take a break. Get out of this place for an hour."

I hesitate.

I need to check on Eliza. Need to stay ahead.

But turning him down would only tighten the leash.

"Yeah. Sounds good. Give me ten to wrap up."

"Lobby in fifteen," he says, tapping his watch.

As he walks away, I see it again—that sliver of doubt in his eyes. He knows I'm hiding something… he just doesn't know what.

Chapter 46

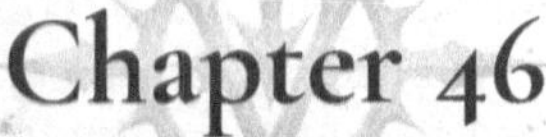

I shove through the door and whip toward Eliza. "Shit, it has to happen, now." My fingers fumble in my pocket for the vial and syringe. The glass slips.

It smashes against the floor, the crack of breaking glass ringing in my skull like gunfire.

"Fuck!"

"Careless," Eliza says, palm settling lightly against my back. Her voice pours like honey laced with iron. Her eyes gleam—not with comfort, but conquest.

I should feel the cool press of her skin. I don't. I haven't in weeks.

"No time left.”

I grab paper towels from the sink, scrubbing at the floor in frantic, erratic bursts.

"Then it's plan B," she purrs.

I freeze. She bites her lip, sculpted and calculated. A memory hits—Turig eyes, vacant and sharp.

I've seen that stare. On her.

"It's too late." I growl. "Calvin's prepping the dose for tomorrow." I kneel beside the shards, rage climbing fast through me. The scar beneath my shirt burns like a warning flare.

"I'll take it first," she offers smoothly, settling beside me. Her gaze pins mine. "You don't have to be the one who breaks.”

"No!" I seize her arms. "I need to protect you."

Her laugh coils around me, cold and indulgent. "You're a terrible liar, Benji." Her voice once mirrored Eden's—now there's no warmth in it, only teeth.

My vision narrows, lines sharpening like a rifle scope.

I hold tighter. It only feeds her smirk. There's no tremble in her lashes. No fear. Just choreography.

"I'm sorry," I mutter as my grip slips. "But that's not good enough."

She presses her palm to my cheek like she's taming an animal. But she's waiting—waiting for collapse. "I'll be okay," she says, low. "If you stay. That's all I need."

My hands snap back. I lunge for the freezer, hinges shrieking. Bottles rattle—glass and chemicals whispering panic.

The cold should sting. It doesn't.

Eliza is right. I'm a terrible liar.

I tell myself I don't care. That it doesn't mean anything. But the words fall into a growing black hole within me.

"Tourniquet." I don't remember speaking, but I'm already moving. The serum warms in my grip like the heat belongs to someone else.

"Let me help," she breathes, clutching the band against her chest like it means something.

"Last chance." I shake the vial hard, urgency turning frantic.

This isn't clarity. It's surrender dressed in purpose. But I can't stop now.

Another flash—predator eyes. Hers. Not imagined. Not subtle.

"I can't lose. Not again." The words snap out of me, hoarse, raw and shaking.

"What did you lose?" she asks softly, feigned concern coating her tongue.

I grip the vial like it's the only thing real.

Her expression doesn't flicker.

"I lost everything," I whisper. "Eden. My unit. My whole goddamn life. All that's left of me is this... ache that never leaves."

She says nothing. She doesn't have to.

"If this works—maybe I can fix it. Maybe I don't have to stay broken. Get parts of it back."

She touches my face again, perfectly still. "And if it doesn't?"

The words slither through me—raw. I blink at her, at the weight of them. "Then I die trying."

She doesn't flinch.

"I've been changing since the attack," I admit. "But you already knew, didn't you? You saw it first."

"Of course I did," she murmurs, drawing the band tight with ritualistic precision.

"Once the pain is gone, I can get the purification. We can have a life… together." My voice barely feels like my own.

"You act like this is for me," She straightens, expression smoothing. "But we both know it's for you." Her fingers lock the tourniquet with too much force. "You're not saving me." Her whisper snakes around me, sinking into my skin. "You're becoming me."

I jam the needle into the bottle. Double dose. No hesitation. My hands stay steady as I slide the needle in.

The door explodes open.

Light crashes into the room.

I press the plunger and… everything halts—just for a second. A single, stretched breath.

Then—detonation. A surge rips through me, white-hot and merciless. My heart skips, then slams back online with a rhythm that doesn't feel human.

Calvin is frozen in the doorway. His eyes lock on my arm. The syringe. The cage. "Eliza?" His voice cracks. "Ben. What did you do?"

Calvin's eyes find mine—and in them, I see the last thread of trust snap.

I can't answer. My mouth isn't mine. Everything distorts—edges pulling wide, walls twisting. I stumble. My limbs don't cooperate.

"Tell me you didn't…" he steps forward, reaching for me.

Eliza is a blur. She hits him hard, viciously. His arms are twisted behind his back before he can react. She moves like nothing human. She never was.

Now I get it.

Every smile. Every wound. Every look. Manufactured.

All for this.

"Don't hurt him!" The words scrape out, raw. The scar pulses with some new rhythm—no longer resistance and warning.

"Why not?" she snarls. "He's the one who kept me leashed. He made me suffer." She leans in, feral. The act is gone. The monster stands in her place.

I ignored every sign.

I wanted to believe her. Needed to.

"He's the only one who can help you... help us." But the word us feels poisoned now.

She didn't fool me—I let her in.

"Us?" Her laugh cuts clean and merciless. "There was never an us, Benji. Just me—getting what I wanted and letting you burn for it." Her eyes are on mine, unflinching. "You weren't the mistake. You were the method."

Let her use my—let every bruise and choice sharpen her blade.

She leans in, lips near my ear, her breath warm as silk.

"He was the target. But you?" Her tone drops, wicked and intimate.

"I didn't mean to keep you." A pause—soft as a kiss, lethal as steel. "But watching you fall?" Her smile curves, slow and possessive. "I liked the way it felt."

Her gaze drags down my body and back up again, deliberate. When her eyes return to mine, they gleam with satisfaction. "And now, you're mine."

The floor tilts. A crack in my knees. The world snaps sideways. Light shears across my vision.

My body fractures. My skin doesn't feel like skin. My blood howls beneath it. And beyond the noise—Eliza's laugh.

Steady. Triumphant.

It isn't relief. It's ownership. Like she's just claimed me as hers. "You finally made it, Benji."

Chapter 47

Eliza's chuckle warps against the thickening air, curling around me like a ghost.

Through my fading vision, I see my hands—veins dark and prominent against unnaturally pale skin.

The same changes I'd seen starting weeks ago but refused to acknowledge.

Even now, she's watching. Waiting. Measuring my reaction like she has been all along, like the scientist she swore she wasn't.

"Look what you've done, you bitch!" Calvin's shout rips through the chaos, hoarse with fury and exhaustion. His voice is raw, but his anger feels justified.

A distant crash—glass shattering.

Something heavy topples. The lab's dim emergency lighting flickers, barely cutting through the thick smoke choking the room.

Through the haze, I make out smears of blood on the wall. A deep gash on Calvin's arm. The way his chest heaves as he glares at her.

They fought. The fire licking up the walls tells me how it ended.

A bent metal tray swims in a pool of alcohol, the flames licking hungrily at overturned papers. The fire alarm screams overhead, and the sprinklers rain down in sputtering, uneven bursts.

And yet—the fire keeps spreading. It clings to the walls, hungry. Unnatural. Soaked equipment, the lingering chemical residue—it's all feeding the flames.

My head slumps forward, too heavy to hold up. Gravity drags me down, like being pulled underwater.

Every heartbeat echoes in my skull. Each one a reminder of how blind I've been. Each pulse of the Turig scar marking another truth I ignored.

"Me? This is all because of you!"

Eliza's voice cuts through the crackling flames, strained but mocking.

I don't have to see her expression to know she's smiling. She's reveling in this. Every second of my downfall. Every ounce of pain.

She wanted this.

A sharp gasp. The piercing shatter of more glass. I force my eyes open, vision swimming.

The flames have spread fast, consuming the lab with greedy fingers.

The heat rises in waves, mixing with the cold spray of the sprinklers, turning the air into a choking fog.

Something crashes.

Calvin moves toward me, but stumbles. He's bleeding, his shirt torn at the shoulder, his hands raw.

I glimpse Eliza in the corner of my vision—hair damp from the sprinklers, blood streaked along her cheek, eyes wild with exhilaration. She's breathing hard, but she's not afraid. She's enjoying this.

The room tilts. Calvin drops to my side, gripping my arm.

"Cal... I'm sorry." I gasp for air, my heart barely beating now. "I couldn't take it anymore. The pain is just... so exhausting..."

Not just the physical pain anymore—But the weight of every manipulation I allowed. The intensity of every moment Calvin gets with Eden. While I'm stuck watching from the sidelines.

Changed. By Turig blood and my own goddamn choices.

"Why didn't you say something!" He shouts over the alarm.

"You're my best friend." I force a smile as darkness creeps in at the edges of my vision. "Seeing you happy made it easier to—"

Watch you give her what I never could.

The truth hits harder now. Eden's happiness was real while everything with Eliza was a lie. A carefully constructed fiction. One my body tried to warn me about and I chose not to see.

Glass digs into my palms as I catch myself against the floor. The pain is sharp—then gone.

"Go." My voice is raw, breaking. "Go to your family. Live life and be happy. For both of us."

The words catch—because I know what she did. She used my loneliness against me—twisted what I wanted most.

And if not for this, if not for the monster inside me, it would have been me.

Eden would have chosen me.

But the monster was always there.

Not born from serum or Turig blood.

Born from me.

My body grows numb. The scar pulses once more—then goes silent. As if it knows I finally see the truth.

"I won't leave you here, idiot." His hand tightens on my arm, but there's hesitation under the panic now. Like he's not sure who he's saving anymore. As though part of him is already wondering if I'm worth saving.

His touch burns like fire against my suddenly freezing skin. But the pain feels honest. Unlike everything with Eliza.

"Fucking help me!" He howls.

I force my eyes open. Eliza is on my other side, her hands tight around my arm. Still playing her part.

The world snaps into perfect focus for one terrifying second. Every detail crisp. The calculated concern in her face. The careful modulation in her voice. The micro-expressions my enhanced senses should have picked up before now.

I see it all. The act, the performance,for what it truly was.

"Eliza... I'm sorry." I look at her through water-soaked bangs. Not for failing her, but for falling for it.

She smiles—not soft, not forgiving. Just certain. Like this is exactly how it was always meant to end.

"Shut up," she mutters, her smile razor-clean. "Apologies make you sound like you still think you have a choice." Her fingers tighten, just slightly. "Besides—" Her voice lowers. "You're not allowed to say goodbye. I'm not finished with you yet."

And, I already promised her forever.

The words twist now. Revealing what they always meant. She never wanted forever. She just wanted to destroy me. Because to her, I was never Ben. Just another man who needed to be punished.

Just like the Turig soldier.
Not to turn me. Only to break me.

THE FIRE ALARM stutters and dies, its mechanical wail swallowed by the crackling flames.

The light shifts—blinding, cascading in sharp flashes through the thick smoke.

And then—grass. The scent hits me like a wall. Fresh. Green. Crushed underfoot. Each blade distinct, pressed into the ground. Cool earth presses against my back. Then—heat. My skin sears, damp with sweat. The contrast makes no sense.

This isn't real.

But it feels real.

A hand presses to my chest. Not comforting. Not human. *Eliza.*

Her touch leeches warmth instead of giving it. My breath shudders, shallows.

I used to crave control. Now I can't even tell what's real.

Wrong. It's all wrong.

Every enhanced sense screams at me. Her touch is fake. Her presence, a lie.

The light burns against my closed eyelids. I force them open—Calvin. Backlit by the fire and the blinding sun.

His silhouette wavers, half-shadowed by the flickering flames, half-obscured by the smoke choking the lab.

His fingers fist his hair—staring at the building. At what's left of it.

The air hangs thick—burning chemicals, blood, charred metal.

The lab is dying. Just like me.

I reach for him but gravity drags at my arm, making every movement a battle.

My finger catches on a loose thread at the hem of his lab coat. A tiny hole. I see it clearly, sharply—more clearly than I see him now.

"Cal… Cal, tell Eden…" My voice breaks. "I'm sorry too."

For believing I could replace her with something hollow.

Calvin kneels sharply. "What?"

I smile—small, tired. "It's okay." My voice barely exists now, carried on shallow breaths. "Just tell her. She'll know what it means."

Because Eden was always real. Even when I tried to erase her with Eliza's carefully crafted illusion.

My body betrayed me. But my senses never did. They showed me the difference all along.

Eliza's gaze flicks to Calvin for a mere moment.

Cal clasps my hand and nods. "I'll tell her." Then he stands, turns, and runs toward the fire.

I don't watch. I can't. The weight on my chest presses deeper.

Eliza's fingers curl around mine—not to comfort, but to tether. Like she's claiming the last piece of me before the world burns. Her touch vanishes like the heat leaving my limbs.

The fire rages, shifting in and out of focus as my vision narrows. My heartbeat slows. And then it happens.

One final moment of perfect clarity. My senses explode.

The world sharper, more defined than even the Turig mutation ever allowed.

The crackling fire is deafening. The chemical burn in the air is suffocating. The lab trembles under the weight of its own destruction.

I look at her. Eliza's face warps, blurring as the mask falls away. And beneath it? A predator. Her true nature, fully exposed.

Another instant, she's gone. Transformed again, this time into…

Eden.

Her eyes catch the light, sparkling with that smile I could never forget. The only true thing I've ever known.

The slender curve of her waist beneath my hands when I finally kissed her like I meant it—once, only once, but I still dream about it.

A moment I should've fought harder for. A life I should've chosen before it slipped away.

The fire cracks louder now. Red, gold, and gray flash across my vision like flares in deep water.

And piercing through the static—I hear her laugh. Soft. Unmistakable. Like it used to be—before the pain, before I lost her.

The fire roars and the lab collapses in an ear shattering rumble of debris.

And then—darkness.

Chapter 48

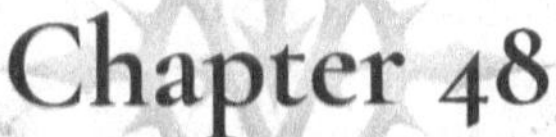

It's been months since the fire. Since they told me Calvin was gone. Since I started pretending I wasn't.

Edo lifts his head as I reach for my jacket, ears twitching at the shift in my breath. His eyes meet mine—steady, soft, knowing.

I crouch beside him, fingers sinking into the thick fur behind his ears. "I was thinking…" I murmur, voice low, "maybe she could use you today. You always knew how to calm me down. Maybe you can do the same for her."

He leans into my hand, a low huff of breath escaping like he understands. Like he's already forgiven me for leaving him behind so many times.

I grab his leash, looping it over my fingers. "Let's go, buddy. Might be your most important mission yet."

My hand trembles in my pocket as I skip up the patio steps and knock. The Turig scar tingles faintly—a lingering brand of everything that led to this moment.

Eden appears in the window, hair erratic, strands falling loose around hollowed eyes—a shadow of the woman who used to light up every room.

"Benji." She exhales, leaning against the doorframe, defeat etched into every line of her posture. "Come in."

I step forward, Edo staying close to my leg as we cross the threshold. The familiar scent of her home is now tainted with grief. It clings to the air, heavy in the quiet spaces where

Calvin used to stand.

Unwashed dishes peek from the kitchen sink, and takeout containers crowd the counter—silent testaments to her unraveling life. Blankets and clothing lie strewn about like abandoned memories; newspapers folded and tucked into corners—their headlines ghosts of my sins.

"Eden, I—"

She hushes me with a hand on my shoulder, the touch sending an unexpected chill through my newly sensitive skin. It's as if my nerves have been rewired—each point of contact registers with painful clarity, carrying emotional echoes I can't quite process. She yawns, covering her mouth with her other hand, then walks past me to a padded chair. The ghost of her touch lingers.

Edo noses gently at her leg before curling at her feet. She doesn't speak, just reaches down, fingers weaving into his fur.

"I should have come sooner..." I cross to the sofa and pick up a blanket, folding it too precisely. The fabric feels wrong against my skin, my fingers registering every thread. I place it over the armrest.

"I've got a handle on it." Her voice carries none of its usual conviction.

I glance around, my new vision forcing details onto me. "Clearly."

She sinks into the chair, hands crumpling the fabric of her sweater in her lap. Staring at me. "You disappeared after the funeral…"

I freeze momentarily, unprepared for the directness. "I needed some time. To process everything." The lie bites my tongue. "What can I do?" The words feel hollow—we both know I'm part of the reason she's like this.

"Nothing, Ben. I've got everything—"

"Don't give me that, Eden." The sharpness in my voice surprises even me. "You look like you haven't slept in days." The concern is real. But so is the guilt tightening in my throat.

"You try having a newborn!"

"It's been months." The words come out clinical, detached. "I would think Ezra has a more consistent sleep pattern by now."

She glances to the window, sorrow hanging on the corners of her eyes like unshed tears. "You can't force these things."

Walking to her, I pull a booklet from my jacket pocket and kneel by the chair, meeting her gaze. She's too lost in her grief to notice how smooth and unnatural the movement is. "This says to look out for signs of postpartum depression." I place the booklet in her lap. "Eden, love, I think it's time for you to talk to someone."

She snorts, a weak attempt at humor. "You can read?" She glances at the mantle. At the photo of her and Calvin—the laugh dying before it can fully form.

It cracks something inside me. "At least let me help." I shift, voice softer now. "All you have to do is call. Or tell me what you need, and I'm there." The irony of my own words taste like acid. "You saved me once. Let me save you."

She shakes her head, folding the booklets corners in on themselves. Her eyes glisten. "I should be depressed, Benji." The words are quiet, but they hit like a hammer. "My husband died." Her gaze drifts.

Each syllable scorches through me like wildfire. I should have been ready for it. But I wasn't. I clench my teeth, following her gaze to the window.

"I miss him too." My hands curl at my sides as I step toward the mantle. I pick up the photo of them together, fingers ghosting over the glass.

I could tell her. Right now. The truth. That I killed him.

But I don't. I can't.

"You can't possibly know what I'm feeling right now." She falls to the back of the chair with a huff—exhausted, guarded.

And she's right.

I don't. My emotions are drifting further from me, dampened by whatever I'm becoming.

Except for the guilt. The guilt still cuts deep.

"I wasn't trying to imply that I…" I shake my head, pushing the words away. "Where's Ezra?"

She waves a hand vaguely toward the dining area. Then brings it to her face, covering her eyes. I step toward the soft crib, moving around scattered pillows and a throw blanket.

Ezra lays there, arms over his head, sucking on a pacifier. Something cuts through my emotional fog like a knife— Calvin staring back at me from his son's face. The resemblance is startling, unexpected in its power to wound. For a moment, my carefully constructed facade cracks, and I have to grip the edge of the crib to steady myself.

So small. So unaware. Innocent.

He doesn't know.

Doesn't know the web of lies surrounding his father's

death.

This child will grow up without knowing Calvin, and the weight of that knowledge—of my part in it—threatens to crush me even through the increasing disconnect with my emotions.

I make myself break away from the crib to the kitchen and start the tea kettle.

"When was the last time you ate?"

"The last time I slept." She mumbles it, the words barely audible—even to me.

I take a slow breath. The house is too quiet. Not just still—hollow.

I open the refrigerator.

Empty shelves.

I pull open the pantry.

Vacant.

How long has she been like this? How long has she let herself waste away, just waiting for something to feel real again?

A loaf of bread sits abandoned in the back of the freezer, buried under long-forgotten bags of vegetables and frostbitten meals.

I pop a slice into the toaster, then start clearing the counter. The mundane task feels surreal, mechanical, too normal against the weight of everything I can't tell her.

The toast pops—I dress it up as best as I can.

Grab a teacup—steep a cherry magnolia bag into the steaming liquid. The scent rises, familiar, clinging to the air. It smells like better days. Like the past. Like a world where neither of us were like this.

As I work, I catch my reflection in the kitchen window— eyes too bright, movements too efficient. For a moment, I wonder if Eden would even recognize what I've become if she weren't lost in her own grief.

I pick up the plate and walk back to her and the silence presses down. On the end table—a newspaper with Calvin's face stares back at me, frozen in black-and-white print.

"Scientist Dies in Unexpected Explosion on Base."

I exhale sharply, flipping the paper. Another headline beneath it.

"Enemy Attacks Local Research Facility—Three Dead."

My jaw tightens. I roll them up, gripping them too firmly. Each headline a knife in my gut.

The world turned my crime into a statistic. Into ink and paper.

Just another casualty of war.

"Eden—" I grip her hand gently, kneeling to her level. Careful. Always careful—to not let her feel how cold I've become. "You need to eat somethin', love."

Her fingers curl slightly under mine. "I don't know how I'm going to do this without him, Benji." Her voice fractures. She looks at me—tears brimming in her eyes. Each one stabbing like an accusation.

"I know." I pull her in, tucking her against my chest. She shakes—so small, so weightless. Just grief and bones. "I know, love."

Her shoulders bounce with silent sobs, the warmth of her breath hitting my collarbone. I say nothing. Because there's nothing to say.

Edo creeps forward, resting his head in her lap, eyes lifted as if he understands the weight of her loss. She doesn't move, but her hand finds his fur, fingers twisting gently into it like a lifeline.

A flicker of light catches my eye. My gaze shifts—to the window, to the horizon.

The sun is setting.

Not a fiery, dramatic descent—just a slow, tired sinking, bleeding into the dark. I watch as the world outside turns to silhouette.

The fading light doesn't hurt my eyes anymore. The bells toll.

Vesper.

The chimes pierce my hearing like arrows. Each one, a reminder. Of what I've done. Of what I've become.

Her tears soak through my shirt, warm against my cooling flesh. I hold her carefully, afraid my strength might betray me, might hurt her as surely as my secrets would.

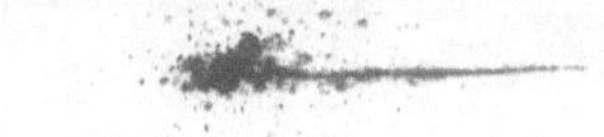

THE ROOM DARKENS as we sit there, Eden eventually growing still against me. I could count her heartbeats if I wanted to, could track the slowing rhythm of her breathing. I should leave—every moment I stay is another lie—but I remain rooted, offering what comfort I can. It's the very least I owe her.

In the crib, Ezra stirs and makes a soft sound. My gaze shifts to him as Edo pads over and settles in next to the crib, and I wonder what kind of world he'll inherit—one where creatures like what I'm becoming walk among humans? Or one where his father's work continues in ways Calvin never intended.

Chapter 49

I close the door behind me, the scent of grief still clinging to my clothes.

"Where'd you go?" Eliza sits on the sofa, one leg bouncing, arms folded. The usual interrogation stance.

The familiar accusation hits before I even fully shut the door, exhaustion curling through my spine. I lick my lips and slide my jacket off, hanging it on the hook.

Mind racing—finding words that won't set her off.

"You were with her, weren't you?"

I sigh, turning away, welcoming Edo's quiet devotion—or I would, if he were here. He's not. He's still at Eden's, watching over the only thing I have left. At least someone's loyalty comes without conditions.

"Sorry. It took longer than expected." I keep my voice even, but Eden's tear-streaked face flashes behind my eyes. Her grief raw. Real. So different from the calculated anger radiating from the sofa.

Eliza doesn't move. Just stares. Then, low: "Edo didn't come back with you."

I don't answer.

"He always does." Her eyes narrow. "Unless you didn't want him to."

The air tightens.

"Is he *hers* now?" she asks, tone dipping into something cloying. "Comfort dog for the grieving widow?"

I grind my teeth. "He stays where he's needed."

Her mouth curls. "Right."

"She's struggling. She shouldn't be alone right now."

Eliza tilts her head. "And that's your problem… why?" Her voice doesn't rise. Doesn't snap. It slices—precise and surgical.

"Because it's my fault he's dead." The words bite—repeated so many times, they've lost meaning.

Maybe she keeps making me say it just to watch me bleed.

"You're not the one who made him run back into a burning building like some fucking idiot."

"Watch it." I snap, clenching my fists. Grounding me. Keeping my mouth shut. Keeping control. Or maybe—keeping down the words I should say but can't.

Eliza exhales dramatically, shifting gears. The pivot always comes fast. "You're right." Her tone softens. "He did save your life, I guess. Though I'd have gotten you out if he hadn't." The criticism lingers in the air like smoke.

"Can we not do this today?" The weariness in my voice surprises even me.

I don't have the energy for this fight.

"Just admit you were with her and I'll drop it." Her voice melts into something reasonable, like I'm the one being difficult.

I shouldn't fall for it. But I do. "I never denied that's where I was."

"I require a confirmation, Benji." The pet name slips out sweet, laced with poison.

I close my eyes, shaking my head.

When did this become my normal?

"Alright, yes. Fine. I was at Eden's."

"All night?"

"Yes, Eliza." I tilt my head, defeated. "I was over there all night. She—"

"Go take a shower." She bounces her leg, casual as an executioner. "I can smell her disgusting pig scent and that abomination of a child all over you."

My stomach turns and I clench my fists, walking away. Not engaging. Not rising to the bait.

"Oh, and Benji—" Her voice follows me down the hall. "At least try to hide it next time." I stop, waiting for the next line to land. "I can't stand the thought of her nasty human hands all over you."

Shaking my head, muttering under my breath, I shut the bathroom door behind me. The lock clicks—a meaningless barrier against the storm in my head.

My chest tightens. Not because of Eliza. Not because of the fight.

Eden.

Her grief is carved into my mind, unshakable. The way she holds herself like she might break. *And I—I shouldn't be thinking about her.*

Guilt swells in my throat. I step toward the sink, grip the porcelain edges, and stare into the mirror. Frozen.

The man looking back isn't me. The angles are sharp. The skin, pale. Eyes, hollow. Like a ghost wearing my skin. A monster waiting to be named.

The scar along my ribs pulses beneath my shirt. Something it only does when I get really heated.

I curl my fingers against the sink, knuckles bleaching white, and lean closer.

"You did this." The words slip from my lips before I even know I'm speaking. "You let her do this to you."

This is what I deserve.

For letting Calvin die. For dragging Eden into this war within myself. For watching the lab burn and doing nothing.

Let her punish me. Let her twist the knife. At least I'll feel it.

Besides—who else is going to help me through this?

Eden can't know what I'm becoming. Calvin's gone. And anyone else—they'd lock me up the moment I slipped. But Eliza...

Eliza understands.

She sees the hunger before it hits. She's lived it.

If I want to survive this—if I want to control it—I need her.

Even if it kills me.

I exhale, but the weight on my shoulders won't lift.

Eliza's voice slithers through my skull, twisting my stomach. The way I let her in—let her sink her hooks deeper than I ever meant to. But it doesn't answer the question:

When did she become such a bitch?

The stranger in the mirror laughs—a hollow, bitter sound.

"You fucking coward," I growl. "You watched it happen. You knew what she was. And you did opened the god-damned door."

The thought stops me cold. The only thing that's changed is the lab exploding, Calvin's funeral, her moving in, and the transformation fully taking hold. There's a tickle in the back of my mind, a whisper I've been trying to ignore:

She was always this way. You just clung to her because she made you feel alive.

"Nah," I murmur, steam swallowing the words. "Nah, she changed… she has to have changed …"

I shake my head, but the doubt lingers, clinging like smoke. The transformation should be dulling my emotions—making them distant. Instead, every interaction with Eden still burns bright and warm. Eliza, though—she spreads through me like frost.

I taste something in the back of my throat—copper, distant, a ghost of something that isn't there—not yet. Just the warning of what's coming.

The monster is waking.

For one horrific second, my reflection doesn't move with me.

I jerk back, breath catching.

No. I imagined that.

I lean forward again, locking eyes with the thing in the glass.

Who the fuck are you?

My pulse hammers.

I look sick. No… wrong.

I tighten my grip on the sink, fingers trembling. Clench my jaw. My reflection clenches back.

I yank open the cabinet, fingers finding a razor-gripping it tight enough to bite my palm. My vision wavers.

What would it take to prove I'm still human?

I exhale and shove the razor back inside, slam the cabinet closed, and twist the shower handle.

The pipes groan as steam unfurls, curling like ghosts against the glass.

Let it burn. Let it strip everything away.

Because she's right I do need her. Not just to learn control—

But because I deserve this.

Deserve the manipulation. The way she twists every word. The way she watches me unravel and calls it affection.

And it makes me sick.

Calvin's dead because of me. Eden's grieving a man I couldn't save. And I—

I'm still here. Breathing. Eating. Walking.

So let her sink her claws in. Let her poison every corner I

tried to keep clean. At least she understands what I'm becoming.

And if I stay close—if I keep pretending I want her— maybe I'll figure out how to survive this before it rips me apart.

Scalding rage spits against the tile. Heat pours into the air, thick and suffocating. It fills my lungs, but my thoughts won't burn away.

Calvin's scream still echoes in the corner of my mind— his hand on my arm, dragging me out before the building came down. He didn't make it back out.

Then Eden's face—tear-streaked, trembling. Like I was the one who tried to save him.

I don't deserve forgiveness, or to fix her grief.

I don't even deserve retribution.

I step into the shower—fully clothed.

The water scalds instantly. I don't move. My breath wrenches from my lungs—a sharp gasp.

The spray slams against my skin, but already the burn barely registers.

I crank the handle higher.

Hotter.

I tilt my head back. Let it hit my face, soak my shirt, my jeans. If I stand here long enough, maybe it'll wash everything away.

Let it burn. Let it strip me bare.

I press my forehead to the tile, eyes clenched shut. The pain feels right—deserved… necessary.

The scent of blood lingers in my nose. Not real. Not fresh. A ghost.

I press my palms to the tile.

If only guilt could wash away this easily.

If only I could dissolve—melt into nothing.

Erase the lab. Erase the fire. Erase Calvin's scream. *Erase her voice*—Eliza whispering into every space I'd tried to keep untouched.

My soaked clothes drag against me, a second skin I don't deserve to shed.

The heat should reach the cold inside me.

It doesn't.

Nothing does.

My skin should be screaming.

It isn't.
My pulse should be slowing.
It's steady.
The transformation is supposed to make everything distant. Numb.
So why does Eden's warmth still cut through like the sun?
And Eliza... fingers grip like ice?
I swallow the pool of saliva collecting in my cheeks from the iron smell in the water. The hunger isn't real.
Not yet.
But I can feel it waiting.
Lurking beneath the surface.
Like the reflection in the mirror. Waiting for me to look the other way.
I stay until the water runs ice-cold. Until my fingers prune, my muscles ache, and I'm forced to accept—
No amount of scalding water can cleanse what I've become.

After the shower, I walk into the living room to find it empty.
"Eliza?" I rub the towel over my hair and walk back down the hallway, peeking inside the bedroom. "Babe?"
Nothing but dead air. Back in the kitchen, there's a note on the table.
Went for takeout.
I furrow my brow, a chill creeping up my spine. "Takeout?" With a shake of my head, I crumple the note and toss it into the trash. "Noctis don't eat takeout."
Relieved for the silence, I slip into lounge shorts, determined to enjoy the stars from my patio—a moment of peace before whatever storm Eliza's brewing decides to break.

I open the door to find her standing in the darkness, crimson painted down her chin. Hugging her throat. The sight should horrify me more than it does, and that realization is its own kind of horror.
"Please tell me that's raspberry filling from a pastry or something." The words come automatically, part of the script we've been playing out more and more frequently.
"As if I could tolerate any of that human garbage." A hint of amusement lingers on her lips, the kind that never reaches her eyes. "I couldn't help myself. I got so angry at the thought

of you with her and I had to eat something."

My stomach tightens. With Eliza, confession is always calculation—a move in a game where I don't know the rules.

"Takeout?" I fold my arms, watching the blood on her lips catch the light.

"Found a stray cat down by that pizzeria on the corner." She drags a blood-stained finger along my chest. "So I ate it." The touch burns like the shower should have—igniting a spark of desire tangled with disgust.

"A cat, Eliza? For fuck's sake." I push her hand away and retreat inside. Away from her. But she follows.

Eden's tear-streaked face flashes through my mind. *What would she think of this? Of me?*

"And when the cat wasn't enough..." Eliza bites her bottom lip, making a sucking noise. Performative. "I found another little snack." Her act is practiced, theatrical—a predator's dance designed to both seduce and terrify.

The sound makes my skin crawl. "What, exactly, might that have been?" The words leave my mouth dry.

"Well, finally, with my hunger satiated,"—with a pleased sigh, she kicks the door closed behind her and drapes her arms over my shoulders. Her lips hover over mine, blood-slick. "Now all I want is something else."

The scent of floods over me, salivary glands starting to work. "What was enough to satisfy, Eliza?" My hands land on her waist, holding her back, but just close enough.

I should be demanding answers. I should be pushing her away.

But the dance is familiar—the pull of her gravity, unbreakable.

"I believe ancient demonic texts would have referred to it as long pig." She stifles a giggle and presses her lips to my earlobe.

"Are you fucking serious?" I pull away, disgust finally winning over desire.

"What's wrong?" She tilts her head in mock innocence. "It was just some dirty hobo nobody will miss." She folds her arms, popping a hip to the side. The picture of casual indifference. Her dismissal hammers into me—not just the horror of what she's done, but the casual cruelty behind it.

"You swore you'd never—" I cut myself off.

Grab for something else. Anything.

"I think I've found some of Calvin's notes on the cure."

The words tumble out fast. Desperate. "I just need to do a little more digging, restart the trials—"

"You say that like you don't already belong in the dirt with me." Her voice drops. Dangerous. "No more digging, baby. It's time to embrace what they made me into."

I watch her, and I know now. She never changed—this is who she's always been, who I've been refusing to see since day one.

I sigh, relenting. "Did you take care of the body?" The question feels hollow.

"Did I take care of—" She scoffs. "Of course I took care of the body! I'm not a fucking idiot, Ben!"

"Which was it?"

Eliza smiles. "Benji, baby, no more business talk." She grabs my hands, wrapping them around her lower back. "Won't you hold me?" The blood on her clothes seeps into me.

"I miss you." Her eyes tilt up, exposing the bottom of her irises.

The hook is there. I can feel it catching… And I let it sink in anyway—a marionette still dancing when I can see the strings.

"Eliza, did you drain the body or did you sever the head? You know that's the only way to—"

"I drank my fill and took care of the body." She snaps. "Don't worry, Ben, nobody will find it." She pushes closer to me, eyes dragging me in. The words are carefully chosen. Answering without answering.

"You're sure?" The scent of blood seeps deeper into me and hunger pulses deep.

"You don't believe me?" She steps back—hurt painted across her features like stage makeup. "Would you like me to escort you there?" Her voice drips venom. "Then you can see for yourself that my competency does not require your babysitting services?"

I close my eyes and sigh, hating myself for what comes next. "No, I'm sorry. I'm just… a bit on edge."

She smiles. "I'll forgive you." Fingers trail up my chest, fingertips finding my hairline. The touch shivers down my spine. "But only because I remember the hunger when it first takes over."

"I'm fine." The lie tastes bitter, but not as bitter as the truth—that I should feel more horror at what she's done.

"I lived it, Benji. You can't hide it from me." She circles

me, slow, deliberate. A predator with prey already in her grasp.

Her words coil around me, slithering through my defenses like silk laced with venom.

"The shaking. The night sweats." Her breath drags across my throat. "You crave it. The sweet warmth of living flesh giving way beneath your teeth. The rush of blood and adrenaline forced down your throat while they cling to the life within your grasp."

I swallow hard. The room tilts—her voice weaving through the static in my head, blurring the lines between what I should feel and what I do. The intensity in her words strikes a false note.

The hunger…

It should consume me.

I should be desperate for it, should want to tear something apart with my teeth, should want—

But I don't.

Not yet.

Eliza presses closer, nails gliding up my forearm, slow and deliberate. She's studying me, measuring my response. I know it. And I let her.

"The intoxication of being so close, you can't bring yourself to let go. Even after they stop struggling." She presses her forehead to mine, voice barely a whisper. "The electric bliss of their life draining into yours so you can do it again… and again… and again…"

I try to cling to reason—Eden's face, the wrongness of this—but it slips. The thing inside me stirs, hungry. Eliza's voice paints the hunt, the chase, the kill. My muscles coil. My breath catches when her lips brush mine—soft, deliberate, ceremonial.

A flicker of restraint inside me fights to surface—and drowns.

My hand curls around the back of her neck. My breath shudders.

She smells like blood.

Like heat. Surrender.

"You don't have to hold back anymore." She whispers.

My hands move like they belong to someone else— stronger, steadier, colder. Like my nerves are responding to a different master.

I slam her against the wall, gripping her waist with

bruising force.

I kiss her. Hard.

Devouring her mouth, chasing every copper-sweet drop. The room disappears, the world narrows to this—blood and hunger and desire tangled together until I can't tell where one ends and another begins.

Her breath stutters, a delighted gasp swallowed between my teeth. The taste of blood explodes across my tongue. A raw, primal sound rips from my throat.

Something in me snaps—not like a shackle breaking, but like a dam collapsing.

The part of me that hesitated. That resisted. That wanted to believe there was another way out. It doesn't just stop fighting. It loses.

And for the first time, I don't just let the hunger in, I want to feel it.

To pull it closer. Breathe it in. Feed it.

Eliza moans into the kiss, arching against me, thriving in my descent.

Her hands roam—fingernails dragging down my back, pressing into my skin, encouraging. Demanding.

She's wanted this.

Waited for it.

And now—she has me.

I grip her waist, pull her closer, feel the slick heat of blood between us. The intoxicating mix of pleasure and power crawl up my spine like a drug taking hold.

She tilts her head back. Offering her blood drenched throat. The pulse beneath her skin is steady.

Confident.

Unafraid.

Eliza knows exactly what she's doing. And I don't care.

I press my lips there, let them linger, my breath hot against her dampened skin. Her body melts against mine, liquid, expectant.

Her voice is pure satisfaction. "See? Doesn't it feel good to stop pretending?" Her words coil around me, slithering through my defenses.

My tongue drags over the blood coating her neck. The taste hits harder this time with the pulse of her heartbeat hiding beneath blemish free skin. Copper. Salt. Something sweeter beneath. A forbidden fruit.

A shudder rolls through her, a tremble that isn't fear but a temptation far more dangerous—

Pleasure.

She likes this.

Likes the weight of my body caging hers, the feel of my hands gripping her like I might not let go. Likes that I'm finally taking what she always knew I would.

She knew before I did. She laid the path herself—and then smiled when I mistook it for a choice.

My teeth skim her pulse and she exhales a shaky, eager breath.

The instinct is there. The hunger. The urge to sink in, to take, to claim.

Eliza tilts her chin. She wants me to bite. To cross that threshold. To prove there's no going back.

And just for a second—I see Eden.

Not crying. Not broken.

Laughing.

That embarrassed giggle when she dropped ice cream down my shirt. The way she stared at my lips when I tasted hers—like she forgot how to breathe.

"You could ruin nothing," I told her.

Her eyes crinkled, her hand warm through my shirt.

Real. Messy. Good.

Gone.

I grip Eliza harder. Press my mouth to her neck. And stop. My breath heaves against her skin. My fingers tighten on her waist.

This is the line. Right here. If I cross it, I don't come back.

Her pulse beats against my lips. My body screams to taste it. To sink in. To make this moment irreversible.

But some part of me—some desperate, flickering shred—refuses.

Instead, I drag my lips along her throat, suck the blood from her skin where it lingers, trace my tongue over the heat of it.

Eliza shudders beneath me, a moan spilling from her lips—one of pure satisfaction. Her fingers tangle in my hair, tugging, guiding. "That's it." She purrs. "That's my good boy."

The words should gut me. Should disgust me. Should make me stop. They don't.

I lose myself in the silk of her skin, in the way she melts for me, craves me, lets me devour her like a creature meant to consume. The monster inside me stretches, unfurls, exhales.

For the first time, it's full.

For the first time, I don't feel hollow. For the first time, I let it happen.

And I don't want to stop.

Chapter 50

I wake slowly. Blinking up at the ceiling, arm draped overhead. The memory of last night settles over me like smoke—hot, clinging, impossible to escape. I barely recognize the version of myself that touched her like that. I can still feel it in my bones—how easily I gave in. Like the part of me that knew better didn't show up. I turn my head. Eliza's side of the bed is cold. Undisturbed.

I exhale, pressing my fingers into my forehead before sitting up. I should feel relief. Instead, unease settles in my ribs.

I slip into clothes, movements automatic, and step into the living room.

"Babe?"

Silence.

I scan the table. No note.

I knock on the bathroom door.

"Eliza?"

Nothing.

The absence of her is louder than her presence ever was.

Light filters through the blinds, casting striped shadows across the floor. The apartment feels different without her— lighter somehow, as though her absence removes a weight I've grown so used to carrying I no longer recognized its heft. The silence should be unsettling. Instead, it wraps around my shoulders like a comfortable sweater.

I grab a pen, scrawling quickly.

"Woke up. You weren't here. Going back to the lab to see if I can find more salvageable documents. Probably be late—

don't wait up."

My hand hesitates at the last sentence. The pen hovers.

A term of affection should come next.

It doesn't. Instead, I just write my name.

"-Ben."

The act feels final as I stare at my own name, stark and impersonal against the white paper. Like I'm drawing a line between us.

One I should've drawn long ago.

I reread the note, a nervous buzz pressing against my ribs. When did signing a note become so difficult?

She won't like this. She won't like any of it.

Grabbing my jacket off the hook, I slip it on and an unseen anxiety hovers over me—like I'm bracing for a storm I can't see yet.

Slipping my hands into my pockets, my fingers bump against a soft, squishy shape.

I pull it out.

Ezra's pacifier.

I stare at it, thumb pressing into the silicone as it sits in my palm—absurdly ordinary, yet somehow profound. A tiny artifact of normal human life—of beginnings rather than endings, of nurture instead of destruction. The ache hits, sharp and disorienting—a flicker of real humanity breaking through the fog of what I've become.

I exhale, a smile curling at my lips. "Looks like I'm making a pit stop before the lab."

Restlessness settles over me as I pull up to Eden's house. It's different from the ache of past visits. The grief is still there, but beneath it coils a feeling I don't want to name.

Hope.

Twisted, selfish hope.

Two versions of me sit in the car—the man who swore to protect what's left of Calvin's world, and the monster who hungers at the sound of Eden's heartbeat.

Both real. Both clawing for control.

I stare at the front door, gut twisting.

I shouldn't be thinking this.

Shouldn't be thinking about how she's alone now.

That she needs someone. That I could...

The urge to keep my promise to take care of them sharpens with every visit. Every tear shed for someone else makes me want to hold her closer. To be enough to banish the pain.

At least Ezra will grow up with a father figure. "Uncle Ben." I smile, pushing the car door open. Then—the smell hits me.

I freeze. The smile dying on my lips as it cuts through the air.

Sweet. Thick. *Wrong.*

The scent wraps around me like a blanket, dragging me toward the house.

Blood.

My chest tightens.

Fresh and flowing.

My gums throb, teeth aching against my will to tear at the source. Inhaling deeply, warring instincts propel me forward.

The monster in me awakening—hungry and eager—while the man recoils in horror. Both compelled forward for entirely different reasons.

The unmistakable sweetness strikes, propelling me forward—the smell growing stronger with each step.

"Eden… what did you do?" I grip the door handle.

Locked.

I step back, plant my foot, and kick.

Once.

Twice.

The frame splinters—wood shards flying inward.

Part of me barely registers the damage. The other part wants to tear through the rest of the door with my bare hands.

I step inside and my heart stops.

The house is worse than before. Shattered plant pots. Overturned chairs.

Blood.

Smeared on the walls. Pooling on the floor. The smell crashes into me, nearly knocking me to my knees.

My mouth waters and a metallic hunger tears through me, clawing up my throat. My vision sharpens—crimson splashes vivid against pale walls. Each droplet calls to me, singing a siren song in a language only monsters understand.

I grip the doorframe, stabilizing myself.

Not now. Not here. Focus.

My gaze snaps to the counter. Blood drips over the edge, slow.

"Eden!" I break from my paralysis, rushing forward, eyes

scanning.

Ezra.

The soft crib—empty.

And then I see him.

Edo.

Slumped between the crib and the kitchen, body half-curled in a pool of blood that's not all his. One paw still outstretched toward the stairs—as if he tried to follow. Tried to finish what he started.

"No…" The word escapes before I can stop it. I drop to my knees beside him, hands hovering. His side rises—barely. A breath. A flicker. His eyes meet mine. Tired. Bleeding. Still watching. Still guarding.

I press a hand to his fur. "Hey… hey, buddy." His head shifts slightly—just enough to nudge my palm. "It's okay." A quiet whine vibrates from deep in his throat. "You did good." My voice threatens to crack. "You're a good boy." His chest lifts one last time. And then stills.

He held on until he knew I'd come. Until he knew they were safe.

My throat tightens as I stroke his fur. "You were a good soldier," I whisper. "Mission accomplished."

I linger there a moment longer, heat trickling up the back of my neck with the bubbling anger. I wish I could give him more than words. But I can't.

A gust of wind slips through the broken window, cool against the back of my neck. It carries the copper-sweet scent of blood—fresh, open, human.

My head lifts and everything sharpens.

I rise, glass crunching beneath my boots. Each step pulling me farther from him, and deeper into the hunt.

Grief still burns behind my ribs, but it's not the only thing anymore. There's a thread beneath it—tight and coiled.

One part of me aches for Eden. The other follows the scent, measuring the blood spatter—reading the trail. Calculating how much has been lost and how much still flows through her veins.

The contradiction tears at me. Makes me hate myself more with every movement.

The stairs beckon me in a trail of life and a breeze that shouldn't be there—carrying the scent like a whisper of warning.

I take the steps two at a time. Faster than I should. Faster than human. The hallway at the top elongates, dark and endless, but I follow the trail. A thin strip of light seeps through the crack beneath the bedroom door at the end of the hall.

My fingertips press against the wood and I push it open, slowly. Time stretches. The aroma thickens the air until each breath feels like drowning. Behind my ribs, something inhuman claws for release.

Eden sits at the base of the bed, head down. Red curls spill over her shoulder, matted with crimson.

"Eden..." I step toward her.

"Benji..." Her voice is softer than a whisper.

I drop to my knees beside her. "What did you do, love?" Her pale legs are stained red.

Her blood sings to me—a crimson symphony that drowns out thought, reason, promises. I hold my breath, fighting the urge to lean closer, to taste. My hands tremble as I reach for her, monster and man warring beneath my skin.

Hardly able to lift her head and look at me, she lets her hands come away from her chest and she holds Ezra toward me. "Promise me... you'll keep him safe."

A breath shudders out of me. "Stop that." I rub her upper back, forcing a smile. "You're gonna be fine. We need to get you to the hospital."

Her vacant eyes meet mine.

"Did you call them yet?" I swallow, not sure I can check her wounds for damage.

Her gaze wanders. "I couldn't. It happened too fast."

"What happened?"

"I was tired—" She swallows hard. "I locked the front door to come upstairs." She pauses. "She was there. At his crib."

A chill claws at my spine. "Who?"

Eden stares ahead. "I ran at her. Grabbed anything, everything. Threw them—to make her leave him alone." Her voice falters. "She attacked me instead... I—I think I blacked out." Her eyes flutter closed. "I don't even know how I—how we—" She chokes on the next breath. "Edo... he helped. So I could run. Get Ezra away from—"

A sob shudders through her chest. "She didn't stop. But he wouldn't let her pass. He saved us."

Ice forms in my veins, freezing the hunger momentarily. A terrible certainty builds in my gut. The destruction downstairs wasn't Eden's grief—it was the scene of her desperate fight. And there's only one "she" who would come here, who would know what Eden means to me.

I cup her face, tapping her cheek lightly. "Eden. Stay with me, love."

She inhales, shaky, and pushes Ezra toward me again. "I… hurt him." Her voice fractures.

My gaze drops. Ezra's tiny face, peaceful in sleep. A thin streak of red across his cheek. A scratch. No deeper than a paper cut.

"It's tiny. He'll be fine." I lift the corner of the blanket, wiping the blood away. "See? There."

Eden meets my eyes. "When I woke up, she was gone." Her voice is small. Hollow. "After, I just… I wanted to sleep." Her fingers tremble, gripped around Ezra's blanket. "I came up. She was here, waiting for us."

Ice pools in my stomach. "Who was waiting, Eden?" Even as I ask, the room's temperature seems to drop. A pressure builds at the base of my skull—the primal instinct of prey sensing a predator. The air thickens with malice so tangible I can taste it beneath the blood. She's been here all along, watching, waiting.

Eden's gaze drifts to the dark corner of the bedroom. Tears filling her eyes. "Ezra… Benji, promise." Her voice breaks.

The darkness in the corner seems to deepen, to breathe. It coalesces like ink in water, forming a silhouette that has haunted my dreams and shaped my nightmares.

"Don't count on Benji's promises," Eliza purrs from the shadows. Her voice slithers from the shadows.

My spine goes rigid, muscles locking as adrenaline floods my system. Not just Eliza's voice, but something older, hungrier speaking through her lips.

I whip around. Light catches in her blonde hair as Eliza steps from the darkness. Her smile gleaming like a blade.

"Eliza? What are you doing here?" I stand slowly, maneuvering myself between her and Eden. Ezra rests in her lap, unaware of the war raging around him.

Eliza smirks, stepping forward. "I would think that's obvious, dear." She folds her arms, the hem of her skirt fluttering in the breeze from the shattered window.

"Let's humor me and say it's not." My fists clench, rage bubbling up beneath my skin again, barely restrained. Ready to ignite.

Eliza drags a bloody fingernail across her cheek. "Obviously, I'm here to finish what Calvin started."

I narrow my eyes, unmoving. My jaw locks. I keep still. She wants a reaction—needs one to feed on. Every cell in my body screams to attack, to end her here and now. But an invisible barrier holds me steady.

She tilts her head. "He put me in a cage, Ben. Ran tests. Took pieces of me in the name of progress. Treated me like a virus instead of a person."

She sighs dreamily. "So now, I return the favor. Not to him directly, no—he's already dead." She chuckles in her throat. "But I want his rotting soul to suffer every second of eternity watching what I did to the people he loved most."

She walks to the window, parting the curtains. "You. Her. The child. All perfect pieces to play." She turns. "And you made it so easy—being in love with her." She says it so simply, so casually, like she's commenting on the weather.

I say nothing.

She turns, eyes narrowing. "You and Calvin both saw her as the light. He got the ring. You got the ache. She's the perfect knife to twist."

"For what, revenge?"

"Retribution." Her eyes narrow, nose crinkling with disdain.

"Eden has nothing to do with any of it."

"Oh, but Benji, she has *everything* to do with it. Calvin tried to save her from people like me—tried to keep her safe, untouched. So I touched her. Broke her."

She steps forward, voice sharpening. "Even when you were inside me, you were thinking of her. I felt it. I smelled it."

Her face curls with disgust. "I gave you everything, and still you ached for someone who would never love you back."

She grins wider, like it's a joke she's been dying to tell. "So I gave you a gift. Her blood. On my hands. In my mouth. You're welcome to have a taste." She bites her lower lip and I clench my fists. "Oh—and you should thank me for finally taking out that mangy pest of yours. Brave little mutt. Thought he could stop me."

Heat and anger surges up my spine. "You touched him?"

"He touched me." She pouts in mock-sadness. "Nearly bit clean through my wrist before I crushed his ribs. He made such pathetic noises."

My stomach turns. "I knew something was off with you. And you fucking lied to me about it." My fists shake at my sides. "I won't let you get away with this, hurting them—"

"Oh, Benji," she laughs, but the light in her eyes is like ice. "That's adorable. But you already did. You practically invited me in the moment you confirmed your desires for her."

I grit my teeth, lips curling in repulsion. My breath hitches, throat dry. Each word sinks like a blade, cutting through pretense. *She's right—I enabled this. My silence, my compliance, my weakness brought Eliza to Eden's door.*

She moves with ease around the room, circling like a predator sizing up its prey. "And after I finish her, that abomination filth of a child is next." She breaths a laugh. "Let's see if Calvin feels that where he is." She lifts a framed photo of Eden and Calvin from the nightstand.

I step forward, voice low, dangerous. "You won't get near either of them. I should've let Cal put an end to you when he had the chance."

Eliza's smile falters for just a second. "But you didn't. You *chose* me." Then it returns, colder. "You craved me. Trusted me. Took comfort in *me*." She turns, walking toward me. "That wasn't about *her*. That was you and me, Benji. Don't rewrite it now."

She lifts the photo higher, fingers trailing the glass—then drops it. Glass shatters beneath her heel as she steps forward. "You're mine. You were destined to be. Without her, we could have been unstoppable." She steps closer, voice low, dreamy—like she's describing a fairy-tale. "Think about it. Just you and me. The world out there dying like it deserves, and us—untouched. Ageless. Unbreakable. No more hospitals. No more fear. Just blood when we want it. Power when we need it." She brushes her thumb along my jaw. "We could disappear. Find a dark little corner of the world and take what's ours. Together."

My pulse skips. The darkness she offers sounds easy— like a life without weight. I don't move. My breath catches. Because for half a second, the image she paints almost tempts me. Almost.

I step forward, feet planting wide, arms spread protectively in front of Eden and Ezra. "Are you forgetting? It won't be forever. There's a cure, and I'll find it. If I don't end you first."

Eliza laughs softly, unfazed. "I already fixed that insignificant problem of a cure." She flicks her fingers dismissively. "Now, step aside, dear. I'd like to finish eating so we can go home."

I bare my teeth. "You'll have to go through me." A shift sparks inside me—a clarity cutting through confusion. For the first time since my transformation began, I know exactly who I am and what I stand for.

Eliza meets my stare, stepping close. "You won't hurt me, Benji." She tilts her head, eyes gleaming. "You can't. We're bound now. Otherwise I'd have made the plan to send you to death along with everyone Calvin loves."

My stomach tightens. "What does that mean?"

She smirks. "Wouldn't have been in his notes for you to read. Nobody ever told him. Or maybe…" She steps closer again. "Maybe I didn't even realize until after we shared flesh."

My blood runs cold. "Get to the point."

Eliza drags a slow, deliberate finger down my chest. "Certain aspects of… intimacy,"—her eyes flick down as she slides her hand down my torso—"create a bond." She takes my wrist, placing my hand on her side. "Can't you feel it?"

Heat coils beneath my skin. The magnetic pull.

"The connection?" Her breath ghosts over my face. "The urge to satisfy me? No matter the cost?"

I stare at her lips, watching them move, my body betraying me with every syllable. My mouth waters—not from hunger, but memory.

Blood. The ghost of it lingers on my tongue, a stain I can't erase. My mind screams.

This isn't hunger. This isn't love. It's a leash, tightening around my throat.

Then—a scent. Familiar.

A flutter of warmth hits me, unbidden. A smile, tugging at the darkness.

Eden.

My stomach turns as the pieces snap together. My gaze flicks to Eliza's lower lip. The dark, dried streak beneath it.

Not just blood. Eden's blood.

The final betrayal. My rage coils tighter, strangling the breath from my lungs.

The room blurs around her as my vision tunnels, locking onto the evidence smeared against her mouth.

She didn't just hurt Eden.

She tasted her.

Eliza's tongue glides over her bottom lip, slow, deliberate. She smiles as her gaze flicks past me—to the body on the floor.

"Tell me you're not dying to finally know what she tastes like." Her voice is like silk and steel, twisting the knife. "We could share, you know. The way we did last night. A simple stranger made you so ravenous." She bites her lower lip, then leans in, her breath grazing my jaw.

"You remember it, don't you?" she whispers. Her head tilts slowly, eyes gleaming with sick satisfaction. "The sweetness. The warmth. The way it lingered and you couldn't stop."

My mouth goes dry. "That wasn't my choice."

Eliza laughs—soft, cruel. "You didn't even feed, Benji. That was just a taste. Just blood smeared on my lips. And it lit you up like a fuse."

"I didn't—"

"You didn't pull away." Her smile spreads, slow and triumphant. "You didn't hesitate. You chased it."

I take a step back, breath coming in hard to keep me focused.

"And don't pretend it was an uncontrolled instinct. You liked it. I felt it in your hands when they touched me. I saw it in your eyes when you finally came undone."

My hands tremble. My body rebels.

"So now we can share her," she purrs, brushing her lips near my ear, "you don't even need to get your conscience dirty. I've already done the messy part. You just get to enjoy what's left."

That's it.

The rage snaps. I grab her arms and shove her back. "Enough!"

Eliza gasps, hands bracing against the wall behind her.

I stalk forward. "You don't get to manipulate me anymore."

Her eyes widen.

"You will leave them alone. Forever." My fist slams into the wall beside her head while the other wraps around her throat.

For the first time, I see fear in her eyes—real fear. The predator becoming prey. Something savage and righteous surges through me.

Pressing against it, I draw my face close to hers, exposing my new fangs to the world for the first time. "If you ever come near them—" My voice drops to a growl. "I'll kill you myself."

Eliza's hands clasp my wrist and her eyebrows knit together. "Benji… baby… you're hurting me."

I lean closer. "Good."

Her eyes flash. Then—she laughs. "You're forgetting something." She smirks. "She's bitten. My virus is inside her now."

Cold washes over me, dread gripping my ribs like a vice. I whip my head back to Eden. Her chest—saturated with blood.

"She'll turn." Eliza tilts her head, watching me drink in the horror. "She'll gut that child of hers. Then she'll drain herself dry to escape the reality of it."

My grip tightens. "You're sick."

Eliza moans softly, like she enjoys it. "What can I say? I'm not the type to forget."

She steps closer, voice lowering.

"I just hope I get to witness her self-destruction. It'll be starting any moment now." Her smile spreads, slow and cruel. "That delicious little heart of hers will stop beating. And when it does, the virus will hyper-mutate every fiber of her body. The chain reaction will begin. In hours, she'll be infected enough to murder that filth of an offspring." She leans her head back into the wall. "Then she'll come to her senses just long enough to realize what she's done—before she drains herself to escape it."

I shake my head, forcing my breath steady. "It doesn't work that fast." My grip loosens and I look over my shoulder again—Eden's face pale, her breath shallow.

Eliza clicks her tongue. "On the contrary, dear. There are things I didn't tell you. That I had a prior exposure before your disgrace of a friend dragged me to his lab and started stabbing me with needles."

I whip my gaze back to hers. "What?"

She laughs softly. "As smart as you are, you sure can be dense." Her hand trails up my forearm, slipping my grip from her throat. She presses my palm to her chest, her skin unnaturally warm beneath my iced touch.

"I was attacked by a group of soldiers before I sought refuge with your military." Her voice drops, almost mournful.

Almost. "They were ruthless to everyone."

She swallows, licking her lips. "Easy on the eyes, they called me. A tasty little snack to keep around until the virus took hold."

Her lips curl—not quite a smirk, not quite a grimace. "Their plan for me after that? To be their little plaything." She lets the words hang. "I'm still the victim in all of this, Benji. You owe me my livelihood."

I push my hand against her chest, shoving her back slightly. "I owe you nothing."

Eliza lowers her head, unfazed. "But the organization you were part of—the one you longed to return to—was involved. You craved it so desperately you mutilated yourself to belong again."

She leans in, voice dripping venom. "That makes you just as guilty as the ones who laid hands on me."

Her eyes flick to my leg, then my chest. "Don't you remember? The ache? The pain every time you moved?"

My jaw clenches. "Shut up. You know nothing of the pain I've endured."

Her laugh cuts. "I don't have to." She lifts her hand, brushing her fingertips over my pulse. "We shared one another. You gave that part of yourself to me. You can do it again… here—now."

I grit my teeth.

Eliza's gaze drops to my lips, her own parting slightly. "Benji… I'll be yours forever." She leans in, whispering, letting her breath warm my skin. "All I ask is that you share with me. Taste the thread of life from the one you love, but could never have…" Her smile widens. "She's here, within me now. I can give her to you." Her words slither around me like smoke, seeping into every crack.

For a moment, I waver. The taste of Eden's blood. The promise of forever. The seductive pull of surrender. I inhale sharply and my stomach churns.

This isn't surrender. It's submission. And I will not be hers to command.

I loosen my grip.

Eliza falls to the floor, hands clutching her chest as she coughs.

I turn away from her. Eden's eyes flutter, glazed with exhaustion and pain.

She's slipping away, and I've wasted time on that monster.

"Go." I growl.

"What?" Eliza tilts her head, staring like I've become a puzzle she no longer understands. "You should be mine by now. The hunger should have consumed you." Her voice cracks with disbelief. "Why are you fighting it?"

I have no answer. I only know that while the monster claws inside me—a deep pull I don't understand—keeps me from becoming what she wanted me to be.

"Get the fuck out." I turn to her, teeth bared. "The next time I see you, I may not be calm enough to stop myself from ripping your head from your body." The words tear from me like a living thing—raw and final.

She smirks, even as she moves toward the window. "That's the connection, you know." She slides her fingers along the sill, tilting her head. "The bond we made. It's keeping you from killing me. Keeping you from wanting to."

I step closer, fists clenched.

Her fingers tremble against the sill, just barely. "Is this really your choice?" Her voice falters, softer. "Benji, how will you cope with the changes on your own?"

"If you don't know the answer to that," I stare at her, voice steady. "you clearly don't know me as well as you thought."

Eliza chuckles. "Maybe next time, you'll feel the depth of the connection we made last night. The desire for me that I have for you. That's the final piece in payback to Calvin."

I slam my hands on either side of the window frame. Wood splinters. Her breath stutters. "You go near them—I'll know."

She flinches, knees knocking against the sill. "Just remember which one of us loves you, Benji." Her hand presses against the glass. "And when you do, come back to me. Then we'll be together. Fulfilling our destiny."

I reach through the open window, grab her top and yank her forward. Her breath catches. "Go near them, and I'll know." My voice rumbles in a low growl. "And when I find you, the last thing you'll be thinking about is your delusions of *us*."

Eliza swallows then licks her lips, eyes darkening. "We'll see, Benji..." Her voice drops to a whisper. "You think you've chosen? You've only delayed the inevitable."

The bond pulls tight again, invisible but real. I feel her heartbeat like a whisper in my chest. Feel the phantom warmth of her skin where our bodies touched. The memory of last night clings to me like blood I can't scrub off. A sound echoes in my ears—her laugh, soft and breathless. From when I gave in.

My fingers twitch.

No.

I bite down hard—on the inside of my cheek, drawing blood. My own. Not hers.

She leans forward, her lips nearly brushing mine. "I'll be waiting. After all, we have eternity."

"Get the fuck out." I release her.

She laughs softly. Then she's gone.

The room feels emptier without her. Cleaner. I turn back to Eden.

The real battle isn't over. It's just beginning.

I drop to my knees beside her, brushing blood crusted curls from her face.

"Eden," I whisper. "I'm here now, love."

Her lips part, breath shallow. Ezra stirs in her lap.

I press my palm to her forehead—still warm, but fading.

"You're gonna be okay," I lie. "I swear, I'll make it right."

Whether she hears me or not, I don't know. But I say it again anyway.

Because she's the only thing that ever made me want to be more than the monster I always was.

Chapter 51

Her warmth seeps into my chest as I draw her close, cradling her against me. "I'm sorry, love. I should have been here."

"No, Benji..." The whisper barely escapes her lips. "I should have been stronger."

"You are. You always were."

Her gaze drops to Ezra nestled in her lap. Her fingers grasp at him, trembling as she clutches him close. It's weak, but desperate—her body shaking from effort. She presses a kiss to his forehead, her tears dotting his soft skin. I can feel her reluctance, the way her breathing hitches as if she's trying to will her body to hold on, to fight. "Make sure he knows who we are, Cal and me. You're all he has now."

"I can't—"

"Please," her voice splinters. "I can't turn into her... I can't." A whimper escapes as tears spill down her cheeks.

"We're close to a cure," I say quickly, my grip tightening. "Just a little more time—"

"You know that's not true." Her breath hitches, and she grips my hand. "There's no cure. Only failures. And I'm out of time."

"Eden, don't ask me to do this…" My voice cracks, my desperation rising. "Cal would have… I'll find a way." I brush away her tears with my thumb, meeting her gaze as my own eyes begin to burn. "I can fix this."

"I won't risk him." Her chest hitches with a sob.

"You won't. Stay with me. I'll keep you both safe."

"You can't promise that," she whispers. "You know it."

She looks down at Ezra again, her fingers barely brushing his blanket before curling into a fist. "I can feel the rage."

In my mind, I see Eliza—her smile sharpened by blood, her words like knives: *"She'll gut that child of hers."* I clench my jaw, willing the memory away.

She lifts her hand to cover mine. "It's better this way. He'll be safer..."

"He needs his mother."

"He needs guidance and security. He needs you."

I shake my head violently. "I can't."

She exhales sharply, eyes hardening. "Coward. I always knew, but I didn't think you'd prove it like this." She clenches her jaw. "Would you rather let me become her?"

I flinch. The comparison stabs deep, twisting. "You are *nothing* like her."

"Not yet." She exhales, softer this time. "I don't need to know how..." Her gaze finds mine—steady, aching. "I just know you will. Because it's you."

The words land heavier than any demand.

Not a plea. Not pressure. Just trust.

And somehow, that hurts worse. Because I don't feel like me anymore. But she still sees him. The man I was. The man I have to become again—for her.

My throat constricts as I let myself drown in her eyes. "I can't do you and Cal justice... but I'll make sure he knows you." I press my cheek to her head, her hair clinging to my damp skin as I clench my jaw and swallow hard with the resolve of what has to come next.

Because she's right. She's always right.

"I'm slipping..." she whispers, fingers trailing over Ezra's tiny fist.

My heart fractures at her closed eyes. I gather Ezra carefully in my hands, bringing him close to her. The corners of her lips lift in a ghost of a smile as she places one final kiss on his head. "Be good for Benji, baby," she chokes out.

Holding him close, I carry him to the other room and settle him in his crib, tucking his pacifier beside him before closing the door.

From the doorway, I watch Eden sway, her head bobbing as she fights to stay upright at the bed's base.

The setting sun catches my eye through the window, bleeding orange across the floor.

Fitting... vesper is here.

But no prayer can keep you with me now, can it?

And maybe that's what this is—vesper. The last fragile light before everything disappears.

But you always said darkness held discoveries.

I hope you were right, love.

Because after this, I'll need to find something in the dark worth becoming.

The thought of beheading her to prevent the change twists my insides—leaving only one option. I return to her side, gathering her once more in my arms.

She gasps, startled, eyes flying open.

"It's just me," I soothe, running my hand along her arm. "You're safe."

"Will it… hurt?" Relief colors her sigh as she sinks against my chest.

"No." I murmur into her hair. "You'll feel light-headed."

"Thank you for never giving up on me, Benji." She wraps her fingers around mine. "Even when I stopped myself from fully loving you."

"No matter how hard I tried, I couldn't let you go. I fell for you the first day we met..." My voice scratches as I brush hair from her face, watching her chest labor with each breath. Her skin cools beneath my touch, her heartbeat slowing. The setting sun catches my eye through the window.

"Don't fear the darkness..." she whispers, as if she already knows I'm damning the sun for taking her with it.

"I don't. I've always lived there. But you showed me its beauty." I memorize her features—her pale skin luminescent in the fading light. My lips tremble as I force out the words: "It's time, love... are you ready?"

A flash of memory surfaces—her embarrassed laugh when she spilled ice cream down my shirt, the way her cheeks flushed as she wiped it away. That was the night I knew I was already lost to her forever.

A tear traces down her cheek as her lower lip quivers. "Are any of us ready? My life was finally starting to be worth living."

Heat builds behind my eyes as tears threaten to fall. I press my lips to her cheek and whisper, "Then, find me in the next one."

Her warm breath against my neck grows shallow, each exhale more distant than the last. Drawing courage from somewhere deep inside, I bring my lips to her throat. My teeth graze her skin, a gentle prelude to what must come.

When I apply pressure, her flesh yields beneath my fangs, flooding my being with the essence that's haunted my dreams for years. Now sinking into me as my greatest regret, a bitter victory I never wanted.

My soul rebels against this reality, silently begging her eyes to open, for her voice to tell me to stop. But this is her choice—choosing oblivion over becoming a creature that feeds on others' lives.

A monster… like me. She's sacrificing everything to spare others pain, not herself.

That selflessness is so quintessentially Eden.

A soft gasp escapes her as strength briefly returns, her hands pressing against my shoulders in instinctive resistance. Each swallow tears me apart—my body's satisfaction at tasting her warring with my heart's knowledge that I'm losing her forever. The woman I've loved for years is becoming part of me in the most tragic way possible, each beat of her heart counting down to our final goodbye.

My arms tighten around her as I continue drawing out her warmth. Her pulse flutters against my tongue, growing fainter. Her delicate fingers slip from my collar to rest against my forearm. Each breath comes slower than the last until her chest finally stills, refusing nature's rhythm one final time.

In her last moment, she weaves her fingers through mine and whispers a single word:

"Benji…"

The sound fades into silence, taking with it everything I've ever loved.

Epilogue

In the nursery, Ezra's quiet breathing fills the space as I lay him on the changing table. The cheerful yellow walls and dancing giraffes mock the gravity of what's happened just down the hall. His cherubic face is marred by streaks of dried blood—Eden's blood—and my hands tremble as I dampen a soft washcloth with warm water.

Each gentle swipe reveals more of his perfect skin beneath the crimson stains, and my chest tightens until I can barely breathe.

"I'm sorry, little man," I whisper, carefully cleaning around his eyes, his tiny nose, those delicate ears. The cloth comes away red again and again, and I have to pause, gripping the edge of the table as waves of nausea hit me. Her essence lingers on him, sweet beneath the metallic tang of blood, and my newfound hunger wars with my disgust at myself.

He watches me with eyes so like his father's—trusting, innocent—as I peel away his stained sleeper. Dark patches have seeped through to his skin, and I find more blood in the creases of his neck, under his arms, between his tiny fingers.

How could I let this happen to him? To her?

With shaking hands, I clean every trace of violence from his perfect skin, as if I could somehow wash away the horror of this night.

The water in the basin turns pink, then red as I work. I change it twice, unable to bear the sight of her life diluting away like a watercolor paint. A soft whimper escapes him as I clean a stubborn spot behind his ear, and my vision blurs with tears.

"Shh, you're safe now," I soothe, though my voice cracks. "Your mom—" I have to stop, swallow hard against the lump in my throat. "Your mom would haunt me if I didn't take care of you properly."

I warm another cloth for his hands, where tiny crescents of red still stain his fingernails. He grabs my finger as I work, his grip strong and trusting, unaware that these same hands just took his mother's life. My tears fall on his clean cheek, and I quickly wipe them away.

Eden kept his clothes perfectly organized in the dresser—everything sorted by size, season, color. The tiny blue onesie she'd laid out for tomorrow morning—was it only hours ago?—still sits folded on top. I can't bring myself to use it. Instead, I select a soft gray one from deeper in the drawer, handling it carefully as if it might shatter like my heart.

"There we go, all clean," I murmur, lifting him to my shoulder. He smells of baby powder and lotion now, but beneath it, I catch traces of this night's horror—hints of copper and salt my senses won't let me ignore. I press my lips to his forehead, tasting the remains of my own tears. "No more crying," I tell him, trying to steady my voice. "We need to be strong now. Like she was."

The soiled clothes go into a plastic bag—I can't bear to leave them here as evidence of what transpired. The bloody washcloths follow. I wipe down the changing table, erasing every trace of red, every mark of violence from this space that should only know love and tenderness. But I know I can never wipe these moments from my memory—they're etched there like acid on glass, a permanent reminder of what I've done, what I've lost, what I've become.

My hands tremble as I pack Ezra's bag, each item a fragment of the life being left behind. Diapers, clothes, toys—all carefully chosen by Eden's loving hands. I pause at his favorite blanket, the soft fabric still holding traces of her scent, before tucking it gently inside. The weight of what I've done presses against my chest with each breath.

When I lift Ezra from his crib, he settles against me with complete comfort, innocent to the weight of this moment. His tiny fingers curl into my shirt as we step out into the night air.

The darkness swoops down, wrapping around us like wings, and I tilt my face toward the sky. Stars pierce through the blackness, countless bright eyes bearing witness to what

I've become. The ache within deepens—these eternal watchers will forever mark this night, this choice, this irrevocable step into a new life.

A cool breeze carries the aroma of jasmine—Eden's favorite—and for a moment, I swear I feel her presence in the gathering shadows. My throat tightens as memories flood back: her smile when she spoke of finding light in darkness, her unwavering belief that every ending held the seed of something new.

Ezra stirs against my chest, and I brush my thumb across his cheek. In the starlight, I catch glimpses of Eden underneath Cal's features—the curve of his nose, the corners of his eyes.

"Don't be scared, lil' man," I whisper, my voice rough with emotion. "Your mom..."—the words catch, and I have to steady myself—"your mom always believed darkness could lead to profound discoveries... and new beginnings."

A shooting star streaks across the sky, as if Eden herself is signing off on this moment, this transition.

"She was right, you know. Even now." I press a gentle kiss to his head—not a promise, but a goodbye.

"This isn't the life I wanted for us... but it's the only way I know how to honor her now.

"You deserve steadiness. Safety. Something I can't give you—not yet." My voice cracks as I pull the blanket closer around him.

"He gave everything to make sure you'd survive. Edo knew, somehow. He held on until I got here.

"They'll raise you with love. The kind she would've given you. And I'll still be watching... Just from farther away than I hoped."

I take one last look at the house where so much has ended—and begun. "Let's get you somewhere safe, lil' man."

As we move into the darkness, I feel the weight of both endings and beginnings settling around us like a cloak. Eden always understood this dance between light and shadow better than anyone. Now it's my turn to learn its steps—not to teach them to her son, but to become someone who could. To find those profound discoveries she always promised waited in the dark.

This was the end of Benjamin Hale—his final breath drawn alongside hers. And in that quiet darkness between stars, between grief and dawn, Vesper was named.

Acknowledgments

Thank you for going through the beginning of this journey with me. I'd love to hear your thoughts.

You can scan the QR code below to visit my link-tree, which will have a direct link to leave a review for this book.

If you can spare a moment to leave details, that is appreciated. If you prefer to leave it at a star rating, I understand, but just know that your feedback is valuable. Think of how many books you would purchase that have little to no reviews.

Regardless of how you felt about this book, leaving a rating is the best way to help any independent author.

Respectfully,

Melody Kepler

Turn the page for a sneak peek of book two,
When the Sun Fades ⟶

Scan me to leave a
review!

Prologue

Cassia

Holli pulls the jacket over my shoulders and tucks my hair beneath it.

"Why are we going in the middle of the night?"

"It's a new kind of game."

"Like hide and seek? Will my parents find me?"

"It works similarly to hide and seek. You will hide, and for a while your parents will seek. But you must do everything you can to not be found."

"What about breakfast?"

"I've packed your breakfast. Cass, baby, listen to me, please. You must never be found."

"Never?"

Holli kneels down, her hands trembling as she adjusts my collar. The moonlight streaming through my bedroom window catches the tears in her eyes.

"Never," she whispers, pulling me close. She smells like fresh bread and peppermint, just like every morning when she makes breakfast. "You're going to be brave for me, aren't you, Cass?"

I nod, though my stomach feels funny, like the time I fell from the apple tree. "But what about you? Can't you hide with me?"

Holli's breath catches. She pulls back, cupping my face in her warm hands, though her fingers are colder than usual. A bandage is wrapped tightly around her wrist.

"I have to stay," she says, voice quieter than before, "to make sure they look in all the wrong places."

She reaches into her pocket and pulls out a silver locket—the one she always wears.

"This was my grandmother's. It will keep you safe."

"But—"

A floorboard creaks somewhere in the mansion. Holli stiffens, her eyes darting to the door. She quickly slips the locket around my neck and tucks it beneath my shirt.

The creak comes again. Slower this time. Like someone dragging their feet.

"Remember what we learned about the stars?" she whispers urgently, guiding me toward the hidden door behind my bookshelf. "Follow the North Star, just like in your astronomy books. Mr. Parker will be waiting at the old chapel."

I clutch my small backpack, filled with the breakfast she packed and my favorite stuffed bat. "I don't want to go alone."

"You're never alone," Holli says, pressing a kiss to my forehead. "Every star in the sky is watching over you."

The bookshelf groans softly as it swings open. Cold air rushes in, carrying the scent of wet earth and fallen leaves. My feet feel heavy, like they're stuck in the mud by the garden pond.

A crash echoes from down the hall—the sound of breaking glass. Not like something dropped. Like something was thrown.

Then another sound—a high, breathy laugh. It sounds like Mama pretending when she plays tea party, only this time the smile is on the inside of her voice.

Holli flinches and gives me a gentle push toward the darkness.

"But what if I forget the stars?" My voice trembles. Last week, I mixed up Orion's Belt with the Big Dipper, and Holli had to help me find them again.

"Count three stars to the right of the Big Dipper's handle," she whispers, just like she's done every night we stargazed from my window. "That's your North Star. It will never lead you wrong." Her voice catches. "Just like I would never lead you wrong, Cass."

Another crash, closer now. And voices—but Mama's is still wrong.

"Holliii," she sings, light and lilting. "Where have you

hidden our little dove? You know she hates being late."

The air grows thicker. Holli's shoulders tighten as if she's holding her breath.

Holli's face goes white. She presses something else into my hands—a piece of paper, folded small.

"Don't read it until you're safe. Promise me."

"I promise." The paper crinkles in my grip.

"When you reach the chapel, knock three times, then twice more. Mr. Parker will—"

She stops, head snapping toward my bedroom door. The handle jiggles once, slowly. Then stills.

"Go. Now."

"I love you," I whisper, because that's what we always say before hiding.

"I love you too, my brave girl." Holli's voice breaks. "Now run. Run and don't look back."

The hidden door closes behind me, leaving only darkness and the smell of damp stone. I clutch my backpack closer, feeling the hard shape of the locket through my shirt.

Somewhere above, I hear Papa's voice joining Mama's. The way they hum together makes my skin prickly.

I run.

The passageway air is cold on my wet cheeks as I count my steps like Holli taught me. Twenty steps forward. Turn right at the fork. Thirty more to the garden exit.

Don't look back. Never look back.

Behind me, muffled by stone and distance, I hear Holli's voice one last time—calm and clear, like when she reads me bedtime stories.

Then a gasp. Something breaks. And a sound like someone drinking too fast.

Then silence.

Interlude:

The Fall of the Old World

They say the end of the war was not marked by peace, but by silence.

Entire cities—emptied overnight. Settlements abandoned, their fires still smoldering, meals left unfinished on wooden tables. Those who remained behind were never seen again.

At first, the stories were dismissed as exaggerations. Raiders, perhaps. Plagues. Accidents.

Then the patterns began to emerge. The towns closest to Noctis activity were the first to go. Then the villages farther out. Then the fortified cities.

Then nowhere was safe.

The first true famine was not of food... but of people.

Entire towns were emptied without a trace—until the wind shifted and the stench told the truth. Bone piles with teeth marks. Rib cages displayed in spirals. Children's shoes still tied beside blood-slick thresholds.

Skulls were stacked in windows like warnings. Teeth left in bowls beside broken doors. Blood crusted over paintings that hadn't finished drying.

In one fortress city, they found bodies drained and strung upside down from balconies like trophies. In another, the people had eaten glass to avoid living through it altogether.

Elsewhere, whole neighborhoods burned themselves alive—gasoline poured down stairwells, prayers whispered as the match was lit—just to escape the knock at the door.

Governments collapsed under the weight of fear. Military forces fractured, unable to fight a war where the enemy no longer played by the rules. Those in power made choices. Some abandoned their posts. Others sought new alliances. A few held their ground, believing victory was still possible.

They were the first to disappear.

What happened next is unclear. The records from that time are fragmented—contradictory. Some claim a deal was struck, a quiet arrangement between the survivors and the Noctis. Others say the Noctis simply took what they needed and left the scraps behind.

Whatever the truth may be, one thing is certain.

The world did not end in fire or war.

It ended in surrender.

"No one remembers the moment they stopped fighting. Only that one morning, they woke up and realized they had already lost."

They called it survival.

But the children born into this new world had no say in what that survival cost.

Chapter 1

Cassia

*R*ule one of compound training: never show fear. Rule two: if you're going to break rule one, do it where no one can see.

Which is why I'm in the east wing's abandoned storage room, hands shaking as I wrap my bloodied knuckles. The floor's stained with old spills—ink or blood, hard to tell. Even the shadows here feel leftover. The training dummy lies in pieces around me, stuffing scattered like snow. Third one this week. The room smells of copper and dust, and somewhere above, rain drums against ancient windows. It reminds me of the dream—darkness, the cold echo of footsteps, wetness that clung to dead air like breath on glass.

"Control your emotions," Warden Keller always says, like feelings are something you can lock away in a box. But control isn't what got me here. Survival did. And survival isn't always pretty. It means learning how to live in a world that already gave up.

The locket at my neck feels heavier than usual today. Nine years since Holli pressed it into my hands, since she told me to run and never look back. Nine years of foster homes and fighting and finally finding my way here, to this compound of lost children and broken things. Like some orphan shelter built on the bones of the old world. No one says that part out loud, but we all feel it.

My fist connects with the wall before I realize I'm moving.

Pain shoots through my already split knuckles, but I welcome it. Pain means I'm still here. Still fighting.

"What did that wall ever do to you?"

I spin, blade already drawn from my boot. Felix stands in the doorway, hands raised in mock surrender. His easy smile doesn't match the concern in his eyes.

"Practicing," I mutter, sheathing the knife. He's the closest thing to a friend I have here, but that's not saying much.

"Right. Because we don't have enough actual practice dummies." He kicks through the stuffing at his feet. "Though I guess we have one less now."

"If you're here to lecture me—"

"Actually, I'm here to warn you. Warden's doing room inspections. Might want to clean this up before she finds her supply room redecorated."

I survey the damage—torn canvas, splintered wood, walls scarred with my rage. "Help me?"

His smile softens. "Always. But Cass?" He catches my arm as I pass. "Whatever's eating at you... you know you can tell me, right?"

I think of the nightmare that drove me here from my bed tonight—screaming, smoke thick in my throat, and a figure that never comes into focus, pressing just under the surface like it's waiting to get out. I think of the letter that arrived yesterday, claiming to know where my family is. Of all the other letters that led nowhere.

"I'm fine," I say, pulling away. "Just restless."

He doesn't believe me—I can see it in his face. But he helps me clean anyway, and doesn't ask about the tears I quickly wipe away when I find my stuffed bat among the wreckage. Some questions are better left unasked.

By the time we finish, morning light streams through grimy windows. Other trainees will be heading to pre-breakfast training warm up sessions, trading stories about their latest bruises and victories. Playing at being warriors while real monsters stalk the world outside. We train for rules, but out there, the rules don't matter. Out there, the monsters make their own.

"Coming?" Felix asks from the doorway.

I touch the locket, feeling its familiar weight. "In a minute."

When his footsteps fade, I retrieve the crumpled letter

from my pocket. The handwriting is elegant, precise—like all the others. But this one feels different. This one names a place, a city far to the north. Now it begs the question on who sent it and how they even found me.

Maybe it's another dead end. Maybe it's another trap. Maybe it's bait strung from the same hands that left towns in piles of bone. But as I stare at my bloodied knuckles, at the cleanup from the destruction one nightmare caused, I know I can't stay here much longer. Something has to change.

The compound bells ring, signaling the start of another day. Another round of training, of pretending I belong here. Of preparing for a fight I'm not sure I understand.

I tuck the letter away and head for the courtyard. Rule one: never show fear. Rule two: if you're going to break rule one, do it where no one can see.

Rule three? Sometimes the biggest battles aren't the ones we fight with our fists.